MAGICAL CHALLENGE

"I need a volunteer from the audience." Dozens of male hands shot up as she playfully talked her way down the aisle.

Straight toward him.

She held out a gold-dusted hand. "How about you, sir?"

Hugh's mouth dried to ash. Getting up onstage in front of several hundred people was his idea of a nightmare.

All around him people clapped and urged him up onstage. Dia touched him, and heat blasted through him at inferno strength. Hugh rose, drawn not by the clamorous audience, but by the wink she gave him, the seduction of her voice and the compelling need to keep anyone else from taking his place.

The silver lamé didn't hurt either.

Dia's smile widened as he accepted her challenge. Onstage the lights shone upon him, hot and blinding. He squinted under the blazing candlewatts, seeing only Dia. . . .

Other *Love Spell* books by Kathleen Nance:
THE WARRIOR
THE TRICKSTER
MORE THAN MAGIC
WISHES COME TRUE

The Seeker

KATHLEEN NANCE

LOVE SPELL   NEW YORK CITY

For Sara, David, and Carl, and all their friends.
How else would I have known about the Twinkie Project?

A LOVE SPELL BOOK®

January 2002

Published by

Dorchester Publishing Co., Inc.
276 Fifth Avenue
New York, NY 10001

ISBN 0-505-52465-1

The name "Love Spell" and its logo are trademarks of Dorchester Publishing Co., Inc.

Printed in the United States of America.

Visit us on the web at www.dorchesterpub.com.

The Seeker

The Myth of Leda
and
The Myth of Hades

Leda, Queen of Sparta, wife of King Tyndareus, drew the attention of the amorous Zeus with her kind and nurturing soul. While she bathed at the side of a river, he came to her in the guise of a swan. She petted him, and he preened. The god beguiled and bewitched the trusting lady, then, resuming his human form, became her lover.

Hera, wife to Zeus, was furious at her husband's continual infidelity.

In time Leda was delivered of a blue egg and gave birth to four children—two boys and two girls. Zeus was the father of two and the King Tyndareus sired the others. Two would be immortal, two were destined for the realm of Hades.

The wrath of Hera remained unavenged.

Thus was the legend of Leda set forth.

* * *

Hades, god of the underworld, master of the realms of Tartarus and the Elysian Fields, Soul Seeker for the gods, fell in love with the daughter of Demeter, goddess of the seed and the plant.

Though Zeus gave his approval, Demeter refused to sanction the union between her daughter, Persephone, and the Soul Seeker. One day, seeing his love picking lilies and violets in the field, Hades rent open the earth. He sprang from beneath the soil, his chariot pulled by four black steeds, his iron-colored reins urging haste. He gathered his love to him and carried her off to his domain of dark caves and glittering gems. There, he made her his.

Demeter searched everywhere for her daughter. Her fury punished the earth with famine and cold. At last a river nymph braved the wrath of Demeter to tell her what she had seen. Persephone dwelled in the realm of Hades, reigning with him as queen.

When Demeter heard this, she stood as one stupefied; then she turned to Zeus and demanded the return of her daughter. Seeing the suffering of the Earth, he consented with one condition: that Persephone had not eaten during her stay in the lower world. Hermes was dispatched to demand the return of the maiden, but discovered she had sucked the pulp from six pomegranate seeds. The god of the underworld had won her heart.

At last a compromise was reached. Persephone would spend half the year with her beloved husband in his underground lair and half the year with her mother. Thus ended the myth.

Deep within each story lie seeds of truth, truths that bear fruit to this day.

The blue egg, however, is sheer fancy.

Prologue

Zeus squinted into the mirror in the presidential suite at Jupiter Fireworks, trying out the visage of a boar. *Too squat. Too hairy. Too . . . boarish.* Lifting one hoof to his lightning-bolt ring, he altered his image. Lightning sparked and crackled, and he became a bull.

Strong shoulders. Long horns. Virile. Much better.

This new ring had potential.

"Mr. Jupiter." The efficient voice of his secretary sounded over the intercom.

"Yes, Mrs. Hunsacker," answered Zeus absently, studying the bull. Maybe thicken the—

"*Mr. Jupiter?*" His secretary's shocked response jolted him.

To him, his voice sounded normal. To her, it would sound like the bellow of a bull. Swiftly he dissolved the image and resumed normal human form. Zeus—or Zeke Jupiter, as he was now called—coughed and cleared his throat. "Sorry, Mrs. Hunsacker. Caught a chill in my throat. Made me hoarse."

"In June, sir?"

"Summer cold." Settling into his leather chair, he swiftly changed the subject. "Did you want something?"

"Ms. Juneau is here—No, ma'am, you'll have to wait." Mrs. Hunsacker sounded harried.

Harriet Juneau had that effect on some people. The name might have changed, but she was still Hera, once queen of the gods.

The outer door opened. "Mrs. Hunsacker, I rarely wait," said a cool, feminine voice, and then his wife of uncounted years strolled in, smiling. Chic in trim aqua and heels, Hera looked better than most women two-hundredths her age. His chest tightened. By Tartarus's depths, many females had fanned his passions, but none had captured his heart and soul like Hera.

And that was the problem.

"It's all right, Mrs. Hunsacker." Zeus waved a hand, silencing the protest of his guardian secretary. "She's expected."

"You should tell me your appointments, sir." Mrs. Hunsacker sniffed and shut the door, leaving them alone.

Zeus steepled his fingers. "Really, my dear, if you'd told me you were flying in from Chicago, I could have warned Mrs. Hunsacker."

"I thought I'd surprise you." Hera perched on the edge of the desk. "Was that a lion I heard in here?"

"A bull."

"A bull? You tried that one with Europa."

"Just practicing, my love." He twisted the lightning bolt, and a golden aura surrounded him, brilliant as the sun.

Hera squinted against the splendor. "Can you tone it down?"

Zeus muttered a profanity. The rings were the source of their powers, powers that long ago had made them king and queen of gods, but these recent replacements of the original jewels were temperamental. He adjusted the ring, and the gold became a sheen blanketing his skin. "The powers in this new ring are raw."

"So you find that, too? I nearly flooded the Chicago River when I first raised a rainstorm with mine."

"I read about that and wondered." He watched as she fidgeted with the cloud ring on her finger. Outside the sky darkened, and swollen clouds clustered over the Rocky Mountains. He tilted his head to the window. "Going to engulf Denver?"

"Sorry." Quickly she stilled her restless movement. "On d-Alphus, I heard whispers that the new crystals contained more powers than expected, but I didn't have time to find out more before I was sent back here."

Millennia past, he and his followers had been exiled from d-Alphus, their homeworld, to ancient Earth, where they'd been hailed as the gods of old. Ah, those days had been exciting. There had been much to cherish, some to regret, but all of it was lived to the fullest. In time, though, human technology had usurped their mystique, and his followers had descended from Mount Olympus to live among the humans. Even Hera had left him—not that he blamed her, he had given her much cause in those heady days. Eventually he, too, had abandoned Olympus to live a hundred lifetimes among the humans, amassing a fortune and, in the process, gaining a little wisdom and a little guilt.

Though always Hera was part of his soul, their lives had taken separate paths for many centuries. Perhaps too many to overcome. Only recently had she sought him out, but not to resume their lives together, as he had hoped. Instead she had abandoned him for a pardon and a return to d-Alphus, then shocked him, some months later, by her unexpected return.

"You don't regret your reinstated exile?" he asked.

"Not for a moment." Hera laid a hand on his and gave him a wicked smile. "Now that Peacock Cosmetics is back to full steam after my absence, I thought perhaps I'd take a little vacation." She leaned forward, her lips but a breath from his. "An isolated mountain meadow, thick with wildflowers, surrounded by impenetrable fog. That bull, as I remember, was quite potent. I could take on the form of a pretty little heifer and . . . ?" She lifted a brow in invitation.

Ah, but she tempted him. For a moment he gave in and tasted the nectar of her kiss. Then he leaned back in his chair, softly breaking contact of lips and hand.

That second time she'd left him . . . He'd thought he'd seen too much, felt too much ever to experience such pain.

He would not risk that experience again.

14

"Or we might continue with my matchmaking project," he suggested, stroking his salt-and-pepper mustache.

During his glory, Zeus had enjoyed many women. He still remembered fondly the nurturing Leda, the charms of so many others. Yet his actions had left an unexpected legacy in his lovers' descendants. Love, the deep and long-abiding kind, eluded the women who fell in love with the wrong man, or chose unwisely, or listened to the drum of practicality instead of the flute of desire. They did not trust the magic that was love.

Of late, the sting of unexpected remorse and the creeping of age—he had only three or four hundred years left—compelled him to make amends by uniting a descendant of each line with her true love. He'd been successful, with the help of Hera.

It was a lot more fun with her, too.

Zeus and Hera. Zeke Jupiter and Harriet Juneau. Together they had passion and amusement.

What he didn't know yet was whether they had sufficient trust, could yield to each other with sufficient abandon, for their lives to entwine again.

Hera accepted the suggested change. She lifted a polished Petosky stone paperweight on his desk. "You have anyone in mind?" she asked, her thumb rubbing the brown pattern.

"A woman of Leda." Zeus set a sparkling white geode atop his desk and sprinkled the far-see crystals atop it.

The paperweight dropped to the desk with a thunk. "Dia Trelawny." Hera groaned. She'd once seen Zeus and Dia share a passionate kiss. That it

15

was all—or mostly all—in the name of his match-making project, she ignored.

"Yes." Continuing the far-see ritual, he wrote Dia Trelawny's name on a piece of paper, then tossed it onto the crystals and paused. "I told you, I'm faithful now."

Hera had to believe that, or there could be no future for them. Zeus leaned back, stroking his mustache. "Besides, we agreed: my choice this time."

"I know." Hera scowled. "Oh, all right."

Smiling, Zeus rubbed the ring on his finger. The spark of electricity ignited the far-see crystals, and a curl of cedar-scented smoke rose from the geode. The paper caught fire, and the image of Dia Trelawny appeared in the smoke.

She was onstage, performing her magic with sensual energy, high-powered grace, and a lush body encased in a silver bodysuit. Her long blond hair spun about her, and her smile was as wide and genuine as any he'd seen on a woman. It warmed his heart and touched a fire in a few other places.

If ever there was a woman designed to tempt a man from monogamy, it was Dia Trelawny.

"This will be easier than we thought," Hera said, pointing to Dia's assistant, a muscular male as blond, and almost as pretty, as Dia. "He's from the line of Apollo."

They'd discovered that the curse Zeus had left in the lines of the earth women could be broken only by matching the females with a son of Olympus, a man descended from one of the other gods. A descendant of Apollo seemed logical, but . . . Zeus frowned. "The blood of the gods is very weak in him."

"It doesn't have to be strong. Just there." Hera turned away. "This matchmaking should be over soon."

Unwilling to trust the easy answer, Zeus spread the view of the far-see smoke. His breath caught, and a sliver of ice lodged in his belly as his eyes were drawn to a man in the audience. Hair black as an unlit cave, a gem in his ear, surrounded by people yet with an aura of solitude that commanded attention. The man sat entranced by the woman onstage.

Hades! The Soul Seeker, guardian of Tartarus and the Elysian Fields, which the humans had called, with a lack of understanding, the underworld.

Not the actual Hades, but Hugh Pendragon, a man Zeus had met but once. Yet those seconds of introduction had crackled with the Soul Seeker's power. The seed of the gods blazed in this one. Zeus looked from Hugh to Dia. From solitary male to vibrant female.

A Soul Seeker did not gaze with such intensity without purpose. He had more on his mind than enjoying her performance.

This was not going to be as simple as Hera thought.

Chapter One

Dia Trelawny spun in a flash of strobe light and glitter. Smoke roiled across the stage, and a frenetic rock beat vibrated beneath her feet as she vaulted onto the steel-pipe stand. She raised her hands and planted her feet in triumph and confidence. Her lungs sucked in breath but her grin, a mix of show and genuine delight, concealed the exertion.

Behind her the whirling blades edged closer. Her blond hair whipped around her neck and shoulders from the force of the generated wind. Dia shook her head, tossing the untamed curtain back while Paolo, her assistant, snapped her wrists into the shackles above her head. She struggled and writhed against the iron, a vivid demonstration that she could not escape the deadly bonds.

All part of the effect.

Throbbing drums mixed with the exhilaration of performance. Sweat enveloped her, hidden beneath her silver bodysuit. Before her, beyond the blinding stage lights and the insistent music, the audience waited, eyes on the stage, while Paolo clicked panels shut around her, encasing her body while leaving her head visible.

For one second Dia wondered if her sister had used the complimentary tickets—the lights kept her from seeing out into the audience—then the question gave way to the demands of her performance.

Metal cut the air behind her, and the skin on her back prickled from heat and adrenaline. Those blades were real; the illusion would be meaningless without that very clear threat. The lady-sawed-in-half updated to the lady-shredded-by-a-jet-fan.

Dia flashed her grin again while she tensed, waiting for the dazzling flares of light. Waiting for the flash, her cue, the perfect moment to complete the illusion.

No flares. No flash.

Smile frozen, Dia cursed. Her lighting tech had begged for one more chance, and she'd given in. It was her fault for being fooled by his excuses.

She *hated* being tricked.

The whoosh of the blades grew closer. Paolo hid his worried look behind an athletic flip. *Abort the blades?* his look asked. *Just do the escape?*

Behind the continuing stage performance, Dia gritted her teeth and gathered her strength. She gave a nearly imperceptible shake of her head. Her show would not be second-rate because she'd fallen for a line. She could do this without the flash. The

19

timing just had to be faster, and she'd have to ignore the painful twist in her shoulder the move would require.

Dia took a breath, flexed her muscles, and—

Now!

With an earsplitting whine, the blades penetrated the surrounding panels and emerged to the front. Spinning metal pierced her right through the belly.

Or at least that was what the audience believed, judging from their collective gasp.

Perfect.

Luckily, the smoke came as planned, and the lady escaped from both bonds and blades. Dia jumped off the platform with a flourish, displaying an intact body. As she took her bow to the precious sound of applause, she grinned in relief and utter joy.

Hugh Pendragon watched the finale of the magician's act, knowing it was an illusion, yet still unable to dismiss the cramp in his gut when it looked as if the blades had gone through her.

Or the heat when she'd flashed that high-voltage smile.

Smoke erupted onstage; then a split second later Dia Trelawny, free of all bonds and dangers, sparkled through it. She spun and bowed.

The lady was good. A mistress of illusion.

Hugh doubted anyone else in the audience realized there'd been one tiny kink in the performance. He wasn't sure what exactly had gone wrong, but he'd seen the split second falter in Dia's smile, and his muscles had felt the alteration of her rhythm.

His cell phone vibrated in his pocket. Amid the thundering applause, Hugh slipped from his seat, glad to escape the confines of the crowd and the blood-rousing sight of Dia Trelawny in silver lamé. Offstage she was charming, but onstage she was mesmerizing. He'd bet a blood ruby that every man here was feeling something erotic.

Unwanted fantasies about Dia were a complication he didn't need in his life.

In the quiet lobby, he glanced at the caller ID: Armond Marceaux. Last week the FBI agent had come to him with a missing persons case, a young woman believed abducted by a coworker and taken out of state. Only Hugh's long-standing friendship with Armond had persuaded him to take the case and risk another failure.

Had his one faint vision been enough? Dense trees, the woman's damaged face—too little to go on when she hadn't much time left.

His chest tightening, Hugh flipped open the phone. "Pendragon."

"We found the lady," Armond told him. "She was right where you said she'd be, in his hunting cabin near the Canadian border."

"Alive?" asked Hugh, gripping the phone. Bars of cold iron banded his chest until his breathing almost stopped. He forced himself to drag in a painful breath.

Armond hesitated. "She was alive, but just barely. We almost didn't make it in time."

His breath came easier. *Almost* was too close, however. Next time he might interpret the scant image wrong—

"Thanks for telling me." Most of the law-enforcement types who consulted him were too busy to get back to him. He was used to their am-

21

bivalence and discomfort about asking for his help in the first place, but he disliked discovering the results in the paper. Or in his dreams. Armond understood, perhaps because he had talents himself.

"You deserved to know. Thank you. It's good to know I can count on—"

"I'm retired," Hugh interrupted softly.

"I didn't think you were serious."

Hugh edged away from the stream of bodies leaving the theater. "I did this last one only because *you* asked it."

"You can't retire from yourself. Trust me, I know."

"I can, and I have. How's Callie and the baby?" Hugh changed the subject.

"Both well," Armond answered with a touch of pride. "Louis is almost sleeping through the night, and Callie is preparing to film more of the video series."

"I saw the first show. It was good; I went and bought a case of wine."

Armond laughed. "I'll tell her. Hugh..." His voice sobered. "Take care of yourself. If there's anything I can do—"

"All I need is some solitude." Then maybe his failures would cease haunting his dreams. Gently he flipped the phone closed.

Bodies from the departing audience brushed against him, the small touches disquieting. He moved away into a small, protected niche until the lobby of the theater emptied; then he prepared to leave.

The door to the theater swung open to disgorge a final straggler, and Hugh slipped inside to stand at the rear. Dia strode across stage, already changed into shorts and a lacy top, her blond hair pulled into a ponytail. She passed through a beam of light, shimmering and glittering as he remembered.

For six months, one vivid image had haunted him—Dia Trelawny passing through a beam of candlelight as she strolled, hips swaying, across the room at Armond's wedding party. For that one timeless moment, she had seemed to glow like amber.

When he'd seen that she was performing in Chicago, he'd come, hoping to exorcize the lingering image. Instead the amber image now glittered with diamonds, and he was more than a little aroused.

Hugh cast one last glance at the curtained stage, then left. He'd had one of his increasingly rare dreams last night. His dreams were sometimes prophetic, sometimes insightful, often painful and confusing, but they were rarely wrong.

Dia Trelawny would soon come to him.

He could wait.

Backstage, Dia plunged into the after-show bustle. At least they'd be playing this venue for several performances, so they didn't need to knock down everything, just reset the props. A tour was exhausting, and with a small crew everyone had to pitch in, but every splinter was worth it. Dia lived for the moments when she was onstage, when her magic held an audience rapt.

What she didn't enjoy were the administration hassles. "Mick?" she shouted, rotating her sore shoulder and looking for her fast-talking lighting tech. "Where's Mick?"

"Mick always disappears when there's work," grumbled Anya, the sound tech, running a hand through her cropped, scarlet-tinted hair.

"He took off before the applause died, because he knew our dear Dia would be fuming." Paolo paused in the process of setting up the massive picture frame Dia used in one sequence. "Good show. You recovered well."

"Thanks."

"But Mick's got the wrong karma; his disharmony disrupts our flow."

Dia cared more about results than karma, and with Mick as her lighting tech, the result was a sloppy performance, discontent among her stage crew, and a pain in her shoulder.

Anya was more blunt. "How many more chances to screw up does he get?"

"None." Leaving her with two problems: finding Mick to fire and finding another tech on short notice.

"Dia!" The enthusiastic call carried through the backstage noise. A moment later Dia was enveloped by soft arms, honeysuckle perfume, and cotton print: Liza, her sister. "I adored your show. How clever of you to take Mother's tapping spirits and turn them into a puzzling illusion."

Dia returned her sister's hug. "Glad you enjoyed it. Where are the twins?"

"Talking to somebody." Liza waved a vague hand. "They are thrilled, and I so appreciate this. You are a lifesaver."

"I'm just glad you could use the tickets. Look, I need to finish—"

"You're busy, and here I am running off at the mouth." Liza made a scooting motion with her hands. "Go ahead. Finish."

"I thought we could get something to eat when I finish."

"Great, teenagers are always hungry. Trust me. Lukas and Cameron drink at least a gallon of milk a day, and Elena devours fruit. Where can the twins wait?"

"I have a dressing area—"

"We'll find it." She gave Dia a kiss on the cheek. "Thanks again. You don't know what this means to me."

Dia watched her departing sister, bemused. Such enthusiasm over tickets and a family weekend in Chicago? Why hadn't she thought to do this earlier? Liza probably didn't get a chance to get out much.

Anya paused in coiling a wire. "Relative of yours, Dia? She looks like you."

"My older sister."

"Is she a magician, too?"

"No." She and her sister looked alike, but the temperament genes had split down the middle. "Liza's into motherhood and macrame."

"How many kids she got?"

"Four. Two sets of identical twins. Fourteen and twelve."

"Ouch. Better her than me."

Dia laughed. "Me, too. She's a single mom, and I don't know how she manages, though they're basically good kids."

The crew, without the errant Mick, worked efficiently and were soon set up for tomorrow's performance. "Dia," called Paolo. "We're about finished. Everyone's heading out for drinks and a meal. You'll join us?"

"Not tonight, I've got plans. Tomorrow though." Dia hurried over to her tiny dressing room, anxious to spend the rest of the evening with Liza and her nieces and nephews. How long had it been? Last December?

The boys, fourteen, hadn't bothered to wait in the room, she discovered as she rounded the corner to the narrow hallway. That wasn't surprising. Her main impression on her last visit had been one of endless motion and restless energy. If the twitchings of a teenage boy could be harnessed, there'd be no energy crisis. Cameron was dribbling a miniature soccer ball, feinting left and right against an imaginary defender. Lukas slouched against the wall, his foot tapping to the music that must be playing through the headphones hanging in his ears while his fingers manipulated the controls of a hand-held electronic game.

"Hey, guys." Dia gave them each a hug, figuring they wouldn't mind with no one to see, and tousled their identical red hair, dislodging Lukas's earphones. "When did you get taller than me?"

Cam rolled his eyes. "Mom asks that all the time. I expected something original from you, Aunt Dia."

"Awesome show." Lukas's eyes gleamed.

"Thanks."

"You use computers to orchestrate it?"

"Some. Where're the girls?"

Cam jerked his head toward the dressing room.

Inside, Elena sat at Dia's dressing table, trying on makeup, while Claire sat curled in one corner, reading and twisting a strand of her brown hair. Where

26

Cam and Lukas mostly ignored being identical twins, except when it suited their purpose to trick someone, Claire and Elena fought it, highlighting their differences with clothes, hairstyles, hobbies, and attitudes. Today Elena wore tight shorts and a handkerchief-print shirt with an extra button undone, while Claire was in black with three narrow braids dangling over her shoulder.

Elena leaped up when she saw Dia. Her face glittered. Blue pencil and shadow outlined her brown eyes. "Aunt Dia, this sparkle foundation is sooo fantastic. Can I borrow it, puh-leeze?"

Dia plucked the bottle from Elena's fingers. "That's stage makeup, sweetie. Too strong for street wear. Besides, aren't you too young?" She gave her a hug. "How's things?"

"I am so glad school is out; it is so boring. And I'm twelve. Old enough for makeup."

"Not that kind. Why don't you try that remover? It's good for your skin." Dia turned to her other niece, who was still sitting quietly. "What are you reading, Claire? Must be good."

"It is." Carefully Claire put her bookmark in her page and closed the book. "It's the diary of a young woman written during her twelve years in a mental institution."

"Oh." Not sure what more to say, Dia looked around. Cam and Lukas propped up the doorway, Elena smeared cream on her face, and Claire was stuffing her book into a small pack. "Where's your mom?"

"She couldn't wait," Cam answered.

"She said to tell you she was sorry, but the plane was leaving," added Lukas.

Dia blinked. "Excuse me? Leaving?"

"She's going off for romance and adventure." Elena sighed. "Just like Grandma."

"Going off?" Dia cleared her throat. "Where? How long?"

The four looked at each other blankly. "I don't think she ever said," said Cam at last.

"It's some wilderness trek," Claire said.

"She said she'd keep in contact by e-mail," Lukas offered.

"Mom gets this way every so often." Claire was utterly matter-of-fact, and the others nodded in easy agreement. "All gooey-eyed over some guy. Don't worry; she'll be back before school starts."

"Who's picking you up? Who's watching you for the summer?" Dia's stomach knotted. No, Liza wouldn't do this to her. Liza had the maternal instincts; Dia couldn't keep a goldfish alive. Liza knew that.

Four pairs of eyes, two feminine brown, two masculine blue, turned toward her.

In unison, four mouths uttered the dreaded words: "You are, Aunt Dia."

Blood rushing south to her toes, Dia dropped to her chair. "No. I can't. I've got shows scheduled all over the Midwest—"

"We're supposed to go with you," Claire said. "Mom thought it would be an education."

"Look, it's impossible. She should have asked me—"

"She did. Mom said she talked to you, and you agreed," Elena accused.

"I didn't . . ." Dia's voice trailed off. Liza *had* called last month after a show, when Dia was bone tired. Her sister had a tendency toward many words and little substance, and Dia had long ago formed the habit of listening only to the cadence of her sister's ramblings as her cue for a polite murmur.

One of those, Liza must have taken as a yes. Or she'd heard what she wanted to hear, not what was said, another of Liza's tendencies.

"I'm sorry; I can't keep you with me." *Especially not now.* "We'll have to find someone to stay with you. What about Grandma?"

"Grandma's off on one of her spiritual treks." Claire hitched her pack onto her back.

"Still?" Dia bit her lip. Her mother, Adele, had surfaced a month ago asking Dia to wire funds to Thailand, but Dia thought she'd come home since.

"We got a postcard from Nepal last week," answered Lukas.

"Mom couldn't find anyone to stay with us," said Cam. "That's why she asked you."

"There has to be someone." But there were no other relatives to call on; the twins' father hadn't been heard from since the girls were two. Dia sorted through her acquaintances, but couldn't think of a single one who'd want the job. "Maybe we could put out an ad."

Claire's eyes widened. "And possibly turn us over to the care of a criminal?"

"We'll check references."

"Do you know how easy it is to forge something like that?" asked Lukas.

Dia had the distinct impression she was being manipulated. "All right." She stopped the cheers with a lifted hand. "I'm in Chicago for two weeks.

29

You can stay with me for that long." How was she supposed to fit four kids—especially two the size of Cam and Lukas—in her efficiency sublet? "But when I find someone, no protests."

"You won't find anyone who'll keep us for the summer," predicted Lukas.

"Then I'll just have to find your disappearing mother, won't I?"

Chapter Two

Hugh Pendragon lived, and worked, in the house of her childhood fancies.

Of course, her fancies had centered on haunted houses, not fairy castles.

Behind her sunglasses, Dia contemplated the mansion, which was barely visible behind the trees and bushes. She'd never been the picket-fence-and-roses type. No, she had dreamed of gothic turrets and octagonal rooms with concealed doorways in the fireplace and hidden passages and mysterious cellars. This house embodied it all.

June in Chicago was sultry, filled with the close stench of exhaust and oppressive heat, but this place looked as if snow should be lining the roof, like the cap on a remote mountain.

She shook off her fascination. No matter to her if

he lived in a Victorian dream or a wigwam. This was business; her sister was missing.

Dia had spent the morning on the phone, but Liza wasn't at any of the vacation places Dia thought she might frequent, nor did any of her neighbors or friends have a clue where she was. The police were singularly unimpressed with her dilemma, since the evidence said her sister had left voluntarily, and even the kids weren't concerned.

Dia could not afford to be so blasé. Even if she could keep the twins with her—and she didn't see how that was possible, given her schedule—they had to be long gone, and far away from any risk, before her performance at Demetria Cesare's remote estate.

That left Hugh Pendragon, the best at finding a missing soul, according to the bored police officer she'd asked about a private detective. Or, in his exact words, "The guy's weird, but you won't find anyone better."

For a detective, though, Hugh was remarkably elusive. When his office number proved disconnected, she'd tracked down his whereabouts using the trusty friend-of-a-friend method: her best friend Mark Hennessy had asked his friend, FBI agent Armond Marceaux.

Dia settled her sunglasses, fluffed her hair, and tugged the hem of her shell over the waist of her denim skirt, surprised at the flutter in her belly, akin to the one she always got right before she went onstage. The cause she knew—Hugh Pendragon. They'd met once before, and she'd never known a man who had so lingered in her dreams after a single, short introduction.

Business only, she reminded herself again.

A wrought-iron fence surrounded grounds thick with trees and bushes. Only a six-foot strip of grass separated the fence from the jungle. Drawing a breath and forming a smile, she rang the bell. In response to the buzz, leaves rustled and shook, branches swayed, and an eerie baying rose to the heavens, sending a chill down Dia's spine.

Suddenly, out from the trees bounded a hound of hell: ferocious teeth, red eyes . . . three heads? No, one head, big enough for three. Barking furiously, he leaped for the fence.

Dia shrieked and staggered backward.

Still barking, Hellhound raised front paws to the fence and tried to stick his head through the bars. His massive hindquarters quivered, his tail swishing with the thrill of the impending kill.

A whistle cut across the grounds, repeated, and, with a whine, Hellhound dropped to all fours. Dia drew in a ragged breath, her hand resting above her racing heart, and watched the whistler scurry down the grass.

Not Hugh Pendragon. The newcomer was stocky, with gray hair and muttonchop sideburns, strong hands and large knuckles—Dia always noticed the hands. And an apron?

"Cerberus, be gracious." His cultured accent was a decided contrast to the rough-and-ready body. English, maybe.

Cerberus gave a single bark and stayed put. Barely. His rear end still wiggled as if he was ready to pounce, and his blazing eyes were fixed firmly on her head.

"Good morning. My apologies, miss. I didn't realize Cerberus was out," the man said cheerily, wiping flour off his hands onto his apron. "Can I help you?"

With one cautious eye toward Cerberus, Dia answered, "I'm here to see Mr. Pendragon."

"Do you have an appointment?"

"Um, no, I couldn't reach him, but I need to see him, Mr. . . . ?"

"Ronald. I am Mr. Pendragon's housekeeper."

Dia smiled at him, finally taking her eyes off the huge dog. "Ronald. Hi, I'm Dia Trelawny. My sister's missing and Mr. Pendragon was recommended—"

Sadly, Ronald shook his head. "I'm sorry, Mr. Pendragon has retired."

"Retired?" Her stomach plummeting, Dia gripped the wrought-iron bars, eyeing Cerberus to make sure he didn't take offense. She gave Ronald her most beseeching look. "Please. I've got to see him. I heard Hugh Pendragon is the best."

"Yes, he is. Or was. I'm sorry, Mr. Pendragon is very firm in this decision." Ronald gave a long sigh, and it was clear he did not agree.

Hot metal cut into her palms as Dia gripped the wrought iron. Armond *had* said she should call first, but Dia believed face-to-face worked to her advantage. She'd feared she wouldn't have enough to pay Pendragon, or that he'd be too busy to take on her case. She'd never thought she wouldn't even get to see him. "Please? She has four children, and she's my only sister."

Ronald wasn't immune to the plea or the blue

eyes. He rubbed a hand across his thick sideburns, looking torn.

"Could I at least talk to him? Can you tell him I'm here? We met last December." Maybe Hugh remembered it as vividly as she did.

"Oh, dear, I—"

"It's all right, Ronald," came a low voice. "I'll see her. Hold onto Cerberus."

"Very good, sir."

While Ronald slipped a hand through the dog's gem-studded collar, Dia watched Hugh emerge from the growth of trees. Her breath stopped right at the level of her throat, and the sultry morning had nothing to do with the rush of heat she felt.

It had been six months since their single, chance meeting at Armond and Callie's wedding party, and she'd convinced herself she'd glamorized the impact Hugh had had on her. Dia straightened, dropped her death grip on the fence, and then gave herself a mental kick.

Deceive the audience, never yourself.

Like that night, the only color about him was the blue diamond in his earlobe and the brilliant emerald of his eyes. Then he'd been dressed in black; today it was gray—T-shirt, shorts. Their loose fit only emphasized the toned body beneath. His hair was still as velvety black as she remembered, especially against his pale skin.

He moved with quiet economy, his bare feet barely disturbing the blades of grass as he came to pause beside the gate.

"Come on in, Dia," he invited, unlatching the gate.

Said the spider to the fly. Dia's body went on alert status. She met his gaze, refusing to lower her eyes before its commanding intensity. "You remember me?"

A smile played over his lips. "I saw you perform last night."

"You did? I hope you liked the show."

"Very much. There was a hitch with the finale, wasn't there?"

"Oh, phooey, I was hoping nobody noticed that."

"I doubt anyone else did. I'm . . . observant."

"You would be, in your line of work."

They were sparring, she realized, making conversation to cover the unexpected, unwanted tug between them.

Or at least she was. With Hugh it was hard to tell. She stepped around the gate and immediately was surrounded by the sensation of utter quiet, as though the world outside did not exist.

Until Hellhound emitted a roaring bark and bounded toward her, escaping from Ronald's grip. Dia screeched and stumbled backward, right into Hugh. His hands gripped her arms, and his body braced her upright, keeping her from falling. Hard, solid, smooth, firm, heated—the impressions tumbled into her.

Cerberus leaped and his front paws landed on her chest, crushing out the air and sandwiching her between masculine strength and canine fur, between faint woodsy aftershave and doggy breath. Dia gasped, her hands rising in futile protection of her face. Cerberus opened his mouth . . . and gave her a sloppy lick on the ear.

"Cerberus! Down!" Hugh's low voice commanded. He didn't need volume to make his point. Immediately the dog dropped to all fours. He settled down on his haunches, an inch from her feet.

"Are you all right?" Hugh asked, still in that low, rumbling voice. His hands stroked gently along her arms, perhaps testing for damages, definitely soothing.

"I . . ." Dia drew a shaky breath, not focusing. "I'll . . . Fine."

As if suddenly realizing what he was doing, Hugh ceased his gentling and shifted away from her with unflattering speed.

"Oh, Cerberus, you naughty dog." Ronald grabbed the collar again and tried to tug the immovable dog farther back. "I am so sorry, miss. He's not usually like this. He's quite taken with you."

"He *likes* me?" Dia scratched out. Lord help her, how did he act if he didn't like someone?

"If he didn't," Hugh murmured, "you wouldn't be inside the gate. Don't you know, Cerberus was the dog of myth, the triheaded monster who guarded the gates of Hades?"

"Sir, don't try to frighten her. Miss Trelawny, his tail is wagging," added Ronald. "He won't hurt you."

Dia finally looked at the massive dog. He quivered, waiting, at her feet. His ears were perked, his eyes focused on the ear he hadn't yet anointed, and from his mouth dangled . . .

"He's got my earring." Dia fingered the dangling cluster of rhinestones on her other ear, making sure it hadn't been dislodged.

37

"He likes gems," explained Hugh. "Especially shiny ones."

"They aren't real."

"He knows that. He goes for glitter, not value. Cerberus, give the lady back her earring."

The dog whined, his gaze still fixed on the other earring.

"Cerberus."

The dog whined again.

"He wants the other one, doesn't he?" asked Dia.

"Yes, but he's not going to get it. Cerberus."

With a mournful whine, the dog dropped the earring. Sunlight glistened off the rhinestones and dog slobber. Cerberus's ears drooped in mournful loss, and he sprawled down, resting his head in sorrow on his front paws.

Oh, geez, she'd hurt the dog's feelings. Dia felt about as high as a worm. "He can have the earrings."

"Oh, no, miss, you shouldn't indulge him—"

"It's okay." Dia slipped the other earring from her ear and crouched down, holding it in her palm. Before she could drop it, however, Cerberus stuck his head in her hand. She shut her eyes as the big teeth neared her flesh, but was proud of how steady she held her hand.

Delicately Cerberus took the earring—and no skin—in his teeth, then scooped up the other. Tail wagging, earrings dangling from his mouth, he trotted off.

Reaction set in, and Dia grabbed Hugh's arm to steady herself. Then she quickly dropped it when she felt him tense.

"Are you all right, Miss Dia?" Ronald hovered over her, fanning her with his hand.

"I'm fine," she answered, praying her knees had enough strength to hold her upright.

"Come to the kitchen. I've made fresh tea, and there are cookies—"

"We'll be in my office," Hugh interrupted smoothly. "Can you bring it there, including two glasses of ice water?"

"Of course, sir." Ronald bustled away, following Cerberus.

Hugh stood in silence, as if realizing Dia needed a few more moments to collect herself, then said, "I'm sorry about Cerberus. He has a mind of his own and the manners of a dog."

"He's . . . fearsome-looking."

"But he's a softy for people he likes."

"I'm glad he liked me."

"How could he not?" The question was so low, Dia wondered if she'd heard him right. He touched one finger to the crook of her arm, the tiny pressure warm against her pulse. "You're still trembling."

His touch did nothing to slow her pulse. Dia gave him a slow, lazy smile; she knew how to keep up appearances, how to hide her reactions to him. "He just startled me."

Hugh's hand lifted, and her skin felt suddenly cool. "Not much of an animal lover, are you?"

Dia lifted one shoulder, not liking his astute observation. She'd never felt comfortable with animals, maybe because she'd never had a pet, but very few people knew that. And none on first meeting. "Dogs and cats, we tolerate each other. It's the birds that are the worst."

"Birds?"

"Big birds, mostly." Feeling stronger, Dia finger-combed her hair, smoothed the wrinkles from her blouse, tried to dry the dog slobber. "For some reason, I never quite trust 'em. I always think they're eyeing me for a good peck, and they usually are. I was an assistant to this magician once who used a goose in his act. I hated every minute. That goose was mean."

"A goose? How do you use a goose in magic?"

"Well, I didn't say it was a very *good* act, did I?" Dia answered with a smile.

Hugh laughed, a bursting, rusty sound that seemed to surprise him as much as it did her. Abruptly he quieted and gestured toward a narrow path, a different route from that taken by Ronald and the dog. "Shall we go into my office?"

Feeling confident, Dia started down the path. Things were going well: Hugh would find her sister, Liza would take back the children, Dia could continue her tour as planned.

And she would stop Demetria Cesare's blackmail once and for all.

Dia Trelawny strolled down the uneven, leaf-strewn, wooded path with a sure grace and a subtle sexuality that Hugh guessed was part calculated, part as innate as a heartbeat. He followed, careful not to touch her again, not even by accident. Just watching her, or receiving that high-voltage smile, upset his hard-cultivated solitude and inner quiet.

A single tiny touch shattered it.

Their encounter last December had been brief, two strangers meeting in party mode. An introduction. An electrifying handshake that had disrupted his heartbeat and her breath. Small talk overlying a bone-deep attraction neither had acknowledged. Her stunning good-bye smile. That remembered exit through a beam of amber light.

In his office, Dia glanced around, taking in the modernistic furniture and high-tech equipment. "Somehow I thought your office would be different."

Did she know of his talent? It wasn't something he advertised; most people thought he was simply very good at what he did, but some were aware of it. "You were expecting crystal balls and tarot cards?"

Dia made a face. "No! I guess, with this old house, I expected leather, red velvet drapes, fog rolling in."

"A slipper filled with pipe tobacco and a violin in one corner?"

"Dr. Watson sipping tea." Dia laughed, a sound as shiny as a sunbeam. "All right, I admit, too much Sherlock Holmes."

"The mind is still the key to detective work. We've just updated the tools." He motioned her to a chair, then sat behind his desk, needing a barrier between them. "Why are you here, Dia?"

Before she could answer, Ronald knocked, then entered with a tray loaded with glasses of water, cups of steaming tea, a plate of shortbread, and a bowl of cherries and peach slices. "I thought a little refreshment was in order."

"Thanks, Ronald."

"Thank you," added Dia. "It's hot out there."

"I find there's nothing better on a hot day than a nice cup of tea." Ronald fussed, settling food and napkins, then asked, "Do you need anything else?" At their refusal, he left.

Dia smiled again. "You've got your own Mrs. Hudson."

"He even sounds like her." Hugh claimed a glass of ice water. "Help yourself." When she shook her head, he added, "Ronald will be hurt if you don't at least try his cookies."

"Maybe one then." She claimed her tea and cookie with a graceful gesture, then leaned back, a smile on her face, her blond hair in charming disarray from wind and humidity.

On Dia, wind and humidity looked sexy.

On her a short skirt, bare legs, and a simple yellow top looked sexy, too.

He had a feeling she could make sackcloth sexy.

"But just one," she added with a smile. "After all, I've got to fit into spandex tonight."

A sudden image of spandex and skin and Dia sliced him with a bolt of heat both unexpected and unwelcome. Hugh gulped the ice water. He didn't understand this fascination with her, didn't like that he was probably one of many enticed by her long legs and bewitching smile. He'd desired women before, many times, but this was beyond desire. He felt like a moth, a creature of moonlight and nighttime, circling the brilliant light, about to be zapped.

Unlike the moth, however, he sure as hell knew better than to dive into that enticing glow.

She nibbled the cookie, then set it down, half-uneaten. "I've come about my sister, Hugh. Her name is Liza Swensen, and she's from Wisconsin—"

This had been a mistake. He'd wanted to meet her on his own turf, so to speak. He had been curious about his dream, about why she'd come, and about whether proximity would dull her impact on his senses. Now he had his answers.

She wanted him to find her sister.

And every moment with her, even hearing her speak his name, lodged her more firmly into his memories.

"I can't," he said abruptly.

"Can't what?"

"Can't take your case. I'm retired." He had no other choice but to lay it out flat like that. He wouldn't mislead her, and he sure as hell couldn't take on another case.

Her jaw tightened. "Then why did you invite me in?"

"Curiosity." Hugh traced a thumb through the sweat on his glass, not looking at her. "I won't take your case, but I can offer a few leads, suggest someone you can hire."

Dia leaned forward, the soft silk of her blouse brushing against her breasts. Her subtle scent, part perfume, part woman, enticed him closer. But Hugh didn't move.

"According to the police, you're the best, and that's what I want." Dia brushed back the strands of hair that had curled around her breast. "My sister has disappeared, gone to find adventure, I gather."

"She left voluntarily?" At Dia's nod, Hugh frowned. "I don't see your problem."

"She's got four kids, and she left them with me. I don't do kids, Hugh. I'm lousy at it, and I've got dates booked throughout the Midwest. They can't stay with me. I need her back."

"Are the children worried?"

"No."

"Why not?"

"She's done this before," Dia admitted. "Maybe once or twice."

"Are you worried?"

"No—" Dia broke off, as if struck by a sudden thought. Her next words contradicted her first, automatic response. "Wouldn't you be if she were your sister?"

"I don't have a sister." She was worried, scared, maybe, Hugh realized, but about something other than a missing sister. What?

His curiosity didn't change his mind.

"Your sister left of her own accord; she'll come back when she's ready. Talk to her friends and neighbors; talk to her kids. Think of every place she's ever gone on vacation, even when you were children, and try those."

"I've done that. She's vanished!"

"Check her credit card statements, telephone bills for recent charges or phone calls. Look around the house for travel brochures. Talk to her employer."

"She works for herself. I'm doing a lot of traveling this summer, Hugh. I work nights, sleep days. These performances will be exhausting and time-consuming; there's no place for children."

"Then hire one of these men. They're all good detectives." He scrawled a couple of names on a piece of paper and slid it across the desk.

Without taking the paper, she rose and braced her hands against the desk. "Help me find my sister."

He felt the tug urging him to help her, whispering that this was easy, one last case. He didn't need his disappearing psychic talent to solve this.

There would always be one last case, and he could not risk taking even one more. He met her gaze unflinchingly, hands clasped. "I can't."

Her lips tightened. "I'll be in Chicago for two weeks. Here's my phone number in case you change your mind." She slid the paper to him.

It was his turn not to pick it up. "I won't."

They stood, motionless, determined, until Dia broke the contact by straightening.

"Okay, if that's the way it is. Thanks for your time, Mr. Pendragon." She carefully folded the list and slipped it into her pocket. "Tell Ronald his shortbread is divine." She strode to the door, then stopped, her back to him. "Is Cerberus likely to accost me?"

"No."

"Good. You can mail my earrings to me."

Hugh watched her leave. She had come, he had met with her, and she had left. He wondered if the Fates were going to be satisfied with that.

Somehow he doubted it.

Whatever fate had in store, though, he could not take her case. Not until he found out what was wrong with him.

He'd known most of his life that he was different. Vivid dreams often proved prophetic, once he understood their confusing images, and when he touched objects that belonged to other people, he

saw visions of where they were, what they were
doing. He shared their experiences. Sometimes he
knew other things from the scene—a threat, a joy,
a choice. The visions were unpredictable, depend-
ing upon the urgency of the situation, the strength
of the soul of the person he sought, and the level
of intimate connection between the object and the
missing soul. The visions required effort and intent
on his part, but they were always vivid, never
wrong, rarely missing.

Six months ago, everything changed.

The psychic talents that had defined him began
seeping away, fading like old photographs exposed
to time and sun. He hadn't realized how much a
part of him they were until he could barely find
them. It was a bleeding of his soul that he didn't
know how to stop.

He'd tried to keep working, but too many of the
cases he accepted were those beyond the realm of
the usual detective. Too many required his extra
talents, and he could not help those he'd been hired
to find. He'd helped Armond only because the faint
vision had contained dense trees, and when he'd
learned the abductor was an avid hunter, he'd
found the deed to the Minnesota cabin.

Dreams of his failures plagued his sleep.

Hugh ran a hand across the files he kept next to
his desk. These were the files of his failures. He
didn't need to measure them to know the stack had
grown in the last six months. He didn't need to read
them to remember; his dreams did that for him each
night.

He did not need to add to the pile. Or to the
nightmares.

The Seeker

Unable to stop himself, he picked up the box beside the files. It held an odd collection—gloves, a glass owl, a wallet, the miscellany of lives disrupted. Without looking, he lifted the item on top: a teenager's diary. He held this small piece of the missing girl's life in his bare palm, the red plastic smelling faintly of talcum powder and Coppertone. Slowly his fingers closed about the stiff cover. He waited, trying to open himself to any sensation, any image, any clue, praying this time would be different. He waited, straining until the effort made his temples pound.

Nothing. Inside him was only blank emptiness and the dry taste of sadness for a missing soul.

Nothing.

Chapter Three

A short knock sounded, and then Ronald poked his head around the office door. "Has Miss Trelawny left, sir?"

"Yes. She said your shortbread was divine."

Ronald beamed, stroking a muttonchop sideburn. "I do pride myself on it. Old family recipe." He began to collect the tray and glasses. "You're not taking her case?"

Hugh shook his head.

"Then this retirement is official."

"Yes."

"What will you do with yourself?"

Try to forget his failures. Regain his balance and his peace. Replenish the well of his soul. Try to find some answers about what was going wrong and why he could no longer tap into the visions and dreams that had always been a part of him.

Ronald wouldn't understand those answers. "Read, write, meditate."

"Become a reclusive hermit? Live in solitude?"

Hugh smiled. Peace and solitude were exactly what he needed. "Something like that."

"You'll think of something else in time, I'm sure. Oh, a courier from the museum returned the gems you had lent them last December. I've put them in your house safe for the time being. And here are Miss Trelawny's earrings." He laid the glittering jewelry on the desk, then picked up the tray. "Do you want me to mail them?"

"I'll take care of it."

When Ronald left, Hugh contemplated Dia's earrings for a moment. Sending them back would remove the last bit of her from his life. He closed his eyes against the sudden punch to the chest. The mere thought of never seeing her again blindsided him and left him reeling. Yet he knew what he needed—solitude, quiet, peace—and Dia Trelawny was none of those. Reluctantly, with the tips of his fingers, he picked up the earrings.

Unseen flames licked up his hand, then his arm, scalding his chest and throat, electrifying his hair. Clogged lungs gasped for air, tasted only smoke. The room faded behind the onslaught, replaced by Dia standing atop a stoop leading to a small house turned into an office.

For the first time in six months, the vision came with vivid clarity. For the first time ever it came unbidden and unsought.

She was frowning. Baking sun, irritating smog, discordant horns—every sensation of the city was transmitted to him. He could taste her frustration.

49

Hugh dropped the earrings, and as abruptly as it had come, the image vanished beneath a wall of fire.

For a long time, how long he didn't know, he sat, too fatigued to stir. He heard the tick of a clock, the hum of the computer, the faint voice of Ronald singing in the kitchen, the passage of air. Bright colors vibrated in his vision, and the chair pressed painfully against him. Even breathing was difficult, for each brush of clothing made his sensitive skin ache. Lingering scents of Dia's perfume and peaches brought on a ravenous hunger—for food, for her.

The aftermath was stronger than he had ever experienced.

Hugh stared at the glittering earrings. Six months ago he had met Dia Trelawny. Six months ago his talent began fading. Now another change—Dia Trelawny again, and a single, potent, unsought vision.

With a piece of paper, Hugh slid the earrings into a small brown envelope. Yet he didn't address or stamp it. He folded the envelope and tucked it into his shirt pocket.

He would return the earrings in person. Tonight.

Of Hugh's two recommended detectives, one was in the hospital with appendicitis and the other was out of town on a case. That left sheer luck to find a replacement.

And Lady Luck wasn't smiling on her search today. Dia paused at the top of the stoop to don her sunglasses. Midday sunshine reflected off the concrete, and waves of heat rolled through the streets. She lifted her hair and fanned herself. At least this last prospect hadn't had cobwebs lining his office. Nor did the rooms stink like antiseptic over urine. She might have hired him, if he'd ever looked above the level of her chest.

She hated when men fell for the stereotype suggested by her looks. Not that she wasn't above using her appeal when it suited her purpose, but she didn't like it.

She glanced at her watch and stifled a yawn. Time to get back. The kids had been asleep when she'd left, but that didn't mean they'd stayed that way. And soon she'd have to leave for the theater. At least she might be able to catch a nap before the evening performance.

In less than an hour she was back at her southside efficiency. Since she'd be touring the Midwest, she'd rented it for three months as a home base. The apartment was small, all she could afford, but it suited her needs. Her work as a magician was intense and required unswerving concentration. Home was a haven of quiet and order, the only place where she didn't have to be onstage, where she could recharge.

Dia opened the door to chaos.

The floor shook with the bass from her stereo. Lukas had plugged in his computer and he sat with his feet propped on the sofa working, his head bobbing to the profanity-laden rap. Elena perched before the television, its blaring volume competing with the stereo, and watched a psychic pretending to contact the spirit of somebody's aunt Barbara. Cam was doing arm curls with her weights. Each lift barely missed toppling a dried fern the previous tenants had left. Claire was immersed in a book.

51

"Hi, I'm home," Dia called.

They all ignored her.

Dia glanced around, frustrated. Clothes were strewn about the floor, a pile of dirty dishes was heaped on the counter, and cups littered the single room.

She'd hoped to recharge? The only thing charging right now was the electric company. "Elena, turn off the TV. Lukas, can you turn that down? *Lukas!*"

That got his attention. "Oh, hi, Aunt Dia."

She mimed turning down the volume.

"Sorry." He turned the dial and a moment later she could hear again. "Hey, Elena, turn off the tube!"

"But I like this show!" Still, Elena snapped it off. "Aunt Dia, can I use your phone? I promised my best friend that I'd call her as soon as I could."

"In a moment." Patience, Dia reminded herself as she rubbed the bridge of her nose. "What have you been doing today?"

Lukas shrugged. "Stuff. What's for dinner?"

Dinner? She usually had a salad, then ate after the show, but they probably wouldn't like to wait. "There's a frozen pizza—"

"We had that for lunch." Cam wiped his face with her bath towel. "With the salad and bread. And cereal. You're also out of milk."

"We would have gone out to find a store, but last night you told us to chill here." Claire's voice was faintly accusing.

"If we're going to be stuck in this dinky apartment all summer, it's going to be totally boring," Elena complained.

"It's too crowded here." They all nodded at Claire's proclamation.

Conventional wisdom dictated getting a bigger apartment; her bank balance dictated otherwise. She'd sunk everything she had into this show. It would either propel her up the ranks of magicians, one of the rare women to crash those upper echelons, or she'd be back to being the eye candy, the beautiful, anonymous, interchangeable assistant, the second bill.

Assuming she could stop Demetria's Cesare's blackmail, that is.

"I can't afford anything bigger. We just have to find a way to make this work until I find your mom. But I've run into a snag in hiring a detective, so it's up to us. Got any suggestions?"

Four pairs of eyes gave her blank stares.

Dia waved a hand. "Maybe you can think of something. Where she might go. Anything you overheard. Any detail. A wilderness trek does not sound like your mother."

"Oh, she's trying to impress this rich guy she's been dating. He's into that kind of thing," Claire said matter-of-factly. "She wants to marry him."

"Where did they go?"

"Brazil."

"Borneo."

"Botswana."

Dia rubbed the bridge of her nose. Obviously the kids weren't up on the location.

"Personally, I think she should have gone with Pan," Elena said dreamily.

"Who's Pan?"

"Julian Panadopolis," Claire said. "The grounds-keeper at the club where she does her psychic readings. They call him Pan because he plays the flute divinely."

"Pan's cool. He gets us passes to swim." Cam headed toward the kitchenette.

"Can we go swimming sometime?" asked Elena.

"I don't know if there's a pool nearby. Now can you think of anything else?"

Shrugs and shakes were her answer. She'd have to try something else.

"Did you put an ad in the paper?" Lukas plopped back on the sofa with his computer. "I tell you, no one's going to want to stay with us in this tiny place."

Cam came back eating a banana. "Fruit's gone. You need to lay in some Hot Pockets, Aunt Dia. When do we eat?"

"When do we leave for the theater?" Claire asked.

Dia focused on the last question in the barrage. "You're going with me?"

"I've been reading about the history of magic," Claire said. "It will be fascinating to see the modern version up close."

Cam kicked a toe against the floor. "I got kind of interested in magic a few years ago, been practicing. Did a show at the school last year—I'd like to show it to you sometime. Lukas is great at the pyrotechnics."

"I'm his beautiful assistant." Elena batted her lashes.

"Beautiful? Not." Cam laughed. "You've got to get a chest first. You're convenient."

Elena flew at him, fists pounding. "You take that back."

Cam continued laughing, holding his hands up to ward off her ineffectual blows, while Lukas pulled her off and immobilized her. Elena refused to give up, kicking out at both of them.

"Ouch!" Lukas shouted.

Dia stared at the chaos, her head throbbing. What was she supposed to do? Was there a parenting manual that covered this?

"Elena," Claire interjected, "no brother is a judge of his sister's beauty."

Elena stopped and frowned. "He's not?"

"No. Cultural taboos forbid a brother from acknowledging a sister's sexuality; therefore he cannot notice her attractiveness."

Elena stuck her tongue out at Cam. "See if I ever act as your assistant again."

Dia gaped at Claire. "Uh, where did you learn that?"

"I read it. Are we going with you tonight?"

She really couldn't keep them cooped up in the apartment for days on end, Dia realized, and she didn't want to leave them alone all the time. "You can come tonight."

"Good." Elena turned the TV back on. The psychic was swaying in her chair, her voice low and insistent.

"I hate shows like that." Dia grimaced and turned it off, then pointed to the dishes and clothes. "Before anyone leaves, that has to all be cleaned up."

"But that's my favorite show!"

"Why? You couldn't have lived with your mom or Grandma and not know how it's done."

"Grandma tells me to let her know what the competition's doing and maybe pick up a few ideas for her. Why don't you like it? You do magic."

"That's not magic; that's trickery. What I do I don't pretend is real." It was an important distinction to Dia. She might fool and misdirect, but she never, ever claimed that what she did was from a power beyond.

"Grandma says you used to design the cleverest equipment, and Mom says you think devious. They say that's why you're so good at your magic."

Dia's jaw tightened. "I'm good at magic because I work hard at it."

Claire tilted her head. "Do you think there are real psychic powers, Aunt Dia?"

"No," she said shortly. "Now get this picked up while I go to the grocery store." As the kids straightened their mess and she headed to the corner market, Dia let her temper cool. She did magic; she performed. She was not a charlatan.

Those who claimed to have psychic connections were fakes; she knew that better than anyone.

Her first memory was of being five years old and sitting in a small space beneath the séance table, tapping or pulling strings according to her mother's cues, and hating it. Not the dark, not the cramped quarters—those she hadn't minded. It was the deception she'd hated from the very beginning.

Honesty had made her an oddity in the Trelawny family. With husbands or fathers usually MIA, the Trelawny women had always lived by their wits. Gypsies, tramps, and thieves, as the old Cher song went. Adele claimed she was helping people, giving them good advice they wouldn't listen to otherwise.

56

Dia loved her mother and didn't fault Adele for doing what she must to provide for her children but as Dia had gotten older her dislike of the subterfuge and the constant skirting of the law deepened. She knew how the tricks were done, but she hated the duplicity.

Dia had left home at seventeen, no longer able to ignore the fact that the deceptions nauseated her. They felt *wrong*.

She'd put her skills—she'd designed many of her mother's best tricks—to work as a magician. It was illusion, yes, but it was honest illusion, and Dia loved it. She loved the crowds, loved the work, loved the stage—front and back. She had dreams and ambitions.

She was a magician and a showman, not a phony psychic or a thief.

It was a perfect afternoon for America's favorite pastime. Organ music swelled across the grass at Wrigley field, *dump-da-dump-dump, dump-da-dump-dump*. Its rising chords incited the crowd to "Go, Cubs!" cheers of support, while the brilliant sun overhead kept the beer flowing. Only a wisp of breeze stirred the ivy coating the outfield fences.

Zeus took a final bite of his chili-laden hot dog. Spicy and steaming hot—just the way he liked it. He glanced over at Hera, still not quite used to shorts, a Cub shirt, and a baseball cap on his usually chic wife, but he was finding he liked this casual side to her. Especially when she had such nice legs beneath those shorts.

Hera jumped to her feet. "He was safe!" she shouted to the field.

"When did you get to be a baseball fan?" he asked, still eyeing her legs.

"I've been a fan since the beginning; I just don't get a chance to come often." She gave a nostalgic sigh as she settled back in her seat, then stretched out her legs. "Remember 1908? The year we won the series. What excitement that was."

"I've been thinking about Dia—"

Hera lips tightened and she turned her attention back to the field. "Later, I need to concentrate. Here, hold my cap."

The fans, including Hera, cheered as the latest Cub darling—Benito "Batting" Blessing, a power hitter with the potential to surpass Barry Bonds and Mark McGwire in home runs—stepped to the plate. The numbers on the ancient scoreboard told the classic tale: bottom of the ninth, two out, man on base, Cubs trailing two to one. A strike. A ball. Then . . .

He swung and connected, and the ball soared across the infield. It was a good hit, but not enough for a home run, until, inexplicably, the wind picked up force. A sudden gale swooped across the field, staggering the players backward, stirring up a choking dust, and catching the ball on an updraft. The ball sailed across the right-field fence.

The fans went wild as the batter trotted around the bases, arms pumping up and down in victory. "Cubs win!" shrieked the hoarse fan behind Zeus. "Man, are these guys hot or what! Even the wind loves us!"

Zeus grinned. He'd been watching Hera, not the batter, and he knew exactly what had happened. Hera had stroked the cloud ring on her finger, providing the gust that had carried the ball. He'd felt it in his ring. He leaned over and whispered in her ear, "Naughty girl. You did that."

She turned and gave him an unrepentant grin in return. "I'm just practicing with this new ring."

He looked at the settling dust and the caps, blown from scores of fans' heads, littering the field. "I think you need to work on the fine-tuning."

"True. You should have seen last week. A mini-tornado spun around the bases. My cap." She held out her hand.

Instead he settled it on her head, then leaned over and kissed her cheek. She smelled faintly of almonds and sunscreen. He felt the flush in her skin beneath his lips, but he took the kiss no further.

"If you're such a fan, why haven't the Cubs had more winning seasons?"

"Cub losses are a tradition. Besides, you know it's better if we don't interfere with such public institutions. Draws too many questions."

"So why now?"

"To practice with the ring, of course."

He gave a snort of disbelief.

She gave him that teasing grin again. "They deserve one spectacular season a century, don't you think? And this year they've got the talent to carry through when I'm not here. Shall we go?"

"In a moment." He laid a hand on her arm. "You can't keep avoiding it, Hera; we're going to help Dia. I've got tickets to her show tonight, and then we'll go backstage."

He felt the tension in her as she nodded. "Do you have a plan for keeping us near her?"

"Not yet, but I'll think of something."

She gave an irritated huff. "Still living in the moment, Zeus? I suppose it's up to me to find a way."

"And I'm sure you'll be brilliant at it, my dear." Zeus followed her from the ballpark. Good, he'd finally nudged her interest. He knew Hera hated it when he refused to make plans, when he trusted in the cosmos to provide the answers, and he'd hoped she would not be able to resist the challenge.

Now to see if she was willing to take the challenge of trusting him.

And he couldn't wait to see her reaction when she found a Soul Seeker thrown into the mix.

"Sorry about last night, Dia." Mick, her soon-to-be ex–lighting and effects tech, lounged against the six-foot picture-frame prop, a toothpick hanging from his mouth. He ran a hand across his shorn head. "When I realized I'd missed the cue, 'bout gave me heart failure, except I knew you'd cover. You really are the best, m'love."

"You didn't stay to set back up."

"Had to go. Promised some friends I'd meet them right away. It won't happen again."

"No, it won't." Dia took a deep breath, ignoring the knot in her stomach. "You're fired, Mick."

He straightened, his eyes narrowing. "You can't mean that. Anya asked for some help, and I got a mite distracted. That's not enough to fire me."

"Not if it was the first time. We've played five performances, and you've been careless in each one. Last time it happened I told you no more chances."

His lip curled, yet he managed to keep the toothpick in place. "Where you gonna find someone to replace me?"

She had no idea. Mick's claim to fame had been his availability when no one else would take the job. "Not your problem, Mick." Dia handed him an envelope. "Here's your severance pay."

Mick ripped open the envelope. "This ain't enough."

"It's all you're getting." Dia knew she'd been more than generous, under the circumstances. "Now go."

"Two hours before a performance? You're nuts; you can't go onstage without me."

"I'll manage."

"You'll be sorry." Mick crumpled the check. "You'll be begging me to come back. No one's gonna work with you after I put out the word what a demanding bitch you are."

Even considering the source, his slur hit a nerve. She knew she wasn't the motherly type, that her drive put off a lot of men, but to hear it in such vulgar terms . . . "Just get out of here."

His answer came straight from the gutter; then with a snarl he stormed off the stage, pushing past Anya and the twins.

"I heard what he said," Anya told her. "I didn't ask for his help."

Dia let out a pent-up breath and swallowed against the sour taste in her mouth. The unpleasant duty was over; it was time to think about the show. "I know. He's right about one thing, though: the performance tonight won't be easy without a lighting tech. If we leave out the blades illusion and go without the extra lights, can you handle it, Anya?"

Anya ruffled her shaggy hair until the scarlet ends stood upright. "I know the show almost as

61

well as you do, Dia, and a hell of a lot better than Mick. Give me an extra pair of hands and I'll get everything done. Even the blades."

Lukas cleared his throat. "Aunt Dia, can I help? I don't know your kind of equipment, of course, but I know my way around a computer."

"So do I," offered Claire.

Dia glanced at Anya, questioning.

Anya shrugged. "Most kids are better at this kind of thing than adults."

"Okay, sure, thanks. Do what Anya tells you, and make sure you stay out of the way of the rest of the crew."

"I'd rather help put on your makeup," Elena announced.

"What? Oh, sure. You can wait in the dressing room," Dia answered absently, her attention already focusing on the show.

Whatever it took, she was going to give a good performance tonight.

Dia hurried off the stage surrounded by an opaque column of smoke. The irritation made her eyes tear and her makeup run, and as soon as she was offstage and had her mike off and the curtain closed, she bent over in a fit of coughing.

Thank the blessed saints that disastrous performance was over!

"Sorry, Aunt Dia. I wasn't sure how much smoke to put out."

Dia waved a hand, reassuring Lukas. "Not your fault," she rasped out, her throat scratchy from the excess of the smoke machine.

"I'm getting a handle on it. It'll go better next time."

"I'm sorry about that urn falling," added Cam.

"Don't worry about it." She was barely able to mask her frustration. It wasn't their fault. She'd been a fool to think untrained kids could handle the intricacies of backstage. They had no place even being there; she'd known that.

From the other side of the curtain the applause died down, replaced by the murmurs of departure. The audience had enjoyed the show, but she knew it had been far from her best. The timing was a shade off, the flourishes not quite right as she worried about the next cue. Then there was that off-stage clang when Cam knocked over the urn. The remains of the smoke wafted offstage, setting off another bout of coughing.

At least all the illusions had had the proper effect; no secrets had been revealed. But she'd been second-rate tonight, and Dia could not accept that. She had to find a new lighting and effects tech, and she had to find a baby-sitter.

Fast.

Without another word she strode to her dressing room to change. A minute to wind down, a minute of solitude, that was all she needed; then she could face the problems.

"Aunt Dia, can I take off your makeup?" Elena bounded up beside her.

"No."

"Are you mad at us?"

"No," she snapped, not looking at her niece.

"You sure?"

Dia stopped and drew in a deep breath. It wasn't them she was mad at—it was herself, the situation. They were just coping as best they could, same as her. She faced Elena. "I'm not mad at you. I just need a couple of minutes alone. I always do after a performance."

"Time-out." Elena nodded sagely. "Mom does that sometimes. She locks the bathroom door."

"Yeah, give me a time-out."

"Okay."

In her dressing room, Dia exchanged her costume for a robe, grateful to peel off the bra that kept her uplifted and in place during the performance. She pulled her hair back with a ribbon, then began to cream off the makeup. Slowly her irritation faded with the familiar motion, leaving behind only questions and dilemmas.

Behind her, on the other side of the screen, came a soft knock.

What now? "Come in."

The door opened, then clicked shut, and she sensed, rather than heard, someone come in. No sound, only a faint whiff of soap, a brush of charged air. Her stomach squeezed in familiar anticipation, while her settling nerves zinged back to high awareness, recognizing her visitor without the need for sight.

Dia faced her visitor as he came around the screen. Black tonight, with the blue diamond and emerald eyes his only color. Calm except for the heat in his eyes.

This time Hugh Pendragon had come to her.

Chapter Four

"Hugh?" Her voice caught on the single word; then she straightened. "I didn't expect—Why are you here?"

For a moment Hugh forgot why he'd come. His mind grasped only one image: Dia, scrubbed, wearing a worn robe and no bra, her hair pulled back. This natural woman was a surprise after the flamboyant performer. An air of vulnerability clung to her, giving her an allure impossible to ignore.

His mouth felt like talc. "Your earrings," he managed as he held out the brown envelope. Their fingers brushed, a fleeting contact charged by two opposites—male and female. "Ronald cleaned off the dog slobber."

"Tell him thanks."

Mission completed; a silence settled over them. What had he expected? Magic answers? He rocked back on his heels, though, reluctant to leave. "Did you find another PI?"

"Not yet."

"The men I suggested?"

"Appendicitis. Out of town."

That about covered that subject. He considered asking her about the glitches he'd seen in tonight's performance, then decided against it. He thought about asking how the search for her sister was going, but knew he had no business asking if it wasn't his case.

And neither were the other questions he was longing to put to her. Why had she invaded his thoughts? Was the vision that had returned after seeing her a mere fluke? He had tried touching the diary again, with no success.

To ask would be impossible. He told few people of his talents. He told no one of their loss.

The smart thing, the safe thing, would be to leave right now, to refuse the siren's call in favor of the healing solitude he needed. Hugh had never believed in unnecessary risks, and he appreciated order and calm.

Yet he couldn't force himself to take the first step.

She clutched the lapels of her robe closer. "Look, I, um, have to get changed. Help with the setup."

And that very neatly dismissed him. His dilemma decided, Hugh took a step, forcing himself away despite the undeniable tug of attraction that urged every muscle to send him in the opposite direction. Only when he reached the door and had his hand safely on the knob did he hesitate for one last look.

It was his undoing. It gave him time for another whiff of her complex perfume. Time to discover that she had moved with him, as though she, too, felt the magnetism between them. Time also to notice the athletic perfection of her legs and arms and to see the faint pulse fluttering in her throat.

"Would you like to go out?" he asked abruptly, surprising himself. He wanted solitude, yes, but he wanted Dia more. A date, a simple date. It wasn't as though he were asking her to move in with him or confessing his deepest secrets.

"Excuse me?"

"Out. With me." Hugh ground his teeth at his tied tongue. He'd never considered himself glib with women, but he usually managed to be more urbane than this.

"A date?"

Her astonishment wasn't too flattering either. "Yes, a date."

The corners of her mouth tilted up in a teasing smile. "Didn't you just refuse me this morning?"

"That was business. This is pleasure. Are you going to hold a grudge?"

"My temper's quick, but short. Pleasure, huh?"

"We could go to dinner or . . ." He tried to think of something going on in town, something that didn't entail several thousand other people being in the same place. "The Steppenwolf Theater. They're doing a midnight performance of *Franco and Billy*."

"I've wanted to see that. You have tickets?"

"I can get them."

"You know a guy." Her smile grew as she echoed the popular Chicago phrase when anything needed to be done.

"Something like that. Tomorrow? After your show?"

"I can't tomorrow—Anya's birthday. She's invited the whole crew, along with half of Chicago, and she's one of my best friends." She paused only a moment. "Would you like to come? With me? Meet the crew?"

A party? A crowd? Hugh batted down a sudden denial. He had a primitive urge to snatch her up and carry her back to his lair and keep her to himself. And he could imagine Dia's modern fury at that primitive, un-PC instinct. "That sounds fine," he answered mildly.

"Good, I—" Her shoulders drooped, and she made a face. "I just realized I can't do either. The kids. My nieces and nephews. Twelve and fourteen, not old enough to stay alone or be out that late."

He liked children, but adolescent chaperones ranked low on his list of desirable dates. "I could ask Ronald to watch them."

"I'd hate to impose."

"I'll ask. I think he will." Hugh had no idea if Ronald even liked children, but he'd taken to Cerberus well enough. Could teenagers be worse than a massive hound who liked to steal jewelry?

He'd offer Ronald extra time off later.

"Great."

"I'll pick you up after the show." Knowing he'd see her soon made it easier to put his hand on the doorknob again. Dia stood beside him. At the vee of her robe, her skin glittered with the remnants of makeup, as if she were sprinkled with diamond dust. Her faint, sultry perfume mixed with the scent of woman and honey in a blend that suggested earthy delights.

He cupped her upper arm lightly with his palm, nonthreatening, nonbinding, simply needing to touch her. Her arm was firm and muscled—he could tell that even with the barrier of her robe—but it had a feminine definition. When she didn't move away or protest, he leaned slowly over. He liked that she wasn't much shorter than he, that he didn't have to bend far to kiss her cheek.

Close up, the scent of her tantalized him anew, and now he had the added sensation of smooth, warm skin beneath his lips. Blood sped through him, found a home as it pooled deep and low. He lifted his head from the kiss, wanting more, unwilling to risk more.

"Until tomorrow, Dia."

She'd accepted a date with Hugh Pendragon? Dia slipped on shorts and a T-shirt, then plunged into the remaining after-performance work, her mind churning, her body still warm from his single touch. What had she been thinking?

Hugh Pendragon saw too much, questioned too much. She was playing with fire, for she could not let anyone find out about her connection to Demetria Cesare.

Face it, her brain hadn't been working when she'd accepted. She hadn't even had enough mental power for complete sentences. One chaste kiss, and her heart was going wild.

Dia considered herself as healthy, as modern, as the next woman. She liked male company, enjoyed kisses—and more—from an appealing man, but she always knew those liaisons were only interludes. She was not the nurturing type, was not the type of woman men wanted to settle with.

She preferred it that way. Nothing to ground her. No one to control her. Only her profession, her ambition, her crew, her chosen obligations as her responsibilities and restraints.

Until Hugh Pendragon's simple kiss spun through her, inspiring lust—oh, how it inspired—and bringing something else, something complex and frightening. Something she'd never felt before, not even with her ex-husband.

The desire for more—more intensity, more depth, more closeness.

Dia attacked the dolly holding the airplane blades, straining to shove it upstage, exorcizing the sudden butterflies in her belly. She wouldn't dwell on Hugh, not when she had shows to perform and secrets to keep. It was a date, a simple date. A date with a good-looking—no, great-looking—guy.

Who happened to kiss like a dream.

She couldn't deny she was looking forward to tomorrow night. "Perversity, thy name is woman," she muttered as the dolly rolled into place.

"Dia, did I not promise you would have an audience in the palm of your enchanting hand?"

Dia spun around at the sound of a familiar, resonant voice, then grinned when she saw the older man. Six months had brought no changes in the salt-and-pepper hair, the trim mustache, the infectious zest for life. She'd known him only a few days and shared a single passionate kiss, but she'd always felt as if their souls had known each other much longer, and she considered him a friend.

"Zeke Jupiter? I thought you were in Louisiana."

"Only temporarily, my dear." He took her hands and kissed her cheeks.

She returned a quick kiss to the lips. "What brings you to Chicago?"

"I'm with a special friend."

Special friend in that tone of voice meant a woman, and she must be special indeed for Zeke Jupiter to speak of her. "Will I get to meet her?"

"Of course. Harriet?" He called to a woman who had her back to them, talking to Elena.

The woman held up her hand, a nonverbal equivalent of *in a minute*. When she finished her conversation a moment later, she strolled over to join them.

By contemporary standards, Harriet was not a beautiful woman, but she had a face that was appealing in its feminine strength, a sophisticated flair for clothes, and a regal carriage that made her a woman who would always be noticed.

She also didn't appear to care much for Dia, judging by the disapproving expression on her perfectly made-up features. Dia gave a mental shrug. She was used to women viewing her with hostility, automatically considering her a rival. She didn't like it, but had learned that only time could change their minds and it was more their problem than hers.

Dia held out her hand. "Dia Trelawny. Nice to meet you."

"Harriet Juneau." She had a firm handshake. "You put on a marvelous show; you have quite a talent."

"Thanks." Dia's brows knitted. "Harriet Juneau, I've heard your name—I know! CEO of Peacock

Cosmetics. I've never found anything better than your makeup remover, and I love the honey scent."

Harriet's reserve cracked. "Makeup should appeal to every sense, not just the visual. Everything about it should make a woman feel beautiful."

Dia nodded. "Who wants to put on a lipstick that feels like a hard shell coating?"

"Or a mascara that clumps and stings the eye."

"True. Have you known Zeke long?"

"Many years," Harriet murmured, glancing at him.

"Are you in town long?" Dia asked Zeke.

He shrugged. "It depends. I've got some interesting projects in the works, but nothing is going forward."

"You wouldn't reconsider my offer to do the lighting for me?" she teased. When she'd last met Zeke, at Armond and Callie's wedding party, she'd been putting together this tour. Zeke ran a successful fireworks company, but he'd just finished doing the lighting for Callie's video series, so Dia had asked him about working for her. After all, nothing ventured, nothing gained. He'd refused, as she'd expected, for Zeke Jupiter's reputation was way beyond what she could afford, and the lighting was only a side business for him.

Now, instead of another gentle refusal, Zeke and Harriet exchanged a glance; then he asked, "What do you mean?"

Could he be interested? Suppressing anticipation, Dia answered, "I had to let my lighting tech go."

Zeke exchanged another look with Harriet, his smug, hers annoyed; then he stroked his mustache. "Jupiter Fireworks is experimenting with a new type of firework. Smaller and without the extreme heat. Something to be used indoors, for shows like this. If you'd be willing to let me do some field tests, I'll handle the lighting."

"Willing? It sounds perfect."

Harriet cleared her throat. "My company is developing a line of cosmetics for performers. I tried out the natural looks with Callie. I'd like to do testing on the more dramatic products—glitter foundation, gold-dusted lipsticks. If you'd be interested."

"Would I? Of course." Then Dia's enthusiasm plummeted. In her life, good things always came with a catch or a dark side. "I can't afford—"

"Money." Zeke waved a hand. "Pish, don't worry about it. We want only one thing—for Harriet and I to travel with you."

"And freedom to fully test our products," added Harriet.

"As long as it doesn't adversely affect the performance," Dia cautioned.

"Of course."

"Then I guess . . . sure. Welcome aboard! I can't believe how this all worked out."

Zeke and Harriet exchanged another of their enigmatic glances. "Neither can we, m'dear," said Zeke with a wide smile.

"I'm lost, Soul Seeker."

"Find me. Bring me home."

"Too late."

"You should have done more."

The voices and faces became confused. A young child spoke with a crone's tremor. A man's words cracked with

73

a teenager's angst. Too late. Too little. Too late. Too little.

Their misery was a common note, each word a hot coal of accusation.

He'd never seen them alive, only as pictures from happier times used to ID. Hands reached out and grabbed him, pleading for an anchor, for a harbor, for deliverance.

And he could not. I don't know how anymore, he screamed in silence.

"Where am I?"

Bodies returned to a single voice: the voice of all those he still could not find. No body, only a voice piercing his throat.

That single voice spread, became smoke, choked him. Suddenly it vanished, and he was running through a place he'd never seen, yet knew intimately. A cave with walls of glistening rock and glittering gems and an opalescent ceiling.

"You need both." A new voice, yet it, too, was familiar. Not one of the victims. A voice of soft knowledge and understanding. "You need both," it repeated, fading as he struggled out of the dream. "Or you need her."

Another face formed in the smoke, too vague to recognize; then it vanished with the coming of wakefulness.

Hugh bolted upright in the chair. Sweat soaked the back of his seat, and his muscles quivered, as though he'd worked out past the limits of endurance. He rubbed his aching chest, then his face, chasing away the remnants of the dream. The memory of its details faded quickly, leaving only the aftermath of fatigue and confusion.

Across the room, the computer hummed. He focused on the painting hanging above the monitor: images of emeralds, rubies, sapphires, and golden chrysoberyl. The familiar images oriented him—his painting, his desk, his office, his home—and his pounding heart slowed. A lightning pain coursed down his neck as he stretched out the kinks from his awkward sleeping position.

Cerberus lay at his feet and, hearing him stir, gave a soft woof.

Hugh reached down to scratch behind his ears, grateful for solid dog. "Well, Cerberus, it appears falling asleep someplace other than bed is not the solution to my problem."

His muscles ached and his eyes felt gritty, but he knew from experience that sleep was over for the night. "You think meditation might help?" he asked the dog.

Cerberus gave a huge yawn.

"Then how about a tussle?"

In response, Cerberus trotted over to a soggy towel. He brought it back and flopped one end onto Hugh's leg. Hugh grabbed the towel and started the tug-of-war game Cerberus liked almost as much as he loved glittery stones. In the absence of someone to share a good workout on the mats, Hugh found it a respectable way to get some excercise.

With pretend growling and planted paws, Cerberus soon tugged the towel from Hugh's grip. The dog dropped the towel and gave an annoyed bark. *Too easy*, he seemed to say. Instead of picking up the towel for round two, he padded to the door, gave a single bark, and then waited. Even in doggy language, the command to follow was clear.

Hugh pushed himself upright and followed Cerberus through the shadowy warren of halls and rooms until man and dog reached the outside doors.

"You want to go for a run?"

Not surprisingly, a bark was his answer. Hugh turned off the alarm, then opened the door. Cerberus bounded outside, ran in a circle, sniffing, and then turned back to Hugh. *Come on*, insisted his bark.

Hugh had changed into shorts when he'd returned from Dia's performance tonight. Now he slipped on a pair of running shoes he kept by the door and headed out after Cerberus. Man and dog wove through the trees at a rapid pace.

It was the zone he sought, that state where the left brain was busy directing the body and the right brain was freed from constraints. The zone was the best place to sort through the images of his dreams.

Or to ignore them.

Sweat returned and dripped down his back as he ran in the city heat, which night had done little to dissipate. The ache in his muscles became a burn, and his lungs worked to replenish oxygen. Hugh relished the feeling, and Cerberus, loping beside him, had his mouth drawn back in what Hugh could have sworn was a grin.

As his body began to move automatically, fragments of the dream returned. He passed swiftly over the first ones; he'd already revisited those too many times in the past six months. Except . . . what had the dream said? Soul Seeker? It was a phrase he'd never heard. The cave was new, too. What had he seen? Gems on the side, especially rubies. Rubies. Gems of fire and protection. A lustrous ceiling. Pearl? Moonstone? No, opal, the luminescent stone of the night.

Rubies and opals. The combination rang with familiarity; it was something he'd seen before, something important.

Hugh snapped out of the zone.

Rubies and opals. Gems. The Pendragon legacy. The gems he'd anonymously lent the museum for a six-month display called Treasures of the Underworld. A fanciful reporter, not knowing their source, had dubbed them the gems of Hades. Ronald had told him the gems had been returned today. Was that the message of the dream?

Abruptly he whistled for Cerberus. "Time to go back, boy."

The curtained secured room—not even Ronald had the code to enter—held the treasure and legacy of Pendragons from time unmeasured. Gems. Gems uncut, gems in lavish settings, gems of all colors and shapes. Gems, beautiful and unchanging.

He brushed the blue diamond that adorned his ear. So far, this and a topaz ring had been his additions to the Pendragon collection.

Before him on the small table sat the chest he had retrieved from the house safe. He traced the strange carvings in the wood: pictures of caves and horses whose hooves sparked lightning, foreign words nearly worn away with time, flecks of color hinting at vanished splendor. The air surrounding him seemed full of anticipation. With a faint click of the lock, he lifted the lid. Inside rested two wristbands—the gems returned today from the museum: a copper armband set with a flawless ruby, and an opal set in silver.

He lifted them both from their casket, welcoming them home after their six-month absence, and rested them in his palms. The silver band felt strangely heavy and sticky. Frowning, Hugh set the two side by side, studying them in the narrow beam of light.

Greek letters wound across the upper surface of the two bands. No pictures or decorations, just two words: *Elysium* and *Tartarus*, the domains of the underworld, the realm of Hades. One for reward, one for punishment, an early pagan version of heaven and hell. He rotated the bands to look on the interior. Etched into the metal were supposed to be symbols.

The concealed etchings were missing on the opal. Swearing, Hugh grabbed the band and held it closer. There was no depth, no fiery color in the milky opal. The gem was fake.

It must have been switched during the display.

He rubbed the smooth facets of the ruby. Perhaps it was his imagination, but it seemed the ruby's fire had clouded. Did it long for its heart's companion? Family legend held that the ruby and its now-missing companion, the opal in the silver wristband, were the beginning of the collection, the treasure of the first Pendragon.

His father had warned Hugh, as fathers of Pendragons had always warned their sons, of three truths about the gems: Each generation must add to the collection, choosing special stones. The gems must be cherished. Finally, they must be guarded.

He had kept faith with two out of three.

Who might have taken it from the display? How? Where was it now?

A lot had happened in six months. He'd been robbed. He'd suffered the fading of his talents. He'd met Dia Trelawny.

Were the events connected? He didn't see how that was possible.

He slipped the ruby band onto his wrist, and in a choking flash the last fleeting image of the dream came to him. The face in the smoke.

The face of Dia Trelawny.

You need both. Or you need her.

Chapter Five

Hugh enjoyed the quiet of his house. Like order and space, it was something he accepted as normal. Yet this morning, as he shifted through the motions of his morning martial arts routine, he found it not rejuvenating, but empty, as though the air itself were waiting for something.

Or someone.

His smooth motions faltered, and, his centering lost, Hugh ended the routine. As he wiped himself with a towel and watched a morning sunbeam cross the mats, he decided that the dreams were turning him into a fanciful fool.

He headed to the dining room, where Ronald had a pot of tea waiting. Hugh poured a cup and settled at the table.

"Sourdough was fresh this morning." Ronald set a plate of toast and sliced melon in front of him. It was part of the morning routine Ronald and Hugh's father had shared, and when Hugh came to live with his father fourteen years ago Ronald had deftly included the son in the ritual. Ronald never acknowledged that Hugh was capable of getting his own breakfast or of eating in the kitchen, and Hugh chose not to usurp what Ronald considered the duties of a ... whatever Ronald considered himself. "Here's your paper, sir."

For once Hugh found himself reluctant to follow the routine. "Ronald, sit down a moment, will you?"

Ronald gave him a startled glance, then perched on the edge of a chair. "Yes?"

"Do you like children?"

"Like? In what sense?"

"Do you like to be around them? Do things with them?"

"I've never really thought about it. Your mother allowed your visits so rarely after the divorce, I'm used to only adults."

"You've never spent time with children?"

"My brother has six. I'm always grateful to get back here to our peaceful grounds after an extended visit, but I don't *dislike* them. I quite enjoy them, as a matter of fact." Ronald's brow wrinkled. "Why?"

Hugh crumbled the edge of his bread. "Dia—"

"The delightful young lady who was here yesterday."

"Yes. I'd like to take her out tonight, but she's got charge of her four nieces and nephews for the summer, and I—"

Ronald beamed. "Certainly I'll watch them for you and Miss Trelawny."

Hugh blinked at Ronald's ready acceptance. "You don't have to. It's not part of your job, and if you've got other plans, fine."

"Sir, I'm delighted you've decided not to be a hermit. Do you wish to bring them here?"

"I'm sure they'll be more comfortable at Dia's; they're familiar with her apartment."

"Very good." Ronald rose to his feet. "Is there anything else?"

Hugh rubbed the ruby at his wrist, then shook his head. Some part of him kept silent, unwilling to admit even to Ronald the loss of the gem or the true reason for his retirement. "Thanks for baby-sitting."

"You're welcome."

Silence once more enveloped Hugh when Ronald left the room. The vibration of the air-conditioning, Ronald bustling in the kitchen, the old house creaking, none of it disturbed him. Yet a restlessness built inside Hugh, unsettling and disturbing. In response, he picked up the paper.

Usually he turned directly to the police reports, but this morning Hugh fought the habit. He was retired. He didn't need to find out if the bad guys he'd identified had gone to trial and been put away. He didn't need to wonder which headline would be his next case, or which victims who weren't making the paper would need his services.

Instead he turned to the entertainment section, where he found a review of Dia's show. The reporter complimented the performance and recommended it to his readers. That was good, but Hugh's irritation rose as he continued to read. The most effusive comments were reserved not for the illusions, but for the allure of the star. Hugh's jaw tightened as he tossed the paper to the table. He glanced at his watch—too early to call Dia about tonight. He required very little sleep, but he doubted she'd be awake yet.

In the meantime, he'd make a few discreet inquiries about the museum display.

"I had an e-mail from Mom."

Dia raised one eyelid and waited for Claire to come into focus. "What time is it?" she mumbled.

"Eight."

"Morning?"

"Uh-huh."

Dia groaned and buried her head in the pillow. Mornings were the scourge of the day, and this was the second day she'd seen the dawn side of noon. "I thought teenagers liked to sleep late."

"I'm twelve; I still get up early. Mom said to tell you hi."

Dia shoved herself upright as Claire's words finally registered. The sofa cushions beneath her skidded, but stayed on the furniture. "You've talked to her? Where is she?"

"E-mail. She says to tell you thank-you again and that she won't be in touch for several days. There's no e-mail in the jungle. She says it should be quite romantic. Sounds boring to me."

Jungle? That narrowed it to several hundred possibilities. "No other clues where she is? Nothing about the e-mail I sent her?" The desperate, get-back-here-now e-mail.

"Nope."

That was Liza: ignore the unpleasant. Dia flopped back onto the sofa. The cushion slipped off, landing her on the springs, and she snorted in annoyance.

Cam, sprawled on the floor in a heap of blankets and a pillow, groaned. "Crap, it's hard to sleep here." He unfolded himself from the bedding, then stretched, his boxers showing above dangerously low-riding soccer shorts. Before Dia could say anything, he poked a toe at the second bundle of sheets. "Hey, bro, wake up. I'll play you in NOX."

Lukas's answer was an incoherent grunt.

"Yeah, I know." Scratching his chest, Cam padded to the bathroom, pausing only once, to switch on the stereo. Metallica's bass guitar vibrated through the room.

"Looks like our day's begun," Claire said cheerily. "So what are the plans, Aunt Dia? Can we tour Chicago?"

"Plans?" Dia rubbed the sleep from her eyes, then raked her tangled hair from her face. Her brain could focus on only one plan. "Coffee."

Once her caffeine level was finally high enough to do some good, Dia thumbed through the Chicago guidebook, desperately seeking *something* to do with four adolescents. Staying in her apartment for the day was not an option. "The Museum of Science and Industry," she declared at last, though museums were usually at the bottom of her list of favorite places to visit. The guidebook said it was interactive, kid-friendly, and big enough to take most of the day.

"A museum?" Cam's scorn was evident. "Boring."

"I'd rather go shopping," Elena declared.

"With Cam and Lukas along?" Claire lifted one brow.

"Eewww, no."

Dia closed the guidebook. "The Museum of Science and Industry or the Art Museum. Choose."

"Science and Industry." If not exactly deafening, the chorus was in agreement.

When the phone rang, Dia grabbed it with a breathless hello, praying it was Liza.

"Hello, Dia?"

Not Liza. Hugh's quiet voice settled across her with a calming rumble.

"Ronald says he'll watch the children for us tonight."

"He will? That's really generous of him."

"He seemed eager. I think he wants me to get out more." An edge of humor tinted his words.

"I have the opposite problem. People claim I'm hard to reach because I'm never home."

"So was I lucky to catch you?"

"Yup. The Museum of Science and Industry in one hour."

"My father used to take me there. I remember being fascinated by the coal mine."

"Will teens like it?"

"I didn't go during those years. My parents were divorced when I was five, and my mother took me south. I've heard it's for all ages."

"Would you like to come with us?" The impulsive words were out before Dia could examine them. If she wanted to keep Hugh Pendragon at arm's length, this wasn't the way, yet the solid sound of his voice was a pleasure she could not deny herself. And she wanted the solid feel of him beside her when she heard it.

She thought the question startled him, too, for he hesitated a moment before answering. "Yes, thanks."

They made arrangements to meet, then hung up. Dia turned to see Claire's solemn stare.

"We're not going with you tonight?"

Dia ran a hand through her hair. "I thought you'd get bored backstage every night."

"And being *baby-sat* here is a thrill? Cam's really excited about the magic, and Lukas loves computers. Didn't you notice?"

The accusation ground into Dia, for she realized she'd noticed, but had assigned no special importance to the facts. "The hours I keep aren't for people your age."

"Mom's loose on bedtime rules, and we're used to traveling around to Mom's and Grandma's séances. Guess I'll get ready for the *museum*."

"It'll be fun."

"Sure." Claire glanced over her shoulder as she left to dress. "Don't try so hard, Aunt Dia. We know you don't really want us here; we'll find things to do."

"No—" She was speaking to empty air. Dia's stomach clenched at the kids' simple acceptance of the upheaval in their lives. *We know you don't really want us here.* More proof that, even at the best of times, she was unsuited to the delicate balancing act of living with four teenagers.

True, she didn't want them here, but not for the reasons Claire probably thought. Because sharing her life was not a healthy exercise. Because Demetria Cesare lurked as an ever-present danger.

How could she tell them that?

The uneasy feeling of being watched started in the coal mine.

Until that point, the trip to the museum had gone more smoothly than Dia had expected. They'd met Hugh as scheduled and she'd let Cam and Lukas go off on their own, agreeing to meet at the *Mercury* capsule in three hours. The girls stayed with her and Hugh. From the fairy castle to the replica of Main Street to the coal mine, with sundry displays between, Claire had marched them on a planned course. For someone who dressed in goth black and espoused free choice, she was a decided martinet about some things. In the coal mine, however, she slowed, intent on absorbing each fact, while Elena happily flirted with the gangly teenage boy in the family ahead of them. The boy, in turn, seemed fascinated by Elena's bare midriff and legs.

The coal mine was cool, shadowy, and made Dia feel a little claustrophobic. The faint scent of Hugh's aftershave teased her when he leaned closer. "Both of those girls act older than twelve." His voice resonated across her, and the base of her spine tightened.

"Claire has the seriousness of a thirty-year-old activist and Elena's got the hormones of a randy sixteen-year-old. They're as different from each other as Liza and I are."

"But look." His cheek brushed her hair, the first time he'd touched her all morning, stirring *her* hormones to rampant life. "Elena never gets far from

87

Claire. She flirts, yes, spreads her wings, but she knows where her haven is."

"She'd protest if you pointed that out to her."

"Of course. I doubt she's even aware of it." His hand rested on her shoulder. "Neither does Claire realize that she sets her pace for Elena to keep up, at least when they're out like this."

With Hugh's solid strength close, Dia eyed the two girls. It was true; Elena and Claire performed a subconscious dance that kept the two of them firmly in proximity.

Had she and Liza done the same?

Dia looked up at Hugh. He'd worn white today, but he seemed to blend with the darkness. She saw only the shadow of his face and the intense green in his eyes, the blue of his earring, and the wink of a red ruby at his wrist. "You *are* observant."

"I've trained myself to be." Hugh's hand shifted from the edge of her shoulder to a more intimate position beside her neck—a subtle gesture, but one that suggested a possession she refused to acknowledge. So far he'd been circumspect, not touching her, more alert to the crowd than to her.

Here, though, beneath the ground, something changed in him. Now that he was surrounded by the glistening rocks of black coal, his wariness faded. All his power—body and spirit—focused. On her. Fire spread from his hand, baking into her like the familiar heat of a stage light, and she wondered which of them was the true magician.

At that moment of vibrant awareness, the prickling at the back of her neck began. It was a wary feeling, as if someone were watching, and it doused the heat. She shivered in the cool cave and glanced around. Nothing she saw, no one she noticed could be pinpointed as the source of her unease.

That did not reassure Dia. As a magician she was well aware how the attention could be misdirected, how easy it was to hide in plain sight. One further scan, then she turned back to Hugh, striving to regain her calm. "This was your favorite exhibit? I bet you could tell me exactly what's going on here without reading the signs."

"It's a bet you'd win." He accepted her change of mood and pointed to the display. "They separate the ore from the rock. . . ."

Throughout the remaining tour, that odd prickling, that feeling of being watched, grew. When they emerged and continued the tour of the museum, a sweet odor assailed her: the scent of lilies. A flash of green caught the corner of her eye, gone as soon as she turned.

Her stomach clenched. Demetria? How could she have known . . . ?

In the stairwell Claire stopped to view the stories-tall pendulum that swung there. "It tells the time," she read from the guidebook.

Elena leaned over to see the clock face at the bottom of the stairwell. "Wow, dizzy time. This is sooo cool. Look, Claire."

Claire hung over beside her sister. "Do you know how it works, Hugh?"

When Hugh began a patient, simple explanation of how the rotation of the earth kept the time, Dia lagged behind.

"They're lovely girls," came a low, feminine voice from a gallery off the stairwell. "You should tell them to be careful about leaning over."

Dia's stomach hit her heart as she strode into the gallery. She was not surprised to see the woman sitting patiently on a bench. Her fists clenched. "Don't you dare threaten them, Demetria."

"I would not *ever* hurt them." Her answer came swiftly and vehemently. "Growing things are under my protection. That was not a threat; it was a concern, pure and simple."

The outrage convinced Dia that she intended no physical harm to the girls. There were other kinds of damage, though, other dangers, and she advanced warily, glad for the stage training that kept her thoughts hidden.

Demetria rose and lounged against a display. "You've lost your edge, Dia. I thought you'd realize I was here much sooner."

"I don't live my life looking over my shoulder."

Demetria laughed lightly, a sound like wind through dried leaves. "Neither do I."

Dia tilted her head to study her adversary. In the years since they'd met, Demetria Cesare had never aged a minute, and six months hadn't changed that. Her face was firm, her carriage erect, and her hands unwrinkled and unspotted, although Dia suspected the trick was aided by hair dye, plastic surgery, regular exercise, and good genes. Demetria wore her signature green, a simple dress designed to convey traditional values and trustworthiness, and her expression suggested friendliness. She was holding a bird of paradise bloom, so fresh the colors were a bright splash in the monochrome museum.

Her eyes gave her away, though. They were the ageless green of moss and held about as much human warmth and compassion. Unfortunately, Dia had recognized that fact too late.

Dia matched the other woman's casual pose. "What do you want, Demetria?"

"Nothing, now. I simply wanted to make sure you didn't have second thoughts about playing my party."

"I don't cancel performance dates."

The dry laugh came again. "Always the professional, Dia. I like that about you. After that performance, we'll talk."

"We have nothing to talk about."

"I'd suggest you reconsider that."

"Why, Demetria? Why did you pick me for your schemes?"

"You have talent and you're ambitious. With me you could go far, to the top of your profession, and you know it. You know I can be a very good friend."

And a worse enemy. Dia's jaw tightened, but she was proud of her even tone. "Six months ago I told you I won't do the transmutation illusion again."

"Pity, it's such a clever one. But we had to figure out something new anyway. It's wise to keep fresh."

Tension stiffened her spine like a steel rod. "I won't let you use me to steal anymore gems."

Demetria stared at her a moment; then a cold smile crossed her face. "The alternative is jail. You'll lose *everything*: your reputation, your success, your freedom, your magic."

Dia's stomach burned. She hated deceptions, even when Demetria gave her no choice. The woman had to be stopped, but she needed more time. Abruptly Dia gave a sharp nod. "I'll . . . think about what you've said."

"You'll be interested in what I have planned. I know you, Dia. You want to reach the top, and I can help you."

You don't know a thing about me. Digging fingernails into her palms, Dia refused to look away. "We'll talk after my performance at your party."

"In the meantime, if you say anything to anyone . . . Such a shame if police attention were brought to your mother and your sister. I doubt their activities would tolerate too much scrutiny."

"Dia?" Hugh's voice drifted from the stairwell.

"Over here," Dia called, her eyes still fixed on Demetria.

The mask slipped as Demetria glared in the direction of the unseen detective; then she turned to Dia. "One month. You have one month to think about what I can do for you. Or against you."

"Which gallery are you in?" Hugh's voice was insistent, urgent.

Dia called in his direction, and when she turned back to Demetria, the woman was gone.

Lilies. A faint aroma of lilies lingered in the gallery. Hugh hated lilies; they reminded him of funerals.

Dia stood alone in the gallery, her fists clenched until the skin turned white. She was safe and unharmed, but she looked scared.

"Are you all right? We lost you."

"I wondered what was in this gallery." She turned and gave him a brilliant smile that didn't fool him for a second. "I warned the girls about wandering off. Guess I should have listened to myself."

"No harm done." The urgent compulsion that had sent him looking for her faded, along with the flower smell, but the strange feeling that something was wrong—that danger waited, that Dia knew it and was scared of it—did not.

Chapter Six

Bracing her hands against the sink in the museum bathroom, Dia drew in a deep breath, battling nausea in the aftermath of the confrontation. First priority—the children had to be protected. Nothing else was as important.

She knew enough about Demetria to believe the woman wouldn't physically harm them, but she might try to seduce them with her schemes. The veiled warnings left a sick knot in Dia's stomach, for she knew firsthand how convincing the woman could be. For a brief moment Dia allowed herself to be sucked into the past—a place she rarely visited.

They'd met when Dia had performed at a breakfast-food-industry trade show and Demetria had invited her to do her magic at a party. The performance went well; the guests were appreciative. Dia knew her success was due to her own effort and talents, but she'd been grateful for the recommendations Demetria sent her way, grateful her help never contained the sleazy strings that so many men attached to their "generosity."

Grateful. Wasn't that a laugh? Demetria had been biding her time. Waiting for her opportunity.

It came in the form of a museum charity fundraiser Demetria had convinced her to do. It was an exhilarating night, and the culmination was a dazzling, surprise finale using real diamonds, the pride of the museum. Dia could still remember the single light shining on her, the sweet-scented profusion of flowers, the rustle of the tuxedo-and-sequin-clad audience as she transformed the diamonds into a bouquet of lilies, then made the flowers vanish. When she made them rematerialize, she converted the flowers back into the gems. A jewel expert confirmed their authenticity, and the diamonds were returned to their high-security velvet display.

The transmutation illusion. She'd been so proud of it. It had drama, flair, and baffling sleight of hand. She'd been proud enough to use it four more times, the last occasion six months ago here in Chicago at the opening of the Treasures of the Underworld exhibit.

It was at that performance that she'd realized, for the first time, that something was wrong. Something about the wristband she'd handed back to the curator was off. It simply hadn't felt *right*, although she hadn't been able to pinpoint why during the demands of her performance.

The next day she found out. When Dia was well and truly compromised, when the jeweler died suddenly from complications of pancreatic cancer, Demetria dropped the bomb: the returned gems were fakes, and the jeweler's signed confession implicated Dia. If Demetria allowed that confession to be found, if she put out word to have the gems reauthenticated, then Dia would be spending years in jail.

Confronted with the scheme, she had threatened to expose Demetria's involvement, but it was an empty threat. They both knew Demetria was the one who had the proof, who held the power with the authorities, while Dia was the one who had actually handled the gems.

After all her years fighting against a life of deception, she'd been neatly snared.

Acid burned Dia's throat at the mere memory. She bent over the sink and cupped her hands to take a sip of water and rinse her mouth of the bitter taste.

Demetria's silence would come at a high price—Dia's continued cooperation. And that cooperation had promised rewards: success, acclaim, a life dedicated to her magic.

A life of deception.

Dia hadn't heard from Demetria in six months, but she knew the woman was simply biding her time, waiting for a suitable target to emerge before she forced the decision. When she called Dia's agent to book the party, Dia knew. The waiting was over.

Dia shook her head. Her agent thought she was nuts to agree. She was a stage performer; this tour was graduating her from small venues to the larger arenas, he insisted indignantly. Private parties weren't in the plan anymore; they'd both agreed on that. Dia had listened calmly, then told him to go ahead and book. He'd soon been distracted by feelers from one of the television networks about featuring her in a special.

Dia had recognized the dangling carrot, even if her agent hadn't.

She dried her hands on a paper towel, and a series of deep breaths controlled her raw frustration. She had a plan—sort of. During her stay Demetria's, she would look for that confession and destroy it. And she was working on a new illusion that would expose Demetria when she made the switch. If only she could figure out how Demetria had switched the gems.

Dia looked in the mirror and carefully reapplied her lipstick. If she failed, she'd lose everything, for she could never look herself in the mirror again if she agreed to Demetria's plans.

She put the lid on the lipstick with a snap. Full circle. This had started with a private performance. It would end with one. She had one month before the curtain rose.

What she hadn't planned on was the twins coming. Her jaw tightened, and Dia stood straight, her nausea conquered. Nothing would happen to those kids, not while she had breath in her body.

She'd cancel the appointments she'd scheduled with potential sitters. She couldn't be sure whatever stranger she hired, even one with references, wasn't in Demetria's pocket.

Should she send the twins away?

Where? Where could she send them and be sure they were out of harm's way?

Tonight they'd be safe with Ronald, and afterward she'd keep them with her somehow. Even if it meant taking out a loan or eating soup for the next few months, she'd find a new place to live, one with security.

"Aunt Dia?" Elena poked her head around the door. "Are you done? We're hungry."

Dia settled her purse on her shoulder. "Coming."

It turned out that Cam and Lukas were not only hungry, but they insisted they needed sustenance now and could not possibly survive until they reached the apartment. The smell of grease at the museum restaurant, however, set Dia's stomach roiling. She wanted to get out, to shake the crawly sensation left from her meeting with Demetria.

"I know of a place nearby," Hugh suggested. "Italian. Huge, cheap calzones and fresh salads."

The children okayed the choice before Dia could say a word. Hugh glanced at her, brows lifted in silent question.

"Are they fast?" Dia glanced at her watch. "We have to leave in an hour so I can get ready for the show."

"They can be."

"Then it sounds good."

Mario and Maria's turned out to be a nondescript hole-in-the-wall decorated with the requisite checkered tablecloths and redolent with the aromas of garlic, olive oil, and tomato sauce. The restaurant was crowded, despite its being just past the main lunch hour and too soon for supper.

"Hugh!" A man bustled forward, wiping his hands on a spotless white apron. "Finally you come visit. Maria was asking the other day why you never come, and after saving our lives." He beamed at Dia. "You bring such a beautiful lady with you. And her children?"

"My nieces and nephews." Dia returned his smile and his hearty handshake.

"I see; come sit. Sit." He ushered them to one of the few empty tables and set down menus. "Shall you start with an antipasto? And my special garlic bread?"

"We're in a bit of a hurry, Mario," Hugh told him.

Mario's face fell. "But I had hoped that you were here to sample all our dishes."

Dia gave him an apologetic smile. "Blame me. I have a performance to get ready for, but the kids are hungry."

"Then may I suggest two meat pizzas, extra large, bread sticks, and an Italian crab salad. This can be ready pronto."

"Pronto sounds good," said Cam, and the others agreed.

"You're an actress?" Mario asked her.

"A magician."

His eyes grew wide. "A magician. Never have I met one."

"She's very good," added Hugh.

"Then I must come to see you. Now excuse me while I tell Maria you're here."

Moments later a woman of equal roundness joined them from the back. She was carrying a sleeping baby. Maria, Dia guessed, by her effusive greeting.

"Who's this little charmer?" Hugh asked, patting the baby's back.

"Our newest grandson. Vincenzio." She held out the baby.

Hugh readily took the child, surprising Dia with his ease. The baby made a gurgling sound and snuggled contentedly into Hugh's shoulder. "He's a fine son," Hugh said; then he asked Dia, "Do you want to hold him?"

She held up her hands and shook her head. "Babies always cry when I pick them up."

While Hugh and Maria chatted and the kids attacked the crackers at one end of the table, Dia sat back and let the conversation flow over her. She felt the tension seep from her neck. Coming here had been a good choice. For a while—for this meal, for one month—Demetria Cesare was out of her life. She could live, she could enjoy, she could ignore the waiting threat.

After Maria left with the baby, Dia rested her arms on the table and grinned at Hugh. "You saved their lives?"

Hugh, leaning back in his chair, rubbed a hand across the back of his neck, and Dia could have sworn she saw a tinge of red on his cheeks. "Not in the literal sense." When she cocked her head in question he continued, "They were in some financial troubles a couple of years back and I invested in their restaurant. It's taken off since then."

"So you're part owner?"

"Silent partner."

"He saves this restaurant, our life's work," said Mario, setting down the bread sticks. "No questions, no strings. Only help. When we have trouble with our supplier, Hugh fixes it. Now things go well."

100

"It's succeeded, Mario, because Maria is a fabulous cook, and because you are hard worker."

Dia chuckled. Hugh was definitely embarrassed by Mario's effusive praise. This was a side of him she'd not seen in their brief encounters; and she found she wanted to see more. In a different time, a different place, she'd enjoy getting to know Hugh Pendragon.

She ignored the small voice that insisted time and place and convenience were irrelevant, that her attraction to him was as inevitable as the sunset.

Their meal did come pronto, and it was as good as Hugh remembered, even though he hadn't been here in a long time, as Mario had pointed out. The kids attacked the pizza with gusto, while Dia nibbled at the crab salad and Hugh ate the antipasto Mario had included. Dia made a very pleasant dinner companion, he discovered, relating with humor and charm the trials of a brief stay on an ostrich farm for someone who hated the big birds, asking about what she might do with the children in Chicago, and finding a mutual interest in politics. They were almost finished when Maria, without the baby, rejoined them.

"Are you really a magician?"

Dia nodded, setting down her fork.

"My grandnephew. He's nineteen and that's all he does. Magic, magic, magic. Practice, practice, practice. Never a real job."

"Sounds like he knows what it takes, although he's got to step out there and perform. If he wants to stop backstage after one of my shows, I'll be glad to talk to him."

Kathleen Nance

"Oh, could he?" She clasped her hands together. "Could you show me something? A trick so I could tell him I have seen a real magician at work?" Then her face grew distressed as she noticed the barely eaten salad. "Oh, I'm sorry. I shouldn't have asked while you eat. Eat. Finish."

"No problem. I don't eat much before a performance," Dia answered with innate graciousness and a high-voltage smile.

"You probably get asked that a lot when people find out your profession," Hugh guessed.

Dia nodded. "I enjoy it. The motions of magic are a joy. Now I need a prop . . ." She glanced around the table.

"Do you need some cards? A wand?" asked Maria.

"Nope. A good magician can use whatever is at hand." She took the linen napkin and spun it into a rope. "Now this is your napkin, right? No holes, good solid fabric."

"Of course!"

"So if I knot it like this, then it's knotted. No flaws?" She held up the napkin, demonstrating the knot in the center.

"Yes, it is knotted."

"Are you sure?" Dia ran a hand across the napkin and the knot shifted from the center to the end, then back to the center and then to the other end.

Maria gaped at her and Mario stopped taking another order to watch, too.

As Dia went through the brief routine with the napkin, Hugh sat back and enjoyed the flow of her patter, the motion of her hands.

102

She fascinated him in a way no other woman had. She was exciting, yes, but he responded not only with excitement, which he recognized, but with an unfamiliar blossoming need to get to know more, to delve deeper, to learn what made her tick and what frightened her.

Vaguely he noticed other patrons also watching in fascination, but Dia's focus remained on the woman in front of her. It was easy to see she loved this, yet not every performer would have agreed to the small request so spontaneously or so graciously.

Dia flipped the napkin open. "But the napkin is sm—Oooow. Oh, no!"

Dia's sudden cry interrupted the pleasant flow of her words.

"My hands," she said in a moan.

Hugh realized instantly what had happened. A waiter, anxious to see what she was doing, had leaned over and his coffeepot spilled its hot contents on Dia.

Hugh reacted instantly. He cupped her hands in his and poured his ice water over them.

"Oh, miss, I'm sorry. I'm so sorry." The waiter dabbed her with his towel, repeating his litany of apology. "I'm so sorry. I'm sorry."

"Not your fault," Dia managed through gritted teeth, then grimaced.

Hugh grabbed the towel from the ineffectual waiter and wrapped it around Dia's hands. He took the glass that Cam held out and poured more ice water over the towel.

"A doctor! Mario, call a doctor!" Maria shouted.

"No doctor," insisted Dia. "The burning's lessened."

Mario and Maria fluttered. The waiter apologized. Hugh urged her to her feet. "The bathroom, Dia. Run them under the cold water. Maria, bring ice. Kids, can you finish up?"

His quiet commands broke through the chaos. Maria hurried off. Dia rose to her feet, her lips pressed together. "Please, I'm fine. Just let me dry off." She hurried to the bathroom.

"Is Aunt Dia going to be all right?" Cam asked. "A magician's hands? That's her lifeblood."

"I think she'll be okay." Hugh reassured him with a hand to the shoulder. "The burn looked superficial."

When Maria brought the ice, Hugh followed Dia into the bathroom. She was running the water at full force and holding her hands under it. He saw the track of a tear down her cheek, though she refused to acknowledge it.

"How do they look? Do you want some ice?" He held out the bucket.

Dia drew in deep breaths, then pulled her hands out of the water to examine them. The skin was reddened but not broken. She flexed and stretched her fingers, wincing a bit at the motion.

"My range of motion is intact. The coffee seemed to hit mostly my left hand; and luckily I'm right-handed." The relief in her voice was palpable.

Hugh took a towel Maria had given him and patted her hands dry. Then he rested them in his palms, examining first the backs, then the fronts. "They look sunburned."

"And I've worked with that before." There was some hand cream on the sink. Dia poured a generous amount into her palms and began working it into her hands. "This will help."

Hugh braced a hip on the counter and watched. He'd never watched a woman put on cream, and it seemed to him a very feminine gesture, appealing to a man by its very foreignness. Her fingers massaged every inch of skin, and each stroke filled the air with the aroma of honey and peaches.

Damn, everything the woman did was arousing.

"You know, you're in the women's bathroom," Dia said at last.

"And I've learned they're a lot cleaner than the men's rooms usually are." Mesmerized by the rhythm of her hands, he felt in no hurry to leave.

She added another dollop of cream, and Hugh felt his mouth go dry.

"You handled the situation very graciously," he managed at last.

"What do you mean?"

"Those are very clever hands, essential to your profession. A burn could be disastrous. Yet you didn't blame that clumsy waiter."

She shrugged. "Yelling at him wouldn't accomplish anything, wouldn't take away the burn. He didn't do it deliberately, and he felt bad enough already. Heck, it was my fault anyway for performing in the middle of the restaurant."

Hugh shook his head. "We all enjoyed it."

"I'm not sure the twins would agree with you. Don't you remember? Teenagers hate being the center of attention.

"I remember." He'd spent his entire life avoiding attention.

Dia studied her hands. "I think they'll be okay. Maybe a little sore tonight, but I can work with that." She glanced at her watch. "Oh, shoot, the time! We have to get going."

Hugh walked Dia and the kids back to their car, then watched them leave. He'd be seeing Dia again in a very short time, a fact that tempered his reluctance to let her go. They had a date tonight, and already he tightened in anticipation.

That afternoon Hugh sat at his desk, sorting through his mail, both snail and electronic. For someone who was retired, he'd found himself sitting here too often of late, he decided with a touch of humor. A variety of social invitations, which he routinely turned down, and charity requests, to which he routinely donated, took little time to handle.

His call to the art museum that had held the Treasures of the Underworld display was equally fruitless. The curator and the events planner were both out, and the assistant had not attended the function.

"Just leave a message for them to call me," Hugh requested.

"I do hope there wasn't a problem with the return of the gems. It was a rare privilege and quite a coup for us when you agreed to let them be displayed."

"They were delivered as scheduled. By the way, did anyone else know that I was the donor? A reporter called, and I wondered if he'd gotten my name from you."

"Of course not! You requested anonymity, and we respect our patrons' wishes."

"That's what I figured." Hugh rubbed a finger along the ruby at his wrist.

"I'm sorry I missed the opening party. I heard it was spectacular, and the entertainment superb."

"Entertainment?"

"A jazz trio and a magician."

His gut knotted. "A magician? Do you know who he was?"

"I'm afraid not."

Maybe Dia would know something. The magic community was a tight-knit one, he guessed. "Was that the only time the band was out of security?"

"Yes. Mr. Pendragon, is something wrong?"

"A bit of tarnish on the band," he said easily. "I thought maybe it was exposed to air."

There were a few more moments of chatter while the assistant tried to extract a promise of another donation and Hugh made vague promises; then they hung up.

For a moment Hugh sat quietly, rubbing the ruby. It was about time to get ready for the evening. Then, like a dental patient unable to stop tonguing a sore tooth, he pulled out the box atop his unsolved case files. He couldn't deny the vision he'd seen when he picked up Dia's earrings yesterday. If the diary didn't elicit a response, maybe something else would. He chose the tiny glass owl.

The woman who owned it was very familiar to him, though he'd never met her. He'd seen pictures of her, talked to her son, learned about her life. He knew that she canned tomatoes and that she worked as a bank teller. Hugh's thumb rubbed against the tiny head of the owl. This owl was the first in her collection, and she liked to hold it when she was thinking, or sad, or excited, her son said. It should be imbued with her spirit, yet he felt nothing. She was a strong-minded woman, yet he couldn't find her.

Still rubbing the owl, he relaxed, opened, pictured the woman he sought. He needed some clue to her whereabouts, some hint whether she was even alive. The back of his neck throbbed from the effort.

Nothing. The walls of the room mocked his efforts, refusing to give way to a vision. He clutched the owl in futile strain. Still nothing.

Hugh leaned his head back in the chair, and his throat choked with feelings of loss and failure. Inside him, a vital piece of his soul—the defining part of him—had been torn away. No matter what he did it remained missing, and the emptiness tasted like ash.

The one blazing vision of Dia must have been a mere fluke, a last hurrah, like the solar flare of a dying sun. Unless . . . Physical touch had always been a necessary part of his visions. Was that the key? Did he need to be connected with Dia for it to work?

Hugh dropped the owl into his pocket.

"Oh, dear." Ronald's gentle comment echoed Hugh's dismay as they stepped inside Dia's apartment.

Dia lived in a cracker box of chaos. There were bodies everywhere. Elena sat painting her toenails in front of a stereo blaring out high-voiced males singing in harmony. Claire sprawled on the sofa and read the *Chicago Tribune*. Next to her, Lukas had hooked his computer up to the phone line, while Cam was stretched out on the floor sleeping. Where there weren't bodies, there were clothes, cups, and the detritus of young people strewn across every available surface.

Elena glanced up. "Hey, Hugh. You must be Ronald. Is it okay if I call you Ronald? That's the only name I know, and Mr. Ronald sounds like a hairdresser, and you don't look like a hairdresser."

"What do you think I look like?"

Elena tilted her head. "A chef. Or a boxer."

"I've been both."

"Claire," said Lukas, "ready for input."

Claire tossed the paper to the floor. She unwrapped a chocolate snack cake, studied it a moment, then bent to see Lukas's computer screen. "Put in that they don't get moldy, not even after six months in the sun."

Lukas's hands flew over the keyboard.

"Don't forget to add about the microwave."

Lukas gave a hoot of laughter. "Definite 'at-your-own-risk' material."

Curious, Hugh moved so he could see the screen. "What are you working on?"

"My Web page," answered Lukas. "I'm updating the Freak Facts. Things you'll never find in a textbook."

"Microwaving of snack food?"

"Yup. I plan to link to the Twinkie Project page. It's a cool site from two dudes with all kinds of stuff about Twinkies. Want the URL?"

"I'll find it if I need it."

"We're expanding the info to include Ho Hos, Rice Krispies Treats, Ding Dongs, stuff like that."

"What happens in the microwave?"

Lukas flashed him a grin. "Mom gets mad and Claire gets a mess to clean up."

"Do you know exploded chocolate is yuck to get off the walls?" added Claire.

"I didn't know that." Hugh perched on the sofa arm. "Where's Dia?"

As if on cue, Dia appeared from a room off the small hallway. She was casually dressed in shorts and an undershirt, with no makeup, but her hair was fashioned into the more elaborate style she wore onstage. She was looking down at her flexing fingers and hands. Gold nail polish glittered, while the earrings he'd returned to her yesterday sparkled like tinsel under the room lights. His gut tightened as nerves sparked to life.

"Don't forget there's frozen egg rolls and burritos," she was saying, "and be sure you offer Ronald some."

Hugh felt Ronald wince at the mention of eating frozen burritos.

"I would be pleased to furnish them refreshments, Miss Trelawny."

She glanced up from her nails and smiled. "Ronald! I didn't hear you come—Hugh?"

"I thought I could give you a ride to the theater. Save us having two cars afterward."

"That will get you there awfully early. I was about to leave."

"My evening is free."

"May I make a suggestion?" Ronald absently stacked loose cups. "Take Miss Trelawny's car. Leave the one we came in. Perhaps the young ladies and gentlemen will wish to go out with me later."

"Yeah—"

"No!" Dia touched her hand to her throat, inter-rupting Elena and surprising Hugh with her vehe-ment refusal. "Um, I mean, you really don't have to do that."

"I merely planned to take them to the estate." Ronald's gaze swept the room, then returned to Dia. "I'm more comfortable in my own kitchen, you understand."

Dia gave a rueful grin. "Very smooth, Ronald. Make it seem like I'm doing you a favor, when I know this place offends every genteel sensibility you have."

"Not at all. I thought ... we have all the elec-tronic equipment for their entertainment."

"And in another room, I'll bet."

"Well ..." He glanced at Hugh. "Do you mind, sir?"

Hugh tried to wrap his mind around the idea of four adolescents invading the peace of his home. The disorder here offended his eyes and ears like a discordant piano, yet ... Children in his home? Children of Dia's line? Was it so impossible to imagine?

Inner peace? Hell, that had gone out the window six months ago. And calm surroundings hadn't pro-duced results yet.

Besides, it was only for a single evening.

"Mind? No, sounds like a good idea."

Hugh drew in a breath and caught Dia's now-familiar scent: perfume and woman. He hadn't imagined Dia's ashen face, nor the fleeting, raw fear in her first refusal, nor her relief when Ronald ex-plained. Curious. What was Dia Trelawny not telling him? Old hunting instincts bayed inside him, as primitive and basic as mating or arousal.

Fool! From her side of the plush, half-circle divan, Demetria Cesare glared at a swaggering Mick Masterson. Not only had he forgotten the simple fact that she was supposed to contact him, not the other way around, but he had chosen this smoky, pretentious bar to meet.

Sometimes, however, you had to humor the minions. She clasped her green mesh gloves together and waited for the idiot in front of her to continue.

Mick wiggled the toothpick he held between his teeth. "Don't worry; I'm still keeping an eye on her. I got connections. Of course, you realize those kind of connections cost."

Enjoy your moment of bravado, for it will not last. Mick was supposed to be watching Dia; instead he'd managed to get fired the first week into the tour. The only question was how to turn this to her advantage.

Her silence must have gotten through to him at last, for he gave her a wary glance. "Learned a couple of interesting things."

Demetria waited, silent and cold.

"Seems she's taking care of four kids this summer. She don't look none too happy about it, either."

Tell me something I don't know.

"I also know who she hired to replace me. Man named Zeke Jupiter. Runs a fireworks company out of Denver. Him stepping in so quick, there's got to be somethin' coming down there."

Demetria sucked in a breath. For once Mick had managed to surprise her. Zeus? What was that meddlesome troublemaker up to?

"She also had a man in her dressing room. He stayed awhile, too. Interesting fellow." Mick gave her a smirk, then fell silent, trying to play the game.

She'd been at it a lot longer than he. "You're wasting my time." She stood to go.

"Wait!" He laid a hand on her arm. Demetria's eyes narrowed, and he hastily removed his hand.

The toothpick waggled again. "I got expenses," he whined.

Demetria reached into her purse, then laid two hundred-dollar bills on the table. When they disappeared into Mick's pocket, she snapped her fingers for the waiter to refill Mick's beer.

He took a long swallow before setting the mug down with a satisfied belch. "Cold and no foam. The way beer should be."

"Who was the man?"

"I never met him."

She made a sound of disgust.

"A friend of mine had a run-in with him," Mick added hastily, "and I recognized him. Name's Hugh Pendragon. He's a detective. Damn good one, too."

Hugh Pendragon. A Soul Seeker, though Hugh doubtless didn't realize what that meant. She felt a familiar lick of rage, but in the millennia since Hades had taken her daughter, she'd learned to control it and channel it.

Demetria Cesare, once Demeter, goddess of the fields and the forests, knew how to be patient.

113

"Yes, he is," was all she said. "So you do nothing. You're finished. Stay away from Dia Trelawny."

"But—"

Mick's protest was lost as she strode from the repulsive bar. Her driver pulled up at once, and a moment later she was ensconced in the back, returning home. A sumac vine, its leaves dark green with toxins, snaked from the planter beside her. Its tendrils gripped the edge of the window. Although she had bred this one for its virulence, it would never dare to harm her.

Her mind turned over what Mick had told her, and suddenly she gave a low laugh. Dia Trelawny and Hugh Pendragon together? For more than a simple date, too, if Mick's information was accurate. *How ironic.*

It had all started so simply. Jewel theft, something to amuse a goddess. A magician, a woman who reminded her so much of her stolen Persephone, groomed for greatness. Then she had found her chance to take a long-nurtured revenge when the talisman of the Soul Seeker's power—the gems of Hades—went on public display.

Here was the opportunity to possess the power of the Soul Seeker by possessing his wristbands. If she could not destroy Hades, the man who had bewitched her daughter, then she would render his line impotent.

She needed the second wristband to complete the process.

She had recently added a new challenge to her amusements: she wanted Dia Trelawny back, body and soul. And if she took her away from a Soul Seeker? It would be perfect justice.

Demeter chuckled. Suddenly this affair had gained new promise. She would be patient, wait for the right moment.

And in the meantime she would find out what that troublesome Zeus had up his sleeve.

Chapter Seven

Zeus loved the bustle of readying for a performance. Whether it was with Apollo tuning his lyre for a feast or setting up shells and mortars for a fireworks display or checking the lights before the cameras rolled, he thrived on the anticipation and excitement.

Backstage was dim and close, but not too crowded; most of Dia's crew had yet to arrive. Script in hand, Zeus perched on a stool making notes, while Dia and Paolo ran through the sequence of illusions for him. Standing beside him, Anya explained the backstage logistics. A lovely woman Anya was, with scarlet-tinted hair, a color beloved by her ancestress, Danaë. Now there had been a woman of character and stoic calm, even if her father was a bit of a scoundrel. And Paolo embodied the grace of Apollo.

116

"This is a quiet portion, Zeke, so backstage can prep for the finale," Dia said, moving toward the front of the stage as Paolo exited stage right. "I bring up a volunteer from the audience, and we don't want to scare off a stage neophyte."

"Startled deer in the headlights isn't a pretty image onstage," commented Paolo.

"Dia's a master at getting people to relax up here, but we try to make it as easy as possible for her," added Anya, her hands moving over her console as her body bounced in time to the music in her headphones. "Hey, Dia, I'm going to start the music another ten seconds sooner. You've been moving faster onstage."

"Good. Say, did you see that the Cubs won another?"

"Yeah, it's World Series this year. I can feel it."

Zeus sighed in pleasure. A descendant of Leda onstage, a descendant of Danaë and a son of Apollo, all three working together in a spectacle for the masses. Truly an Olympian moment.

"Zeke, five minutes, then I'll be stage left." Dia strode to her position. "That's your cue for the spots."

Zeus hit the stopwatch and noted the timing on his script. "We could add a little color to the flares. Maroon and emerald, I think."

"You can do that?"

"That's some of the new technology I'm trying. Like fireworks, but without the danger of the heat."

"No changes for tonight," Dia decided. "Let's put it in next for Evanston, since we've got a couple of days off after tonight."

"I've got some other plans I think you'll like." Plans for the show, plans for her—it was time to give things a little push. Zeus rubbed his lightning ring and the air in the theater crackled.

Dia jerked around. "What was that? Problems with the sound?"

Anya gave her a mock scowl. "You expect anything but perfection with me?"

Dia laughed. "Sorry, oh perfect one. Of course not."

"What's biting you, pal?" Anya ran a hand through her hair, making it stand straight up. "Where's the when-I'm-onstage-no-distractions-Dia I'm used to? You're jumpier than a kid needing to pee."

"You think Mick might be up to some dirty work?" asked Paolo.

"I doubt it. He's too cowardly."

"Who's Mick?"

Hugh's quiet question startled Zeus, for he had not heard the Soul Seeker move closer. When Zeus arrived, Hugh had been lounging in the shadows of the stage, watching, not participating with the other three onstage. Zeus twisted on his stool to eye the man, curious to see him with the others. Though the question was directed to Paolo, it was Dia who held Hugh's focus, and it was she who answered.

"Mick Masterson. The lighting tech, until I fired him yesterday."

"You think he might cause problems?" The question was put to Paolo. Hugh crossed his arms, and Zeus noticed the flash of red at his wrist: a ruby set in copper.

Hugh Pendragon wore one of the wristbands of Hades—the ruby, which kept him grounded. Where was the opal? The source of his ability to seek?

Casting a sidelong glance at Dia, Paolo rubbed a hand against the back of his neck. "If he gets some drink in him, he's unpredictable."

"This kind of thing happens all the time in this business. I'm not worried about Mick."

"What *are* you worried about?" The words were a barely audible challenge. Hugh's stillness seemed to command the air around him to quiet, too, waiting for her answer.

He used the Seeker's power, drawing on that source within. Did Hugh know what it was he did or were his responses sheer instinct? Instinct, Zeus decided. The Soul Seeker was on the hunt. Sweat rose on Zeus's skin. He would not like to be Mick Masterson should harm come to Dia.

Dia met Hugh's stare with one just as bold; then she broke the tension between them. "I'm worried about getting this show to run tonight. Let's get back to work."

Hugh nodded once, as though his question were answered, then glided toward his seat.

Dia pivoted toward Zeus. "Paolo does a sequence here while I get ready for the airplane blades. His act is different from mine, otherworldly and mysterious. We're trying to figure out the best way to showcase the differences, and him."

Zeus turned his attention back to the stage. "What about a single column of gold light?"

They finished the run-through; then Dia rested one hip against Anya's console. "You're good, Zeke

119

Jupiter, so why pick my show? You could work anywhere in the business."

"To tell the truth"—Zeus fingered his ring—"you and your crew remind me of people I once knew."

"People you miss? Friends lost?"

"For the most part." A few he didn't miss, like Demeter. In a group of self-absorbed gods, she was the worst.

Anya laid a hand on his shoulder. "Why don't you and Harriet come to my birthday party tonight? It'll be a mix of family, crew, and people from the city. Dia's even letting me leave early to get ready for it."

Dia leaned over and gave him a kiss on the cheek. "Chill, make new friends."

A crash at the back of the theater spun them around. Hera had arrived, stumbling over a row of chairs in the process.

"Are you all right?"

"What happened?"

"What was that noise?"

Hera ignored the questions. She dusted off her sleeves and straightened her jacket, while Hugh, who'd moved to her side with singular speed, picked up her satchel and handed it to her. She gaped at him a moment before giving him a gracious thank-you. Her gaze latched onto the three onstage. "Are you ready for makeup, Dia?"

"Harriet, hi! Half an hour," Dia answered. "Are you okay?"

"Fine, I knocked into a chair. I'll wait."

" 'Scuse me, ladies." Zeus was off his stool and over to Hera faster than thunder after lightning. "What happened?" he whispered.

"The ring," she spat, shaking her hand. "I did a far-see, and very interesting it was."

A far-see? Zeus fingered his mustache. Had she seen Dia's kiss? Hera glared at him. She'd seen, and she was definitely annoyed. He refused to apologize, though, for he had done nothing wrong. "Why the noisy entrance?"

"I tried to transport here. The energy exploded, out of control. And what do I find when I get here? A Soul Seeker!"

Zeus shrugged. "These humans have an annoying free will. She has raised his interest."

Hera rolled her eyes. "Your curse is broken only with a son of Olympus. I thought we agreed on Paolo. Can he compete against a Soul Seeker?"

"Why do you think our choice should be the son of Apollo?"

"Apollo was beloved by us all. I'm sure she would be happy with him."

"But Dia is a magician. She needs mystery, secrets."

"What if we fail?" she asked in a hoarse voice. "What if the Soul Seeker falls in love with her? What if she is not strong enough to break the curse you left? We'll be condemning him to a life without the pleasures of love."

"He will sire a child, no matter what. He will love that."

She shook her head. "It's not the same."

"No, it's not." Zeus laid a hand over hers. "When your own love rejects you, it is a pain not easily forgotten."

Hera flushed, obviously remembering her rejection of him. "I know," she whispered, tearing a small piece of his heart away. She had known his rejection as well. "Do we have the right to meddle in this, Zeus?"

"Pish, the gods have always meddled in the affairs of humans. It's fun." He laced their fingers together, then kissed the knuckles of her hand. "It is not yet love between Hugh and Dia. Without love, any attraction can be severed or diluted. The bond can still be broken, leaving them free to choose elsewhere. Watch them for a while; then tell me which man is right for her. I'll abide by your decision."

He had no doubt that she would eventually agree with him.

The instinct to mate—and to sire—had been awakened in the Soul Seeker. And that was a powerful force indeed.

Hugh had seen Dia's performance three times, yet he remained entranced. Her skills as an illusionist were exemplary—he still could not figure out how she accomplished the sleight of hand. No two performances were exactly the same. Within the framework of her show, she played to her audience, shifting her patter and smaller illusions according to the crowd's mood.

Like now. She came down the steps into the audience with the sexy, effortless glide of a Hollywood femme fatale. Hugh's gut tightened as he watched the rhythm of her hips, and the room heated up as her full lips tilted in a mischievous smile.

"I need a volunteer from the audience." Dozens of male hands shot up as she playfully talked her way down the aisle.

Straight toward him.

She held out a gold-dusted hand. "How about you, sir?"

Hugh's mouth dried to ash. Getting up onstage in front of several hundred people was his idea of a nightmare.

All around him people clapped and urged him up onstage. Dia touched him, and heat blasted through him at inferno strength. Hugh rose, drawn not by the clamorous audience, but by the wink she gave him, the seduction of her voice, and the compelling need to keep anyone else from taking his place.

The silver lamé didn't hurt either.

Dia's smile widened as he accepted her challenge. Onstage the lights shone upon him, hot and blinding. He squinted under the blazing stage lights, seeing only Dia. When she shifted position, he followed her motion, and to his relief suddenly found he was able to see the stage, the lighting no longer directly in his eyes.

Thank you, he mouthed.

"You're welcome." She held a microphone for him to talk into. "And what's your name?'

"Hugh."

"All right, Hugh. Is this an ordinary deck of cards?" She handed them to him. "Take a look; do you see anything unusual? Examine them all you want."

"It's an ordinary deck of cards," he answered after a cursory examination, uncomfortably aware of the audience watching his every movement.

"Good. Ever wanted to be a magician, Hugh?"

"Not particularly." To his surprise the audience laughed.

"Well, you're going to be the magician here. Do magic with this deck of cards." She fanned out the deck. "I want you to pick a card. Whatever card you want."

He picked the ace of spades, but before he could show her, she put her hand on his. That heat, that incredible, charging heat spread through him, to lungs and throat and chest and toes.

"Don't show me," she told him. "Show the audience only."

Dimly he followed her instructions, aware of little beyond the melody of her voice and the tingling of the copper band at his wrist. Show the audience the card, write his name on the back, tear it up—she led him through the steps.

"Now I want you to put it in your pocket. Do you have a pocket, Hugh?" She was keeping up the show alone, for he was contributing little, and he heard a note of frustration in her voice.

For Dia, Hugh tried to shake off the heat stealing his senses, and for the moment he succeeded. "Yes."

"You don't know it, but that pocket is magic, and I'm going to prove it to you. Put the pieces in your pocket."

He did so, with a little flair that had the audience chuckling in appreciation, and his fingers brushed against glass. The small owl. Quickly he pulled out his hand and showed the audience his empty palms.

Paolo picked up a tray of bottled drinks, which had been sitting within view at the side of the stage, and brought it over. Dia waved her hand over the array. "This magic takes a few minutes to work. Would you like something to drink while we wait? Milk, pop, wine, juice, beer."

"Juice?"

"Now, I would have taken you for a wine man, myself, but we've got some good orange juice here. You like orange juice?"

"Served by you? Yes."

The audience laughed again, and Dia gave him a grin as she chose a carton. Paolo removed the tray. She set the carton beside a glass and started to open it, then paused. "I think this trick's about ready. I want you to reach in your pocket and give me the pieces like this." She held out her closed fist, fingers down.

Hugh complied, avoiding the glass owl this time, then held out his fist, the papers mashed beneath his fingers. Dia cupped his hand between hers.

The heat exploded within him, and the dying ember of his gifts shot to life again.

For an instant he channeled through her. He saw her through his eyes. He saw himself through Dia's eyes. Knew danger. And fear. He could barely breathe. Something in Dia's Trelawny's life was terribly wrong.

She let go of his hands and the image disconnected. Through a haze, he watched her hold up an empty hand; the pieces had vanished. She teased him about the magic pocket, about not giving the pieces to her, and somehow he must have responded appropriately, for the audience clapped. He watched her pour the juice, watched her retrieve the card, intact, from the previously sealed carton, watched her hand him the card to verify his signature.

"Check your pockets one more time," she said, her voice seeming to come from a distant tunnel. She laid a hand on his arm. "Are the pieces gone?"

Only that teasing voice got through the haze, except now it held a touch of worry. He followed her directive blindly, checking his pocket once again. "The pieces are gone." His fingers touched the glass owl.

Heat. Another explosion. Burning, clogging his lungs, sapping his strength. He willed himself to stay upright as the vision closed around him.

The missing woman. He could feel her, hear her, see her. She was in pain, but she was alive. She planned escape, but her hope was fading fast and she could not last much longer.

He had to find her.

Hugh staggered offstage amid applause while Dia skillfully covered his sudden, silent departure. The crew, all busy, paid him little mind as he stumbled toward the solitude of Dia's tiny dressing room. He examined the vision for answers, hoping his strength lasted, and trying to touch the lost woman, to give her the fortitude to endure.

Hugh slammed the door shut behind him and the sound reverberated in his ears as his senses heightened with the clarity of the vision. He dropped into a chair, wincing as the stiff vinyl jabbed his sensitized skin. *Let me see.* A seedy room, a captor—a customer at the bank. The vision expanded, and he recognized the Chicago landmarks. He knew where she was.

As the vision faded, he blindly groped for his cell phone, grateful the police number was on speed dial.

"It's Pendragon," he said in a gasp when the lieutenant came on. "I know where Marcia Zebolt is." He rattled off the location. "Hurry."

This officer was a good woman; they'd worked together before and she'd come to trust Hugh, even if she didn't understand. She'd have a patrol there in time. Hugh hung up, collapsed back in the chair, and gave himself to the aftermath of sensory overload.

At the close of the show, as the audience exited, Dia hurried backstage. Dear Lord, what imp on her shoulder had urged her to bring Hugh Pendragon onstage with her? She'd nearly dropped the torn card at his touch.

No man had ever made her lose control of her magic, not like that.

What had it been? An urge to shake up his self-control? A desire to have him share her spotlight? A need to have him close?

And what the heck had happened at the end?

"Where's Hugh?"

Anya jerked her head. "In your dressing room. For a beginner, he did pretty well out there. Who'd have suspected he had stage presence?"

"Something spooked him, though."

"We thought the bit ended too abruptly. I knocked and he said he was fine, a case of stage fright. It happens."

Dia had seen plenty of stage fright in her time. He'd started out awkward, but he'd begun to overcome it, begun to warm up to the audience—he had a dry sense of humor that came across well—when something made him beat a fast retreat, and it wasn't stage fright.

The room was dark; only a single bare bulb in the minuscule closet was lit, and Hugh had set the door so only a crack of that light came through. Warmth filled the small space, a heat that wrapped itself around her. Dia closed the door behind her with a gentle click and drew in a breath. A faint, foreign scent was mixed with her perfume. Masculine. Soap and lime.

"Hugh?" The darkness absorbed her soft question.

"Here."

Her stomach fluttered as she sought the source of his low voice. As her eyes finally adjusted to the dimness, she saw he was sitting in her chair. No, not sitting, lounging, claiming his rightful spot with one leg thrown over the chair arm and one dangling hand holding a cell phone. Spots of color shone like gems against velvet: copper and red at his wrist, blue from his earlobe, green in his eyes.

The fluttering strengthened and her insides tightened. She had enough experience with men to recognize that look. Normally she handled it with ease, either accepting the invitation or turning it away with a deft charm.

With Hugh, though, normal was nonexistent.

"Are you okay?" She went closer, leaning against a small table. *The spider and the fly*; the phrase echoed once more in her mind.

"Fine."

"What happened?"

He didn't bother to deny the strange stage ending. "A sudden inspiration about an old case. It was something I had to follow up at once."

She didn't really understand, but sensed that was the only explanation she would get. Dia reached over to turn on the light, needing something to dispel the cotton that seemed to have replaced her brain.

"Don't." Hugh laid a hand on hers. "My eyes feel a bit . . . sensitive."

Cotton? Hell, it was sexy silk substituting for brain power.

The cell phone rang in a barely audible tone. Hand still clasping hers, eyes locked with hers, he answered the phone. "Pendragon." There was a moment's silence while he listened. "Thanks, Lieutenant. I appreciate knowing." Another silence, then, "I'm glad, too." He flipped the phone closed, still never breaking eye contact.

"The case?" Dia asked.

Hugh nodded. "They found her."

A deep satisfaction filled his voice. He turned his hand to lace his fingers with hers, then lifted her hand to his lips. His mouth brushed across her knuckles in a soft kiss that barely touched her skin, yet managed to stir something deep within her soul. He kissed her again, then gave a soft, appreciative purr. "You taste like honey, Dia."

"It's the new makeup."

"I don't think so."

When he rose from the chair, she went with him. They faced each other in the heated room. The ribbon of yellow light, the spots of color, the glimmer of her costume blended to become a mosaic of color

129

and light against the shadows. Dia saw his nostrils flare slightly as he drew in a deep breath, and she wondered if he knew how intoxicating the scent of him was.

"I want to kiss you, Dia. Do you mind?"

Mind? Her insides softened at the thought and her body opened in preparation. "No."

To her surprise, he didn't move directly to the kiss. Instead he drew her flush against him and wrapped his arms about her. Masculine strength and that strange, incredible heat surrounded her. He had the body of a champion runner and the temperature of a furnace.

Unwilling to give him total control over the embrace, Dia bracketed his face, urging him to the next step. The faint scratch of beard tickled her fingers. Tall as she was, she still had to look up a short way to see those emerald eyes, and her stomach muscles tightened. If gems could burn, they would look like his eyes. His hands shifted until one splayed across the small of her back, holding her flat against him. The other hand cupped her head and dislodged the fastenings that controlled her hair onstage.

Distantly she heard the sounds of her crew knocking down the sets and knew she should change, get out there to help.

Hugh's had lowered toward hers.

Later.

Their lips met halfway.

If she tasted of honey, then he tasted of something more exotic, like kiwi or dark chocolate. Dia gave a soft moan of pleasure and moved closer, reveling in the feel of him pressed against her and the excitement he made no attempt to hide. He was a man adept at using his mouth and coaxing a woman's response, she found. His hand stroked down her hair and across her neck in a tender dance. Or maybe it was only *her* response that he coaxed.

It wasn't nearly enough. Dia gripped the muscles of his arms.

A rap sounded on the closed door. "Dia," called Paolo. "Zeke was asking about packing the lights."

Not enough, but for now all it could be.

She pulled away from the kiss.

"She'll be right there," Hugh answered.

"I have to change," she whispered.

"Let me help." Without moving away, Hugh deliberately but deftly unfastened the back of her lamé suit. Dia clutched it close, holding it up at the neck. For one too-brief moment his hand lingered, warm and strong, at the nape of her neck; then he leaned over and kissed her bared shoulder. "Mmmm," he said in a growl that curled her toes. "Do we have to go to the party?" His low voice hummed inside her.

"I do," she said under her breath, although at this moment she'd never wanted to party less.

"Then I'll wait." His lips found a sensitive spot, right where her neck and shoulder met. Dia shivered at the soft touch of his tongue. "Tomorrow. Come to me. We'll talk."

"Talk?" His lips did delicious things to her neck and the lobe of her ear. He blew gently and it was oxygen on the sparks of desire. With a single kiss he promised so much more than talk. "About what?"

"Your sister. I'm taking your case."

Chapter Eight

To Hugh's astonishment, Dia jerked back and ripped herself from his grasp.

"So that's what this is? A bargain? You find my sister in return for a little sex on the side?"

"What!"

"I don't deal like that, Hugh Pendragon."

"I'd be disappointed if you did."

"I thought you were different," she said with quiet bitterness.

He met her furious gaze with one of his own. "I kissed you, Lydia Trelawny, for one reason and one reason only: because I wanted to. Because you happen to be the sexiest woman I've ever met. Finding your sister is *business* and has absolutely nothing to do with whether you kiss me or sleep with me or tell me to F-off."

"Yeah, I've heard that before. 'Come on, Dia, a little kiss and I know a guy who can make you a deal.' Or 'I can do big things for you, baby doll.' Or 'You know the way the game's played, honey.' Well, I don't work that way."

"And I don't traffic in blackmail."

"That's not what you said."

Hugh raked a hand through his hair, trying to remember what the hell he'd said. Sweet kisses, the aftermath of the vision, the urge to be alone with her and not at some damn party, the elation that he might be able to help her and all the others now, all blended together. Okay, maybe she had some basis for misinterpretation. "I'm sorry if that's what it sounded like, but it's not what I meant. I wasn't talking with my brain right then, and I'm surprised anything coherent came out of my mouth. I'll still take your case, if you want. The other . . . we'll work it out as we go. Mutual agreement only."

She was silent a moment. "You called me Lydia."

"That's your name, isn't it?"

"Nobody's ever called me that. I'd almost forgotten it was on my birth certificate."

"I thought it might get your attention."

"It did." She caught her lower lip between her teeth. "You must've been doing some research already. Why?"

"I was intrigued." Out of curiosity, he'd done some poking around this afternoon, and had been surprised by the lack of info about where Liza Swensen had gone. Usually people left a trail of reservations and credit card charges when they traveled. "But I don't take cases unless I think I can help. I think I can now."

"Oh." She paused another moment, then lifted her chin. Faint spots of color showed under her makeup. "I'm sorry I assumed the worst."

He nodded in acceptance. Working in the entertainment industry, looking the way she did, he expected Dia had received more than her share of ugly propositions. In what ways had she been hurt? Forced to give in or compromise? Whatever the answers, they wouldn't change his opinion of her. The questions only exposed a fierce wellspring of anger at those unknown males and a decidedly uncivilized urge to tear into a few.

"Tonight we're going on a date. Tomorrow we'll talk business. Come at ten."

Dia groaned and rolled her eyes. "Not another morning."

"Then make it eleven. And I'll get Ronald to keep the coffee hot."

After the equipment was loaded onto the truck and everyone left, Dia dashed back into her dressing area to change out of her working shorts, and Hugh prowled restlessly about backstage. "Do you have a picture of your sister?" he asked through the door.

"Yes, I'll bring it," she called back. "She looks like me. Mom always said I was supposed to be Liza's twin, I just came six years late. We're the only Trelawny generation without a set of twins."

Since Liza was thirty-two, that made Dia twenty-six. "I thought twins skipped generations."

"Not in the Trelawny family. Twins everywhere you look. Maybe that's why the men always get spooked. Too many twins. Can you call Ronald and make sure everything's okay?"

"Will do."

The phone call took only a few minutes as Hugh verified that yes, the children were at his house, and yes, Ronald was having a smashing time with them.

"Everything's—" Hugh turned at the sound of Dia's door opening behind him, and the words faded away as his body burst into life.

Black leather skirt. Silky blouse with a dangerous V neck. Hair drawn back by two glittery clips. Thousand-watt grin. She was a fantasy in a warm, breathing package.

". . . fine," he finished weakly.

She came to his side, and only when she brushed his shoulder did he smell the rich musk of her perfume, a tantalizing scent meant only for someone she allowed close.

"Are you ready?" She linked her arm with his.

Hugh looked at the black leather, the dangling earrings, the high heels. "More than ready."

The party was in full swing when they got to the rental hall. Family and friends crowded the room, clustered around the food and drink tables scattered about and dancing to a rocking deejay. Hugh had been expecting a simple party with a two-layer cake and a chorus of "Happy Birthday." This was an event.

Generally he avoided crowds and parties. He disliked the press of bodies, preferring the more satisfying interactions of small groups. In crowds, on very rare occasions, he'd been beset by an unexpected vision generated from someone he'd touched.

Apparently Dia had no such qualms. As Hugh strolled in behind her, he was amazed by her unself-conscious sparkle as they eased into the crowd. She greeted friends, spoke with strangers, and drew attention without effort or deliberation.

Anya spied her and made a beeline over, greeting them both. "I'm so glad you came, Dia. You're almost a member of the family."

"I wouldn't have missed it." Dia exchanged a kiss on the cheek with her friend and handed her a gift bag. "Happy birthday."

Anya peeked inside, then lifted up the porcelain penguin. "It's beautiful; thank you! You remembered I collect penguins."

"This is quite a party," he commented.

"Rostovs know how to throw a bash." Anya rubbed her head, spiking her already mussed scarlet hair. "My folks are worried. No prospective husband for Anya, so they're trotting out the eligible sons of their friends to give me a little nudge. I'm supposed to dance with each one. Better watch out, Hugh, or you'll be added to the list."

"Who's tops on the prospects list?" Dia teased.

"No one." Anya made a face. "Marriage is an institution that would put me in the institution. I figure it's just a good opportunity for a party, although I did tell Paolo that if I did this"—she rubbed a finger along her chin—"he was supposed to create a diversion."

"Anya," called Paolo. "This dance is mine."

"I was just demonstrating."

He laughed and swung her onto the dance floor. "Not getting off that easy, beautiful."

"Just make yourselves at home," Anya called back. "Hugh, Dia can introduce you around. Anyone she doesn't know won't be a stranger for long."

Hugh met and listened and managed the party chat, kept Dia supplied with club soda, and was tolerant when she danced with someone else—she tried to get him out there with her, but he'd refused—and wondered how soon before he could leave with her.

Too many questions haunted him as he endured the party. Had his talents come back? They could be unpredictable at the best of times, so it was hard to tell. Could he see visions only when he was in contact with Dia? Did she somehow channel for him? Was Dia in some kind of danger? Did her sister's disappearance have anything to do with it?

Hugh spotted Paolo Phoenix, alone for once as he claimed a root beer, and meandered over to join him.

"Hey, Pendragon. How's it going?"

"Phoenix, going fine." Hugh nodded in response. On the dance floor, he saw Dia with one of the stagehands. She didn't look tight or worried about any mysterious danger, but Dia was good at illusion. Hugh traced a finger through the sweat on his glass. "Paolo, do you know if Dia is worried about anything?"

"Like the tour? She's betting everything she has on its success."

"Nothing else?"

"Not that I know of. Why?" His eyes narrowed. "You know something we ought to know?"

Hugh shook his head. "She asked me to find her sister. I'm just looking at places to start."

"That's right; you're a detective." Paolo tilted his head to study him. "Pendragon. Your name seems familiar. I grew up in Chicago. You been here long?"

"The family's been here six generations at least. Before that, family history gets a little skimpy." He'd always figured some ancestor along the way had a few skeletons to hide and created a new identity for the Pendragons. "I came back about fourteen years ago."

"I remember now. My old man used to talk all the time about a Daniel Pendragon. Said he made a killing in the commodities exchange, had the golden touch about what and when to trade. Dad made a mint following his leads. You any relation?"

"My father." His father had ignored the family talents—especially after his first wife died and he married Hugh's mother—except for one: Pendragons had a gift for making money. "So is Paolo Phoenix your stage name or your real one?"

Paolo laughed. "Paolo Phoenix né Colavincenzerelli. It seemed a bit much for the marquee. I worked as the uninspired Paolo Colo until I joined with Dia and became Phoenix." He took a swallow of root beer. "It seemed appropriate."

"Appropriate?"

"Phoenix. Rising from the ashes." He held up the root beer. "This is the only beer I drink these days, but it wasn't always so. I literally owe Dia my life."

"How so? If you don't mind my asking."

"It's no secret. She confronted me about the drinking, got me into a treatment program. More important, she gave me a reason to work at it."

"You're in love with her?" Hugh asked tightly.

"Hell, yes. What hetero male wouldn't be?" He gave Hugh a quick glance. "But we know where she draws the line. What I meant is, she helped me get back in touch with what was important. You see, performing can be a real trap. You have to be so on, so focused to make it all work, that when you come offstage . . ." He shrugged.

"It's hard to wind down?"

Paolo nodded. "My relaxation aid of choice was alcohol. But Dia reminded me what started it all. The magic. The joy of a perfect false shuffle. The fun of listening to people gasp when you totally surprise them. The beauty of a cups-and-balls routine. She also took a video of me trying it with my hands shaking and my voice slurring. It wasn't pretty to watch." He took another gulp of root beer. "So I quit, and when I got dry, she hired me for this gig."

Hugh guessed it was much harder than that, that Paolo was downplaying his own efforts, but he figured the magician had said all he wanted about the subject. "What's Dia's relaxation aid of choice? Partying?"

"People," corrected Paolo. "She enjoys partying, but it's the interaction with people she needs. You're not much into this scene, are you?"

"Is it that obvious?"

Paolo shrugged. "You play the game okay, but you don't let loose and enjoy. Not like our Dia. You want some advice?"

"Not particularly."

"Well, Dia always says I talk too much, so I'm going to be real generous and give you some anyway. You won't make any points with Dia Trelawny if you don't at least make an effort to look like you're having fun."

The music changed to a slow beat, and Hugh glanced over to see Zeke Jupiter eyeing Dia. Maybe he should listen to a little unsolicited advice now and then. "Phoenix, maybe you're right. Tell me if this works."

Hugh set down his glass, and a moment later he reached Dia and swung her into his arms. "Would you like to dance?"

"I thought you couldn't dance."

"I said I didn't like it, not that I can't do it."

Dia wasn't really surprised to find Hugh a pleasure to dance with. She doubted he'd have asked her onto the floor if he hadn't mastered the techniques, and she'd seen that he moved with a fluid, masculine grace. Their smooth steps felt like they had danced together for years, instead of mere minutes. The fact that she enjoyed the feel of his arms about her and the rhythm of their bodies moving in concert was an added plus to the sheer joy of the movement.

Another couple that seemed to have a distinct match in dance technique was Zeke Jupiter and Harriet Juneau. When he twirled her around, it was obvious they had danced together before, and often. Their movements were practiced, but it was not a dance step she recognized.

Hugh didn't seem to want to talk, and his expert technique kept them from accidentally bumping into other couples, cocooning them in quiet. Dia gave herself up to the joys of the dance.

All too soon the song ended and the deejay switched to the latest line-dance craze. Hugh led her to the side of the dance floor. "Thank you for the dance."

"Aren't you going to do the Salsa Stomp?"

"Not my kind of dance."

Dia swung her hips in response to the driving beat.

"At least not in public," he added.

"Ah, it's fun. And easy. All you have to do is sway like this, shoulders move this way, then down, up, step, turn." She demonstrated the rhythm, enjoying the Latin beat of the song.

He hesitated a moment until she thought he might let loose a little, drop that quiet control; then he shook his head.

Paolo grabbed her hand. "C'mon, Dia, let's dance. Good first step, Hugh, but you need to work on your follow-through."

As she followed her friend, she gave Hugh a laughing warning. "Someday, Hugh, you are going to do the Salsa Stomp with me, and in public."

"So what do you think?" Zeus whispered to Hera.

"Give me time. I haven't seen enough of them."

"This is their third dance—"

"Only the slow ones."

"And the only other person he's chosen is Anya."

"I've lost count how many partners she's had."

"Twelve, and none were as well matched to her as Hugh," Zeus insisted.

"The Furies danced well together, too, and they hated one another."

141

"All women, so it doesn't count." He whirled her around so she could keep an eye on the couple in question.

"Stop twirling," Hera complained. "I didn't mean I had to keep them in sight the whole time they're on the floor."

"You love to whirl; admit it." He gave her another spin. "You love to dance, and I'm the best partner you ever had."

"Apollo and Pan were good."

"Not as good."

Hera just shook her head.

"Ha, you're just afraid to admit it. Do you trust me?"

"What?"

He spun her around, then without warning lowered her into a dip. It was a smooth move only if she trusted him implicitly, trusted him to lower and raise her easily and without letting go, and if he fulfilled that promise.

The dip was a masterpiece of grace.

Zeus grinned at her. "We're making progress."

Hera stepped on his toe, and Zeus turned to see what had caused her to miss the step.

His blood ran cold when he saw the woman entering through the doorway.

"Demeter," Hera said in a hiss beside him.

"I thought she'd returned to d-Alphus."

"She did. When I was there, though, they exiled her back here. Said she was being disruptive." Hera cast a worried glanced toward Hugh. "They said she never got over her dislike of Hades."

142

"Dislike? By Olympus, it was hatred." Zeus stared at the woman. The myths had portrayed her as the benevolent goddess of the Earth, a goddess who looked out for the needs of humans by providing food.

Benevolent, ha!

And she was heading straight for the dance floor.

Hugh's arms around her, Hugh's shoulder beneath her cheek. None of her other partners, as polished as some had been, had felt so right. Dia smiled and lifted her head from Hugh's shoulder to glance into his emerald eyes. As always they were focused on her, although he must be aware of the other dancers around them, as he deftly avoided them.

A flurry of green at the door caught her eye. Dia glanced over and stiffened.

Demetria Cesare. Her green dress billowed about her like rippling aspen leaves, and her hands, covered in thin, green mesh gloves, held the stem of a large, brilliant orange, poppy-shaped flower.

What was she doing here? Wasn't this morning in the museum enough?

The music stopped and Hugh led Dia off the dance floor. Zeke and Harriet also left with them, she noticed idly. Hugh stiffened as he saw the woman closing in on them.

Did he know Demetria? She was almost on them. What did she want?

Cold encased Dia's stomach, and her fingers slipped from Hugh's grasp. He draped an arm around her shoulder, the heat and strength of it a welcome support. She saw Demetria's lips twist

Kathleen Nance

and saw her finger the unusual poppy bloom.

A sudden crackle of electricity sounded through the room. Overhead, a single light exploded in a shower of sparks. The smoke alarm blared, and seconds later the sprinklers began to drench the party.

Chapter Nine

"By the laws of the Oracle, what were you thinking, Zeus?" Hera shook her damp skirt as the firemen declared a false alarm and left.

"I didn't intend to set off the alarms; I only wanted to distract Demeter. I thought she was going to use one of her infernal plant toxins on Hugh." Fingers still tingling, Zeus shook his hand. "It's this ring."

"Well, well, well. Zeus and Hera. Fancy meeting you here." Demeter's amused voice broke through their conversation.

Zeus turned in concert with Hera. "Demeter. You're looking unruffled."

"A little indoor rain doesn't bother the goddess of nature." She glanced away at Anya, who was still laughing about the sudden disruption. "The sprinklers. Zeus, that was very naughty of you, although

I must admit, you always did have a knack for livening things up. The question is why."

"Why do you think?" He crossed his arms.

"I haven't decided yet." Demeter ran her gloved hands along the stem of her poppy. Despite the dimness of the indoor lighting, the mesh gloves glowed. The gloves of Demeter, forged by the gods, had miraculous power over plants.

"Don't try it." Hera shook her head.

"Try what?"

Zeus wasn't fooled a minute by her feigned innocence, but he decided to let Hera carry the conversation. He'd never understood why, but Hera had always gotten along better with Demeter than he did.

"Letting the poppy spray us with its pollen." Hera rubbed her ring and a gust of wind carried an orange cloud of pollen from the flower to land in one of the puddles. The orange color faded.

Demeter gave an annoyed *tsk*. "Now, what did you do that for?"

"Removing the temptation. What sort of venomous effect have you bred into it?"

"I wouldn't call it venom. More a kind of . . . truth serum. One poof and your secrets are mine."

"And what truths did you expect to get from Hugh Pendragon?"

"Who said I planned to use it on Hugh?" She ran the flower across her lower lip, studying them. "I must admit, I'm curious to see you together. Wasn't it just last century you were pining for the pleasures of home, Hera, dear? Saying you planned never to see him again?"

"Heat of the moment; we're still working things out."

Zeus eyed the two women with interest. Last century? Hera and Demeter together? Doing what? Apparently he and his love had some catching up to do.

"I thought you were safely ensconced on d-Alphus," Demeter continued. "You were still there when I left."

"I didn't stay long; it was a mistake to think I could."

Demeter gave a low chuckle. "In other words, they kicked you out for being a disruptive element, just like me. Hera, we have more in common than you admit."

Zeus decided he was tired of being left out, tired of the artificial humor and the mask of banter. He slid a hand around Hera's waist. "She is nothing like you."

To his annoyance, Hera stepped away from his embrace.

Demeter smiled and tapped the poppy against her thigh. "So is it Hugh Pendragon or Dia Trelawny you're interested in?"

"Both," answered Zeus, not surprised Demeter had figured out that much.

"Don't interfere with us, Demeter," added his love.

"I could say the same thing to you. My plans have been years in the making. Don't try to stop me."

"From what?"

"New ventures. The cereal business got too boring." She smiled, as humorless as the plants she developed. "I don't think I'm ready to share more. Unless you want to go first?"

"Zeus is still your leader," Hera said softly, her fingers rubbing her ring. A wind tugged against the poppy, pulling off a petal. "And I am your queen."

Demeter responded with a disbelieving roll of her eyes. "Oh, stop living in the past. You have no ascendance over me. That ended when we left Olympus." She handed the poppy to Hera. "So let the games begin. Shall we?" Without another word, she strode away.

The wind died. Hera ran a peacock blue nail along the poppy stem. "You know, my love, this is becoming vastly more entertaining. You were right; Dia and Hugh belong together."

"What made you decide that?"

"Because you think it true."

Zeus laughed. "And you are looking forward to a battle of wits with Demeter."

Hera looked at him from the corner of her eye. "You know me too well."

"You continually surprise me. That's part of your appeal." Yet he was satisfied. Whatever the reasons behind her decision, they were working together, and she acknowledged his authority.

It was progress.

"That was fun." Dia leaned against the headrest of Hugh's car, enjoying the leashed power of the purring engine and of the man at her side. For a few more hours she would not think about Demetria or gems or anything but this moment. "I love parties. Don't you?"

"Even when the sprinklers came on?"

"Oh, that was fun, too. The presents got a little soggy, but nothing was damaged. Anya said at least her parties are memorable. I'm sorry if I'm getting your seat wet, though."

"We're both damp. Are you cold?"

"The air-conditioning's a bit high. I'm fonder of fresh air anyway."

Without another word he turned off the AC, and they rolled down the windows. The air was city-hot and still humid. Night offered little relief from the baking day, but Dia drew in a long breath.

They talked desultorily about the latest election, sights Dia planned to see in the various Midwest towns where she'd be playing, and the fact that neither of them had had time in months to see a movie. In the moments of silence, though, Dia found she was unable to turn off the restless energy, forged of worry and work, that still vibrated inside her.

Hugh turned down a road that traveled the lakefront, and she peered out at the street signs. "I don't know a lot about Chicago yet, but isn't this out of our way?"

"Yes, but I'd like to show you something." He parked in the parking lot of a small marina, then came around to open her door.

"Isn't it all locked up?"

"I have a key." He held out a hand. "Trust me; no one will toss us out."

Dia hesitated a moment, then put her hand in his and let him draw her out of the car. Still holding her hand, Hugh unlocked the gate, then led her across the stony shores of Lake Michigan and down a weathered pier. He stopped in front of a sailboat.

"Yours?" she asked.

He nodded, stepped easily onto the deck, and held out his hand. "Come aboard."

"Hugh, I'm in heels and a tight skirt."

"Take them off. The heels, that is, although I wouldn't stop you if you chose the other." He flashed her a teasing grin.

"We're going out?" She eyed the boat uneasily as she slipped off her shoes.

"Is that a problem?"

"I was born in Nevada. That's desert. No boats. I don't know how to sail."

"I'll do all the work."

"I might get seasick."

"The way you twirl about onstage? I doubt it, but if you do we'll head straight back in."

She placed one hesitant foot on the edge, uncertain of her footing on the damp, bobbing boat at night. Suddenly Hugh gripped her on either side of her waist and swung her aboard. Frantically she grabbed his shoulders, and a second later the deck was beneath her feet. Hugh planted a light kiss on her hair, then released her too soon.

"Sit there." He pointed to a cushioned seat behind a large steering wheel, if that was what it was called on a boat. "There's a life jacket if you want to put it on. I'll have us out of here in a jiff."

"Is the water warm?"

"Judge for yourself. There's a bucket to dip over the side."

Dia dipped up a pailful, then stuck her hand in the water. Immediately she pulled it out. "That's cold!" She shook off the numbing water and glared at a laughing Hugh. "You could have warned me."

"Lake Michigan never gets very warm."

"People swim in it."

"Midwesterners are a hardy bunch."

With a *hmpf*, she sat. She watched his easy, practiced movements as he coiled ropes and motored them out of the yacht basin. Still another facet to Hugh Pendragon. Here he looked relaxed, almost lighthearted, as if getting away from shore and the human masses released some unconscious inner control.

Once beyond the buoys, he turned off the motor, hoisted the sail, and then came to sit beside her. With one hand on the wheel, he wrapped an arm around her hip and urged her against his lean, hard side.

It was so quiet here. The only sounds were the easy rhythm of Hugh's breathing, the occasional whistle of a steamer, and the lapping of the waves against the boat. The expanse of water was vast—not as big as an ocean, but from here it was impossible to tell the difference, except the breeze was fresh, not briny. A sliver of a new moon failed to dim the brilliance of a sky's worth of stars. The only other time she'd seen so many stars was on the desert.

"Do you—" Dia began.

"Shhhh," he murmured. "Listen to the waves."

Hugh laced their fingers and rested their hands on her thigh. His palm was warm and dry and strong—a solid man's hand that anchored her firmly to this time and this place.

In the silence the whirl of worry found root in her again. She was beset by questions she couldn't answer, not tonight. Problems she didn't want to think about, not now. Yet they wouldn't go away. She shifted impatiently on the seat.

"Dia," he said, with a hint of amusement, "I can almost feel your thoughts, they're churning so hard. Calm your mind; be quiet. I came to refresh my soul. I brought you here for one thing only: to enjoy."

Embarrassed that he'd read her so easily, she sat stiffly beside him. The silence deepened as the waves formed a soothing parade of foam. It was cooler here, damp and with a faint smell of fish. The sail flapped a little in the easy breeze. Little by little as her hand warmed and her heated body cooled and no demands were made of her, as the rocking of the boat lulled and soothed her, the questions and the tension seeped out, swept away by the wake of the boat. Mostly, though, it was Hugh—his easy posture, his even breathing, his rock-steady presence—who grounded and quieted her.

At last Dia released a small sigh and leaned her head against Hugh's shoulder.

He murmured his approval and drew her closer. So warm he was, so solid. Her lids drooped and she burrowed closer. He tilted her chin up and kissed her, a light kiss that slowly, inexorably deepened and pulled her into a whirlpool of need. That fast, that easily, peace left and desire demanded her full attention.

Dia turned, her fists bunching the fabric of his shirt to pull him against her. She didn't understand this wild, fiery fascination he held for her, this need to hold him tight. She only knew she wanted him. She wanted his body pressed on hers, in hers, her aching breasts against his naked chest, her tongue tasting his. She moved against him, invited him.

His hand slid up her thigh, beneath the leather skirt, caressing and teasing. His little finger brushed against her silk panty, while she used mouth and breasts to tantalize him.

"Oh, Dia," he whispered. "You're already wet for me."

"You turn me on," she answered, her voice husky with need, and this time she initiated the kiss, while her hand reached down to caress him through his pants. "No fair; you've got easier access."

Slowly he lifted from the kiss, his green eyes mesmerizing her. One hand cupped her cheek, while his other hand, still beneath her skirt, caressed the silk. "Unless you want to make love to me tonight, on this boat, on this seat, then I suggest we slow things down." His voice was ragged and heated, his hands were tempting, and he left the choice all up to her.

Did she want this? The primitive part of her shouted, "Yes, yes, satisfy me. It's only sex," but something else held her back all of a sudden. Something that urged caution and care. This was too soon, too fast, too dangerous to her tenuous peace of mind, it insisted.

Hugh read her reluctance, even without any words. He exhaled in rueful acceptance as he slowly withdrew his hands, then gave her a friendly kiss on the cheek.

"I'm sorry," she whispered. "I'm not a tease."

"And I didn't intend to come on so hard and fast."

"I wasn't fighting."

They sat in silence again, cooling and slowing, until Hugh said, "All I intended was a sail in the moonlight."

"Uh-huh, and you had no idea how romantic it would be."

He gave a half laugh, then settled back in the seat, both hands on the wheel. "Believe it or not, you're the first person I've brought on this boat."

"Really?" Dia matched his easy stance, propping her feet up, grateful he was taking away the awkwardness of her withdrawal. "Not even family?"

"My father liked the water, but he got deathly seasick on boats, and my mother won't set foot in Chicago."

"They're divorced?"

"When I was five."

"Tell me about them."

He hesitated, setting the boat on a different tack.

"Tell me a story about your father," she urged, curious about the forces that had shaped him. "Something that illustrates the kind of man he was."

"My father took me to the lakefront right before my mother moved us south after the divorce," he said at last in his low rumble. "He said the waters were all connected—Lake Michigan to Lake Huron to Lake Erie to Lake Ontario, then onto the Saint Lawrence Seaway and the Atlantic Ocean and the Gulf of Mexico—and if I went to the Gulf and put my toes in it at five in the evening we'd be sharing the same water, for he'd do the same. According to Ronald, he went every day. You see, he knew my mother would resist letting me come back, and he wanted to let me know we were always connected."

"Their divorce wasn't amicable?"

"My mother was hurt and angry. She always said he was still in love with his first wife, that he'd married her only because he wanted a son. There must have been some truth in the notion, because my father never tried to talk her out of it, only fought her in court for custody."

"He lost?"

Hugh nodded. "It was years before she let me visit, because she was afraid he wouldn't give me back. Maybe her fears were real; as soon as I could I came back to my father."

"How sad for them. And for you."

His hands curled around the wheel. "I'll never do that to my child. He'll have two parents, full-time."

His child. Looking away, Dia fingered the hem of her skirt. "Do you still see your mother?"

"I get down there a couple of times a year. She's remarried and happy now with her new family."

"Your father. Is he . . . ?"

"He died. Three years ago."

"I'm sorry."

"We had several good years together."

Hugh got up to tighten a rope, his hands moving with deft skill; then he sat back beside her.

"If your father hated boats, how'd you learn to sail?"

"My mother insisted, probably because she knew how much my father detested it. She never knew one of the reasons I liked it so much, why I refused to come back before five o'clock, was because it tied me to him."

His voice faded away, and the waves took over the silence between them. After a few moments Hugh exhaled and rubbed a hand against his neck. "Sorry, I didn't mean to ramble. I'm sure you're not interested in my family history."

"It's a lot more fascinating than mine."

"It's late. We'd better turn back."

During the quiet sail back, Dia found the peace of the lake short-lived. Not because of the questions and problems waiting for her on shore. Not because of the sexual chemistry that still vibrated, unfulfilled, between them. Those she could handle.

Emotions were the problem. Hugh's story of his family had touched something in her—a companion isolation. Her feelings were running deeper than the lighthearted, surface-only relationships she allowed herself.

She had neither time nor desire nor talent for anything serious. Quick and easy worked best. Get out before someone let you down and someone got hurt.

Dia glanced over at Hugh. He was not a quick and easy man. He was complex, mysterious, honest, and bone-deep appealing. And he wanted children and marriage.

She was an itinerant, determinedly single magician who couldn't raise a philodendron and an unknowing thief who might be facing a jail sentence in just one month.

Yet she knew she was glad that tonight was not the end. She would be seeing him tomorrow.

Hugh poured himself a snifter of brandy, then offered a second to Ronald. Cerberus plopped himself on the rug. "How did things go?"

"Fine, sir."

"The house seems to have survived."

"That it did. And I enjoyed the company. They are good children, although"—he took another sip of brandy—"I do believe they are feeling a trifle unsettled."

"Unsettled?"

"About their mother leaving; Miss Claire especially misses her. About Miss Dia traveling so much. Children need security. Resilient as youth are, they are scared."

"You got all that in one night?"

Ronald gave a tiny laugh. "Your father did say I tend to go on a bit, and my imagination always did seem a vivid one. Likely it was nothing, sir. Now, if you'll excuse me, I think I will turn in."

"Sounds like a good idea."

Left alone, however, Hugh made no move toward bed. Instead he took the brandy into his office and opened the box next to his unsolved cases. Eagerly he grasped the leather diary. Tonight, onstage, his talent had come back, and it had felt so good. He'd solved one of the cases. He'd gone to the party to keep his promise to Dia, recentered himself after the disorder of the night, shared a magical interlude, and then found himself eager to get back here.

Tonight he'd find the girl who'd written this diary, the girl taken by her noncustodial father.

Hugh relaxed into the chair, holding the diary, waiting. He smelled the Coppertone and talcum powder, saw the tiny hearts that dotted her *i*s.

Cerberus gave a doggy huff and turned Hugh's feet into a pillow. Hugh stroked the dry leather of the diary. Waiting for some clue. Waiting for the choking, burning vision.

Nothing. Inside he was dead quiet. Hugh swore and dropped the diary to the floor. He tossed back the remaining brandy, feeling nothing but the burning of alcohol in his throat. Nothing.

Except another series of nightmares that night.

Chapter Ten

At least her mother answered e-mails, Dia mused the next morning, even if Adele's reply was that she couldn't possibly return to the States to watch her grandchildren, for she was on a new path of spiritual openness, and the flowing energies heightened her psychic connections to the ancestors of the gentleman who was her sponsor.

In other words, her mother had found a new pigeon.

At least she'd sent the phone number Dia had requested. She copied it, then turned off her computer and glanced at her watch. It was almost time for her meeting with Hugh. She'd make this call on her cell phone on the way. It was a conversation she didn't want the kids to hear.

The number belonged to a man known only as the Brick, and as far as Dia knew, no one had ever seen him. His business was conducted by phone or e-mail—with the contact numbers routinely changing—and his commodity was information. If the Brick couldn't find out, the information didn't exist. She needed answers to a few questions about Demetria Cesare. She pushed her chair away from the computer. "I'll be back in a couple of hours," she called to the four kids. "I have a meeting with Mr. Pendragon."

"Can I go?" Elena asked. "Please, please, please?"

"Sorry, sweetie. This is business."

"Pleeease? I wanna go. Ronald said I could come again sometime," Elena whined. "Why not now?"

"Because it's not a good time."

"Well, when will it be a good time?"

"I don't know," Dia snapped, then gritted her teeth. The kids were as tired as she was of the cramped quarters. "When I come back we'll do something."

"Not another museum," complained Cam.

"You find something." Dia's jaw was starting to ache.

"We'll only have a couple of hours before you go to the theater," Claire added.

"Then I'd better get going or we'll have even less time." Dia closed the door on their protests. Definitely, she had no patience for kids.

Dia rang Hugh's bell promptly at eleven. No sooner had the sound died away than the moonstruck baying echoed across the grounds. This time, however, she was prepared for Hellhound leaping from the bushes.

"Hello, Cerberus." Laughing, she patted him on the head through the fence. "Look what I brought for you." She held up a pair of earrings. The direct summer sun caught the zirconium facets, and a rainbow of colors sparkled across the greenery. Cerberus backed to his haunches and gave an eager whine.

"You spoil him." Ronald opened the gate and let her in.

"They're an old pair I don't wear anymore." Dia braced herself for Cerberus. He bounded to her, stopped just short, licked her hand, and then tilted his head back in a howl loud enough to have come from three throats. "I hope that means he liked the earrings."

"It does. Mr. Pendragon is waiting for you in his office."

The office. Remember, this is business.

She gave Cerberus the earrings, watching with a smile as the dog trotted off, his tail wagging, then followed Ronald inside. At once, two sensations struck her: coolness and quiet, like a geode-lined cavern she'd once toured. As Ronald led her through a labyrinth of corridors, she caught glimpses inside the warren of rooms and was entranced. Last time she had come to Hugh's office from the outside and she had not realized that the inside of his house was as odd, and as intriguing, as the outside.

Just like the man who occupied it.

One room was decorated in a Japanese motif—very sparse except for a mat, an inked picture, and a black pot holding a carefully raked rock-and-sand display. No curtains shielded the window, so sunlight became a mobile structure in the room. In contrast, the next room she saw was crammed so full that she barely took in the suit of armor, the stack of spears, and the gigantic, blue-bowed teddy bear before she'd passed. A heavy steel door with no visible lock or handle guarded still another.

"I've left a pot of coffee," Ronald said at last, opening the door to Hugh's office and ushering her in. "Please feel free to help yourself. There's cream and sugar on the tray and a plate of scones with blackberry jam and lemon curd."

"I come over here too often and you're going to make me fat, Ronald."

"I doubt that very much, Miss Trelawny. If there's anything you need, please ask." He left, closing the door softly behind him.

Hugh was sitting behind his desk, leaning back in the chair, his hands steepled, and her insides did a little flip at the sight of him. Wearing a charcoal suit, he blended into the shadows except for those jewel bits of color and the paleness of his face. The curtains were drawn, but narrow-beamed lights afforded necessary illumination, glinting off the blue diamond earring and the ruby-and-copper wristband he seemed to have taken to wearing. His lids were half-lowered, and the slits of green glittered with laser intensity. Lines of fatigue radiated from the corners of his eyes. Wordlessly he motioned her to a seat.

"Are you feeling all right?" she asked.

"Too little sleep."

She didn't believe that was the entire reason for a minute, but decided Hugh was as entitled to his secrets as she was. "If this is a bad time, I can come back."

"No. I said I'd help and I will. Tell me what you know about your sister's disappearance." He picked up a pen and balanced a pad of yellow paper on his knee.

Dia summarized what she knew. Her sister was on a wilderness trek with a man considered one of the movers and shakers of Madison. She was looking forward to the trip into the jungle, according to friends and family, but no one seemed sure exactly where it was. The kids thought it began with a *B*. "This is the e-mail she sent," Dia said, handing him the printed post. "I tried also to get in touch with a man named Julian Panadopolis, but couldn't reach him. He's a groundskeeper at one of the clubs where she works. The kids say he's fond of my sister. And here's the picture of her you asked for." She handed him a photo of Liza and the kids at the beach last summer.

He glanced at it. "What does your sister do?"

Dia hesitated a moment, then decided it wasn't any secret. "She's a psychic. Reads palms and tea leaves."

"And you don't approve?"

Dia shrugged. "She's got to provide for the kids."

"No husband?"

"He hasn't been heard from since the girls were two. He got the odd notion that the girls were not his and simply walked away."

"Any truth to the idea?"

"No! Besides, that was a decade ago. What does that have to do with her disappearance?"

"Probably nothing. Just getting the whole picture. Any other relatives?"

"Just my mother. She's in Nepal, I think. We never knew our father." Men didn't have a habit of sticking around in her family.

"How long has your sister lived in Madison?"

"About two years."

"Before?"

"A variety of places. My mother moved us around a lot, and Liza's followed her pattern." Dia scratched her cheek. "Liza sometimes runs afoul of the local ordinances." In other words, she was always one step ahead of the law.

Hugh made no comment. "Do you have a key to your sister's house? I'll need the address, too. Also the names of friends and places she might frequent."

Dia fished through her purse, found her ring of keys, then pulled off one and handed it to him. "You're going up to Wisconsin?"

"I'd like to nose around. See what I can find. Talk to people."

"How long do you think you'll be gone?"

"Two or three days." Deliberately he set down his notes and fixed her with an emerald stare. "Dia, is there anything else I should know? Anything else that might be going on?"

Dia hesitated. She hated deceptions, but there was no way she could come out and say, "Yes, oh, by the way, I'm a jewel thief." Yet if there was something more behind her sister's disappearance . . . Hugh deserved to know. Otherwise he might be walking into a real mess, where ignorance meant danger, not bliss.

Hugh sat motionless, waiting with patience and utter silence. He knew, she realized with a sudden squeeze of apprehension. Somehow he knew she was hiding something. How?

He's observant. That was all it was.

"You might see if there's any connection to Demetria Cesare," she said at last.

"Why do you think she's involved?" His voice was clipped, colorless.

A faint shudder ran through Dia, a vulnerability she hated. A sudden urge to confide in Hugh, to share her burden, swept through her, but she ruthlessly squashed it. This was business. She trusted business arrangements a lot more than she trusted personal commitments. She believed in Hugh Pendragon, but tell a man who put criminals behind bars, who'd been best man for an FBI agent, that she was a thief? *I don't think so.*

Besides, it was her life to run or to ruin, and she'd never depended upon anyone else. Briskly she ran her hands over her arms, warming the flesh. She was hiring him to find her sister, not solve her problems.

"She hired me a few times when I was getting started. I think she fancies herself a mentor type."

"Funny, she never seemed that selfless to me."

"You know her?" She remembered his reaction to Demetria last night.

"Yes." He fingered the ruby-and-copper wristband. "My father had business dealings with her, a partnership that went sour. Only time my father lost money; he suspected she was double-crossing him."

165

From the tone of his voice, Dia could tell Pendragons did not take kindly to a double-cross. "Could be he just didn't want to admit he'd made a mistake."

"Could be." He fingered the wristband again. "I thought she'd be older."

"Well preserved, I guess."

He made a noncommittal sound. "What might she want from your sister?"

"I don't know." Her insides twisted in frustration. "Demetria wants me to work for her."

"You don't want to." It was a statement, not a question.

"No." Dia took a sip of her now-cold coffee. "But I don't know how far she'll go before she accepts that."

"Does she have some hold over you?" He crossed his arms, pushing back the sleeves of his charcoal jacket. The light reflected off the ruby at his wrist.

"No," she lied, her mouth puckering with the bitter word. One more item of business remained. "About your fee—"

"I'll bill you, but only when I find your sister."

Dia bristled. "I don't want favors."

"It's my standard procedure. Do you want references?"

She had to smile at the clipped offer. "You came highly recommended." She fingered the strap of her purse. "When I do get the bill, though, I'll have to pay on installments. I'm a little . . . strapped right now. But I will pay," she hastened to assure him. "I always pay my way."

For a moment he didn't answer, and Dia's stomach tightened. What if he didn't agree?

Then she'd manage some other way.

He held out his hand. "I'm looking forward to working with you."

Hugh liked to keep his life compartmentalized and tidy. He never mixed business with pleasure, and Dia was now in the category of business.

Yet when he shook her hand and the musky scent of her perfume curled around him like the tantalizing incense from a genie's lamp, he was not thinking about business, only of the known pleasures of the taste and feel of her, the imagined pleasures of sharing his bed with her.

And they scared the hell out of him.

Since she had strolled into his life, the things he'd always depended on—his steadfast order, his unique talents—had been turned inside out. Even his plans for retirement hadn't lasted more than four days when Dia asked for help. She invaded his waking thoughts and teased him with her vibrant smile. His detective instincts were roused by the curiosity to know more about her and to learn her secrets. He wanted to experience more with her, go deeper than he'd ever gone with a woman. His hand tightened around hers, muscles tugging her closer, business distance be damned.

"You going to keep that hand?"

Dia's playful question brought him out of the well of sensation. He shifted his hand so his fingers laced with hers. "I thought I might. I have this collection, you see. Every client donates a hand to it."

Dia laughed. "Why, Hugh, are you teasing me?"

"Is that so surprising?"

"A little." Gently, almost reluctantly, she pulled her hand from his. "I have to get going. Let me know when you find out something?"

"I will." Hugh released her, resisting the urgent need to call her back, to keep her safe at his side and wild beneath him. He doubted she'd be thrilled with those primal instincts, which seemed to be what drove him these days.

So he kept silent. He would see her again; he could wait. In the meantime he'd protect her by doing what he did best: keeping his promises and finding answers.

After she left, Hugh settled back into his chair, but he didn't pick up the phone to make his plane reservation to Madison, letting the faint alertness and arousal, which seemed his constant companions whenever she was near, abate. It was hard to think logically when all his blood was heading south.

At last he drew in a deep breath, made his reservation, then studied his notes. It wasn't the errant Liza Trelawny Swensen, however, that pricked at him. It was Dia's reaction to Demetria Cesare's name. He couldn't escape the crawly feeling that the older woman offered a distinct threat to Dia. There had to be more than a mentor–protégé dynamic between them. While he looked for the sister, he'd also investigate why Dia was frightened of Demetria Cesare.

He stroked the smooth surface of his wristband. He had a few other questions plaguing him as well, like what had happened to the opal and why his talents were so erratic. For a man who was supposed to be retired, he certainly had plenty to keep him busy.

And overriding everything was one blood-boiling, erotic need: he wanted Dia sharing his bed.

To Dia's surprise, the apartment was quiet when she got back. "Cam, Lukas? Elena? Claire?" Fear washed through her, weakening her knees and spine, when no answer came back. Her heart spinning faster than airplane blades, she raced through the apartment, looking for her nieces and nephews.

It took fifteen seconds, tops. The apartment was deserted, and they weren't in view of the windows.

Where could they be? Had something happened while she was out? Wouldn't they have left a note? Had Demetria come for them? Had she been so wrong in thinking that Demetria would not harm them? Her hand shaking, Dia grabbed her keys, ready to start knocking on doors and scouring the neighborhood.

The front door opened, letting in a wall of heat and a teenage boy.

"Cam!" Dia laid a hand on her chest. "Are you all right? Where are the others?"

He seemed surprised by her vehemence. "Out."

"Out where?"

"With some dudes we met." He detoured into the kitchen and opened the refrigerator. "What's to eat?"

"You know what's in the fridge. Dudes? Old dudes or young dudes? Male dudes or female dudes? Where did you meet them?"

He gave her an annoyed look as he pulled out a carton of milk. "What is this? The inquisition?"

Jaw tightening, Dia handed him a glass before he could drink from the carton. "No, it's your aunt coming home to an empty apartment, no note, and wondering where you were."

"Mom doesn't get this bent out of shape." He downed the glass in one gulp.

"Liza knows your friends and your haunts."

"We were safe." He turned his back on her, heading toward the living room.

"I didn't know that. When I go out, I let you know exactly where I am, how I can be reached, and what time I expect to be back. I expect the same courtesy, Cam." Dear Lord, she was starting to sound shrill. She did not do shrill. Dia took a deep breath as she hurried behind him.

"Sure. Whatever." Pulling a deck of cards from his pocket, he headed onto the tiny balcony, then closed the door in her face.

Dia gaped at the glass, counted to ten, and then shoved the door along its tracks. The frame rattled with her anger. "Cameron Swensen, I've had to put up with a lot of overbearing, overheated, over-obnoxious people in my life, but I will not tolerate rudeness at home."

"Well, I don't want to be here, so what do you plan to do about it?" he asked, his tone holding a touch more curiosity than belligerence.

Dia's mind raced, searching for a suitable punishment for someone who was taller than she was.

"I won't buy you any more Ding Dongs or Hot Pockets."

Cam gaped at her a moment. "How about Pizza Rolls?"

"Nope. Yogurt and organic carrots only."

"I happen to like organic carrots." He looked out over the scraggly trees set in the concrete sidewalk. "We met some dudes—a guy and a chick," he corrected. "About our age. They live in the first-floor apartments."

Dia remembered the names on the mailbox—Goldstein and Joseph—and vaguely recalled seeing a dark-haired boy and a girl big enough to be on her way to the WNBA.

"They asked us to go to the VR arcade. Sorry," he mumbled. "Guess we shoulda left a note."

"Yes, you shoulda. Where are the others?"

"Still at the arcade. I didn't feel much like playing."

"Are you sick? Do you have a temperature?"

He tolerated her hand a moment before shrugging it off. "I'm fine. Just want some time to myself."

Dia watched him a moment while he kept his gaze steadfast on the unfascinating street. His eloquent silence hinted at something wrong, but he gave no hint of what it might be. "Is there something you want to talk about?" she asked hesitantly.

He gave a grunt of denial.

Feeling totally inadequate, Dia was at a loss for what to do next. She felt more like Peg Bundy than Carol Brady, unable to come up with just the right thing to say that would let him open up with a touching heart-to-heart in which she solved all his problems by the end of the hour.

Besides, she figured the kid deserved privacy.

In the end she settled for merely saying, "If you need anything, I'm going to be in the living room, practicing. I've got this sleight of hand with candles that I'm trying to add to the act. If I can figure out how to keep from catching my bodysuit on fire, that is."

Not even that got a response.

By the time the other three exploded into the room, exuberant with their afternoon in virtual reality, Dia was sweaty, her fingers ached, and she was still in danger of setting herself on fire—if she'd been practicing with lit candles. Before she could say a word about their carelessness, Elena turned on the TV and Claire flopped into a chair, her face in a scowl. She snatched up her book.

Lukas headed straight for the balcony and Cam. "Hey, bro, you left too early. You missed some definite streetables. Whoo, were they hot."

Claire made an annoyed noise.

"Streetables?" Dia asked her.

"Their classification system for girls. Meetable, streetable, deletable. Men can be such pigs," she shouted toward her brothers.

"You're just mad because Benjamin and Dan were more interested in the Dragons of the Mist game than in you," answered Lukas. "Bro, trust me when I tell you these were butt-hugger shorts and skimpy tops."

"I think I'll become a nun," muttered Claire.

"There are no Lutheran nuns," Elena loftily informed her.

"I know that! I'll start my own order. Or better yet, become so rich and powerful that it'll be me doing the classifying and rejecting."

"You go, girl," said Dia, privately resolving to have a little chat with her nephews later. "By the way, is something wrong with Cam?"

Claire's lips pressed together. "I don't gossip."

"I do," said Elena. "For a price."

"What's your price?" Dia crossed her arms.

"A new bottle of nail polish."

"You can use my gold glitter. Once."

"His girlfriend sent him an e-mail breaking up with him. Said she wasn't going to sit home dateless all summer."

"Oh, geez, no wonder he was in a bad mood. I'll go talk to him—"

"Don't." Claire's command interrupted Dia's stride. "Lukas knows what to say."

"He'll handle it better than you," added Elena.

So much for any votes of confidence in her parenting talents. Definitely she fell into the Peg Bundy school. She looked at the two red heads close together outside. Lukas was talking with animation and graphic gestures. Cam was listening with more interest than he'd given her.

Dia wasn't ready to give up so easily, though. Later, after sending Lukas and Elena to the nearby grocery and Claire to get the mail, she found another chance. Cam was still sitting out on the balcony. His hands were working the deck of cards, practicing a phony riffle shuffle. He wasn't bad at it, and she remembered he'd said he was interested in magic.

She grabbed a deck of cards and headed to the balcony. Sitting beside him, she held out the deck. "Pick a card."

He glanced at her with curiosity, but said nothing as he picked out a card.

"Look at it, now put it back in the deck." After he complied, she shuffled the deck, then picked up the top card. It was the card he'd chosen.

"That's the basic phony riffle shuffle you were trying. It works easier if you hold your hands like this." She demonstrated the technique.

"I never saw that in the books."

"That's because magicians don't put the best stuff in books. We make up our own techniques or learn from each other, one-on-one. Try it."

Cam practiced until he acquired fairly good control. "That gives better control. So who'd you learn from?"

"My friend Mark Hennessy. Other people along the way. What else have you been trying?"

He demonstrated a very credible version of the cups-and-balls, with a cute, unique twist at the end.

"That's good. Cam, I'm performing at a little girl's birthday party next week—"

"I thought you didn't do parties anymore."

"This is special. Would you like to come with me and do that?"

He brightened for the first time that day. "I'd love it."

"Then we'll do it. Oh, and, by the way, on another topic, I wouldn't voice your little classification system too often. Women don't take kindly to being referred to as 'deletable.' "

He gave her an unrepentant grin. "Then don't listen."

She cuffed him on the shoulder, then got to her feet. "Time to get ready for tonight." She might be Peg Bundy in the nurturing department, but she was a darn good magician, and she wasn't doing too badly at the juggling act.

"Aunt Dia!" shrieked Elena, throwing the door open with a bang and racing into the room. Tears streamed down her face and she grabbed Dia's hand. "Aunt Dia, you gotta come. Right now. It's Lukas!"

"Lukas!" Cam shot to his feet.

"Lukas?" Dia's stomach plummeted to her feet, and her icy hands dropped the deck of cards.

"Come on!" Elena tugged at her hand. "He's hurt. He's hurt real bad."

Lukas, it turned out, had been walking home with Elena and the groceries when he stepped off an unseen curb and, in a freakish twist of fate, instead of a simple bruise or sprain, had broken his leg. Elena, of course, had dramatized the whole situation and created instant, terrifying visions of death and dismemberment. Lukas was neither dead nor dismembered. He was, however, in pain and did need to see a doctor. Her pulse gradually subsiding, Dia took him to Cook County ER, and then proceeded to wait; a broken leg, apparently, was low on the triage scale when there were auto accidents, shootings, and knifings to be treated.

Dia glanced at her watch for the uncounted time and bit her lip in frustration. She should be leaving for the theater. She made a quick call to Anya, asking her to get everything set up and ready. She would warm up in the hospital. Her costume was there already—quick change, makeup, hair a little less elaborate. She could do it.

Lukas gave her a weak smile. "Sorry, Aunt Dia."

"Not your fault," she said, tapping her foot. It wasn't, but she couldn't help the anger and frustration and worry roiling inside. She hadn't signed on for motherhood, hadn't asked for this responsibility. Then she noticed the gray lines of pain around his mouth, and she added feeling like a heel to the roster of her emotions.

Dia searched for something to occupy him. She'd already entertained him with every disaster-on-the-road story she could think of that was fit for him to hear, and done every trick she could think of, along with a few extra variations, and gotten them pop from the machines and made up stories about the other detainees.

Briefly she entertained the idea of getting someone else to sit with him. Hugh was out of town. Ronald, maybe? Harriet Juneau? Somebody from Anya's family? Tempting as it was, though, she reluctantly discarded the notion. He was her nephew, her responsibility. She needed to be here with him.

But why did this have to happen on a performance night?

Lukas shifted, then winced. "I'm glad you're here, Aunt Dia. Mom would have been all teary and hyper."

"I'm all teary, too. I'm just better at hiding it." She ruffled his red hair, and she knew how much he hurt when he didn't protest. "Let me see if I can get you something for that pain."

When the triage nurse saw her coming, her look of irritation was all too obvious.

"My nephew is in a lot of pain and his foot is swelling," Dia began. "He needs to have something."

"Not until—"

"—the doctor sees him," Dia repeated with her. They'd been over this more than once already. "I know. So when is the doctor going to see him? How much longer do we have to wait?"

"Cubicle open," called the orderly.

The nurse's sigh was audible. "You can go in now."

"Good." Dia glanced at her watch. *See the doctor, get a cast. Theater, performance, still doable.*

Chafing at the slow process of getting Lukas on the stretcher and into the cubicle, aching to see how much pain he was in, Dia started warming up her hands and rehearsing the night's performance.

The doctor took his time examining Lukas. When he listened to his heart and checked his ears and throat and lungs, she bit her tongue to keep from asking what the heck his tonsils had to do with a broken leg. He was probably looking for an embolism or the start of an infection or something.

"I want to send him down to X ray," the doctor said at last.

"Why?" asked Dia. "It's obvious his leg is broken. Can't you just put on a cast and let us out of here?"

He offered some long explanation filled with medicalese, the bottom line being that he wouldn't do anything without seeing an X ray first. "Then I'll need to see him again in the cast room, and he'll need prescriptions for antibiotics and analgesics . . ."

The words faded behind the roaring in Dia's ears as the inevitable, awful truth gripped her. *X-ray. Wait. Cast room. Wait. Pharmacy. Wait.* The night stretched on before her.

Nausea gripped her stomach and throat. This was why she'd known her commitment to her magic and her career could be her only commitment. At times like this, when two responsibilities clashed, she didn't want to be forced to make the choice she had to make now.

This would not happen again. Ever.

She flipped open the cell phone. Slowly her shaking fingers dialed, and she could barely choke out the awful words.

For the first time in her life, Dia canceled a performance.

Chapter Eleven

Three days later, as Hugh eschewed the O'Hare tram for a brisk walk to the main terminal, he was satisfied with the progress on some of his questions.

Info on Demetria was scarce. The woman was an enigma. Lots of people knew her, but nobody seemed to know much about her except that she spent lavishly, never had visitors to her house, and kept greenhouses on her grounds. There was one instance in which a former employee tried to sue because he claimed that her devil plants had scarred his hands with acid. The lawsuit was dismissed as frivolous, but Demetria had offered "out of appreciation for his years of service" to pay for cosmetic surgery on his hands and the man had accepted.

Demetria as benevolent benefactor? Not in this life, he'd bet.

On the matter of Liza, he'd made better progress. Apparently the man she'd gone with was very rich and very devoted to keeping his privacy when he went out on one of his "adventures," as his staff described it. Nothing Hugh learned about him indicated that he was involved with anything that would pose a threat to Dia or Liza, or was connected with Demetria Cesare; he'd learned only that the man was willful and selfish, and that if Liza chose to marry him, she'd earn her material comforts.

He had finally located the tour company they had used, and although the corporation guarded its guests' privacy and the location of the "secluded, pristine jungle experience" with the tenacity of Cerberus, he figured he could find out with a little more digging.

Julian Panadopolis had disappeared, but from the trail he'd left, Hugh guessed he was chasing after Liza.

It made for an interesting soap opera.

Liza had kept scrapbooks on Dia's career, he discovered, and he'd indulged himself by thumbing through the books, fascinated on a purely personal level. He found pictures of a young Dia onstage with the notation, *Dia goes legit* and an ad bill for a magician and "his beautiful assistant" that featured geese, ducks, and emus in the act. Hugh smiled, remembering the day she'd come to him, and her reluctant admission about her odd fear of animals, large birds in particular. The books were full of newspaper clippings and ads and programs, attesting to her tireless pursuit of success. She'd worked nightclubs and country clubs and twenty-seat theaters all over the country. In the early days she had done school functions, parties, trade shows, and numerous charity benefits, although she'd stopped doing private events, except for charities, in later years.

Dia's career had taken its biggest leap about two years ago, he'd found, when she'd switched agents and taken a job as Mark Hennessy's assistant. He'd drawn in the crowds, but she'd shone in the segments she'd done herself. That led to a series of solo performances in California, which proved she had marquee value, and then to her current tour.

From all reports, Dia was a tireless perfectionist who played as hard as she worked, although, judging by what he'd seen of her, he suspected some of the accounts held a touch of creative masculine bravado. She was honest, straightforward and had a bit of a temper, according to what he read.

Sexy, generous, and *delightful* were his own additions, and suddenly the hungry need was back, tying him in knots.

He flipped open his cell phone and dialed Dia's number. Busy. He wanted to see her, considered going over; then troublesome common sense decided against it. She'd be leaving soon for her performance, and he had some leads he wanted to follow up, anxious to have something definite before he saw her again. He had a ticket for her show tomorrow at Northwestern. He'd see her then.

One strange occurrence on this trip still puzzled him. Liza's home should have been infused with her spirit and redolent with images of her reading for a trip that excited her, but no psychic flashes provided guidance this time. Instead, whenever he'd tried, a sucking, suffocating blackness had oozed over him, refusing to let go until he stopped. He'd known weird in his life, but that odd sensation of drowning in night was definitely one of the weirdest.

You need both, or you need her. The unknown but familiar voice from his dream whispered inside him. Twice now with Dia he'd regained his talents. When he was away from her they seemed dead, more distant than ever. Was Dia somehow the key?

Feelings, whispered the voice again.

Great, now he was thinking in lounge songs.

"Pendragon!" A hearty call shattered his introspection.

Hugh turned and recognized the voice and the tall black man bearing down on him. Benito Blessing, "Batting Blessing" of the pennant-bound Chicago Cubs. He'd met Blessing last year when the player's two-year-old daughter had wandered out of the house. Hugh had found her and brought her back safely before she fell into any harm.

"Hey, man, I haven't seen you in ages. How you been?" Blessing's grip, honed by years at bat, captured him.

"Fine. You're having a spectacular year."

"It's like I got a guardian angel sitting right here." He loosed Hugh's hand to point to his shoulder. "You coming or going?"

"Coming home."

"I'm meeting my mama, but her plane's gonna be late. You got time for a beer?"

"I don't—" A thought struck him. "Blessing, were you at the museum fund-raiser last December? It had a display called Treasures of the Underworld."

"I was there. You, I expect, were among the missing, right?"

"I was busy." A touch of annoyance brushed across Hugh. Why did everyone lately seem to comment on his appearance, or lack of appearance, in public? Or had he just never noticed before? "Have you got a minute for a few questions?"

"Sure. Let's duck in here before we gather too much of a crowd."

They slipped into the airline's Platinum Member Only lounge, the quiet a contrast to the bustle outside, and found a table in the corner. The waiter brought their order—and a request for an autograph from "Batting"—in record time, then discreetly left them.

Hugh took a drink of the dark lager, then began. "A magician performed that night. Do you remember anything about him?"

"Even after all these months, I sure do. Not a him. A her."

The beer slipped down without a swallow, icy cold that froze his chest. "Do you remember her name?"

"Nope. I wasn't paying attention to the name."

"The performance that good?"

"The magician that fine. Blond and a set of tits beautiful as I've seen." He cupped his hands in front of his chest in a crude display.

Hugh's jaw tightened, but he reminded himself it wasn't Dia whom Blessing was talking about.

Or was it? The question did a dropkick on his gut. Hugh carefully set down his glass. "Do you remember anything about her performance?"

"With all that distractin' me? All I remember is, she looked spectacular."

Hugh's insides tightened. "Did she do anything with the display?"

Blessing scratched the side of his nose. "Yeah, come to think of it, she did. She made a silver bracelet—a valuable one, from what I understand—change to a white lily-of-the-valley. It was a real flower, too. I could smell it. I tell you, it was spooky how she did it. Not just me, everyone felt it, 'cause it was real quiet-like in the room." He took a long gulp of beer. "Then she turned it back and the show was mostly over."

Overhead came the announcement of a flight arrival. "That's my mama's flight," Blessing said, and tossed back the remaining beer. "Don't be such a stranger 'round town, Pendragon."

"Maybe I won't."

After Blessing left, Hugh sat for a few moments, finishing the beer. Was the performer Dia? He dismissed the idea that she could have stolen his band; Dia was too honest. If he suspected anyone, he'd prefer to zero in on Demetria Cesare, although he'd found nothing connecting the theft to her.

Everything seemed to circle back somehow to Dia. Was all of it—the sister, Demetria, the theft, the loss and erratic return of his gifts—connected in some obscure way, with Dia at the center?

Weary and frustrated, Dia trudged up the stairs to her apartment. She'd spent the morning looking for a bigger, more secure apartment, and her luck was nil. Too expensive, too long a lease, or too disgusting. She'd have to look beyond the city next. Dia rubbed a hand over the back of her neck, trying to ease the tension. She just didn't have the time, and she couldn't afford to cancel another performance.

She wondered if Hugh had found out anything about her sister. He was supposed to have returned last night, but he hadn't called, so she assumed that meant his luck had been as bad as hers.

A scrape sounded on the steps below just as she reached her floor. Startled, Dia peered over the banister. No one. "Great, now I'm jumping at shadows," she muttered. She was going to need a room with padded walls and no sharp objects before this was over.

At least Hugh was coming to the show tonight. She found herself smiling as she let herself back into her apartment. Despite all the reasons why she shouldn't, she was anxious to see him again. Three days and she was missing him.

Dia stopped inside the door, caught by a vague sense of unease. Something was wrong. The apartment was quiet. . . .

Suddenly she laughed at herself. The apartment was quiet. She'd gotten so used to the noise of the kids, quiet now seemed an aberration. It was supposed to be quiet. The twins had gone with the two "dudes" from the apartment below to spend the day at the Indiana Dunes. Even Lukas had gone, not wanting to miss out on ogling the "streetables" and "meetables," although he had to be careful with his cast.

She had a whole afternoon to herself.

A scrape sounded outside the door, and she whirled around, her heart pounding. She had to stop doing that. It was probably someone delivering a telephone book or something.

The door was flung open with a rattle that sent her jerking backward. In the doorway stood Mick Masterson.

"Hello, Dia," he drawled. "I been waiting for a little something that's been coming to me."

"Like a black eye?" Dia's self-defense training took hold. *First defense? Scream.* "Help! Fire!"

Mick seemed undisturbed by her yell. "Now that all those stupid kids are gone, building's empty this time of day."

Mind racing, Dia sought options. She was stronger than most women and knew how to inflict damage, but Mick was ruthless and bigger. She didn't want to start a fight she might lose. *Second defense? Escape.* Could she get past him?

"Been looking for a chance to get you alone. Thought we could spend a little time gettin' to know each other," he continued, swaggering in.

"What a revolting thought." Dia tensed, ready to run.

Mick ignored her comment. "Course, it wouldn't be fair to keep you all to myself." Another man followed him through the door. "So I brung along a friend."

Oh, shit.

So much for self-defense class.

Trying to work was a useless exercise. Hugh snapped off the computer and rubbed his eyes. Damned restlessness had him so edgy he couldn't make a lick of progress.

He knew the reason: Dia. Instead of his notes, he'd see her teasing smile, or instead of the keys, he'd feel her soft skin beneath his fingers. God, but he was a sorry case.

The damnable thing was, regardless of the questions, regardless of the doubts, he still wanted her. Hugh leaned back, his blood stirring. He still wanted Dia in his bed.

Now. Tonight. Soon.

A vibrating energy coursed through him, drawing him to his feet to pace about the room, rubbing his arms. He felt as if he should be doing something, that he was missing something.

"Woof. Woof." Cerberus barked at the closed door, then nudged it open with his massive head. Nails clicking on the hardwood floor, he scrambled over to Hugh, a pair of rainbow earrings dangling from his mouth.

"Are those Dia's?" A heart-squeezing dread overtook him.

Something was wrong with Dia. That aura of danger he'd seen!

"Woof," answered Cerberus, dropping the earrings into Hugh's hand.

The vision exploded over him.

Dia. Two men. Her apartment.

He could feel her panic, knew that she hadn't given in to it. Taste the blood where she'd bitten the inside of her mouth. Hear her harsh breathing and feel the stitch in her side. Smell the stink of sweat and garlic and hot city.

Hold on, Dia, hold on.

Hugh fought the effects of the vision, struggling to his feet and pulling in deep gulps of air that seared his lungs. He couldn't give in to the sensations or the pain. Blindly he punched in the police on his cell phone as he raced through his house toward the car and prayed someone could get there in time.

Two pictures appeared before his eyes: Dia, the men, the apartment. Himself, his house, the kitchen.

Ronald washing dishes. "Sir, is something wrong?"

Hugh didn't stop. "Dia," he said in a gasp.

Ronald dropped his dish towel and kept pace. "I shall come with you. Give me the keys."

"Need speed."

"I am quite capable of speeding, and you know your sight is impaired during these spells."

The grounds around his house. Dia, the men, the apartment. Two movies playing simultaneously and in full Sensurround. Greenery faded under the drama of the apartment. They were circling her. She wasn't making it easy.

Hugh tossed Ronald the keys and flung himself into the passenger seat. Ronald had the car started only milliseconds later.

"Step on it. Dia's apartment."

"Very good, sir." Ronald peeled out of the grounds.

Hang on; I'm coming.

Dia inched backward, away from the door—not the direction she wanted to go, but the two men had effectively boxed her in. Her fingers were cold, her pounding pulse in her throat. *Keep the bastards in sight.* It was not easy as they circled around her, intending to commit mayhem and rape.

Hold on. Don't make it easy. Don't give in.

Mick's friend feinted, snagging her attention, and Mick lunged forward. He grabbed her hair and wrenched her head back. Pain shot up her neck, burst from her scalp. Dia scratched rough skin, kicked something soft. Mick staggered back, doubled over and cursing, and let go of her hair.

Dia ran for the door, too breathless to shout.

The friend caught her, tried to throw her to the floor.

She was stronger than he expected. Fueled by adrenaline, she stayed upright. Dia fought back, straining for escape. His sweaty hands slipped. *Almost. Almost.*

Hang on. She heard not so much words, but felt a strength from within. A promise of help. With a burst of power she broke free and headed for the door.

Mick recovered. The two men were mad as hell.

She was slammed from behind up against the wall. Her head cracked against the doorjamb, dazing her. Her arm was wrenched brutally up her back, her legs shoved forcefully apart, a male body flattening her to the wall. They cursed, vile promises of what they were about to do. Blood ran into her eye, blinding her.

Dia twisted, kicked, struggled, but she could not best two of them.

The door flew open and cracked against the opposite wall.

Hugh! He burst into the room in a fury of action Dia could hardly comprehend. The attackers were pulled from her. It was still two on one. Released, Dia turned and tried to help, but her knees were weak. She braced herself against the wall, refusing to collapse, unable to move.

Hugh had help already. Dia blinked, wondering if she was hallucinating. Ronald? Ronald with fists up, dancing around Mick's friend and jabbing. Connecting, too, while Hugh pummeled Mick.

The would-be rapists were beaten, and they knew it. They took off at a run out the door.

Hugh raced over to Dia and gathered her into his arms. Dia collapsed against him. Oh, dear God, he was warm and strong and here.

"The ruffians?" asked Ronald.

"Let the police get them," Hugh said in a snarl. "She's bleeding."

Dia refused to faint or throw up. The shaking she seemed to have no control over. "My head hit the door."

"Oh, miss, are you . . . Did they . . . ?"

Over Hugh's shoulder, she saw Ronald, hovering and looking blurry. She tried to smile, to reassure them both, but her lip hurt. "No damage."

"No damage! You are bloody and bruised and trembling." Hugh leaned back, not releasing her, just far enough for him to see her, and for her to see his grim expression. He wiped the blood from her face with a tender touch.

"Thank you," she whispered, swallowing hard against the wellspring of tears clogging her throat.

"You're welcome." Gently he pushed back her hair to examine the cut. "It's not too deep, but it's turning a very vivid shade of purple."

"She should see a doctor, sir," added Ronald, still hovering, but a little more in focus.

"She will."

"I don't want—"

Hugh quelled her protest with a single look. "You'll see a doctor."

"I was going to say, I don't want to go to Cook County."

"I'll take you to my physician."

"And I'm not staying the night in any hospital." She could have also added that his warm touch did more to restore her than any doctor's remedy could. "I've got a performance tonight."

"You can't even stand without support."

"I've performed with a fever of a hundred and two, with a broken finger, and with scalded hands. I'm more shaken than injured. I will not cancel the performance." She willed herself to push away from the wall.

"Stubborn woman."

"I've been told that's one of my most endearing qualities."

"I think you're right." For the first time a faint smile softened his ferocious expression. After brushing a kiss to her forehead, Hugh shifted and gave her room to move. He stayed close, however, one comforting hand on her shoulder.

With effort, Dia let go of the wall and of Hugh. She swayed, she swallowed rising bile, but she stayed upright. Avoiding looking into the room, afraid of reliving the horror, she took a step forward and a deep breath, then winced at the pain in her chest. She hoped it was only bruised, not a cracked rib.

Hugh gathered her close again. "You've proved you can walk by yourself. Now let me help."

191

For once in her life Dia gave in to weakness. After all, she'd need her strength to make it through tonight's performance.

"I think I hear the police coming," said Ronald.

"Are you ready to face them?" Hugh asked.

Are you ready to relive the attack? Dia swallowed and nodded, discovering new pains in her head and neck. "Let's get this over with."

"Police, then doctor."

"All right. Hugh, I'm glad you were here," she whispered, then frowned. "How did you know something was wrong?"

"Cerberus told me. Ronald, can you wait here? I want you to tell the kids what happened when they get home, then pack them up and bring them to the house. I'll watch Dia tonight."

"Very good, sir. I think that's a wise decision."

Dia started another protest, then bit it off. She'd be foolish not to accept Hugh's offer. She had not only herself, but the children to think of, and until the police picked up Mick Masterson, she'd feel safer with them in Ronald's care.

After all, it would be for only a day. Two at most.

She was in his home. She was in his bed.

Hugh tucked the covers around a sleeping Dia. Granted, he wasn't under those covers with her, but after what she'd been through today, he'd be a real beast to desire anything more. For the moment it was sufficient that she was here, though his body still thrummed from the aftermath of the vision and the fight.

Now he would have to figure out how to keep her here.

He let himself out of the shadowed bedroom and glanced at his watch. He'd promised Dia he'd wake her in one hour, and though he chafed against it, he'd keep the promise.

The police had taken her report and put out an APB on Masterson. The doctor had pronounced that there were no internal injuries, but a possible concussion. He'd prescribed painkillers, a sedative, someone to watch her tonight, and several days' rest.

At Hugh's insistence, Dia had had the prescriptions filled, but she hadn't bothered to take one of the tablets. She'd been fussed over by the twins when they arrived and had spent an hour on the phone with Anya and Zeke Jupiter, making changes to her show to accommodate her aches. She only at last consented to a nap when he told her she looked like hell and she'd scare away her audience, then held up a mirror to convince her.

"Woof?" Cerberus was in the hallway, waiting. "Woof?"

Hugh scratched him behind the ears. "She's okay. Stubborn as hell, but okay. She'll heal, and she's resilient."

Cerberus gave a sound that almost seemed like approval, then burrowed his nose in Hugh's pocket.

"Wait a minute, wait a minute." Hugh fished in his pocket and pulled out Dia's earrings. No visions this time; the crisis was over. "Is this what you want?"

In answer, Cerberus licked his hand, then took the proffered earrings. He trotted off, the sparkling jewelry dangling from his massive mouth.

"I'm just glad you had them." Hugh paused a minute, listening to the quiet of his house. There were extra noises now from the activities of Cam, Lukas, Claire, and Elena. Rather than disturbing him, however, the sounds added a curiously welcome lightness to the house.

Hugh headed toward his workout room. Physical release, the mindless zone was what he needed. Later he could deal with the aftermath and the questions. Now one thought continued to buzz through him.

Dia was here.

Chapter Twelve

Dia awoke feeling confused. Her body hurt like hell, and this wasn't her bed. Gingerly she moved her arms and found they worked, but her head and neck weren't faring so well. What party had she been to?

No party. The events of the afternoon flooded back, bringing with them a wave of nausea. Dia breathed deep through her nostrils until the queasiness receded, then opened her eyes.

She was in Hugh's house, in one of his bedrooms, one of his beds. Like other rooms she'd seen in this house, the room had a unique, thematic decor. Ancient Greece ruled here, with a wall mural of the Parthenon, an urn in a classically arched recess, a collection of books on mythology and statuary, and lifelike stallions pulling a chariot carved into the headboard.

She burrowed under the covers a moment, resisting getting up. It smelled so clean here, sounded so peaceful. She hadn't experienced this much quiet since the twins came.

When her eyes started drifting shut, though, she forced herself to get up. "Performance tonight," she muttered. "Warm-up. Mental prep. College campus and they'll be expecting energy and pizzazz."

Her body protested the motion, and when she rotated her shoulders, her neck and back spasmed. "Ow!" Dia rubbed the knot, grimacing at the pain.

A faint knock sounded on the door. Following her call to come in, Hugh entered. Dressed in black shorts and shirt, he glided through the shadows with his emerald eyes fastened on her. "You're up."

"Just."

"How do you feel?"

"A little sore. Mick wrenched my head back, and it pulled muscles in my neck and shoulders."

His response was a short, furious expletive. "We haven't found him yet, but trust me, we will."

She wouldn't want to be Mick if Hugh found him before the police did. A slight trembling coursed through her. Having someone champion her was a rare experience. It made her uneasy, yet she couldn't regret that Hugh was here.

He held up a white jar. "I thought you might be a little stiff. This works wonders for sore muscles. Would you like me to rub some on?"

"Sure." The scents of rosemary and honey wafted into the room when he opened it. "What is it?"

"A family recipe. According to family legend, an early Pendragon was an undertaker. This balm relaxed the muscles and preserved the skin of the dead."

"Hugh, that's macabre. You aren't serious?"

"Family legend. Personally, I think a knight's lady fashioned it to ease the aches of her lord and master. And his horse."

Dia burst out laughing. "That's a little better. I think."

With a gentle hand, he guided her to the bed. "Take off your shirt."

Dia complied, refusing to catch Hugh's gaze, feeling strangely shy as her laughter faded with the sudden fluttering in her belly. She had few qualms about displaying her body, but generally there was the barrier of silver lamé, or she was with a man only out for some fun, a man she could control.

Hugh was different. He was too strong to be controlled, too assured to abuse his power, too compelling to be dismissed or forgotten. *Big-time mistake*, she thought as she sat on the bed and twisted her hair onto her head. Yet she would not give up his touch for all the common sense in the world.

Hugh settled behind her, his weight dipping the mattress, so she slid against him, her hips against his leg. "Let me." He cupped his hand over the mass of her hair, cradling her head in his large palm. "You hold the jar."

With one finger and the barest of touches, Hugh lowered the straps of her bra, baring her shoulders. Dia's breath caught as she anticipated his next move. His fingers dipped into the jar she held, then touched the side of her neck. She started from the electric charge of his touch.

197

"Are my fingers cold?"

"No." *Far from it.* They were warm as he slowly spread the creamy salve over her neck. They stimulated the fibers of muscle and nerve, soothing the aches and igniting other basic responses. "They're magic." She sighed.

"I'll take that as a compliment, coming from a mistress of illusion." His fingers stroked shoulders, shoulder blades, and neck, his touch delicate and thorough.

"It is."

Whatever the origins of the cream, it worked. His large hands knew precisely how much pressure to apply. Under his ministration the knots eased, yet he seemed in no hurry to abandon the massage.

"Does any other place hurt?" he asked softly, his breath brushing her neck.

Excitement gathered at the base of her spine. "My arms."

With him still at her back, his hand slid from the side of her neck to the front, then feathered down her arms. Rhythmically he dipped into the jar she held, then spread the cream. One hand massaged, one hand held her in place for his attentions. The shift was subtle but unmistakable—his touch had gone from soothing to arousing.

Dia made no move away. She wished he'd stroke lower, touch her tingling breasts. Hugh was observant; he could see over her shoulder. He had to see her nipples straining against the thin silk of her bra. Yet he did nothing to ease the aches he'd created.

Normally Dia preferred to be an active participant, but the pleasure she felt now was too deep to move and risk breaking the spell. For once she was content to trust in the solid strength of a man.

"You should patent this formula." The words were a bare whisper. Even the muscles of her throat seemed to have relaxed. "It would make you famous."

"I prefer anonymity. Pendragons guard their privacy." His fingers tightened in her hair. "And their prized possessions."

Dia stirred uneasily beneath the ferocity of his low words. Immediately his hand relaxed and he murmured, indistinct but gentling sounds. She relaxed against him, her body molding against his thigh, his flat stomach, his shoulder. His sex stirred against her buttocks.

He would make no move, she realized, until she did. Deliberately she set down the jar of cream. "We should lie down," she whispered.

"Are you sure? You're feeling better?"

"Much." She shifted her hips, a deliberate movement against him.

His hand brushed against her hair. "No residual . . . hesitation? From this afternoon?"

"That was violence. This is pleasure."

Together they sank down to stretch out atop the bed, Hugh still at her back. He let go of her hair, burying his face in it as his arms wrapped across the front of her, enveloping her with his body and his power.

The copper of the band at his wrist was slightly cooler where it touched her bared ribs. Seeing it this close—the shape of it, the etching, Dia realized it was familiar, but couldn't immediately remember why.

The thought vanished under Hugh's sleight of hand. His breath warmed her neck, his hands warmed her arms, and all the blood inside her pooled deep.

Not a single ache remained from her ordeal this afternoon; they'd been replaced by new, far more exciting aches. That he wanted her as much as she wanted him was abundantly clear from the bulge pressing against her bottom. His hips tightened and shifted, tiny movements that rubbed against her, brought them closer.

"I want you. I want you sharing my bed. You know that, don't you?" His low voice slid inside her, part of the spell he wove around her senses.

"Yes. I want you, too." His arms held her, keeping her from twisting to face him, doing delicious things to her fingers and the inside of her thighs.

"So much I can barely breathe."

Dia reached behind her to cup his cheek. The skin was masculine, roughened by the shadow of whiskers. "Now is a perfect time."

"I don't want only these minutes. I want more. A whole night. Longer."

Dia sucked in a breath, assailed by images of Hugh naked, Hugh reaching strong arms toward her and tumbling with her among black silk. Needing him, afraid of the deeper needs pushed to the fore, she twisted in his arms, and this time he let her go. With an agile move, she pushed herself upright and straddled his hips, her skirt hiking to her hips.

"Not into quickies?" She tried for a light tone, indicative of a casual relationship, the only thing she was capable of.

"I like quickies. I just don't want that to be all we have, Dia." He wasn't backing down.

Dia took a deep breath. "Offstage, I don't fool anybody, Hugh. Long-term leases aren't my style. I'm not into marriage, family, or kids because I'm on the road three-quarters of the year, committed to my magic. I don't own furniture or dishes, and my address is a Las Vegas post office box." Her declaration might have been more effective if her body weren't still crying out for him.

"I was talking about sex, Dia."

"No, you weren't." He was demanding far more than she ever gave. "You want too much."

"We'll see. Let me worry about it." Only small bits of late-afternoon sun escaped around the drawn curtains, enough to glint across the jewels of diamond and ruby. A sudden humor lit his emerald eyes. "In the meantime, we'll have this much."

In a smooth move, he rose and slid her onto his lap, snug against him, while he leaned against the headboard. "Pretty," he murmured, looking at her breasts, and his lips curled upward in a smile that lightened his face and took him from handsome to devastating.

Dia's heart squeezed; her chest was filled with the emotions clamoring for release inside her. It was as he had said; she wanted him so badly she could barely breathe, and the very power of her need scared her. It begged to stay, to settle, to lodge deep and never leave.

Hugh bent her back, setting her slightly off balance. His sex pressed close to hers and all she knew was the heat of him searing her as he lowered his lips to the curves above her bra. His tongue traced the hem of fabric, delved below to tease sensitive, waiting flesh.

Sex. This she understood. This she could handle. This was what she wanted.

Hugh lingered over her and teased her, as though her acquiescence gave him those hours and nights he'd demanded. He touched and kissed her in places she'd never realized were erotic until he discovered them: her temple, the top of her ear, the tip of her shoulder, the crook of her elbow.

Her fingers gripped his thighs, kneading the strong flesh. *Now*, she urged him. Yet he continued his leisurely, erotic exploration. The corner of her eye. Her knee. The sides of her breasts. Dia reached down to stroke him through the soft fabric of his shorts.

A faint tapping sound broke into her consciousness. *Tapping?* Hugh quieted and, staring at the door, brought her upright with a short curse.

The tapping was repeated at the door. "Aunt Dia?" came Cam's whisper through the wood. "Are you awake?"

The door opened.

Darn, darn, darn! Desire fled as Dia grabbed for her shirt and flung it on. Beneath her Hugh started shaking. The wretch was laughing, not helping a bit.

Cam came in and paused, searching the gloom. "It's almost time for you to leave, and I wondered if I—" He caught sight of the two of them on the bed. "Oh, um, sorry." He started backing off. "I so do not need to see this."

At least she'd gotten her shirt back on and was off Hugh's lap with her skirt down. Dia had always thought she was pretty open about sex, but she discovered openness didn't include almost being caught in the act by her nephew. She gave him her brightest smile, fervently glad the bed was in the shadows. "Hugh was just leaving. He wanted to make sure I was awake."

"And I guess we've established that fact." Hugh took his cue and rose from the bed with an easy move. The loose cut of his shorts almost disguised his lingering arousal. At least *he'd* still had his clothes on. "I'll take you to the theater when you're ready, Dia."

"It's not necessary."

"It is as long as Mick Masterson is at large." He nodded to Cam as he passed by him in the door. "See you later."

At least one of them was being nonchalant. Cam avoided looking at her while Dia shoved back the tangled mass of her hair. "So what did you want, Cam?"

"I was wondering if I could go with you to the theater? You said I could do a bit at that party, and I thought I might pick up a few tips."

"Sure, tell the others they can come, too."

"All right." He left without meeting her eyes.

At least her neck wasn't still sore.

Despite being frustrated as hell, Hugh was well pleased. Dia was here, and it was gratifying to know she was no more able to resist the siren call of desire than he was. Soon she would share his bed.

As for anything else, he would take it slow, woo her carefully. She was skittish and wary and reluctant to see beyond the pleasures of a short affair. That was understandable. They hadn't known each other for long, and he'd never considered a long-term relationship with any of the women he'd dated, either. He couldn't explain how he was so sure about Dia, but somehow her presence here seemed inevitable and right.

Cerberus joined him, padding beside him. Hugh scratched the dog's head. "She belongs here, Cerb, old buddy. Just like you."

He just had to convince Dia of that.

Dia discovered she was more tired, that the day had taken more out of her, than she'd realized. Her body ached with strain and her muscles shook with fatigue. Her performance that night was serviceable, but not inspired, and afterward she had no trouble refusing the invitations of her crew and heading straight home.

Home. Not her home, Hugh's home, yet it seemed a haven to her tonight.

Only Cam had come with her and Hugh to the theater, and she let him take the front seat in the car, too tired to carry on a decent conversation. Hugh and Cam had no problems in that regard, and she leaned her head against the seat back, lulled by the sound of their voices. They certainly found enough to talk about.

She must have fallen asleep, for the next thing she knew, Hugh was giving her a kiss on the temple and telling her they were home.

"It's time for bed, Dia."

She gave him a sleepy smile. "Are you coming with me?"

He shook his head. "You need your rest."

He was right, of course, and a few minutes later she was in bed, alone, and sound asleep.

Dia felt much better in the morning, if one considered noon still morning. In the kitchen she found Ronald putting some meat into marinade and Hugh drinking a cup of coffee and reading the newspaper.

"Miss Trelawny, I do hope you are feeling better."

"Much, and call me Dia."

"Can I get you something to eat, Miss Dia? Would you prefer lunch or breakfast?"

"Breakfast."

"I have fresh muffins, or if you prefer an omelet, it will be ready soon." He pulled out a cloth napkin and a luncheon plate and headed toward the dining room.

"You don't have to wait on me. I'll just pour some cereal and eat here."

"Miss Dia, you should have a proper breakfast."

Hugh looked up from his newspaper. "How about a compromise? Ronald cooks and serves; Dia eats in here."

"Very good, sir."

Dia poured her own coffee right away, and a short time later Ronald set a plate with two warm bran muffins and a fruit cup in front of her. He left the kitchen, and they were alone.

While Dia speared a piece of pineapple and ate it, Hugh continued to look through the paper. Suddenly he made a disgusted noise and tossed down his paper to take a drink of coffee.

"Unhappy news?" Dia asked as she attacked her bran muffin.

He pointed to an article. "They're letting this guy out of prison early for good behavior. Apparently he's been an exemplary prisoner and is reformed."

"You don't think people can be reformed?"

"Not this guy. I was the one who put him behind bars. I know what he's like. Pardon boards can be so gullible."

Dia crumbled bits off her muffin. "You don't believe in pardons?"

He thought a moment. "I believe in justice and in allowing the victims their moments of empowerment. I believe that wrongs need to be righted and paid for, and I've seen too much hideousness in my work to condone letting a true criminal off with a slap on the hand."

Dia pushed her plate away, all of a sudden not hungry. She clutched her coffee cup instead, anxious to change the subject. "Did you find out anything about my sister?"

He summarized his findings, ending with, "I've figured out some of the places they might be."

"Can we go after them?"

He shook his head. "These outfitters travel all over the world. I have to pinpoint which site first."

Dia sighed. "Then I guess I've got children awhile longer."

"Uh-huh, but it won't be so bad now that you're here. How did Lukas break his leg?"

She told him.

"I could have told you not to go to Cook."

Cam burst into the kitchen, with Lukas close behind, hobbling on his walking cast. "Hey, Hugh, it's time to go."

Hugh looked as his watch, then downed the last of his coffee. "You're right."

Dia looked at them curiously. "Where are you going?"

"Hugh's taking us to the tae kwon do class he teaches."

"Is it safe for you?" she asked Lukas, nodding to the cast.

"He can help with arm strengtheners. The boys have taken enough martial arts to be a help." Hugh bent over and gave her a quick kiss on the top of her head. "I'll see you when we leave for the theater."

The three left with the boys excitedly asking Hugh about what belt he was and what routine he would do.

Numbly, Dia brushed crumbs off her hands, finished her coffee, then tidied up the kitchen. A thoroughly domestic scene this had been, the two of them sharing breakfast, him dashing off with the kids and a good-bye peck.

It was not her scene. And if she'd ever hoped that this affair she and Hugh were starting, this affair that she could not seem to resist, might have a future, those hopes had been destroyed when she'd heard him talk about justice.

She wasn't needed backstage, Hera decided during their second performance in Evanston. She perched on a stool positioned to keep both the backstage chaos and the performance in view. Dia could do her own makeup using the experimental products Hera had provided. The crew had their assigned work. Zeus was intent on his lights and explosions.

Even Cam and Lukas had responsibilities, and Hugh had rolled up his sleeves to provide added physical labor.

It was time she approached the matter of Hugh and Dia from another perspective.

"Miz Juneau, can I sit with you?" Claire stood beside her, clutching a book to her chest. "I was reading, but I need a break and it's boring by myself."

"Go ahead."

Claire pulled over an empty stool and hopped up beside her.

"How are you enjoying your stay in Chicago?" Hera asked, not sure what to talk to such a young person about.

"It's okay. I miss my mom. Aunt Dia's cool and all, but she's kinda busy right now. Too busy for us."

"Your aunt cares for you."

"I know, but she is so not ready for a twenty-four/seven family."

True, and Hera feared that included a husband. And love. "Do you know how she got the bruises on her face?"

"Some guy she had to fire did it. Guys can be jerks sometimes."

Hera glanced over at Zeus, in animated conversation with Anya. "Yes, they can."

Claire sighed. "But Hugh came and saved her. That was so romantic. I just love romantic stories."

Hera had the feeling that there was more to the story, but grilling a twelve-year-old romantic wasn't going to reveal it. "What's your favorite romantic story?" she asked, surprised to find she was actually enjoying the conversation with Claire. There was something refreshing about innocent candor.

"My favorite romantic story? That's easy. Hades and Persephone."

"*What?*"

Claire held out her worn book of mythology. "We studied all the myths in school last year and I just loved them." She opened the book to a picture of a man in a chariot controlling four straining steeds. "See, he fell in love with her at first sight and whisked her away. Her mother was mad."

"I always thought Demeter sounded like the inspiration for all those nasty mother-in-law jokes," Hugh's low voice commented from behind them.

"She was. I mean, I thought so, too." Hera turned as he joined them. Hugh had brought Dia to the theater, stayed until her crew arrved, and then went back for Claire, Cam, and Lukas. Elena, apparently, had elected to stay with Ronald. Hera hadn't been surprised to hear that Dia and family had moved into Hugh's house, only at how quickly the Soul Seeker had gotten them there.

"Did you have a favorite myth?" Claire asked Hugh.

"Not really."

"Who was your favorite goddess?" Hera asked lightly. "Hera?"

Claire made a face. "She was mean. I liked Athena. And Hades was my favorite god."

Hera's jaw tightened, and her foot tapped against the rung of the stool. Always she was portrayed as the cow-faced, jealous goddess. "The mythmakers

209

got it all wrong. Athena wasn't real. They created her from parts of Ares."

Claire and Hugh stared at her.

"I've read some of the ancient texts," she muttered in explanation, then tried to distract them. "Did you know the original title for Hades was not god of the underworld, but Soul Seeker? The translators got it wrong."

"Soul Seeker?" Beside her, she saw Hugh tense. Had he somehow heard the term?

She nodded. "Soul Seeker. The gods took journeys through the soul, not through the physical body. All gods did, many times in the course of a life, to renew the spirit. Sometimes they visited places of joy, an *elysial* journey, but sometimes a more difficult examination of painful places was needed and corrective actions were required. This was a *tartus* journey. The Greeks turned those words into Elysian Fields and Tartarus. Heaven and hell."

Claire was wide-eyed. "What did the Soul Seeker do?"

"His was a unique, uncommon talent to connect with the spirit. Aided by his talisman, the Soul Seeker was the gods' guide, their companion, and their anchor. He shared what they experienced, found lost wanderers, and gave them the strength to endure. But to seek and locate and touch the souls was not enough to make a true Soul Seeker.

"What more was needed?" Hugh asked, his voice rough.

She glanced at his wristband, then into his eyes. "Duality. A Soul Seeker needed to wander through the *celestium*, but he also needed to be anchored,

210

grounded in reality so he could return the soul to the body. It was that dual nature that was so rare. And so necessary."

"I like it better when he's god of the dead. That is so cool," Claire declared, then jumped down from her stool. "I guess I'll read some more."

"You seem to know a lot about things that are not mentioned in mythology," Hugh observed quietly to Hera when they were alone.

"Spirit walking is part of the myth and culture of many societies. Besides, you don't believe ancient knowledge is always openly shared, do you?" Hera gave him a steady look. "I've studied the subject extensively, consulted sources hidden from most, and I've formed my own conclusions."

Onstage, the airplane blades emitted their high-pitched whine. Hugh spun around, his attention drawn to the stage, his fists clenched. A burst of white sparks dazzled the audience as the blades spun through the spot where Dia stood. She sprang to the stage, intact and triumphant, lifting her arms and performing her bow to the applause of her college-age audience.

Hugh's fists relaxed. Hera eyed him closely. Such intensity. Even while he'd conversed with her, his attention had remained on Dia.

Dia gave the crew a brilliant smile as she strode backstage. "That was great! You all are super. Every cue right on, and Zeke, your heatless fireworks are fabulous. I am so pumped." She noticed a group of fans gathered in the wings. "Do you all mind doing the postshow reset without me?"

"Go ahead," Anya answered for them all. "Customers pay our bills, and customers come to see you."

Dia detoured by her dressing area long enough to throw on a black robe before joining the fans—mostly good-looking, twenty-something, testosterone-laden males. Immediately she was surrounded by them. It didn't take long, Hera noticed, for her to have them mesmerized by her animated conversation, vivacious flirting, and big laugh as she signed autographs and talked about her magic.

Nor did it take long for Hugh to start frowning.

She'd seen that frown. It was precisely how Hades had frowned when he'd found Perithous trying to abduct Persephone. Hades had abandoned his rival to the hell of a *tartus* journey for his temerity. Poor Perithous had learned it wasn't wise to counter god in love.

A god in love? Hera sucked in a breath and studied Hugh anew. By the sirens' song, had the Soul Seeker fallen in love? A Soul Seeker would love but once. Was Dia Hugh's chosen? She sidled up to Zeus and whispered, "Look at Hugh. What do you think?"

He turned and studied the couple. "He's in love," he said flatly.

"You don't sound too excited. Didn't you hear? She's in Hugh's house. They're making it easy for us."

"Are they? Watch them, my love."

Dia managed to usher out the fans with a gracious wave while the crew finished, trickling out one by one, until only Zeus, Hera, Hugh, and Dia remained. Hugh gave them an irritated look.

"Just leaving," said Zeus brightly and dragged Hera around the corridor corner.

"You said watch," Hera said in a hiss.

212

"And so you shall." He held up his ring. "What shall it be this time?"

Hera smiled. "Mist."

They activated the rings, and gradually Zeus and Hera disappeared behind a thin veil of mist. The mist crept down the hall, back toward the dressing room, and hid in the shadows.

Hugh was waiting for Dia when she emerged in heels and a silky red dress held up by two thin straps. The Zeus mist gave an appreciative sigh. Hera elbowed him quiet.

Hugh's frown deepened. "You're going to a party?"

"Not exactly. I'm going to do a little P and P."

"P and P?"

"Publicity and promotion. There's a press party tonight I have to attend."

"You didn't mention it to me."

"I thought you'd taken the kids home."

"I called Ronald and asked him to pick them up."

"You know I usually go out after a show."

"I was planning a quiet dinner for two and a bottle of Bordeaux." He paused. "We could finish what we started yesterday."

She sucked in a breath, and Hera saw a tint of red flood her cheeks, but she shook her head. "Hugh, this is my work. I have to go."

"You can't—"

Beside her, Hera heard Zeus make a disgusted noise and mutter, "Inept." She stepped on his toes to quiet him.

Dia's eyes narrowed. "I can't what?"

"You can't get a taxi this time of night."

Good recovery, thought Hera.

"I'll manage. I know you don't like parties, Hugh, but this is what I do."

He paused, mulling over what she'd said, then nodded. "All right. Mutual pleasures later. First I'll take you to meet the press."

Dia shook her head. "Don't do this, Hugh. Don't get all possessive."

"Who said anything about possessive? I'm simply protecting a client. Masterson's still out."

"I'm not going to live my life scared of a worm like Mick Masterson."

Hugh took her elbow. "You don't have to," he said calmly. "Taking care of him is my job."

"I thought I hired you to find my sister."

"You're on the comprehensive plan."

They left, snapping out the lights and locking the door behind them. When the stage was silent and eerie-still, the mist coalesced into two figures. A lingering glow from the power surrounded them.

Hera looked after the two lovers. "See, he has chosen."

"But she has not."

"He excites her."

"Remember the curse I left in her line, Hera. Descendents of the women I wronged do not trust in love; they do not make wise choices. She may care; she may even fall in love. But she may not be able to commit the way he needs. Will she be able to sacrifice what she cherishes most for him?"

"Without that, the union with a Soul Seeker cannot last." Hera sighed. "I fear you're right."

Zeus rubbed his chin. "So we need to prod her a bit. Isolation works—a fog, a rainstorm?"

"Been there, done that. Do something different."

"Like what?"

Hera shrugged. "I'm sure you'll think of something."

"What, Hera not planning everything?"

"I'm leaving it up to you. I'm not going to be here."

The gold aura surrounding Zeus flared with diamond brightness. "What!"

"Demeter. Someone needs to find out what she's doing."

"That someone doesn't have to be you."

"You're going to become her bosom buddy?"

Zeus thought a moment. "She does have a very nice bosom."

Hera gave an irritated snort.

"So what do you plan to do, my love?"

"She knows of my jealousy. She knows of your philandering ways—"

"I'm faithful!" Zeus sputtered. "Why can't you believe that?"

Hera laid a hand on his cheek. "I'm working on it. After all, you are quite convincing, my love."

Zeus settled down, somewhat mollified.

"But Demeter does not know that," she continued. "She will believe my ire has been raised once more, that I have turned to her and against you. It might help if you could flirt just a little bit more."

Zeus laughed. "Now, isn't that a twist?"

"*Only* flirt," she warned.

"Of course."

"You, in turn, must trust that whatever I do or say, our goal is still the same. You must trust me."

She waited a moment, breath held, until he picked up her hand and kissed her fingers. "I have always trusted you. In the meantime I shall occupy myself with a scheme to unite our lovers. It's too bad kidnapping isn't allowed these days. Hades had such luck with it."

Chapter Thirteen

Hugh had thought he was thoroughly experienced, but Dia showed him new pieces of life. A press party was one adventure he'd missed.

He couldn't say he regretted the lack. Conversation based upon the goal of self-promotion, free-flowing alcohol, trays of hors d'oeuvres, uninspired music. He did not belong here, and Dia—despite her flash, her easy laugh, and her savvy—was a world away from this artificial scene.

Yet Dia seemed to blossom as she made her way around the room, fatigue falling off her like a discarded coat. He downed his drink in a single gulp and gave the glass to a passing waiter, recalling what Paolo had said to him at Anya's party. Dia needed people. And he should try to look like he was having fun.

Had he really gotten that stuffy, that reclusive, that he could not even find a single moment of pleasure here? It was not a picture of himself he liked. His father's last years had been spent in isolation; he'd even refused to leave the house. Hugh loved his father, but he did not want to suffer that same loneliness.

He shoved his hands in his pockets, then spied a reporter from the *Tribune* whom he knew, one who covered the art scene. Perhaps she would know if the theft of his gem had been a one-time affair or part of a pattern. He tended to believe he was not the only one who'd been hit—the switch was too polished to have been a single score. Dia'd had him so tied in knots the last two days that he hadn't followed up on what Blessing had told him. It was time he did his job.

Half an hour later he'd learned of a couple of possibilities. He'd also fended off a request to open his house for a television program called *Unusual Abodes*, discovered that Demetria Cesare had made her first fortune in the cereal industry and her second in natural pharmaceuticals, got annoyed by a woman dressed in a caftan and gold chains working the room to promote her public-access palm-reading program, and interested a morning television reporter in having Dia on his show.

Hugh shifted his shoulders against the press of fatigue. He'd had about all the party fun he could handle for one night.

He spied Dia across the room, the red of her dress a homing beacon for his eyes. When he'd first seen her in that dress—silky, scarlet, two thin straps—it was like being hit by the boom of his boat. Everything vital was covered and her makeup was subtle, but with her hair loose about her shoulders and those long legs made even sexier by high heels, she was a package of pure temptation.

He wound his way to her side. Waiting for a lull in her conversation, he laid a hand on her shoulder. When she glanced at him, he leaned over and whispered, "Which sounds more appealing right now? That warm beer you're nursing or a promise of mutual pleasure?"

She sucked in a breath and finished her conversation with graciousness and speed.

Resting his hand between her shoulders, he guided her through the crowd. Her silky hair caressed his arms, and with one finger he rubbed lightly against her skin. He liked the texture of it, smooth and firm. As her flesh warmed, he detected the enduring scents of rosemary and honey.

Something dark and heavy lifted from inside him. Maybe it was the grounding Harriet Juneau had mentioned in that odd story about the Soul Seeker. No more feet stuck in the rock.

Whatever, it left a shining desire in its wake. He wanted Dia with a need that had no parallel in his life. Just watching the sway of her hips beneath that red dress was enough to do him in. His hand drifted lower, from her neck across the smooth bare skin of her shoulder blades. When he reached the edge of her top he caressed beneath it, claiming the unseen. Her hips swayed again, red silk brushing against him in invitation. His hand trailed down, atop her smooth dress, until it came to rest at her waist. His fingers splayed on the supple indentation. She looked up at him and shared an intimate, sexy grin.

Tonight she would be his. He felt light with anticipation and readiness, as arousal spun through him.

Despite the sultry city night, the air was fresher and cooler outside, and the din was definitely diminished. Dia took a deep breath.

"I like the night," she observed. "It's exotic and embracing."

"I've always found it a dangerous friend."

"The danger is part of the mystique, don't you think?"

"Only if the danger doesn't get dirty, doesn't actually touch you."

"True. You do have to point out the practical flaws, don't you?"

And talk about banishing the mood. Smart move, Pendragon. He was saved from answering by reaching his car and the mundane routine of settling in and starting it. But as he turned onto Lake Shore Drive—preferring the slower, scenic route along the shore to the interstate—the comment still rankled. Were they that different? Was *he* that different? "Did you really enjoy that party?"

"What's not to like?" she asked lightly. "Music, drinks, conversation, people. Did you find anything to enjoy?"

"I liked being with you."

"Nothing else?"

He thought a moment. "The drinks were icy cold, I had an interesting conversation with a reporter, and I liked one of the songs that was played, but I don't know the name." He hummed a few lines.

"That sounds like 'Kryptonite.' Three Doors Down. So it wasn't a total bust?"

"No."

"If I had wanted to stay longer, would you have?"

"I wasn't going to throw you over my shoulder and carry you off, if that's what you mean." Although the urge would have been quite tempting. At night, primitive instincts didn't seem to recognize the correct behaviors of the day. "But I could see you were getting tired. And you neatly turned away my question, by the way. Did you enjoy yourself?"

"I really do like meeting people," she said after a moment, "but a press party is working, not playing. I've just done it so long it's second nature now."

"If you were to have an afternoon, or an evening, that was just for yourself—no *shoulds* or *musts*—what would you do?"

"I'd eat ice cream," she answered promptly. "Every flavor I could find. I adore ice cream, but I watch what I eat pretty carefully, so I don't indulge myself very often. And when I do, it's a single scoop."

"Where would you have this ice cream?" They passed a sign for the Lincoln Park Zoo. "The zoo?"

She shuddered. "Me and animals? I'm the one who hates big birds, remember?"

"Then I guess Sesame Street on Ice is also out of the question."

She laughed, that big, full laugh that filled the car and his chest. Hugh felt himself stir all over again, and heartily wished they were home and in bed.

"Lord, yes. Where would I have ice cream? In Chicago, I guess it would be either a blues concert or a Second City comedy performance. First choice—Second City."

"And here I was hoping you'd opt for the blues. I enjoy the smooth rhythms of a good bluesman."

"Have you been to the famed Second City?"

"Once. It was entertaining, but uneven, at least the night I was there." Of course, the woman he'd been with wasn't Dia, either, and the affair had been winding down, so that might have colored his view. "I'd give it another chance."

She leaned her head against the seat rest and closed her eyes. "My ex wouldn't have." She opened one eye. "Did you know I was married before?"

"Yes." He didn't mention that the fact had come up while he was researching her, not her sister. "He was a magician, wasn't he?"

She nodded. "A good one, too. We had a lot in common. Or so I thought at eighteen."

"What happened?"

"I mistook lust for love and a common interest for compatibility. Turns out we didn't want the same thing at all. He thought success was his due, and that my role was to admire him and bear his children. Things went downhill the night I came home with my first win in a magic competition. He asked for a divorce six months later and it got pretty ugly. He said I was sabotaging his career for mine and accused me of sleeping my way up."

"Sounds like a jerk."

She shrugged. "In the modern vernacular, he had issues. We weren't working on the same stage."

"Where is he now?"

"California. He bills himself as 'The Persian Mystic' and is still waiting for the big break. Every so often he calls and asks if I'd like to do a tour with him." She raked a hand through her hair. "Sorry, I'm sure you didn't want to hear all that, and I certainly don't usually blather like that. You're too good a listener, Hugh."

Or maybe you were warning me? Don't mistake lust for anything more. Don't expect too much.

"I'm not your ex, Dia," he said softly.

"I know. You know, he didn't like parties either." She laid a hand on his arm, and from the corner of his eye he saw her grin. "He never went to one just because I wanted to go."

The warmth of her smile and touch roused the sleeping beast of desire. Hugh gripped the steering wheel with one hand, grateful for the sparse traffic, and captured her hand. Eyes on the road, he lifted it to his mouth and kissed her palm, then her wrist. When he glanced over, he saw his need echoed in her. Desire roared through him in an undeniable rampage. *Do something*, it demanded, *something utterly crazy.*

Now!

With a short curse, he pulled the car into a deserted lakefront parking lot. The tires protested as he jerked to halt. A line of trees shielded them from the view of the street, and before them spread the dark, rolling waves of the lake. If she thought all they had was lust, then that was what he would take. What he needed. Feed the desire, bind her close to him with the velvet ties of sex.

"Hugh?"

He rolled down the windows, turned off the car. Steamy June spread in, replacing the cool air. Outside was quiet, with only the faint whoosh of cars behind and the low whisper of the waves ahead.

"I'm glad I don't have a sports car," he muttered; then with a swift movement he tilted the steering wheel out of his way and turned to Dia.

She was leaning against the door and smiling again.

He matched her pose. "Come here, Dia. Come to me." Somehow it seemed very important for her to come to him. For her to acknowledge that this burning need was mutual.

He waited, his entire body tense but still while her gaze brushed across him, took in the straining fabric below; then to his utmost relief, she closed the gap between them. She leaned over and kissed him, her lips soft, her tongue tracing an invitation.

Hugh's body tightened and hardened. "Do you have any underwear on beneath that dress?" he whispered against her mouth.

"What do you think?"

"I think it's a saucy bit of silk that you need to take off right now."

Her laugh was low and throaty as she reached beneath her dress and slipped off her panties.

"Good. Straddle me."

"Eager?"

"Yes. I've waited too long."

"You've known me a week."

I've known you forever. "Not a week. I first met you six months ago, and I wanted you then."

"So did I," she admitted as she settled down onto his lap, the red silk rising to expose her long, firm thighs. Hugh captured one hip with his palm, anchoring her to him.

His sex rose eagerly, only to meet the unyielding, uncomfortable barrier of his zipper. *Soon*, he promised.

"What shall I do next?" Dia asked, teasingly. "Since you seem to be into commands."

"At least you know the proper response. Obey."

"A fleeting aberration. Enjoy the moment."

"I will. Lower your straps."

She did, and he discovered she was wearing only a thin, strapless strip of silk there—an instant turn-on. He didn't bother to move the silk before his mouth found the tip of her generous breast. He gave it a quick nip, pleased to feel the tense nipple; then he took the breast in his mouth and suckled.

Honey . . . she tasted of honey and silk. Her other breast was heavy in his hand as he rubbed the nipple with his thumb, and her soft sighs pirouetted straight to his groin.

Mouth and hands explored. He learned the soft down of her skin and the firm curve of her muscles and the exquisite pleasure of her hands tunneling through his hair as she held him close.

He lifted his lips to her mouth and plundered. She had come to him, had surrendered, yet still she demanded and met him with a fierce, matching desire. Dia moaned against him and her hands, normally so sure and clever, fumbled at his zipper.

Now!

He sprang forth, so ready that Hugh had to grit his teeth not to spill himself. That was all he'd need. He held still, willing the rampant need under his control.

"Now," she echoed, breathless. She gripped his arms and her fingers hooked into the copper band at his wrist. Dia rose, then glided onto him as he guided himself inside.

Hugh gave a soft moan of pleasure, echoed by Dia.

She felt so good. Tight and wet and welcoming. He gathered her in his arms and held her close. She buried her face in his neck, her breath coming in short pants as her excitement gathered. He moved, thrusting deep, taking control, claiming, flying. In his arms Dia trembled, then tightened with a gasp.

Hugh thrust forward, pumped, felt the gathering explosion. Where he was seated deep within her, Dia convulsed around him in a scorching, endless tremor, and he silenced her shout with a kiss. Then he was flying with her, released from his shackles. Glittering lights, bright as gemstones, led the way, led him back to earth, before twinkling out with his satisfied moan.

She blanketed him, boneless and soft. Damp skin pressed against damp skin, and her slowing breath tickled the sensitive skin on his neck. Hugh wrapped his arms around this woman who had stormed into his life to turn it topsy-turvy, and he held her close.

"Mmmm," Dia murmured in satisfaction.

Hugh bracketed her face with his palms and gave her a tender kiss. "Mmmmm, indeed."

Her smile contained nothing of the practiced showman or of the teasing vamp. It was pure satiation. A beam of light passed across her face, and she flinched.

"I think we're about to have company," Hugh observed as the blue car pulled into the lot. "Chicago's finest."

With a short curse, Dia scrambled off his lap and pulled straps up and skirt down. While she finger-combed her hair, Hugh zipped himself; then she gazed nonchalantly out the window.

Rubbing the bridge of his nose, Hugh watched the bear-sized officer get out of the car and lumber toward him. Hugh rested an arm on the door. The light swept through the interior. From the corner of his eye Hugh saw Dia surreptitiously slide her underwear under the seat with her foot.

"What are you folks—" The light stilled. "Hugh Pendragon?"

"Hi, Patrick." Hugh had helped him with a case last year.

"What are you doing out here, Hugh?"

"Just watching the waves."

The light flashed briefly on Dia, who treated him to a smile. "Uh-huh," answered Patrick, clearly not believing his explanation.

"We'd just finished communing with nature."

"Probably a good thing I didn't disturb you folks five minutes ago, while you were, uh, communing."

"Probably right."

"We were about to leave," added Dia.

Patrick gave a chuckle and called to his partner, waiting cautiously behind, "They're okay." The two officers got in their car and left.

Dia gave Hugh an incredulous look while he started their car. "Communing with nature? Come on, Pendragon, couldn't you have come up with something better?"

227

"My blood wasn't exactly in my brain at that moment."

Dia laughed, a laugh that came from deep inside her, and Hugh joined in.

"Besides, I didn't hear you chiming in too quickly, Trelawny."

"My brain wasn't working too well either. One of these times we've got to get behind a locked door."

Still laughing, Hugh pulled back onto Lake Shore Drive, feeling immeasurably satisfied.

When had he last laughed with a woman like this? Especially right after sex? He should be embarrassed as hell to be caught necking like Cam or Lukas, but instead he felt as though a burden had been lifted from his soul. "Kryptonite" was the name of that song he liked, Dia had said, and tonight, fanciful as it sounded, he felt like Superman, as though he could see and hear beyond the realm of normalcy.

As though his talent had returned.

The car swayed slightly, but Hugh corrected it before Dia noticed.

She had her head back against the seat rest and was chuckling. "I had forgotten what a bitch sex in a car can be. You gotta keep an eye out for the police *and* the gearshift."

"Sounds like you've had experience."

She looked at him out of the corner of her eye. "You mean you never . . . ? In a car . . . ?"

"Not all the way. A plane, yes. A car, no."

"A plane? Someday you'll have to tell me about it."

"No. I don't think I will." *Show you, yes.*

She laughed, as he'd hoped, but the sound faded as she worried her bottom lip. "Hugh, there are things in my past, things that aren't too savory—"

"You don't need to tell me." His hand grazed her cheek in a tender caress. "What happened before doesn't matter. What matters is now." *And the future.*

He supposed she thought he might be upset about her previous experience, but he wasn't. Besides, he guessed she was a lot more show than action. In this day you had to be stupid to risk sleeping around, and Dia wasn't stupid. She was an entertainer; she presented a good show, but in the end she was backstage alone.

Just like him, in some ways.

What happened before doesn't matter. For a brief moment the words shuddered through him, calling out the heaviness that had plagued him of late, the coldness that he thought he had just banished. Hugh thrust it away.

Whether he was the first wasn't important. What he wanted to be, what he would be, was the last.

What happened before does *matter.* The voice from the cave of his dreams reshaped his words and sent them back.

Chapter Fourteen

Dia leaned back against the headrest as a pleasant exhaustion settled across her, the lingering ache between her thighs a reminder of the wild moments just past. Hugh turned on the radio and changed stations until the low growl of blues filled the car. Apparently he was content with the silence between them; his mood of satisfaction needed no words.

She, too, needed the quiet, for despite her body's languor, despite the lulling drone of the engine, her mind could not be still.

Tonight she should have been able to keep things cool and in her control, but Hugh defied every one of her expectations. He was honest, no deceptions. He kept his promises; he didn't trade on favors or expect sex as payment. He kept her off balance in a way that no man ever had, even while he filled her with a strange, deep contentment.

Dia took a deep breath. *Get a grip. It was sex.* She could handle that. Quick, awkward, frantic, exciting, mind-blowing sex.

Yet it was more than physical. This connection with Hugh fulfilled a need that had cried out for release and now demanded more.

More what? She didn't know. She'd gone from hiring him as a PI to living with him to having sex in the front seat of his car in the space of a few short days. What more could there be?

Permanence?

Not for the likes of her; she'd always known that. Not for a gypsy Trelawny. She had too many places to go and things to do to want a place or person that anchored her and drew her back.

Yet for the first time in her life the idea didn't seem so frightening or so impossible.

Because of Hugh.

Mentally she shook herself. *Fool the audience, never fool yourself.* Right now she had too many distractions, too much trouble, too much baggage in her life to want added complications.

But perhaps in the future . . . ?

"Dia," Hugh began, sounding almost hesitant.

"Yes?" She turned to see him gripping the wheel.

"Back there. We didn't use any protection. I'm not usually so careless—"

"I'm on the pill," she assured him. "I don't leave something like that to the heat of the moment."

"Oh."

"You sound almost disappointed."

"Not really." He gave her a fleeting smile. "Definitely much too soon for anything like that."

"It's much too *never*," she answered. "Motherhood and magic don't mix, not for me. If having my nieces and nephews here has shown me anything, it's that." She tilted her head, remembering how he'd held the baby, how he'd been so gentle with her brood. "Do you think of yourself as a father type?"

"Yes," he said softly, "I do."

And she heard a depth of longing in his voice that could not be denied.

Future dreams, future plans faded in a puff of magician's smoke. She and Hugh could have these few days; then she would confront Demetria and either be in jail or be free to pursue her success, and Hugh would be free to find a woman who could share his home for more than a few months and who would bear his child.

But, oh, the path to the top suddenly looked very lonely.

Dia leaned her head against the headrest, tired to her bones, then turned her head to look at Hugh. She hadn't deceived him. He knew where she was coming from. They could have these days if he wanted.

As they traveled the miles to home, the streetlights highlighted the movement of his arms and glinted off the ruby at his wrist.

Again she was struck with a sense of déjà vu. That wristband. She'd seen it, or something like it, somewhere. "Your wristband. It looks old. Is it an heirloom?"

"It's been in our family as long as any Pendragon can remember."

"Can I see it?"

He slipped off the band and handed it to her.

The copper was warm from his skin and the ruby was a deep red, without a hint of light reflecting off it. Strange etchings covered it, both on the top and on the inner band, and it was surprisingly heavy. Copper and ruby, elements of the earth. Ageless constancy; she knew it by mere touch. Her breathing slowed; her mind settled.

Idly she turned the band in her hands, her fingers skimming the etchings on the inside. She could slip it here; her hands worked the movement. Do a sleight of hand to—

Dia sucked in a breath as a wrenching truth jammed into her stomach. She had held this wrist band, or rather a companion to it. Silver. Opal. Same etchings on the top. She squeezed her eyes shut, unable to look at Hugh, and her throat clogged with horror.

Six months ago she'd performed at the opening of a display called Treasures of the Underworld. It was at that performance that she'd found out what Demetria was doing—found out too late, for the opal and silver bracelet had already been switched. She'd never learned who was the anonymous donor-victim.

Until now.

The last gem she'd unknowingly helped Demetria steal belonged to Hugh Pendragon.

Blood roared in her ears as hot shame filled her. She had stolen from the man she'd just made love to.

Each unholy second of that last performance played in her mind. She'd loved the feel of that band, loved its mysterious look, which hinted at secrets and moonbeams. When she'd held it, her magic had been more seamless and captivating than she'd ever known.

Perhaps that was why that illusion, that gem, had been different. The four others she'd unknowingly exchanged were simply a means to an end, a part of the illusion. That wristband, however, had been a joy in itself, something that had taken her attention away from the illusion for the precious seconds needed to notice the switch.

"It's unique," she scratched out, handing it back to him with hands suddenly numb.

"Almost," he said, snapping it back on his wrist. "There's a companion piece of opal and silver."

Any faint hope that she'd remembered wrong, that someone else might own the other gem, died, leaving only an ashen taste.

Did Hugh know? Know of the switch? Know of her role? How could he? Easily—he was a detective and a gem expert. So why hadn't he said anything if he knew? Why had he opened his house to her and the children if he suspected? Was it some bizarre scheme to trap her? To entice her into committing another theft? The unpleasant questions whirled in a mad frenzy.

One question of them all dominated: what did Hugh know?

"The companion. You don't wear it?" she asked tentatively.

He shook his head. "Two is too many, and I prefer the feel of this one."

He didn't sound like a man who knew he'd been robbed. Unable to face him, Dia stared straight ahead, seeing only a blur of nighttime lights.

If Hugh knew, he wouldn't pretend. He wouldn't have made love to her. Of that she was sure to her bones. Private, reclusive, yes, but his dealings with her were straightforward and his passion had been blunt and honest. If she believed in anything, she believed in that. No false promises, no cons, no fake claims.

She should confess, be done with the lies. Enlist his skills, as she had been tempted to do so many times.

Don't be a fool. When he found out, Hugh would want nothing to do with the woman who'd stolen from him. She remembered his comments about justice, about pardons.

Besides, she never depended upon anyone else. Stopping Demetria was her responsibility. And if she couldn't get back the gems, she'd take responsibility for that, too. She should leave his house, though, stop taking advantage of his generosity.

The faces of Cam, Elena, Lukas, and Claire swam before her eyes, blotting out the darkening landscape as Hugh turned into his drive and the security gates closed behind him. She couldn't leave them and make Hugh take responsibility for them. And if she told Hugh, and he turned her in . . . Oh, she couldn't believe he would, but could she take that risk? What would happen to the children with Liza missing?

She couldn't think, couldn't decide what to do, not tonight. Not when she was so tired. She would sleep on it. Nothing would happen tonight, and tomorrow she could decide.

Lies. Deceptions. Trickery. She hated them, but she was trapped back in the world she thought she'd left for good. Damn Demetria for pulling her back into the life she thought she'd escaped, and damn herself not finding the way out.

One thing was immediately clear: she would not compound her sin by making love with Hugh again.

Her body thrummed in protest, remembering the delights of his touches and his kisses, of his warm hands caressing her and the fullness of him inside her. Dia pressed her lips together against bleak frustration. Such a short time she'd known him, but of all the things she had faced and done this was the hardest.

Hugh cast a wary sidelong glance at Dia. Rarely did she hide behind silence, yet she had said nothing after handing him back his wristband. The hum of wheels on pavement and the soft purr of the engine were normal, welcome sounds, yet tonight they made a poor substitute for her throaty laugh, her easy conversation, and her cries of completion.

What was she thinking? He couldn't fathom, except to know her thoughts brought a downward tilt to her lips and a crease between her brows.

Not the reaction a man wanted to see after making love to a woman.

He pulled into the shadowy garage and closed the door, leaving them in a darkness relieved only by the faint moonlight filtering through narrow panes of glass. He turned off the engine, and the silence ballooned.

"Penny for your thoughts," he said quietly, capturing a strand of her hair and running the silk through his fingers.

"They aren't worth even that."

"They are to me."

Dia sucked in a deep breath as his fingers grazed the smooth strength of her shoulder; then she straightened and shifted from beneath his caressing stroke. Before he realized her intent, she was out of the car and heading inside. "Thanks for tonight," she mumbled.

Hugh caught up to her in the deserted kitchen. " 'Thanks for tonight'? That's your reaction to what happened? I thought what we had was pretty damned incredible."

She flushed. "I meant about taking me out."

"Ah, that was my pleasure. As was this." He gathered her hair in one hand, anchoring her at his side, then bent down to kiss her, craving the tastes of honey and Dia.

She broke away. "I can't. We can't."

"Why?" Frustration bit at him.

"The children."

"Are asleep in a distant part of the house. We'll be discreet."

"I don't want to."

"I don't believe it. When I run my hand down your arm like this, you tremble and your breath catches. When I touch your breast like this I can feel your nipple harden."

She sucked in air, and her eyes fluttered shut for a moment before opening to fix him with a blue stare. "My body wants you. I don't."

The bald declaration stopped him. When a woman said no, it meant no, regardless of where and when and how. At least, he'd always followed that rule before.

Principles were a damn nuisance sometimes.

His hand dropped and he stepped away, knowing that if he touched her again, if he smelled that sweet honey, he'd be lost to reason and principle.

"Why, Dia?" he asked quietly. "Not half an hour ago you were shuddering in my arms. I deserve an explanation."

"You do, but I can't give you a good explanation."

"Can't or won't?"

"Both."

He was losing her. Hugh fingered the band at his wrist, the weight of it dragging at his arm. A vise squeezed his chest. "I've never made love to a woman in a car, yet you tempt me beyond all common sense. And I'm not alone in that feeling."

She shook her head, although whether she was agreeing or disagreeing he couldn't tell. Her gaze swept across him, her blue eyes as steamy as hot springs, across his face, down to the band at his wrist. She stilled, her shoulders straightened, and when she met his gaze this time, her eyes were blank, hiding all thought and emotion.

"You want more than I can give, Hugh." Her voice was flat. "You're a permanent kind of person, and I'm a gypsy through and through. I'm bailing out before one of us gets hurt."

"So this celibacy thing is for my benefit?"

She refused to acknowledge his barb. "I know I should move my things out tomorrow, but the children . . . With Mick still out there, I don't want to expose them to him or his friends—"

"No."

She gave him a startled look, at last jerked out of her annoying monologue. "The children? I was hoping, for their safety—"

Irritation overlaid the frustration. "Of course the children can stay. So will you. You're their relative, the one they know. You need to be here."

"Thank you." She laid a tentative hand on his arm. "I'm sorry."

Heat exploded within him, and Hugh cursed the fact that he had so little control over himself. He fingered the cooling metal on his band, the etchings familiar and soothing. "Don't touch me, Dia, unless you're issuing an invitation."

She dropped her hand at once. "Good night, Hugh." Without another word she left the kitchen.

Hugh stood a moment, looking after her, his detective instincts kicking in. He didn't buy her explanation. Oh, it was probably true as far as it went. He did want more than she did. Just what, he wasn't sure yet, but he knew he couldn't let her go out of his life, his soul, so easily.

Dia was running scared. But there was something she wasn't telling him. When she'd first come to him, he'd had the impression she was hiding something, and that suspicion was stronger than ever.

The click of nails on tile drew him up. As if sensing that his master was now alone, Cerberus trotted into the kitchen. Hugh gave him a rub about the neck.

"Cerb, do you like Dia?" Hugh interpreted the single bark as an affirmative. "Well, they say animals have good instincts, and I like her, too. Do you think she needs to stay longer?"

Cerberus gave another bark, and his tail wagged.

"Wouldn't be because she feeds you treats, would it? Is it because those four kids are playing with you?"

Cerberus butted Hugh's thigh with his head.

Hugh scratched the dog behind the ears and motioned with his head toward the office. "C'mon, Cerberus. Let's figure out what she's hiding. If she's going to be running from me, I want to know all the reasons."

Demeter loved the forest at night, when it was cool and only the leaves whispered their secrets. Foolish humans saw monsters in the shadows of her trees, and the idiot beside her chewed nervously on his toothpick. She had chosen the time and place for this meeting, and she had planned well.

"What do you want?" Mick asked her with a touch of belligerence.

"You are a fool," she spat. "Did you think I wouldn't find out?"

He shifted. "Find out what?"

"Your attack on Dia. Now you've driven her into Hugh Pendragon's house." *And into his protection, where I can't easily get to her.*

"I was just having a bit of fun. Getting my own back. I thought—"

"No, you didn't. From now on you think and do only what I say."

"I don't take orders from no woman." Mick's toothpick dropped from his mouth as his lips curled into a sneer. He stepped forward, looming over her and touching a finger to her arm. "Seems to me you made a mistake coming here alone. You're kinda old for me, but it's dark, and you know what they say: even an ugly woman's good in the dark."

Demeter shrugged off his repulsive touch. Just because she was short, people always underestimated her, and Mick had just guaranteed himself a reminder who was in charge. She reached one gloved hand to the sumac vine climbing the tree beside her. Oh, the power tingling through her was a better aphrodisiac than any man's touch.

Mick, the fool, wasn't even aware anything was wrong until the vine curled around his feet and his throat.

As she strode from the park, Demeter smiled. It had been a good night's work, and she would turn this unwanted development to her advantage.

Chapter Fifteen

Dia rolled over, looked at the clock, and then groaned. Morning. If she kept this up, she was going to do serious damage to her night-owl reputation. Worse, she felt as though she'd gotten all of five minutes' sleep last night, and in those precious moments of oblivion, Hugh had invaded her dreams.

His intense green eyes had held her rapt while he stroked her inside and out. Her skin still tingled from the remembered weight of his hand. His low voice crooned and excited with its raw sensuality.

I deserve an explanation. He deserved much more than that.

He deserved the truth.

In her dreams she'd confessed all and he'd still taken her into his arms and kissed her and made love to her with hot, raunchy, frantic need.

In reality, the choices were not so clear.

Moaning again, Dia buried her face in the pillow. She had that birthday party today and a performance tonight; she needed sleep.

Sleep eluded her, though. Never interested in lolling in bed alone, she padded into the bathroom and stared bleakly at the face before her. Her eyes were puffy and her skin looked dull. Too much more of this, and she'd have to change her performance look to hag. It wasn't called beauty sleep for nothing.

The morning ritual of cleansing, toning, and moisturizing revived her and made her feel human again. She threw on a shirt and tights, then went in search of coffee.

She found Ronald in the kitchen. "Morning, Ronald. Where is everybody?"

He handed her a cup of steaming java. "The young people are keeping busy with a computer activity, and Mr. Pendragon is teaching his tae kwon do class."

The decisions could be postponed awhile longer. "I'll bet he's a good teacher."

"Quite so, I gather. These are children with learning problems, and he hopes it will help them gain self-assurance. He enjoys being with them."

"You admire him, don't you?"

"I wouldn't work for him otherwise. Mr. Pendragon gives more than people realize. His work is quite taxing, and he is most generous."

"I imagine working with missing persons cases all the time can get gruesome. Is that why he retired?"

Ronald gave her a curious look. "He didn't tell me his reasons. Can I get you anything? Something to eat?"

So much for pumping Ronald for info. "Just some juice, thanks."

"Pomegranate, mango, or orange?"

"Into the exotic? I'll stick with orange."

As he handed her the glass, he added, "You had a phone call this morning."

"I hope you don't mind that I forwarded my calls to this number."

"Certainly not. He said his name was the Brick, and he refused to leave a number or a message." Ronald sounded faintly disapproving.

Dia didn't enlighten him. "Is there someplace I can make a private call?"

"Mr. Pendragon's office."

"How about a place where I can work out? I need to warm up, work out the kinks."

She also needed to perfect a very special new illusion. If she failed to find what she needed at Demetria's estate, she knew there would be another call, another command performance to do. Then she'd have to choose—refuse and be arrested or go along and give up any hope of leaving behind the life of lies she hated.

Dia didn't like either option, so she was preparing another: an illusion to trap a thief.

"Mr. Pendragon has a workout room," Ronald told her, and gave her directions.

She thanked him; then, with a large glass of orange juice in hand, Dia headed to Hugh's office. She heard the voices down the hall and detoured there first. Claire was hunched over the computer; Lukas sat beside her, his cast resting on another chair.

"Still working on the fast-food project?"

"Yeah," Lukas called over his shoulder, "some dudes in Germany added to the data on our Web page, so we're talking to them about what to do next."

"Where's Cam and Elena?"

"Cam's on the phone persuading his girlfriend that a few weeks apart will only make coming together that much sweeter. Elena and Cerberus are exploring the house."

That dog would keep her out of trouble.

"Have you found our mother?" Claire asked, still hunched over the computer.

"Not yet. She's still on the wilderness trek, and the outfitters refuse to contact them or tell us where they might be. They say it would destroy the experience for her and the others. Are you worried about her, Claire?"

"No, but I miss her." She turned then and fixed Dia with a stare. Her all-black attire made her face pale and her eyes huge. "I want to leave."

"Chicago? You want to come when I start the touring?"

"I want to leave this house. I don't belong here. None of us do. Except you."

"We can't go back to the apartment."

Claire sighed, rolled her eyes, and then pivoted back to the screen. "I want to go home, but I'll manage."

Dia's jaw tightened. Before she could answer, Ronald poked his head in the door. "Ah, Miss Dia, you have a phone call. A Mark Hennessy."

"Thanks, Ronald. I'll get it in the office."

"Very good." He disappeared back down the hall.

Dia gave a frustrated glance at Claire's gothic back, then sighed and went to talk to her friend, Mark.

"Hello, darlin'," Mark drawled. "Who's the cultured English voice that answered the phone?"

"Ronald. The majordomo."

Mark gave a low whistle. "You must be doing well if you can hire staff."

"I'm staying with Hugh Pendragon. Remember Armond's best man?"

"I remember him, darlin'. I saw you meeting him, too. Plenty of sparks there, but I hadn't realized you were living with him." There were currents of amusement and curiosity in Mark's voice.

"It's complicated."

"I expect to hear all about it one day." He respected that her private life was private, and switched subjects. "You know I'm counting on your joining me in Paris this fall. We start rehearsals in one month."

Dia rubbed a hand over her eyes. She had known Mark for many years and owed him a lot. When everyone else had seen her only as a body, he had hired her as his assistant and arranged a segment in his show to feature her magic. This fall he was planning a European tour, a real coup for him and for any magician with him, and he had asked her to go with him, not as his assistant, but as second bill. She was just beginning to make her name; Mark was approaching the ranks of the master magicians. It was the chance of a lifetime.

Her mouth dried. She could not. Mark was a friend, one of the good guys. She wouldn't risk exposing him to Demetria's vengeance; she couldn't ask him to wait until she had things resolved.

"You'd better find someone else, Mark."

There was dead silence for a moment. "Can't do that, darlin'. You're already listed on the billing."

"I'm second; you can always promote an understudy."

"But I don't want to, love. So why don't you tell me what's going on?"

"How's Joy doing?" Dia asked about his wife of a few months.

"Restaurant's going strong and so's she. Keepin' me fed, happy, and comin' home."

"Now, *that's* an accomplishment."

"And you're changin' the subject."

"Yup. Can't fool the magician."

He laughed. "I get the picture." There was a moment's pause, and when he spoke again, the easy humor had been replaced by concern. "You take care of yourself, Dia, love. You know I'm here if you need someone."

"I know, Mark, and I appreciate it."

But she knew she wouldn't call him for help. After hanging up, Dia sat a moment, then dialed the Brick's number.

"What do you hear?" she asked when he answered with his characteristic grunt.

"None of them's surfaced."

Dia gripped the phone. "None? No one's tried to fence those pieces? Are you sure?" The silence on the other end told her she'd offended him. "Sorry,

T. B. Why would someone steal priceless gems and not try to sell them?"

"Because they like to own things." He sounded totally disgusted with the idea. To the Brick, possessions were not important, only information and the means to acquire it. "About your other questions. I've got the guest list. You got a fax?"

Dia gave him the number on Hugh's machine and a moment later the info started coming through.

"Nobody knows where Demetria Cesare has been the past six months or what she was doing. You need anything else?"

"Not—"

He grunted and hung up before she could say another word or thank him.

Dia looked over the list of invited guests. None of them was connected with the gems she'd taken. And Demetria hadn't sold the stolen gems—which meant she still had them. For the first time in a long time, Dia felt a ray of hope. If she could get hold of one of those real gems, find someone on the list who would recognize it, perfect her new illusions, she might have a chance of escaping, her reputation intact.

That was a lot of ifs, though.

The exercise room was a dream, she discovered. A thick mat took up half the floor space, and the rest contained free weights and a weight bench. Nothing fancy, but everything necessary. Despite the baroque-gothic architecture surrounding him, she was finding the Pendragon estate's current occupant had a decidedly practical bent.

Hugh. She'd really bungled last night. She'd hurt him, and she'd never wanted to do that, but there was no way to make it right. Acid etched her stomach. Hugh wanted more, deserved more than a casual friendship, and though something deep and basic urged her to give in, to submit, she could not do it. It wasn't right for her; it wasn't fair to him.

She traced a hand over the weights, almost able to feel the imprint of his strong hands on the metal. She remembered how he had touched her, both firm and gentle, physically and emotionally.

Dia's fingers tightened around the heavy bar, and with a grunt she lifted it. She had things to do, and mooning like a puppy over some beat-up weights wasn't going to get them done. As always, action and magic were her solace and her center. Dia set to work.

Poetry in motion did not describe Dia at work. Hugh stood in the doorway of his weight room and watched her twirl two fiber-optic wands in a blur of light. Frenetic rocking was more her style. There was no sound except her breathing, but he could hear the music from her show playing in his memory, its beat driving the illusion forward and stirring his blood.

She stopped once and redid a move, then continued on, finishing with a jump and a whirl. The wands vanished, and she executed an extravagant bow. A sheen of perspiration coated her, and wisps of hair escaped the knot on her head.

He pulled back before she saw him, then decided he couldn't spend his days avoiding her. He came in, and she spun around, holding a towel to her chest. Obviously she hadn't realized he was there.

"Where'd you hide them?" He nodded to the wands.

"Trade secret. You don't tell people how you do your magic of finding people, do you?"

"Rarely. Don't let me stop your cool-down. We can't avoid each other while you're here." Hugh sat on the weight bench and idly picked up a twenty-five-pounder and began arm curls. When he taught, he warmed up, but didn't get a chance to really push himself. He studied her from the corner of his eye as he worked. There were circles beneath her eyes, not fully concealed by her light makeup, yet even tired, sweaty, and disheveled, she was beautiful. His body tightened, wanting her again.

Hugh picked up the tempo of his lifts, hoping she wouldn't notice the bulge springing lower. Last night, when she had convulsed around him—eyes closed, lips parted, skin flushed—she had reached deep inside him and lit a fire that would not be extinguished. When he'd exploded inside her he'd felt more alive, more powerful than he ever had with a woman. Despite what she, and he, had said last night, it was not over between them.

He could be patient, go slow.

She finished wiping the sweat off her face, then reached her arms over her head and twisted at the waist in the start of her cool-down.

Slow was hell.

"Do you practice every day?" he asked, determined to get through this first awkwardness.

"Mostly. Even if I'm not working on something new, I have to keep limber. Along with exercise and weights." She sat on the mat beside him and bent

over her knees, limbering and flexing, loose strands
of blond hair concealing her face.

"Did you sleep well?" she asked, her voice muf-
fled.

"No," he answered bluntly. "I wanted you there
with me."

So much for slow.

"Oh."

"Did you expect me to be able to turn it off that
fast, Dia?"

"No, sorry. It was a stupid question."

"How did you sleep?" he asked softly.

"Badly." Her answer was softer.

It was enough, an admission that she shared this
crazy longing. He eased off, content for the moment.

His frustration and unrelieved body hadn't been
the only problem last night. The nightmare had returned in full color and sensation. As had the
oddly-familiar voice. *You need both, or you need her.*
This time, though, the voice took on a recognizable
timbre: Harriet Juneau.

All in all, for a night that had started out so spec-
tacularly, it had ended up mighty lousy.

"Hugh." Dia sat up and crossed her legs. Her fingers twisted the hem of her shirt. "I need to talk to
you about something—"

Cam poked his head in. "Aunt Dia, when are we
leaving for the party?"

She glanced at her watch, then made an annoyed
tsk. "Twenty minutes."

"Okay. I'll be ready." He disappeared.

She rose to her feet with a lithe movement. "I'd
better get going."

251

"What did you want to talk about?" Hugh asked.

She shook her head. "It'll have to wait. When there's more time."

Hugh lowered the weight, but didn't get up from the bench. "Dia."

"Yes?" She paused in the doorway and looked at him, her blue eyes wide and instantly aware.

"Last night." His fists clenched. Primitive needs howled. He felt the urge to toss her over his shoulder and claim her, despite the memory of her stinging "no." The desire for tenderness and willingness, the need to protect her and care for her, welled inside him, as strong as the rising wildness that demanded sensual release.

He crossed his arms before the urge grew irresistible. "Last night, when we made love, it meant something to me. I don't do one-night stands, and you know I still want you, but I wanted you to know that you're safe here." Safe from Mick, safe from whatever demons drove her, safe from him.

She nodded. "It's a refuge. A haven. But outside that fence is reality, with all its problems and complications, and that's where I have to live, Hugh."

Hugh sat in the weight room alone, listening to the silence left by her departure. Silence, once so welcome, was now so empty. The room seemed dark as a cave, as though by leaving, Dia had taken the power from the sunbeams that filtered across the floor. That was what knowing her did for him; it put sunshine and heat in his life. She brought—

Love.

Stunned, Hugh rubbed his bare wrist. *Oh, hell.* It was insane, too fast, beyond all logic, but the heat in his chest told him it was true.

He had fallen in love with Dia Trelawny.

*   *   *

Zeus peered into the cedar-scented far-see smoke. By Hades, he wished he could hear what those two had said. Hugh had let her leave without so much as a single kiss.

Soul Seekers were such inept wooers; it took a special woman to see past their reticence. True, those women claimed they made excellent husbands, usually following the admission with a blush, but getting to that blissful state was a chancy business.

Didn't Hugh know that the trick was not to give a woman time to think? Give her passion and excitement. Sweep her off her feet. Zeus chuckled, remembering the time he'd changed himself into a bull and kidnaped Europa. *My, what a ride that was!*

Zeus glanced back at the far-see smoke, but the scene remained the same. Boring. Hugh alone, scowling, his hand rubbing his bare wrist.

"Do something!" Zeus shouted, although Hugh couldn't hear him. Or maybe he did, for his face took on a determined cast and he strode from the room. Zeus followed his path for a moment, disappointed when Hugh turned not toward Dia, but toward his office.

Definitely inept. Too bad Hugh couldn't turn himself into a bull and—

Or could he?

A sudden idea swept through Zeus and took hold. His heart sped up as the old excitement rose, and the notion consumed him. Oh, this was a good one. Just when things were getting boring, that was when he got his best inspiration—got into some of his worst trouble, too, but Zeus dismissed that thought.

He rubbed his ring, changing his image. He gave a little honk, testing out the plan, then studied himself in the hotel room mirror. *Perfect. Perfect.* He threw back his head and laughed. It could work, and whatever the result, it would be fun. If only Hera were here, she'd help him perfect it.

Oh, how he wanted to see her. He wrote Hera's name on a piece of paper, then dropped it into the dying ashes. The thinning smoke rose into a thick plume, and the scene changed. He peered into the smoke.

Hera was leaving an old and isolated house, almost invisible from the profusion of plants that surrounded and covered it. He waved his hand, focusing the smoke for a closer view. Another woman appeared in the doorway.

Demeter. She and Hera embraced with air kisses.

So the game had begun, and he would pray that she would be safe. Zeus let the smoke fade away, not needing to see anymore. He glanced over at the mirror and rubbed his ring, erasing the feathered image until his own face stared back at him.

Hugh considered the latest bits of information he'd gleaned regarding the theft of his wristband, a pit of unease centering in his chest.

Starting with the suggestions from last night's press party, he'd located two other instances when valuable gems had been used during a magician's show. He couldn't discover the magician's name in one case, but in the other, when a diamond necklace belonging to Harry Xavier had been used, he did.

Dia Trelawny.

The report also noted that a respected jeweler had verified the authenticity of the gems, but when Hugh tried to speak with him, he discovered the man had died of pancreatic cancer six months ago. His family, however, had been left with a sizable insurance policy that covered the considerable medical and funeral expenses, as well as leaving a tidy college fund.

Six months ago.

One other fact he'd learned: it wasn't on the list of performances posted on her Website, but next week Dia had scheduled a private performance—for Demetria Cesare.

She had told him she would never work for Demetria.

Hugh stirred uneasily in his chair, an uncomfortable prickle warming his skin. When his phone rang, he picked it up immediately after seeing the caller ID. Harry Xavier was a man he'd long corresponded with about gems, a man he'd called, knowing he could trust in his discretion.

"You were right," Xavier said without preamble. "The diamonds are artificial. I can't believe I didn't notice."

"They're hard to detect, especially if you don't suspect anything." Hugh shifted in the chair again; the room suddenly seemed stifling. He could barely draw a breath, and he struggled to focus on the conversation. "I need a favor. Can you keep this quiet for a while? Don't do anything about it; don't bring in the police. There're some other issues here."

"How long?"

"A month. I hope I can resolve it all for you by then, discreetly and to your satisfaction."

"I can wait."

"Thanks, I owe you one." Quickly he hung up, and his jaw clenched tight.

Apparently Dia had been less than forthcoming when she'd hired him, when she'd moved in with him, when she'd shuddered in his arms.

How much did she know about the thefts? What was she planning now?

Was she the one who had stolen his wristband?

Chapter Sixteen

Dia didn't do birthday parties anymore. She'd had more than her fill of them when she was starting out. They were either a joyful two hours or an endless, excruciating pain in the butt. It all depended on whether the child was awed and delighted by the magic or intent on proving it was all just trickery.

This, however, was a special request. The ten-year-old had dreams of being the first wheelchair-bound magician, and Dia had maintained an e-mail correspondence with her over the past year.

Dia sat beside the girl and twirled a CD on her finger, then held a hand above the spinning disk. Red and green sparks shot from the silver disk to her hand, then back in a rainbow of color. Sparks exploded into glitter, showering the birthday girl with shiny confetti. The girl laughed and clapped her hands, and Dia smiled. One of the reasons she'd brought Cam for his first taste of performing was because she knew this would be a child delighted by the magic, and the audience would be sympathetic to Cam.

"I brought a special assistant this afternoon," Dia announced to them. "A promising young magician. Welcome, Cam."

Cam was nervous, she could tell, but he went through his short routine with surprising polish. Dia watched, pleased by the way he concluded with a flourish and a bow to the applause.

"That was awesome," gushed their diminutive hostess. "Will you teach me that illusion? I'll show you one I've done."

Cam was obviously flattered. "Sure. But we have to keep it a secret, just between us."

While the two youngsters huddled in a corner, exchanging tips, Dia wandered through the small crowd of people, exchanging pleasantries. Performance over, she relaxed, feeling the tension seep from her and enjoying these rare quiet moments as she moved away from the guests and their voices faded.

"I thought you would still be here, Dia."

The low voice froze Dia. Demetria Cesare? Here? Was there no place the woman could not find her?

Frantically she glanced around and realized she had ambled toward the front of the house, while the party was being held in the back. Demetria, holding a green stalk covered with tiny yellow flowers, stepped from behind a shrub.

"What do you want, Demetria?" Dia crossed her arms, her face composed, her nerves screaming.

This moment had come sooner than she'd expected; she wasn't ready yet. She hadn't thought Demetria would approach her before the performances scheduled at her estate.

"You're going to do a little favor for me. Have you noticed a wristband Hugh Pendragon wears?" Demetria didn't wait for the answer. "Bring it to me. You'll replace it with this." She held out a replica of the copper-and-ruby wristband.

Dia shook her head, her throat closing around a shout of denial. Demetria asked the impossible. Stealing from Hugh once was bad enough, but at least then she hadn't known what she was doing. To do it twice, deliberately, while she stayed in his house, would be an unforgivable betrayal.

"Principles, Dia? With your background? You've already stolen one from him, I'm sure you've realized. Take the other and I'll leave you alone."

Dia's eyes narrowed. "What do you mean?"

"Exactly that. You and I will go our separate ways. I'll never bother you again."

"You expect me to believe that?"

"I'll give you all the evidence I hold. I'll even arrange for the other jewels to be discreetly returned so that they can't be connected to you. All I want is the two wristbands."

"Why?"

"That's not your concern. You'll be free, Dia."

Dia had been raised on cons and deceptions and knew better than to trust Demetria's promises. Still, it was hard not to feel a flare of hope.

"Do this, and I won't harm you," added Demetria. "Or your family."

The threat was subtle, but unmistakable.

"After all, we wouldn't want something like this to happen to them." Demetria blew softly on the strange stalk she carried. A cloud of gray pollen floated from the tiny yellow blooms and settled on Dia's hands.

Immediately the burning started, worse than anything she'd felt, worse than the scalding from the coffee. She gasped and frantically rubbed her hands, trying to get it off. What was it? What had Demetria done? It felt like acid burning through her flesh, destroying her hands. She had to get it off her hands.

Demetria's green-gloved hands grabbed Dia before she could run. A mossy glow radiated from the gloves and the burning stopped. Demetria dropped her hands.

Dia stared at the reddened skin, unable to believe what had just happened. Suddenly she knew what she had to do.

"All right." Dia held out her sore hand. "Give me the wristband."

"Bring me the real one tomorrow."

"I can't. He wears it all the time, so I'll have to find a way to make the switch. I'll bring it to you next week. At the performance."

Hugh found Harriet Juneau at the Cubs game.

"Good afternoon, Detective." She didn't seem surprised to see him, motioning to the empty seat beside her. "Join me. I've got a ticket not being used."

Hugh settled down behind home plate with her. "Good view."

"I've been a loyal fan for many years. There are perks."

The opponent's long ball, seemingly destined for a home run, caught an errant breeze and dropped into the right fielder's glove.

"Wrigley Field seems to have developed some strange air currents lately," Hugh observed.

"Really?" Harriet answered. "But I doubt you've found me simply to discuss the vagaries of baseballs and breezes."

"No." She wanted direct, she'd have it. "I want to know more about the 'Soul Seeker' you talked about last night."

"You've heard the term before?"

He figured honesty wouldn't hurt. "In a recent dream, a voice called me that. Last night the voice was yours."

She shrugged, her eyes still on the field. "Only because I was the first person you heard use the term." The opponents dropped another ball, which seemed to have developed a mind of its own. She smiled. "Two outs."

"Am I this Soul Seeker?" Hugh asked her.

She turned her attention from the field then. Her eyes searched his face; then she nodded. "The last in a direct line to the original."

Hugh's eyes narrowed as he remembered the story she'd told. "Hades? You expect me to believe Hades was real? And you know of him? How?"

"I'll tell you what I know, not how I know. You have your reasons for secrecy; I have mine. As for the information—use it or not; it's up to you." A shout drew her attention back to the field. "Now look what happened. They got a man on base."

"Harriet," Hugh ground out, "do the wristbands have any power?"

That startled her. She swung around. "What do you know of the bands?"

"I thought you were answering my questions."

She toyed with the silvery cloud-shaped ring on her finger, and the Cubs' opponents got their third out. Organ music sounded.

"All right, Cub fans," came a voice over the PA system, "time for the seventh-inning stretch and 'Take Me out to the Ball Game.'"

Harriet tugged on his elbow. "Stand up. Sing. Benito Blessing's up first. After he bats, I'll answer all your questions."

Annoyed at the delay, Hugh rose and crossed his arms as the organ began the opening strains and the announcer led the crowd in a rousing rendition of the ballpark classic.

"Sing," Harriet said in a hiss.

"For it's one, two, three strikes, you're out at the old ball game." Hugh joined in the final line. To his ears it sounded as if he were booming out a solo.

Harriet nodded as though pleased, and when Batting Blessing hit a home run, she gave a satisfied clap. Then she turned to him. "The wristbands are very old, a legacy. The gems of Hades. They augment the natural power of the Soul Seeker and keep the dualities balanced. The ruby for grounding, the opal for seeking. If one leaves the possession of the Seeker, an imbalance results. However, even without the wristbands, the Soul Seeker would still be powerful, and there is a substitute for each."

You need both, or you need her. "What is it?"

"Two very basic emotions: the anchor of security and the joy of love."

Security? Like his home? And love? Hugh eyed her, but she sat relaxed in her chair, not at all the picture of a demented woman or a woman who pretended to powers she could not possess. She seemed to believe what she told him.

He'd dismiss her words, except what she said seemed so exactly right, so much the truth. The opal band had been stolen and his talents had started to fade. Their return started when Dia reentered his life, when he started to fall in love.

"So if the Soul Seeker falls in love . . ."

She shook her head, then glanced around and leaned closer. Her voice was so low he barely heard her as she said, "A Soul Seeker falls in love but once, and it is eternal. But this alone is not enough. For the joy to last, he must be loved in return, enough that she will choose him above all else, above that which she holds dearest." She turned away, her attention back on the game. Apparently she'd said all she intended to.

It was enough. Denial rose up in Hugh. Regaining his talent depended upon either getting back his wristband or Dia falling in love with him? Keeping her love meant she had to sacrifice something for him. Even if it were true, and he had serious doubts about Harriet Juneau's veracity at this moment, he could not use Dia that way.

As though he could make her fall in love with him, anyway. Love wasn't something to be commanded or reasoned out.

Hugh rose to go.

Harriet laid a hand on his arm. "Watch out for Demetria Cesare. She doesn't like you. I don't know what she's up to, but Demetria's interested in only one person's benefit: hers." She turned back to the field. "He was safe!"

Hugh slipped away. If regaining his power required Dia to be in love with him or regaining his wristband, he'd better find that wristband soon.

Hugh detoured by the museum and found the special-events coordinator, who tried to cover her surprise at actually seeing him. "Mr. Pendragon, I'm sorry you had to make the trip down. I've been out of town and just got your message. We do keep files of all our special events, and I'd be glad to find what you need."

"I'm interested in a display called Treasures of the Underworld."

"Ah, yes, one of our most popular exhibits. It just finished."

"I know. I donated the gems."

She coughed delicately. "Of course. I hope there were no complaints."

He could imagine her horror if he told her about the theft. "It concerns an unrelated matter. I'd like the name of the magician who performed at the opening."

"I don't have to look at my files; I've used her a number of times. Dia Trelawny."

A lump of ice formed in his chest, and his ears roared as facts clicked into place. The way she'd touched his band last night. Her abrupt shut-down. Benito Blessing's crude description of the gorgeous magician.

264

She'd stolen it, and she knew it—knew it was his. Probably she hadn't known at the time, but she did now. And she hadn't said a word.

His words and motions grew slow and deliberate as he disconnected mind from body and heart. This was a case; he was a detective. *Think only of that.* Otherwise, he'd have to acknowledge the pain and that he could not do.

"Whose idea was it to use a magician for the patrons' party?" He could barely form the words.

"Mine," the coordinator answered with pride. "I'd used her before when I was at another position and she was very good. Very popular."

"I'm sure she was if you used her more than once. How did you get so lucky as to find her in the first place?"

"One of our patrons suggested her."

"Oh, who?"

"Demetria Cesare."

Hugh's next stop was the city library. He could search the Net and newspaper databases from his equipment at home, but he wasn't ready to face Dia yet.

He looked first at her past performing schedule. It took some digging and cross-referencing the data from her Web site and the newspapers, but by searching for gems he located one other time—besides his wristband and the one he'd already discovered from his talk with Harry Xavier—when she could have made a switch.

And at each event Demetria Cesare was listed as a patron.

On a whim he looked up Harriet Juneau and her companion Zeke Jupiter. What little data he found was innocuous. Pillars of the community, they were, with a definite knack for making money. Although there'd been rumors about Peacock Cosmetics' stability a short time back, when it seemed Harriet Juneau had vanished, the rumors disappeared when she returned a short time later.

He was surprised to see Zeke's name come up in a Food TV listing, however, and when he checked it out, he discovered the man had been lighting director for Armond's wife's wine video series. *Curious.* Dia had also mentioned meeting him before, something in connection with Mark and his wife Joy.

Talk about a small world. The man did appear to crop up in the most unusual places. Hugh, however, was skeptical of coincidence.

He relinquished the computer, then went outside to the heat and the sunshine. Chicago bustled about him, the city alive and vibrant with people enjoying the summer. He sat on the sun-warmed concrete steps and pulled out his cell phone. His luck held and he caught his friend, FBI agent Armond Marceaux, at his desk.

After a few moments of greeting and catching up, he asked, "Armond, what do you know about Zeke Jupiter and Harriet Juneau?"

"Are you asking professionally or personally?"

"Personally." Hugh knew it was useless to ask about anything Armond deemed confidential. "What's your opinion of them?"

Armond hesitated a moment. "This is just between you and me?"

"Yes."

"There's something strange about them. I can't pin it down, but they seem to know things they should have no way of knowing, be places they shouldn't be."

"Do you know where they came from? I find a lot of current info, nothing biographical."

"Zeke once told me he was from Greece."

Greece? Olympus? No, it was too fantastic even to consider.

It was Hugh's turn to hesitate and consider his next question. Armond had a special talent. He'd never really talked about it, just as Hugh never talked much about his psychic abilities, but the agent had an unerring instinct for evil, for focusing on the guilty. "Have you ever felt . . . Do you think he's up to no good, Armond?"

"He's a pesky troublemaker; my friend Mark Hennessy calls him a gadfly. But he saved Callie's life and my life once and I think he also did the same for Mark. I owe him one, so Zeke and I have an agreement: I won't pry further as long as he doesn't meddle in my life. So far it's worked. But there's no evil in him or Harriet, Hugh, no guilt, if that's what you want to know."

"Thanks, I appreciate it. By the way, have you ever met a woman named Demetria Cesare?"

"No."

"Have you heard about her?"

"Yes."

The clipped answer told Hugh that what Armond knew was FBI business. Hugh gripped the phone, his stomach tangling and his mind racing. "Is it an ongoing investigation?"

"Yes."

Which meant Armond wasn't free to tell him much.

"If you know anything, *mon ami*," Armond warned, "don't keep it to yourself. Let the law handle it."

"Don't I always?"

"No."

"Let me check a few things out first. Can you at least tell me one thing? Is it related to stolen gems?"

There was silence; then Armond apparently decided some information was safe to share. "Yes, partly. We broke up a ring last year, but some of the pieces never surfaced and we suspect Demetria Cesare has them. We've never been able to find any evidence on her. She came to our attention, though, because people who cross her tend to fall prey to strange maladies. Her plant research generates some unusual alkaloids and toxins. Be careful with her."

"I will."

After farewells Hugh flipped the phone shut. For a while he didn't move, thinking. Zeke Jupiter— pesky gadfly, but no criminal. So it was Demetria Cesare he needed to focus on. Even though Armond had been involved in breaking up a gem-smuggling ring last year, he deliberately hadn't told the agent about Dia and his suspicions. Armond would have had to make it an FBI matter then, and that Hugh did not want.

He would not draw the law's attention to Dia.

Not until he talked to her first. The urge to protect her, to keep her safe, welled up inside him. He had told her once that the past didn't matter, and he meant that. Though he hated her deceptions, his consolation was that her thievery had occurred before they had ever met. If she had done it after they had made love . . .

His gut clenching, he shoved the cell phone into his pocket.

It was time for a showdown with Miss Trelawny.

Dia stood at the door leading to Hugh's bedroom. She was alone in the house. Ronald and the kids were at the movies; Hugh was out doing unknown errands.

He hadn't worn the wristband this morning, she'd noticed, so she guessed it was in his bedroom.

This was her chance.

Her moment of choice.

Dia pushed back her sleeve and pulled the fake band off her wrist. She ran it through her fingers, testing the weight of it, seeing the lifeless ruby. The familiar motions of her hands, the loosening of her arm muscles, should have released the tight band across her chest, but it only squeezed harder until she could barely breathe.

One small switch, one last con, and she'd be free. It was a siren's call, so tempting. She'd wanted it for so long—to be free of the past.

Except that there was no way she believed Demetria would simply cut her loose. "Never try to con a con," she whispered aloud, still turning the fake band in her hands.

With this, she held evidence that Demetria was involved in the thefts. For the first time the woman had become directly involved. The band wouldn't hold any fingerprints—Demetria had been wearing those green gloves—but she had to have had it made somewhere. *When working out an illusion, always trace it back to the source. What do you want to show? What do you need to do to get it done?*

The answers would take time. And if she didn't make the switch? Dia clenched her reddened hands, the feeling only now beginning to come back. Without her hands, her magic was impossible. The children were vulnerable, too, and who knew where her sister was, and whether she could be reached by Demetria's poisons?

Dia's hands stilled, and she opened the door. Her body tensed, as taut as the guide wire for the arrow illusion. She took a deep breath and another, trying to force herself to take that first step inside.

"Woof! Woof! Woof!" Barking furiously, Cerberus came scrambling around the corner and down the hall.

She was alone in the house—except for one exuberant dog.

His nails battered against the hardwood floor as he careened forward, still barking. His eyes seemed to glow with hellfire, and he looked huge, especially his head. It seemed as though there were three of him coming at her.

Dia backed up, stumbling into Hugh's room. A frenetic Cerberus followed her. She backed up a farther and knocked into the stand beside Hugh's bed. A metallic rattle drew her attention down.

The ruby-and-copper wristband.

Cerberus skidded to a halt right at her feet and sat back on his haunches. Blessedly he grew quiet. Nor did he jump on her. He seemed to be awaiting her next move.

She picked up the real band.

Cerberus whined.

When it was held next to the fake, even someone unversed in gemology could see the difference between the two bands. It was in the ruby. The fake gem had none of the depth, none of the character, none of the soul of the real ruby. No red fire gleamed from its depths.

The copper felt cold on the fake, while she could almost feel Hugh's body heat lingering on the metal of the real band. The air-conditioning blew across her in a sudden gust, sending a shudder down her spine. It carried the faint scent of Hugh's aftershave, a clean, masculine scent.

Cerberus whined again and gave a tiny whimper. *Don't do it*, he seemed to say.

This band was important in ways she couldn't understand, she realized. Hugh wore it all the time, and Demetria wanted it.

That was something she hadn't considered. Why did Demetria want it?

To take it while she was under Hugh's protection, while she was accepting his hospitality, and then give it to Demetria would be an unforgivable betrayal. Dia's hands started to shake.

The band is a family legacy. The flash of memory seared through her, lodging in her heart. The aching band around her chest loosened as she gulped in air.

She could not betray Hugh.

She had to tell him everything, from the very beginning.

Hugh was an honorable man, more honorable than she. He would let the children stay here to keep them safe, and he would find Liza. Dia closed her eyes, almost able to hear the clang of bars shutting her in. The flesh on her palms burned.

She would not betray him.

Her fingers, normally so agile, seemed cold and stiff and awkward as they gripped the two bands. She tried to return the fake to her wrist but her hands seemed clumsy and nerveless.

Cerberus gave a loud whine, startling her.

Dia dropped the fake band.

With a joyful woof, Cerberus picked it up in his mouth and trotted off.

"No, Cerberus, bring that back." With the real band still in hand, Dia chased after him.

Cerberus looked back over his shoulder, saw her coming, and speeded up. Dia followed, trying to catch up, but the darn dog stayed several steps ahead of her as he wove through the halls.

"Cerberus!" Dia shouted. "Come back here. That is not a sparkly for you."

Cerberus didn't listen.

"I'll give you another pair of earrings."

For a moment Cerberus slowed, as though considering, and Dia almost caught up with him. Then his ears perked up, and he took off at a run.

Dia raced after him. He tore around the corner and gave an excited bark. Dia skidded in pursuit, only to find herself back in Hugh's bedroom.

"Cerberus, you bad dog, give me—"

Her voice died.

Cerberus had dropped the fake band—right at Hugh Pendragon's feet.

"What do you have here, Cerb?" Hugh asked with a laugh, scratching the dog behind the ears.

He reached down and picked up the fake band.

And grew utterly still. He looked up from the band he held and immediately his eyes fastened on the real one she still gripped.

Then his gaze shifted to her.

In his eyes she saw only the cold of a deep mountain cave. No warmth. No light. No joy.

Dia's throat closed around her voice. Inside her a light was extinguished. Hope, once the sole gift in her Pandora's box of troubles, faded, and her body ached with the loss.

He knew.

Everything.

Hugh's fingers closed around the deceptive band. A buzzing sounded in his ears and he gasped for air. The room faded behind a spontaneous vision of his nightmare. Lost souls, the cave, the silver wristband entwined around Dia's hands. Visions swirled around him in a frenzy of smoke and reflected off silver mirrors.

Dia backed up, not looking at him. "I'm sorry. It's not what it seems."

Excuses? More deceptions? Not content with one, was she about to steal his second band? A lick of anger burned through the chaos.

"Stop," he ground out.

She halted, her eyes downcast.

Wordlessly he held out his hand. With the air of one condemned she drew in a long breath, then handed him the band she held. He held the bands in one hand, then took her hand with his other. She lifted her lids and met his eyes with a steady blue gaze.

Two bands. One real, one fake.

And he knew the truth. Anger became an inferno of betrayal. Darkness crashed around him, weighting him, making breathing a chore. His hand tightened around hers and she flinched at the pressure.

"You took the opal."

To her credit, she didn't try to hedge. "Yes."

"And you were after the second?"

"No—"

"Do you still have the silver and opal?"

"No. Hugh, let me explain—"

"No," he spat, flinging away her hand. "Don't. Not now. Maybe not ever."

"Are you going to call the police?"

"No. I don't know."

"I can be gone—"

"No," he interrupted again. "You'll stay here."

And that was the worst of all. Despite her lies and her deceptions, despite her theft and her betrayal, he still could not let her go. Despite everything, he still wanted to protect and shield her.

Hugh's gaze raked across her. Her face and hair were still done up from her performance this afternoon, although not as elaborately as when she appeared onstage. She had on her work clothes, black pants and a black sleeveless shirt, again not as glittery as the night required. Whatever she wore, she was sexy and sultry. Whatever she did, she still smelled like honey and would still taste as sweet.

Desire roared in on the heels of anger.

It wasn't pretty; it wasn't refined. It was raw and needy and demanding.

Hugh's face tightened, and he crowded closer to her. Dia backed up until her legs bumped against his bed. He moved still closer, until their bodies brushed. The tips of her breasts grazed his chest as she breathed. Her long legs were sandwiched between his, and his sex strained to touch her.

He reached up and tangled his fingers in her hair. The only sound was of the air rushing in and out of her lungs. Her blue eyes held steady on his.

"I said I'd wait for an invitation to touch you again. Well, seeing you in my bedroom is all the invitation I need right now."

A low moan came from her, although from desire or despair he couldn't tell and didn't care. His fingers cradled her face, holding her still as his head bent to hers, while his other arm came about her and pushed her hips flat against his. He rubbed against her, letting her feel his arousal.

This is wrong, some civilized portion of his brain insisted, but Hugh wasn't listening to reason. She wasn't saying no. She wasn't stopping him.

He kissed her, deep and hard, with lips and tongue and teeth.

He'd intended it to be a punishing kiss, but he could no more hurt her than he could hurt one of the kids under his protection. Instead the sensual assault coaxed and urged.

Sweet honey and spicy Dia mixed together. She didn't resist. She didn't protest.

She didn't participate.

Her body was tense, and Hugh felt her resisting her own needs. But her tiny shifts and gasps betrayed her growing passion. Slowly he rose from the kiss to look at her.

"You want me to pay with my body?" Her voice was ragged. Her eyes refused to meet his.

"Yes." Anger and desire still raged, demanding their due.

All motion ceased. In her. In him. In the very air.

"No," she whispered, barely audible. She looked at him then, and a single tear rolled down her cheek. "I'm sorry for what happened and for what I did, but I will not prostitute myself."

She pulled from his arms, and he let her go. A second tear followed the first.

He'd never seen her cry before, and apparently she didn't like it, because she erased the tears with an angry swipe as she stalked from the room.

Damn his temper. It wasn't roused often, but when it erupted, it was fierce. Not that that was any excuse. Now all that was left was a bitter regret and a cold lump in his gut.

Chapter Seventeen

Tears were a useless commodity, and crying was like banging your head against the wall: it left raging headache when you stopped.

Dia splashed water on her face, rinsing away the salt, then stared at herself in the bathroom mirror.

She'd been propositioned before. She'd been disappointed before. She'd screwed up royally before. The answer wasn't tears. Always she just picked herself up, figured out the situation, and went on as best she could.

So why was she unable to see or think of anything but the look on Hugh's face when he'd held that fake wristband?

If only she'd talked to him. If only she hadn't used Cam's interruption in the weight room as an excuse to delay.

"If onlys" were as useless as tears.

She couldn't think what to do next. Common sense had departed, leaving behind a whirlwind of hurt. Her body ached with exhaustion, as though she'd performed three shows back-to-back. Inside she felt more hollow and alone than she had ever been in a life spent on her own. Her heart—

Dia dried vigorously with the towel. *Don't think about your heart. Don't think about what might have been and what is lost. Don't think about the years to come without Hugh.*

She was a gypsy and a magician. No ties. Her life was her magic and her career. She had a performance tonight.

For the first time, however, thoughts of her magic failed to absorb her.

Hugh Pendragon had claimed a permanent place in her heart.

The kitchen was awash with kids and Ronald when Dia descended from her useless tear-fest for her preshow juice. The children chattered; Ronald bustled. "How was the movie?" she asked, pouring a tumbler of orange juice.

Their comments and plot summaries swirled about her. The sheer normalcy and energy of the teens made her feel better, while the serenity of the house worked its own brand of magic.

Lukas opened the refrigerator. "Ronald, you said there was some of that beef stuff we had last night left."

"In the blue bowl. I'll heat it for you."

"Nah."

"No thank you," corrected Dia.

"No, thank you. I'll eat it cold."

Claire spread the *Tribune* out on the counter and began to read. Lukas pulled a chair beside her and read over her shoulder as he spooned cold beef Wellington into his mouth.

Ronald set out a plate of cheese and crackers and a bowl of strawberries, then pushed them closer to the kids for a snack. He tilted his head as he wiped his hands on a towel. "Are you all right, Miss Dia?" he asked quietly, too low for the children to hear. "You look—"

"You're not supposed to comment on a woman's looks when she doesn't have makeup on," Dia tried to say lightly.

Ronald flushed. "I'm sorry, miss; I didn't mean—"

Dia laid a hand on his arm. Ronald was a dear, and she wouldn't cause him even a moment's distress. "I'm sorry, I was just teasing you. Don't worry. I'm just a little tired."

"You have been quite busy."

"After tonight's performance I have a couple of days off. I'll get my beauty sleep till noon and it'll be a new woman who emerges."

"Of course, miss." Ronald sounded doubtful that sleep would cure her problems, and Dia silently agreed with him.

"Oooh, this is gross." Claire pointed to the newspaper.

"Hey, Aunt Dia," called Lukas. "That guy who attacked you got his."

"What do you mean?"

"Look at this." He slid the newspaper where she could read it.

279

It took a moment for Dia to find the article. Mick Masterson had been found alive but unconscious in the Forest Preserve and was currently at Cook County Hospital. He hadn't been attacked, though, at least not in the conventional sense.

He'd been hospitalized with poison ivy.

It was no ordinary case, however. "I've never seen anything like this," the doctor was quoted as saying. Apparently Mick had the rash inside and out: skin, lungs, mouth, elsewhere. He was one miserable, itching puppy. He'd been hospitalized so he could be given intravenous steroids and watched for shock and breathing problems. The doctor advised the Park Commission to use herbicide to eradicate the troublesome weed.

Dia slid the newspaper back to Lukas and shivered.

A virulent plant? She detected Demetria's fine hand in all this.

She glanced at the four children. They were so young, with their whole lives ahead of them. A fierce well of protectiveness she didn't know she had arose inside her.

Nothing would harm them. The children came first. And if that meant putting away her own hurts and facing Hugh, making him listen, and enlisting his help, then that was what she would do.

"Ronald, where's Hugh?"

"In his gem room."

"Where's that?"

"I'm sorry, no one's allowed to enter except Mr. Pendragon. You'll have to wait until he emerges."

No, she wouldn't make the mistake of waiting again. If Ronald wouldn't lead her to Hugh, then she'd find him herself.

The Seeker

*   *   *

Hugh tilted the bright, narrow beam of the lamp onto the brooch and studied the jewelry's inlaid emerald design. His father had purchased this collection right before his death and had been excited about its arrival. Hugh had never wanted to look at it while grief was fresh.

He was glad he had taken the time at last. The collection was ancient, although not as old as the wristbands. The pieces themselves were beautiful in their simplicity: a brooch for a toga, a serpentine rope for the upper arm, a pair of looped earrings. All were gold with chips of gems inset in the metal. They were not the polished and elaborate workings of more recent jewelry, but when he held them he could feel their deep connection to the earth and to the continuity of life.

No wonder his father had been excited about the acquisition. At the end of his life, gems had been his only passion.

His only passion. Hugh let the brooch fall to the table.

His father had loved once and had lost that love to death. Yet Hugh had never heard his father say he would have forgone those few years of joy to save himself the remaining years of sorrow.

"And where will your passion be?" Hugh asked himself. The soft fabrics and shadows beyond his single light absorbed the quiet question in this most private of sanctuaries. He held the brooch away from the light, into the darkness, where the gold seemed to take on its own sheen, a single bright spot in a room filled with gems. As he watched, though, the glow seemed to fade. Slowly he brought it back to the light, where it gleamed with a rich shine.

He laid the brooch down in the small circle of light on the table. Gems from beneath the earth; light from the heavens above. Balance.

Just as Dia was his sun. It was a crude analogy, but it worked.

Could he give up on love, on her?

Hugh rubbed the back of his neck. He felt too battered still, too betrayed and unsettled and hurt to take another chance right now. He needed to retreat and bind his heart wounds. Find solitude and peace.

A quiet buzz interrupted him. The intercom. The room's walls were so thick that he wouldn't hear if Ronald knocked, so they'd installed the intercom system.

"You have a phone call," Ronald announced.

"Take a message."

"It's Agent Marceaux, sir," Ronald continued before Hugh could break the connection. "He said it was quite urgent. Oh, and Miss Dia is looking for you."

Hugh broke the connection. He could not face Dia right now, not while the sight of her holding his ruby armband was still so fresh and raw. Instead he picked up the phone on the table. He usually turned the ringer off so he wouldn't be disturbed, but he kept the phone here in order to take care of business without leaving the room.

Armond didn't waste time on preliminaries. "I need your help. A missing child."

"I don't know if I can. There were reasons for my retirement, reasons that still exist."

"I'll take whatever hints I can get. What if you came to New Orleans? Surrounded yourself with the child's things? We haven't got much time on this; I feel it in my gut. The girl is only twelve, Hugh."

The same age as Claire and Elena.

"I'll be there as soon as I can." And maybe, when he got back, he'd be able to face Dia with less anger and pain.

When he left the room, however, he found Dia waiting for him, her hands running nervously up and down her fiber-optic wand. He started down the hall.

"Did you hear me knocking?" she asked.

"The walls are too thick." He kept walking.

"We need to talk, Hugh."

"Not now."

"We have to talk. I can't let you make the same mistake I did."

"Not now!"

There was a sharp crack, and a platinum-bright flare exploded in front of him. "What the hell?" He spun around, blinking the spots from his vision, and saw Dia holding out her fiber-optic wand.

"Zeke's been showing me some new uses for his heatless fireworks."

She hurried to his side and stood in front of him, words tumbling from her. "I stole the gems, yes, but I didn't know I was doing it; not until the last one, yours, when I recognized the difference, but it was too late, the switch was done, and I didn't know what to do about it because it was really De-metria who was stealing them, only she was setting me up and she had proof that I stole them, especially because I did—make the switch, I mean—but I didn't know the gem was yours until last night because of your damned reclusive nature, so the museum listed it as being from an anonymous donor, and I wanted to tell you in the weight room, only Cam came in, and then Demetria met me at the party and told me to switch the bands or she'd hurt my family, and she threw some kind of weird acid stuff on my hands, so I knew she wasn't kidding, but I couldn't do it, I couldn't switch them even after all that, and I am so, so sorry that I didn't tell you."

Hugh stared at her in astonishment as she finally paused for breath. Her words jumbled in his mind. She hadn't known about the thefts? Demetria was behind it all? Threats?

"She threw acid on your hands?" Bile rose in his throat at the thought.

"Well, it wasn't acid, it was pollen, but it hurt just as much." She showed him her palms and he shoved his hands into his pockets before he was tempted to caress away those scalded streaks of red.

"Can you do your show?"

"Yes, but Hugh, that's not my concern right now. I need your help."

He shook his head, unwilling to risk being drawn back to her. "We'll talk about it when I get back from New Orleans." He started to walk away.

That flare stopped him again. Hugh rubbed his eyes. "Dia, you've got to stop that. I just got rid of the spots from the last one."

She stalked closer to him. "I need your help, Hugh. I will not let her hurt my children."

Hugh stopped rubbing his eyes to stare at her around the white and pink dots. "What did you say?"

"I won't let her hurt the children. She's threatened that if I don't bring her the band, she'll do something to them and my sister."

No, that wasn't what she'd said. She'd said, "I won't let her hurt my children." *My children.*

"I've got an idea"— she'd continued.

"Dia," he interrupted. "Start from the beginning. Tell me what led up to yesterday. Tell me everything."

He leaned one shoulder against the wall and listened carefully. Fortunately she was a little more coherent—and slower—this time. The gist of it was that she'd stolen the gems, but she was innocent. Demetria was blackmailing her and threatening her and her family if she didn't come back to work for her, starting with that private party next week. And the current price of Demetria's silence was his ruby wristband.

"You've put her off until the performance at her home?" he asked.

"I think so."

"You've got a performance tonight, another three days off, a week on the road, then her party—that gives us ten days. Dia, what you should do is go to the police. My friend Armond is suspicious of Demetria already."

"FBI?" She shook her head. "No. No law. There's got to be another way."

"Work with them. Cooperate. I know he'll work a deal. They'll give you immunity or a suspended sentence. It's not you they'll want; it's Demetria."

285

"No, I don't trust cops." She kept shaking her head.

"Let me talk to him, then."

"No!" She was trembling, looking at her twisting hands instead of him. "I don't trust justice. I saw my mom get slapped in jail while rapists and murderers with good lawyers went free."

"Dia—"

"One night, when I was about ten, a disgruntled client beat up my mother, sent her to the hospital. The police weren't interested in looking for the guy who did it; he had money. Instead they gave my mother a citation for running a business out of her home. Hugh, I know my mother stole from people and deceived them, but she didn't deserve to be hurt like that."

Hugh's throat closed as he listened to her litany. He hadn't even imagined half of what Dia's life had been growing up, he realized.

She looked at him then, her blue eyes clear and hard. "That wasn't the worst of that night. One of the detectives came to our house while Adele was in the hospital."

Hugh's gut twisted. *Oh, God, no.* She was only ten at the time.

"The detective said that Liza and I would be taken from our unfit mother, that we'd be split up. Sent to foster care. We'd never live together again. Then he closed his notebook, and he looked at Liza. She was young, sixteen, but she was beautiful even then. He said he'd tear up his report, forget all about us. For a price." Dia shook her head, her voice cracking. "I was lucky; the pig of a man

286

wasn't interested in kids. Liza paid the price for us, though, and we stayed together."

Hugh took her icy hands in his. His thumbs rubbed against her, trying to warm her. "Not all cops are like that. Armond's not like that."

"No," she said flatly.

"All right." He dropped the subject, but he knew that eventually—soon—he'd have to let Armond in.

Dia took a deep breath, as if cleansing her lungs. "One thing I haven't been able to figure out is how she made the switch without my knowing it."

"Why don't we run through the routine together? Maybe I can see something you missed. Do you have time before your performance?"

"I'll make time."

Five minutes later they were in the weight room, using the mats as the stage. Dia demonstrated her transmutation illusion with the two ruby bands and a bouquet of wildflowers.

"I put the gem in this box, and pull out the flowers from here," she explained, then gave Hugh a grin, feeling more hopeful than she had in a long time. "You do realize you are very privileged to learn this. Magicians never tell their secrets to anyone not of the brotherhood."

"I shall guard the knowledge with my life," he answered easily. "What happens next?"

Dia finished running through the illusion. "I thought maybe the fake was hidden here, placed so I'd grab it instead of the real one, but I haven't gotten the logistics worked out."

"Was Masterson working with you?"

"Once, but not every time. Maybe she called on someone different."

"Too risky. Too many people to keep a secret. Demetria was there every time?"

"Yes. I thought she was being a mentor."

"She was, but not the kind you expected." Hugh frowned, studying the box. "And the jeweler came on and authenticated the gem each time, but you think he was paid to authenticate the fake?"

"I'm sure of it. Demetria has his signed confession implicating me."

"Run through it again, starting at the very beginning. I want to see something."

Dia picked up the real wristband.

"No, don't start with the illusion. Start at the very beginning, when you're introduced, and run through it all to the last moment when the jewel is locked away. I'll play the various other roles."

They ran through the illusion again, this time with Hugh as announcer, assistant, and jeweler. She and Hugh worked together as though they had been partnering for years, although they were both careful that their touches remained brief and impersonal. Neither was ready for the maelstrom of desire. At last Dia finished and took her bow as the "jeweler" walked offstage.

"Did you see what you were looking for?" she asked.

"I think so. Get the wristband, will you?"

Dia picked it up from the weight bench they were using as a stand-in for the sealed security case, then frowned. It felt wrong. She held it up so the last of the sun's rays fell on the bloodred gem. The ruby was dull. She turned to him. "You switched it!"

He smiled and held up the real band. "That I did."

"How did you . . . ?" Suddenly it dawned on her. "I don't believe it. Misdirection, the stock in trade of every magician. I was so busy thinking I'd switched it that I didn't realize I'd had the real gem all along. The *jeweler* switched them when he authenticated."

Hugh nodded. "It didn't take any major sleight of hand. You command a stage, Dia, and were still doing the final bows, so most eyes were on you. Besides, who would suspect a respected jeweler? People see what they expect to see."

Dia frowned. "But the last time, I realized it had been switched. That's why I confronted Demetria. So how did I know, if I never held the fake?"

"That was a stupid thing to do, by the way, confronting Demetria. No telling what she might have done." Hugh perched on one end of the weight bench.

"I've never listened to caution," she answered absently, replaying the performance in her mind. She snapped her fingers. "I remember. The jeweler started coughing before he could put the band in the case, and the museum events coordinator took the gem from him. She gave it to me to put in. I remember the jeweler started to protest, but it was over and done and the case sealed in a moment. It wasn't until later that it sank in what I'd held."

Dia rubbed her face, unable to believe that in all these months she hadn't seen how the trick was accomplished. It had taken Hugh to open her eyes.

As he'd opened her eyes to a lot of things.

Hugh stilled, as if sensing her shift in mood. The air around them seemed heavy and thick, magnifying each breath in the silence. Dia felt a bead of sweat trickle down her back.

Hugh handed her the wristbands. "Take care of these while I'm gone. Think about what we can do to trap her, and we'll talk about it when I get back."

Without waiting for her answer, he strode out of the room.

Dia rubbed a thumb over the warm ruby in the band, gazing at the empty doorway. He'd given her the band. He trusted her with it, trusted her not to betray him.

Carefully, she tucked the bands into her pocket.

It wasn't often a person got a second chance.

There was nothing more frustrating than having a plan, then discovering that one of the principals involved refused to cooperate and left town for two days.

Zeus sat on a lounge chair at the edge of the Lake Michigan. Around him, children shouted, rode waves on Boogie boards, and tossed sand. Even though the day was waning, the sun overhead was hot, bringing out sweat and making him squint, but the water was chilly and his toes were getting numb. Scowling, he tossed mini lightning bolts to warm the water by his feet. On days like this, he missed the hot springs of d-Alphus.

The warmth lasted only seconds, until the waves brought in fresh cold. Zeus aimed another lightning bolt. Even the water wasn't cooperating.

"You might take your feet out of the water if you don't like the cold."

Zeus turned to see Hera at his shoulder. "Zapping is more fun."

Hera took the folding chair slung over her shoulder, snapped it open, and then sat down beside him. "Do you remember the hot springs of d-Alphus? You used to like it when I made waves like this."

"Those waves were warm. And you weren't wearing a bathing suit."

"I think the mothers here might protest if we turned this into a nude beach."

"Pity." Zeus gave her an appreciative leer. She looked good in a bathing suit, but she looked better out of one. He leaned forward and warmed up the water again. The tiny fold of flesh over the edge of his suit reminded him that perhaps it was best that this beach required covers, and that perhaps he needed some time at the spa. "You missed Dia's performance day before last."

"I'll see her when you leave. I've got some body glitter I think she'll like." Hera rubbed her ring and the breeze died, calming the winds and keeping the warm water circling his feet.

"Thank you, my love."

"Anytime."

"We work well together, don't you think?"

"Quite well, although the current project seems to have stalled."

"Because Hugh left town for two days. But I have a plan."

"You?"

"Of course. I just have to work out a few of the details."

"Of course. What's this great plan?"

Zeus warmed the water a touch more. Not hot springs, but with the baking sun it was an acceptable substitute.

"I'll tell you when you tell me what you learned at Demeter's. Although don't you think the kissing was a little too much?"

"What? How did you know?"

"I'm Zeus, remember? The king of the gods; the all-knowing." A small bit of his golden splendor shone from the shield he kept over it.

Hera gave a snort of irritation. "You were spying on me, weren't you? Using the far-see smoke."

"Guilty as charged." He wasn't the least worried about her anger. He liked Hera when she got angry. She usually did something delightfully entertaining. Like those gadflies . . .

The wind blasted him with cold water and rocked his chair.

"Hades, that's freezing!" Zeus sprang up before he landed in the water. "Naughty, my love."

Hera glanced around at the curious looks coming their way. "Maybe we should talk about this elsewhere."

"I prefer here."

"Why?"

He waved a hand. "Stony beach. No plants." Zeus righted his chair and plunked back down beside her seat. He picked up a plastic bottle stuck in the sand, and then leaned forward. "And I need suntan lotion on my back."

For a moment he thought she might refuse, but she took the bottle and squeezed the white lotion into her hand. She started spreading it on his back.

Ah, that feels good. Now, that was a cool he didn't mind. Her hands were smooth, for she took care to use her Peacock Cosmetics hand lotion, and the peacock blue nails lightly scratched his back.

"Don't spy on me if you don't want to see things that annoy you," she said with deceptive sweetness. Hera was never sweet.

"I was worried about you."

Hera's fingers tightened, pressing her nails into him.

"Careful, my love. They frown at drawing blood on the beach."

"Sorry." Her grip lightened. "You were worried?"

"Of course." He glanced over his shoulder. "Don't you ever worry about me?"

She didn't answer at first, her hands moving slowly over his back, working in the lotion. "All the time."

Now, that was a distinct pleasure to learn. "What did you learn?"

"Not much. Demeter is as closemouthed and crafty as ever. I did find out that Dia is performing at a party she's giving next week, and she asked us to attend. It's quite a coveted invitation, I gather."

"That opinion coming from Demeter, I assume."

She laughed, the low sound stirring something inside him and making him doubly glad that this wasn't a nude beach. "She seems quite proud that Dia is performing, says she's going far. She even had a newspaper clipping with a picture of Dia working at a charity function."

"And how does Hugh Pendragon fit in? You know her plans will include him somehow. She won't be able to resist trying to finally win over the Soul Seeker."

Hera's hands stilled as she sucked in a breath. "That's it."

When she didn't say anything more, Zeus wiggled his back, reminding her about the lotion. Her hands dropped, and Zeus guessed the suntan lotion rub was over.

"That's what, my love?" he asked.

"The gems of Hades."

It was Zeus's turn to suck in a breath. "The wristband that Hugh wears."

"He owns Hades' talisman, the gems."

"Demeter has always coveted the powers they represent."

"And she hates Hades."

"What makes you think she's going after the gems?"

"The newspaper clipping. Dia was holding up a diamond necklace. She'd used it as a dramatic part of something she called a transmutation illusion. Valuable gems disappear, only to reappear. It's a perfect way to steal the gems."

The two gods fell silent. Hera reached down and rinsed her hands in the water. "Demeter has to be stopped."

Zeus captured her damp hands in his. It was a moment for honesty between them. "Hera, I don't want you taking any risks with her. You've come back into my life, and I don't think I could survive losing you again. We've wasted too many years. This is my project. I can end it—"

"This is *our* project," she corrected. "And we must see it to the finish. This is not just about Dia and Hugh; it's about the gods, and we are still king and queen. Besides, a little danger just adds to the excitement, don't you think?" She gave him a lop-sided grin that never failed to add extra beats to his heart rate.

"Passion and excitement?"

"Passion and excitement," she agreed. "Trust that I have no desire to be separated from you again."

Zeus searched her face for the truth and found a revealing fire in her eyes. "Do you believe me when I say I've reformed?"

It was her turn to search for the truth in his eyes. "Yes, I do."

With a satisfied nod, Zeus tucked one of her hands into the crook of his arm. "Good."

"What about our project to unite Hugh and Dia?" she asked. "Those two are living together, yet they seem farther apart than ever. You said you had a plan."

"What do you say we clean the sand off our feet and have dinner at this chic restaurant I found in Tunisia last year and I'll tell you all about it."

And if Hera agreed to his plan, he'd know that her promise of trust was true.

How long had it been since she'd been to an amuse-ment park? After a day at Six Flags north of Chi-cago, Dia came into the kitchen laughing with the four children. Her nose was sunburned and she'd had too many sweets—she'd have to wear black leather instead of silver lamé at her performance tomorrow—but she'd had fun.

It had been a perfect day, except for one thing: Hugh wasn't with them.

She hadn't seen him in two days, and she found she'd missed him.

She'd spent her two days of downtime not with magic but with the children, getting to know them and enjoying their company. Slowly they were slipping into a new dynamic. She was no longer the traveling aunt who breezed into town with presents and funny stories, and they weren't mysterious creatures who happened to have the same last name. Instead they were people, with strengths and weaknesses, and they were family.

The children went off to their rooms, but Dia bent over a pot simmering on the stove. "Mmmm, that smells good, Ronald. What is it?"

"Bouillabaisse, miss. It's one of Mr. Pendragon's favorites, and I thought I'd make it for him."

That quickly Hugh was back in the forefront of her thoughts, for he had never really left them. "Hugh's coming back today?"

"Yes. He should be home in time for supper."

Hugh was coming home. Her insides did a tiny flip of delight. "Was he successful?"

"I don't know."

A yeasty odor tickled her nostrils. "Do I smell bread baking?"

"You do. Fresh French bread."

"You spoil us. I'm going to miss you, Ronald."

"You don't have to leave." Carefully he wiped a wineglass with a towel, not looking at her.

"Yeah, I do. My tour is heading into southern Michigan early tomorrow."

"I meant for the future."

Dia stilled, a spoon dipping into the bouillabaisse for a taste. "What do you mean?"

"I have truly enjoyed having you here. Seeing you together, I had thought perhaps you and Mr. Pendragon . . ." He paused and, except for the bubbling of the bouillabaisse, the kitchen was silent.

"I'm sorry," Dia said softly. "It can't be."

"Because of Mr. Pendragon? His . . . work?"

Why Ronald thought Hugh's being a detective should bother her, Dia didn't know, but she didn't pursue it. "Because of me," she told him. "Because of who I am and what I do and have done."

Ronald studied her a moment. "What you are is a beautiful, talented, busy woman. What you've done? Mr. Pendragon is an extraordinary man, and when there is love . . ." He shook his head. "I am prying. Forgive me." He turned and busied himself at the stove, then immediately turned back. "Oh, I almost forgot. You had two messages while you were out. The Brick, who again left no number, and a woman. She didn't leave a number or name, just a message that she was looking forward to your performance next week." He handed her a piece of paper, not voicing the patent curiosity in his voice about her odd messages.

And she could not enlighten him. She glanced at the paper, not needing a name to know the woman caller: Demetria, warning her that time was running out.

"Can I use the phone in Hugh's office again?"

"Of course."

In the office, Dia called the Brick. "What have you got for me, T. B.?"

He rattled off a name and a phone number. "Makes the best paste jewels in the country, never asks questions, and he's right here in the heart of the Midwest." He paused a moment, then surprised her with an uncharacteristic warning. "Be careful, Dia. If this guy's involved it means big money."

"Thanks, T. B. I will."

After she hung up, however, she didn't leave the office; it was so quintessentially Hugh. She leaned back in his chair, imagining she could feel the stamp of his body in it, that it was his body wrapped around her instead of leather.

She closed her eyes, facing truths. She had missed Hugh. If she knew he was coming back to her, it would be tolerable, but when he came back he'd still want nothing to do with her. Something solid and strong and good had left her life when she'd tried to deceive him.

Love, Ronald had said. Anything was possible with love.

Was it? Did she love Hugh? Enough to believe a future together was possible? Dia realized the idea had been simmering at the back of her mind, as redolent and rich as Ronald's bouillabaisse.

She'd tried marriage once, thinking it was the forever kind of love, and discovered she hadn't escaped the Trelawnys' ill-fated luck in love. Commitment required a lot of changes, and the truth was that she was scared—scared of failing, scared of hurting, scared of committing her heart and still losing Hugh.

Dia turned the ruby wristband around. The band felt heavy about her wrist, a solid link to him, to this house, to possibilities, and she'd found comfort in wearing it.

She had changed, she realized. She didn't find the idea of being united with one man so impossible.

Not if it was Hugh sharing her home or suitcase or hotel room. His job was flexible, she could choose dates, they could find the time to be together. They could have a full, busy life. He was one of the most open-minded men she'd ever met. Could he accept that children and her magic were incompatible?

If they loved each other, the inevitable problems could be worked out.

If they loved each other.

If only she believed in miracles.

A small scrape caught her attention, followed closely by the fresh scent of Winter aftershave. Her muscles tensed; her heart swung into overdrive; her hormones danced to life. Even with her eyes closed, her body recognized him.

Hugh was back.

Chapter Eighteen

At first Hugh thought his imagination had conjured Dia into his office. He'd thought about her enough the past forty-eight hours to make dreams a reality, but she hadn't looked like this in his fantasies. There she'd been bold and strong, stopping him in his tracks with her magic wand, or tense and stricken, as he'd seen her with the bands, or naked and sharing his bed, as he wanted to see her. Here she looked relaxed and so beautiful in her shorts, Tasmanian Devil shirt, and cross-trainers, with her hair pulled back and her nose sunburned. His heart squeezed with the need to hold her in his arms.

How could he think to banish her from his life when he could not banish her from his soul?

Slowly her eyes opened, as though she'd been asleep and waiting for his return to awaken. "Hugh," was all she said.

He came into the room and leaned one hip on the desk. "You've been out in the sun."

"A day at Six Flags with the kids. Did you find the missing girl?"

"Armond did," he said shortly.

His talent had disappeared. Surrounded by the missing girl's things—pictures of her soccer games, stuffed animals, schoolwork, telephone—he'd hoped to find a faint, fleeting touch of her soul. Instead a heavy blackness had reached up from the earth to suffocate him with its weight. All he felt inside was nothingness, as though a vital light inside him had been torn away and extinguished. They had found her, through a called-in tip, but it was none of his doing. He had failed utterly, and Hugh held out no hopes for the recovery of his gifts.

He'd also seen the look in Armond's eyes, which held both realization of what had happened and assurance that he would not call and put Hugh through that again.

Hugh hated that look. He hated the loss and the knowledge that his weakness was exposed, even if Armond was one of his best friends.

He hated more knowing that Dia did not love him. For if she did, his gifts would have returned.

He would not attempt to seek again. Sometimes illusion was so much better than reality.

She was wearing his wristband, he saw. He traced a finger around it, feeling the smooth skin and defined muscles over delicate bones beneath. For one moment his thumb caressed the racing pulse at her wrist; then he released her hand before the urge to pull her closer grew too great to ignore.

He loved her. She didn't love him; he had proof of that.

He still wanted her, and he always would.

Hugh straightened. "Ronald says to tell you dinner is ready."

Night was a friend, but tonight it was a lonely companion. Dia sat in the wing-back chair of her bedroom, looking out at the darkened grounds of Hugh's home. A narrow-beamed light shone on the book in her lap, but the biography of Robert-Houdin, considered by many to be the founder of modern magic and inspiration for Harry Houdini's stage name, held no magic for her.

She would not return to Hugh's home, and her chest hurt with the knowledge.

A light tap sounded at her door.

"Come in," she called softly.

Hugh stood framed by the doorway, a shadow relieved only by those familiar glints of jewels; then he stepped inside and closed the door.

"I saw your light," he said. "We need to talk."

She closed her eyes briefly against the spasm of pain. Only talk. She'd lost any chance at more.

He sat in the chair opposite her. "I need to come with you on your tour, Dia. We need the time to brainstorm, to figure out exactly what we're going to do at Demetria's. We can't go in without a plan."

"All right." She was proud of her even tone. "But we'll need an explanation why you're there."

"Try part of the truth—that I'm keeping an eye out for Mick's cohort."

"Plus, you know the crew already, and you've been around backstage recently. They'll be curious, but if you pitch in and help with the grunt work, they probably won't look too closely at the gift horse." Likely they would think that Hugh was her lover as well, but most showbiz people accepted affairs on the road as routine.

"No problem. I've learned the ropes."

She closed the book and attempted to be brisk and businesslike. "I've been thinking about how to trap Demetria. She hasn't sold the gems—"

"How do you know that?"

"I know this guy. He sells information, always reliable. Name's the Brick."

"I know him."

"You do?"

Hugh gave her a small smile. "I've used him myself."

"Oh. Anyway, if she hasn't sold them, it must be because she wanted the gems for herself, and I figure she'd want them where she could see and touch them—at her house. So while I'm there, I'm going to look for them and the confession. If I can figure out where the gems are ahead of time, I have a couple sequences built into my act where I can get them and be back without her being the wiser."

"Where?"

"Do you remember that illusion where I enter the sealed coffin and Paolo emerges in my place?"

"It gives you time when everyone thinks you're onstage and you're not."

"Bingo. Or we use smoke machines. Too much and it literally becomes a smoke screen."

"So you were going to get past her security and search her house right under her nose while doing a performance?" He made a sound of masculine irritation.

"That's why it was a 'sort of' plan. If it doesn't work, I've got a backup."

"I hope it's a better one than that."

She made a face. "Not much. I'm working on a variation of the transmutation illusion, one that needs an assistant from the audience. The next time she tells me to do a job, I'll bring Demetria onstage."

"She won't agree."

"I'm taking a chance that she won't want to make a scene. I'll plant the real gem on her, then an anonymous tip to the museum and she's on the hook. As far as I'm concerned, she was an audience plant, but I had no idea what she was planning."

"She'll implicate you."

"But she'll be the one holding the jewels."

Hugh shook his head. "Too many ifs. Too many things that can go wrong."

Dia gave him an annoyed look. "Then you figure out something different."

"I'll do that."

She fingered the wristband. Despite the no-nonsense tone of the conversation, his voice lingered inside her like the caress of a long-missed lover. She tried to tell herself that this was as far as it would go, but her body savored the memories of his lovemaking and demanded more.

The plans. Focus on the plans. "I was also trying to trace the fake band. Who made it and who commissioned it. I thought it might be one more lead to implicate her. The Brick says it's the work of Julio Jones."

The Seeker

Hugh sat forward, his knee brushing against her bare leg, his green eyes boring into her like lasers. "Don't even think about going to him. He's a paranoid forger who won't hesitate to drop you in the Chicago River with cement overshoes if he thinks you're a danger to him. Let me bring in Armond to go after him. I have one of his forgeries. It's not impossible that I would recognize his work. He need never know you're involved."

Dia twisted her fingers together. It was hard to shake her ingrained distrust of the legal system, but this wasn't a nameless detective. This was Hugh's friend. Hugh trusted Armond. And she trusted Hugh. "All right. Call Armond. But only about Jones."

Hugh exhaled, as though he'd been holding a pent-up breath. He looked at the wristband she wore, then back at her. "I've been thinking, too."

For a moment she savored the wild hope that he was off the job, thinking of the two of them, and of her.

"You don't need to wait for the next job," he said softly. "She's already given you one. We'll switch the wristbands, and I'll accuse her."

Dia met his eyes, mysterious behind their brilliant green, yet always honest and true. Tonight they told her nothing. Nothing of whether he could see her pulse fluttering in her throat. Nothing of whether he could see her doubts and hopes. "Too many ifs, you said. You could lose both to her."

"I'll take that risk." And behind the words, for one moment, she saw the spark of love. Her heart swelled with the magic of that singular gift—with the magic of love.

305

Seeing him like this, in her room in the night, casually dressed with bare feet, it was like that moment when she saw though the misdirection to the skill behind the illusion. Nothing had changed, but everything was different.

One powerful, too-brand-new-to-believe thought drummed through her.

She was in love with Hugh Pendragon.

And it was no accident that he had come to her room like this, in the friendly dark, even if he didn't realize it.

"I should have figured that out, but I didn't," she said softly, shifting in her chair until her knees touched his.

Hugh watched her without moving, his face closed down again. He gave away nothing, none of the fiery passion that burned between them. He had once again become the recluse.

The first move was up to her, and she'd always been better with action than with words. *Don't blow this, Dia.* Magicians courted physical danger all the time; she could be as brave with her heart.

She got up, went over to the door, and locked it.

She knelt as his feet, reaching up to run a finger along the outside of his thigh, and she saw the pulse throbbing at his throat. Her hands slid up his arms. One of them had to take the chance. "Hugh, is it over between us? I know I've made mistakes, but when I'm with you, all I can think about is how right it feels."

He looked at her then, his burning gaze searching her face. Her fingers tightened around his arms, and she slid closer until she felt his warm breath and smelled the fresh soap of his skin.

She moved into his chair. Her hips scooted closer to nestle against his, and she brushed a kiss against his cheek. He just sat there with all the responsiveness of a marble column. He definitely wasn't making this easy.

Had she read him wrong? Read the night and the moonlight wrong?

Until he told her no, until he left, she had to go on.

The scent, the warmth, the nearness of him all combined to addle her senses. She reached to bracket his face with her hands, feeling as awkward as a kid and as exposed as a magician whose concealed cards had just fallen from his pocket. "If you believe anything about me, believe this."

She kissed him then, giving him her heart and her soul. For one hideous moment she thought he wasn't going to respond, that he was going to reject her, but he gave a groan and his arms wrapped around her, pulling her onto his lap with a ferocious need.

"Oh, God, Dia," he said in a moan. "I still want you."

"I'm here. I'm here." Her hands raced frantically across his shoulders, his back, his thighs, exploring all the dips and bulges that made up his beautiful body. The heat flared between them, igniting fireworks as spectacular as any she ever used onstage. A powerful need arose, and it would not be ignored or denied. Her kisses moved over his lips and his cheeks, then back to his mouth.

He took over the kiss. His hand pulled the band from her hair, then wrapped the loose tresses around his fingers, holding her in place. "If this is what I can have, then this is what I'll take," he muttered.

She didn't understand what he meant. She only understood the desires running through her, the throbbing of her body, the pulse of his hips against hers, and the erection pressing against her, insisting on more.

Hugh tunneled beneath her shirt, rapidly unfastened her bra, and surrounded her breasts with his strong hands. He kneaded them, caressed them, then leaned over to suckle them through the cotton of her shirt. Dia turned to straddle him, then leaned back, bracing herself on his thighs, to give him full access. Whatever he wanted with her body, he could have.

Whatever he wanted with her heart, he could have, too.

"I love you," she whispered, then realized the words had not escaped past the low moan in her throat as he delved beneath her shorts to touch her intimately. All she could do was gasp at the inferno he created.

"You're wet," he said, his fingers making their own magic with her. "You want me."

"Yes," she said under her breath. She wanted every part of him. All of him. No longer content to let him control the lovemaking, Dia shifted, releasing her grip on him to caress the inside of his thighs. Her fingers danced upward, rubbing the ridge beneath his shorts and sliding down the elastic with a determined twist of her wrist.

"Yes." He echoed her need.

Dia leaned forward and ran a string of kisses along his jaw to the back of his ear. "Mmm, you smell good. Taste good, too."

With a growl he stood and pulled her upright into his embrace. Their lips met. As his tongue stroked hers, his lips and hands moved with expert ease, coaxing her response. Dia raised on tiptoe to press against him. Muscle, heat, fleece, silk, whiskers, all joined in a thousand sensations of Hugh. Hot and strong, his hands brought her even nearer, fusing them in the kiss of a sorcerer. Under the sensual onslaught, she moved backward, until she bumped awkwardly against the bed.

Of one accord, they fell to her bed. Clothes vanished under the rush of hands on button or zipper or hem. Here the light from her lamp no longer reached, leaving them in a pattern of shadows. She saw nothing but odd shapes, the thick spread, and Hugh. As mysterious and dark as the room and the house that surrounded them, he lowered himself onto her. Their gazes could no more separate than they could. They were lost in the touch and the taste of one another.

His body, she'd dreamed of his body, so strong and masculine. His erection pressed against her belly, solid and demanding. The line of hair on his chest led to his groin and tickled her as he pulled her close. His legs encircled her, and the rough hairs were a heavy stimulus to her sensitive skin. Dia drew in a breath of sharp need.

Only the sound of breathing and the cries of pleasure and the murmurs of direction or approval disturbed the quiet. For this moment, only this man existed, only this thick, soft mattress at her back, only the stark, green need in his eyes as he settled between her legs.

"Now," she demanded.

Hugh kissed her behind the ear as he tested her with his fingers. "Are you ready?"

"Rhetorical question."

"Remember that. Remember this." With a steady pressure, he drove his thick shaft into her. He filled and stretched her, fit her with solid power and a velvet stroke. "For this, you're mine."

It felt so very good to have him inside her, exciting her, that she didn't even acknowledge his raw possessiveness. He pulled out nearly all the way. Dia gripped his hips, urging him back. He plunged inside her, touching her in ways she'd never been touched before. He stroked; she kneaded the muscles of his back, his buttocks, and kissed his salty-tasting neck.

His strokes and caresses and groans bound them firmly together. Her strokes and kisses and moans raised them, flew them starward. They raced against the mounting urgency, higher and firmer and together, until Dia exploded with white-hot fireworks, crying out her pleasure to Hugh and to the world. Hugh's hips bunched and pounded as he joined her in flight and in fall.

Slowly they drifted to the ground, breath easing, bodies wrapped around each other.

Dia wiggled slightly, shifting closer, unwilling to give up just yet this contact with her beloved. Hugh murmured his approval, and his arm wrapped around her waist, pulling her closer. For long moments Dia could find no voice or breath to share. At last she felt the tension in him recede as it did in her, replaced by the languor of completion.

"One of these times we're going to have to do this slowly," he said with a low chuckle.

"You've seen my show. You know I like it when things move fast and furious." Her hand trailed lazily down his side.

"But even the most frenetic performance needs moments of quiet for contrast." He kissed the side of her neck, then ran his tongue around her ear in a slow, easy motion.

"True."

Replete as she was, Dia felt the stirrings of desire again as he languidly and carefully touched her in ways designed to arouse her. Remembering his pleasure, too, she ran a nail lightly up the inside of his thigh until she encircled his sex.

His abdominal muscles tightened as he sucked in a sharp breath. "Don't start anything you're not ready to finish."

"I don't think it's me we need to worry about being ready."

"Oh, really?" He gave a small pulse of his hips.

Dia smiled with surprise that he was already semihard. "Okay, we don't have to worry about you either."

"And it will be slow," he promised.

He bent to leisurely suckle her breasts, and when he had finished she was open and ready. But Hugh took his promises seriously, and he continued his lazy, overwhelming assault on her senses even as Dia explored and learned him.

Finally he pressed her back against the bed. His fingers laced with hers as she sprawled beneath him and he entered her inch by exquisite inch. Both were primed and aroused, and mutual orgasm came in a long, throbbing release.

Afterward, Dia felt as boneless as a silk scarf, as satisfied as she ever had felt at the end of a perfect performance when the applause swelled across her. She needed no applause, now, only Hugh's soft breathing.

Throughout the quiet night, surrounded by darkness, they loved each other, until the alarm on her watch beeped, startling her, and reminding her of the world outside.

"What's that for?" Hugh asked.

"Time to get up. The crew bus and equipment truck will be coming, ready to hit the road."

He shifted off her, then rose with easy grace to his feet. Dia followed and they began to dress, preparing to face what lay beyond these walls.

Hugh paused as he pulled up his shorts. He smoothed her loosened hair behind her ear. "On the tour you don't have to book me a separate room."

Dia looked up at him, knowing what he was saying, but unsure what he was thinking. To have him share her room was announcing their relationship to the crew and the world. Was she ready for that?

"All right," she whispered. Her hand brushed against the blue diamond in his ear, and the wristband gleamed with soft red light. *Take a chance, Dia.* She grabbed her courage. "I love you, Hugh."

He tensed.

Dia frowned. She had enough experience to know that what had happened between them was special, different. A man wouldn't make love like that and not feel something. Was he afraid to admit it? She raised on tiptoe and gave him a little nip on the ear, encouraging him. "I love you."

It got so much easier to say with practice.

To her surprise, however, he didn't murmur back the words she wanted to hear. Instead he moved away from her and reached down for his shirt.

Stunned, Dia fisted her hands against her waist and stared at him. After all this, he was rejecting her? "Did you hear me?"

"I did." He pulled his shirt over his head, then finally looked at her. "You don't have to pretend."

"I'm not pretending. I don't say those words lightly."

He shook his head. "It's not love, it's gratitude."

"*Gratitude!*"

"Or lust or mutual need. I know for a fact that it's not love, so don't worry about saying the words. I don't need to hear them."

And with that insane statement, he picked up her shirt and held it out. "Your crew will be here soon."

Dia gaped at him. He sounded sad and frustrated and so very sure. A lick of anger wormed in behind the good feelings. How dare he presume? She snatched the shirt from him and threw it over her head.

He was heading out the door when her head emerged through the neck hole.

Oh, no. Reclusive Hugh Pendragon was not going to hide. Not this time.

She raced off after him.

Chapter Nineteen

Hugh heard Dia coming after him. He should have known she wouldn't let him just walk away.

"Hugh Pendragon!"

He ignored her call, knowing he was bungling the whole affair. But after weakening, after making love to her again, after all his defenses against her had been shattered in a single, powerful night, to hear her say the words he longed for—and to know they were not true—was more than he could take.

Love was an absolute bitch. It hurt—badly.

"Hugh." Her voice was low and warning. Dia grabbed his arm and swung him around. She was strong and she was angry.

Too bad. So was he. "Don't push me, Dia."

"Why? You'll beat me?"

"No! I don't want to say anything I'll regret."

"Let me tell you something, Hugh. You've already passed that point."

"You wouldn't understand. You wouldn't believe me."

"I *hate* it when people make assumptions about me. Which one is it this time? Dumb-blond stereotype? Body but no brains?"

"Now who's making the assumptions?"

"Then tell me. Hugh, I just gave you my body and my soul. I tell you I love you and do you say the words back? No, you tell me I'm lying. I deserve better."

"You want to know how I know?" They'd been striding down the halls, voices tense and angry. Hugh realized they were at his office. He detoured into it and snatched up a file. "I know because I can't find your sister."

Dia stared at him. "What?"

He shook the file at her. "I can't find your sister. I can't see or feel a thing. I don't have the talent anymore and I won't get it back until I retrieve the opal wristband or unless you love me. And since I don't, you don't." There, he'd said it. He slammed down the file.

Utter silence followed his admission.

At last Dia scratched out, "What the hell are you talking about?"

Hugh gave her a wary look. He'd never heard her swear before, not even a *hell* or a *damn* or an *oh, God.* His gut knotted.

"My psychic talent. It's dying. Fading out since you took the opal wristband."

"Psychic talent?" Her words were a mere breath.

"If I get the wristband back, or if the woman I love is willing to commit to me, then it will come back. But it hasn't. So I know you don't love me. You aren't willing to commit to us."

"Psychic talent?" she repeated. Dia shook her head in denial, and he saw horror growing in her expression.

The sickening truth dawned on him: she didn't know.

"I thought you knew. I don't advertise it, don't talk about it, but people know."

Her head continued shake, denying his words. "You claim to be psychic?"

"Not claim to be. I am."

"A psychic detective?" She made the words sound as horrifying as if he'd claimed to be a satanic sacrificer.

"Yes," he said defensively.

"Then why haven't you found my sister?"

"I told you. Because my gifts are fading."

"Gifts? Oh, that's right, and you need me to get them back. So either you're a phony psychic—and you must be one of the best if you've fooled so many people—or you're using me. I'm leaning toward the former, but let me tell you, Hugh, neither option is real endearing."

Hugh raked a hand through his hair. He had no way to prove to her the truth. Testimonials and former successes wouldn't sway her. She'd need to see it for herself. To see results in real time. It shouldn't matter if she believed him; it wouldn't change anything, wouldn't make her love him. But somehow it did matter.

The Seeker

Dia leaned one hip on his desk and picked up the file on her sister, idly glancing through it. "You found out a lot even without this 'power.' Is that how you do it? A lot of legwork, and if you don't find the answers, then it's 'Oh, dear, the power isn't working today. Her soul is not strong enough to touch mine.' So, success or failure, you're covered."

After the endless nightmares and the agonies of knowing he couldn't find someone or discovering he was too late, her sarcasm was unbearable. It speared sharp and deep to his failures and fears and emphasized again how far apart he and Dia were. Their differences seemed an impassable chasm. He sat at his desk and buried his face in his hands, unable to look at her and remember the joy they'd known while the loss was still fresh and painful. "I told you, you wouldn't understand or believe."

She picked up a glass paperweight from his desk and began tossing it up in the air. "You've got me curious. So how does this 'power' work? You gaze into a crystal ball? Spirits tap on the window? You go into a trance?"

"I sense things when I touch objects someone's owned."

"Sense as in see?"

"See, hear, feel, taste, smell, experience."

"Ah. What do you sense with this?" She tossed him the glass ball.

Deftly he caught it and set it back on the desk. "Nothing. It's mine."

"Conditions. Yes, there always have to be conditions. What do you sense when you touch me?"

317

"Lust," he said bluntly. "Naked heat. The need to have you beneath me and above me and around me. The desire to be inside you. At least that's what I was feeling about an hour ago."

"Yeah? Well, it doesn't take psychic powers to turn a man on. Only breasts." She spied the photograph of Liza and the children and picked it up. "Is this what you were using as a focus for my sister?"

"One of the things."

"You should have felt something. She loves those kids. Here, show me what you do with it." She held out the picture.

"I told you, it hasn't worked."

"Oh, go on. Do your act for me. If anyone can appreciate a good show, it's me. My mom and sister are in the biz, although some people call it psychic and some people call it a con, and we know the tricks. I set up my mother's séances when I was five. She's in Asia right now, channeling for someone's ancestors, and let me tell you, I learned from the best."

"It's not an act or a con or a fake," he snapped and grabbed the picture from her, ready to fling it down onto the desk.

His lungs felt clogged with smoke. Fire raced along his nerves. Dia, the office, all disappeared to black. The image exploded over him. Jungle, heat, humidity, sweat pouring down his back and sticking his shirt to his armpits, monkeys screeching, sore feet, a brilliant blue bird barely visible in the canopy above, mosquito bites scratching, exhilaration and pride at having made the trek, sheer annoyance at the man walking in front. He felt it all, experienced it all in exquisite detail, every sense primed and powerful.

Dia stared at Hugh. For a moment she feared he'd had some kind of attack or stroke, the way he gasped and stiffened. Then he grew utterly still. His eyes stared straight through her, and his breathing steadied to a shallow rhythm. A trance. She recognized the technique, but even her mother hadn't managed to break into a sweat like that on command.

"Oh, Hugh," she said softly, "you are good."

He didn't answer.

She could offer him a few pointers. "You should talk while you're in the trance, give the audience a few crumbs to pique their interest. Moan or gasp once in a while. It keeps people's attention."

He still didn't answer.

As the silence lengthened, Dia stirred in her seat, the hairs on her arm standing on end, as though he electrified the air with his power. "Okay, I gotta admit. This works, too. It's definitely creeping me out."

Hugh inhaled, long and slow, and his eyes closed. He leaned his head back against the chair as though he were utterly weary.

Dia laid a hand on his arm, concern overriding her skepticism. "Are you okay?"

"Don't touch me," he said in a low growl.

Dia snatched her hand back.

"The aftermath," he offered, his voice still deep and raspy and sexy, as though he'd just woken up. "It leaves me . . . aroused."

If she hadn't grown up the way she had, Dia would have been convinced of the vision thing. Despite everything she knew, she found herself wanting to believe, wanting to trust that Hugh did not live by deception.

"I saw your sister, but there was nothing I could use to pinpoint her. A jungle. It's hot there. She finds the mosquitoes annoying and the birds gorgeous. This trek was some kind of pilgrimage, to prove that she could do it." His eyes opened, and his gaze held her under his spell.

Keen disappointment speared her. Nothing, nothing that he didn't already know or couldn't surmise. She'd seen her mother do it a thousand times. Heck, Sherlock Holmes had perfected the technique in the nineteenth century, always shocking Dr. Watson with his deductions. Except he admitted how he'd done it.

"She does not love the man she's with."

The quiet words spread through her, bringing the ache of dreams lost. Dia swallowed back the tears in her throat. "Another Trelawny fooled by love? It's a family trait, you know. We joke about it. Men wander in, and they wander out. We're a family of wanderers and gypsies."

"It doesn't have to be like that."

"Because you have some vision, I'm supposed to believe all's well?"

"It was real. Stronger and more vivid than I've felt in six months. It may be a fluke; I don't think it's permanent yet."

"Unless I stay and commit to you." She gave a humorless laugh. "Great. Now I'm your path to . . .

whatever. I won't be used like that. Real or pretend."

"I'm not using you." He got to his feet and made it look as if it took a singular effort for even so small an act. "Tonight you asked me to believe. Can you believe in this?" He leaned over and kissed her—tenderly, gently, sensually. No demands, only a gift.

"Sex is not enough," she whispered when their lips separated.

"That wasn't sex. It was love."

She shook her head, unable to voice her pain. An hour ago she would have relished his vows. Instead she felt raw inside, scoured until there was nothing left to give or to risk. Her trust was gone.

She took the ruby-and-copper band from her wrist and laid it on the table.

Hugh drew back. "I can't keep proving myself to you. Either you trust me or you don't." He went to the window and pushed back the curtain. With his back to her, he stared out over the grounds. Outside, it was black and starless, with shapes and shadows only a dim blur. A mantle of darkness seemed to settle over him.

"Tell me something, Dia. An hour ago, before you knew about me, if I had asked you to choose between me and your magic, which would you have chosen?"

"What kind of a question is that?"

"A simple one. If you had to choose, which would it have been?"

"I thought with you I wouldn't have to choose."

"In other words, your life as you have it now, only with me waiting for you to breeze into my bed.

We want different things, Dia. You want me to soar and fly with you, but I also want you to settle with me, give me children."

"I can't do that. Not now." The words were so thin, she barely heard herself.

Hugh's hand fisted against the windowpane, then relaxed. "I'm a good detective, whether you believe in any power or not. I'll keep my promise and finish what I started. We'll finish this tour; then you'll be free of Demetria, free of the children, free of me, free to go wherever your magic takes you. To the top."

"I don't think it's such a good idea for you to go with me."

He glanced over his shoulder at her. "No. We'll finish this once and for all, Dia. No loose ends."

No loose ends, nothing to bring them back together after this was over, a clean, final break.

"All right."

As soon as the words were out of her mouth, Dia felt a clutch of panic. But why, she wasn't sure. Was it because she would be spending more time with Hugh, a man who'd deceived her, yet she couldn't resist?

Or because when it was over he would be gone from her life, taking her heart with him?

Dia set her suitcase next to Hugh's, ready to join the others in the bus. She had one last thing to do before she left. She found the four children together and in characteristic poses and dress. Elena in a hot pink camisole and shorts was watching television. Lukas and Cam wore baggy shorts and soccer camp T-shirts, while one worked on the computer and the other did sit-ups. Claire, in her black tights cut off at the calf and a black poet shirt, sat reading. Cerberus lay snoring in the corner.

She also discovered Hugh talking to them.

Elena grinned at her. "Hugh says Mom's okay. That she's enjoying her trip and they're almost done. She'll be back soon."

"Great." He was even carrying on the deception with the children. Dia forced a smile, even as a small voice told her that Hugh was not the kind of man to deceive children.

"We'll be out of your hair soon," mumbled Claire.

Dia sat beside her and smoothed a hand down her niece's hair. "It's not like that."

Claire flinched away, and Dia lowered her hand. "I'm going to miss you four."

And she would, she realized, as she stood at the door ready to leave. Somewhere in their time together, she'd grown accustomed to them. It was nice coming home, when home was a place that wasn't empty and filled only with things easily moved to the next apartment, the next job. It wouldn't last, she knew. Liza would be back and Dia would leave Hugh's home, but for the moment she would savor it, their closeness—and try to be more a part of their lives in the future.

So why was Hugh really here?

Zeus stroked his mustache as he eyed the couple sitting at the front of the bus. Twenty-four hours into the tour and he hadn't quite figured it out. To provide protection, maybe, but not against Mick's ineffectual cohort. The crew was equally divided between the theory that they were lovers—even though they'd booked separate rooms last night— and the notion that Hugh was researching a mystery novel. Either way, Dia had established him as a working member of the crew, he worked without complaint, and they liked him, so there wasn't anything more to worry about.

The bus pulled into the theater parking lot and the unloading and setup began. When they finished, the crew would have a couple of hours free. Zeus decided he would follow Hugh and see what the Soul Seeker did.

The Soul Seeker did nothing, Zeus discovered. He stayed at the theater with Dia, just the two of them. Of course, the logical assumption was they were conducting an afternoon tryst behind that closed door. Zeus fingered his mustache.

"Take the bull by the horns" had always been one of his favorite human clichés—that he had inspired it during his little escapade with Europa was a secret delight. He knocked, then pushed open the door, remembering that Hera always quoted another cliché to him: "Fools rush in where angels fear to tread."

Dia and Hugh were in chairs too far apart to be deemed intimate. It was definitely not a tryst, more was the pity. They seemed to be in earnest conversation.

"Zeke? Did you want something?" Dia asked.

Zeus closed the door and leaned one shoulder against the jamb. His fingers toyed with the lightning-bolt ring. "Yes. I want to know what you're planning to do about Demetria."

* * *

324

If Zeke had said he wanted to know the best way to use body glitter, he couldn't have surprised her more.

"I don't know what you're talking about," Dia sputtered. She glanced over at Hugh. "You don't seem a bit surprised."

"I think there's more to Zeke Jupiter than he lets us see," Hugh answered calmly, though his body was alert.

Dia's insides shriveled a bit. She'd thought Zeke was her friend. She'd imagined he was here out of friendship and mutual benefit. Was that a deception, too? "Zeke?"

He came over and patted her hand. "I am Zeke Jupiter, owner of the Jupiter Fireworks Company, developer of heatless fireworks that you have generously assisted me in field testing these past two weeks. I am your friend. I just happen to have known Demetria Cesare a lot longer than you, and when I found out you were performing at her home, even though you don't normally do private functions, I couldn't help thinking there was more going on than meets the eye. Perhaps I can help."

Dia wasn't sure what to say.

"My friend Armond vouches for him," Hugh quietly told her, his attention still snagged by Zeke. "In a fashion."

"I thought perhaps you'd done some checking." Zeke didn't seem upset. "I don't offer explanations. I do offer assistance." He sat down and crossed his legs, one finger stroking his salt-and-pepper mustache. "I also happen to think Demetria wants Hugh's wristbands."

Dia's insides shriveled a bit more. Was everybody around her buying into the story of the mysteriously powerful jewelry? "Zeke, do you think those bands have some sort of psychic power?"

"They're talismans, my dear, not brains. Only living creatures can have the gift."

"So you believe in psychic powers?" she asked carefully.

"Of course! Oh, not the one-nine-hundred, twenty-five-dollars-for-one-minute brand." Zeke gave her an apologetic glance. "Sorry, Dia; your family is charming, but they haven't got a shred of the true talent. You see, somebody who does, does not advertise on late-night television. They guard their inner soul most carefully and speak of their gifts only when necessary."

They guard their inner soul most carefully and speak of their gifts only when necessary. Dia slumped back in her chair. He had just described Hugh. Her gaze darted from Zeke to Hugh, her world spinning off its axis once again.

Zeke leaned back. Rubbing his hands together, he smiled at them. "So, what's the plan with Demetria?"

"It's your call, Dia." Hugh arched a brow. "Do we trust him, even if we can't explain him?"

Dia pressed a finger against the bridge of her nose, feeling the beginnings of a headache. But she couldn't afford to turn down an offer of information and assistance, no matter how unexpected the source.

"Let's talk."

Chapter Twenty

A week later Dia sat on a plastic chair outside her motel room door, dressed only in a tank top and gym shorts. The night was hot and still. Her room was dark, and all around her it was quiet. An hour ago the night clerk had turned off the motel's sign, quieting its neon hum. Even the bug zappers were off, and the clatter of the cicadas had ceased. Aside from the almost full moon the only other light was a single beam in Hugh's room.

Idly she ran two coins through her fingers. She flipped one and deftly caught it while she tried a new palm technique with the other. Distraction and misdirection in one complex sequence.

Performers often had trouble sleeping after the demands of the stage, and she was no exception. Whereas she'd seen many turn to drink or drugs or promiscuity as a way to unwind, Dia chose another route. Sometimes she partied with her crew and a club soda, but she always returned to her magic. The practiced motions were soothing.

The tour was going well. She'd had sellout crowds all the way; there was only one more performance to go before the hiatus at Demetria's.

A lightning bolt speared the night sky. No sound, no rain, only a brilliant flash that left charged air, the faint smell of hot electricity, and a vague restlessness. Heat lighting, she supposed.

She glanced once more at the light in Hugh's room. The crew had accepted his presence. She and he had talked with Zeke each night and gradually a plan had taken shape. There were still a lot of contingencies, such as locating the gems and the jeweler's confession. Zeke suggested they use another piece in the transmutation illusion, if they found the gems. Let someone not connected with Dia recognize the switch. They agreed on Harry Xavier, since both Zeke and Hugh knew him, and Zeke promised he'd be there. She had finally agreed to let Hugh contact Armond, and bring him in that night, but she refused to have anything to do with him. The players would be in place. The curtain would go up in forty-eight hours.

After their strategy session finished each night, however, the three separated to their respective motel rooms. Zeke gave her a warm kiss on the cheek. Hugh gave her a grave, "Good night."

It was the way she wanted it, the way it had to be, but chaste got harder every night.

A soft honk sounded, indistinct in location, but definitely birdlike. Dia stiffened, and the coins dropped from her hands with a soft clatter. Not here, too. She hadn't seen a single pond or pool.

Only one odd glitch had marred the days: she was bedeviled by swans.

Every place they went there seemed to be a pair of swans swimming nearby, but she was the only one who ever saw them. Whenever she called one of the crew over, the birds had flown away. Paolo had taken to teasing about her fixation, telling her the mated birds were a symbol of romance and fidelity, and that she'd better watch out or she'd find herself shackled by wedded bliss. *Romance, ha!* The big birds left her with a queasy stomach. She simply didn't like the creatures, which meant, of course, that when she was alone, they always swam directly toward her, their dark eyes seemingly filled with mischief and mayhem.

Maybe stress had driven her into hallucinations.

Another honk was followed by a bird waddling around the corner of the motel, its eye on her. Dia shrank back in her chair, nausea rising in her throat until the bird stood in the parking lot before her room and looked at her, its head cocked.

"Go away," she whispered.

It moved forward.

She glanced at Hugh's room, wondering if maybe his supposed psychic powers extended to receiving vibes of "help."

Nothing moved but the bird.

Get up she commanded herself. *Just go inside.* But she couldn't move. Dia closed her eyes, hoping the bird was a figment of her imagination.

And perhaps it was, for when she opened them again it was Hugh who stood in front of her. Lightning crackled across the sky, illuminating, then shadowing him. He seemed to shimmer in the expectant air, as ethereal as a dream.

Without a word Hugh leaned over and kissed her—thoroughly, passionately, expertly. Surprised, Dia let her eyes drift shut again. She softened and sagged toward him. Regardless of whether he was real or part of her imagination, this dream she would savor.

The kiss was all she had missed, all she had yearned to feel, yet . . .

It wasn't Hugh. It was familiar, but it wasn't Hugh.

A bright light flashed across her lids—lightning again—and the skies opened up in a torrent of rain. She sprang to her feet and discovered she was alone in front of her stark motel room. A cold wind whipped around her and brought the drenching rain under the small overhang. Within seconds she was soaked.

She raced inside, straining to shut the door against the wind, still feeling the tingling kiss on her lips. Confused, she looked out the window at the storm which was dying as quickly as it came. Neither the swan nor Hugh was anywhere to be seen. Even his light was out.

Had she imagined it all? Was she going crazy? Dia rubbed her hands across her wet face. Either life had taken a definite turn for the weird, or else she was completely losing it.

It was almost enough to make her believe in the supernatural.

Hera waved away the far-see smoke with an angry gesture. Her cloud ring swirled and shone as the rainstorm that she'd raised retreated. "The philandering cheat! He told me Dia Trelawny meant nothing to him."

Demeter laid a sympathetic hand on her shoulder as the smoke dissipated. "She does mean nothing to him. But Zeus is incapable of fidelity."

"You told me that, but I didn't want to believe it." Hera was proud of her tone. It captured just the right mix of anger at Zeus and admiration for Demeter. It helped when she remembered how enthusiastically Zeus, in the guise of Hugh Pendragon, had just kissed Dia. He didn't have to get into the part quite that much.

At least he had gotten soaked, too. She wondered if the icy wind had been a bit too much.

"So now will you at least think about what I'm offering?" Demeter asked.

"The partnership in your new greenhouses? Yes, I'll think about it."

"Good. You won't be sorry."

"What I don't understand is why you need Dia."

"That, my dear Hera, you will see in two days."

Not soon enough.

Demeter linked her arm through Hera's. "Come, let me show you where she will perform."

Dia would be coming without her crew, Hera knew, so she'd forgo the biggest, splashiest illusions, like the airplane blades. The stage was wasn't really a stage at all, but rather a raised platform that meandered through the room like a deer path in a forest. It would be a unique showcase for Dia's talents, allowing her to interact with the audience. Throughout the room was a profusion of exotic plants—some Hera recognized, some she didn't—

331

which added to the illusion of a forest.

"Will any of these be in bloom during the party?"

"Some." Demeter stroked the leaves of a small bush. "This one will. It's a variation of the poppy."

"Like that truth serum one you tried to use at Anya's party."

"No, nothing like that," Demeter said with a laugh. "It was bred for its beautiful blooms."

Hera glanced around the room again, suddenly uneasy with the multitude of plants that filled it.

The fireworks exploded in a rainbow of color and brilliant sparks. "Oh, I'm good," Zeus crowed as he checked the timing on the final bank of rockets. Anya switched the music and Zeus stared, fascinated as he had been all week with this new final segment Dia had added to the tour.

At first he'd thought she was making a mistake by not ending with the airplane blades. By Hades, that bit was effective. He had to admit, though, that Dia had the instincts of a true showman, for this illusion embodied the essence of her show. Her fiber-optic wands reflected the colors of his heatless fireworks. The explosions and the music bathed Dia, Paolo, and the stage in a blaze of sound and color, while the wands transmuted into brilliantly hued fake gemstones that appeared and disappeared.

Tonight, on this last performance, it all came together perfectly.

At least something on this *tartus* journey had gone right.

Nothing else had. Hera had not called; he was lonely and forbidden female companionship by his vow to her; even the swans had not had the effect he desired.

Hugh and Dia definitely needed his help. The close confines of the tour kept them together, but rarely alone. They worked side by side, but it was all business. Somehow the two of them had managed to twist their relationship into a Gordian knot of hurt.

He could see that the unguarded looks they gave each other heated up the night. Why couldn't they? Zeus shook his head. Sometimes humans baffled him.

Tonight, though, was the night. This performance was part of the Zoobilation Benefit held at the amphitheater in the local zoo.

All he needed was to get his recalcitrant lovers alone.

Dia took her bows onstage, and Hugh paused in winding up cable, already beginning the show breakdown, to watch her. She never failed to stir him when her face lit up like that.

"Hugh," whispered Anya. "Can you take my console a moment? You just need to cue the closing."

"Sure." After a week on the road, he'd become as familiar with the program as any of the crew.

"Thanks." She patted his shoulder as she went by, a friendly gesture of inclusion. He was one of the group.

In all his life he'd never been one of a group.

Zeke Jupiter sat beside him. "Dia's magic has never been better," he said brightly.

There were times being one of the group could be a pain. Beyond their strategy sessions, it seemed Zeke had dogged him all week with out-of-the-blue comments about how pretty Dia looked in her shorts, or how Zeke once gave a woman he was wooing a shower of golden stars and Hugh could do the same with these new fireworks, or did Hugh know that swans mated for life. . . .

"She loves being onstage," Hugh said. "Her magic is her life."

"True." Zeke glanced at the stage. "But she needs more."

Did she? Hugh's attention followed Zeke's to Dia, who was completing one small illusion as a farewell. She seemed so at home onstage and on tour; he'd seen that during these days. Nothing he offered her could compete with the thrill of performance.

"The curtain always comes down," Zeke said, as if reading his mind. "Just as the Soul Seeker needs to fly, the illusionist needs someone to trust."

She needs someone to trust. Hugh cued the closing music and Dia left the stage with a wave and a "good night." She didn't trust him, and without that trust, she couldn't love.

"Try the zoo," Zeke added. "The Africa compound. It's quite stellar."

"What?" Preoccupied with the music and with Dia, Hugh wasn't sure he'd heard the man correctly.

"I have to put away my equipment." Zeke rose, then leaned over and whispered, "The moon is full and the night is balmy. Take time, Soul Seeker, to hear the lions roar and watch the peacocks strut.

You'll find it quite rewarding." He walked away, calling to the returning Anya, "Anya, love, do you know what state we're in? Farms begin to look the same when you can't tell a soy crop from alfalfa."

"Indiana, I think."

"And the city?"

She gave him a blank look.

Zeke laughed. "We're a fine pair. Don't know what day it is or where we are. What do you say we find a secluded bench and while away the evening?"

"Zeke," she said with a laugh, "you are incorrigible."

"Of course."

"Tell you what. We'll compromise with a dance."

"Excellent, my dear."

Hugh listened to the easy exchange. Zeke Jupiter was pesky and mysterious, but things were never dull with him around.

The curtains closed onstage, and Dia passed him on her way to change out of her costume. Before she disappeared, she gave him a grin, setting a fire low and deep in his belly. This really was where she belonged, he realized. She had a rare gift for bringing wonder and joy and magic to people's lives. To tie her down would be like trying to nail a rainbow or a shooting star to earth.

Backstage sounds, now familiar, swirled around him, and he found himself mentally detailing the tasks ahead. Where once he had surrounded himself with solitude and silence, now he enjoyed the camaraderie and physical labor of being simply a member of the crew.

The Soul Seeker needs to fly.

It was a temporary interlude, he knew, but one he found himself enjoying with a bittersweet pleasure. For when it was over, Dia would be gone.

That last illusion, the transmutation trick, had worked perfectly. She was as ready as she ever would be to meet Demetria. They had one day left.

Perhaps Zeke was right.

They should enjoy the evening and make the most of the time remaining.

Dia watched the truck with the bulk of the equipment disappear around the curve of the road. The bus would return the crew to Chicago tomorrow; most of them had already left for the hotel. Staying behind would be Dia, Hugh, Zeke, and the items of equipment she'd kept for the performance at Demetria's.

All was in readiness. She had tonight to relax, even if it was in a zoo. She looked up at a full moon. The grand illusionist. It was no accident the ancients worshiped and feared it, that *luna* gave its name to *lunacy*. Its brightness hid the multitude of stars, while its silvery light cast shadows and tricked the eye. A tree became a monster, and a monster seemed no more than a mere mound.

Hugh came up behind her. Without a touch, he electrified the hairs on the back of her neck, excited each nerve ending so sensation became more exquisite and more powerful. She smelled the clean scent of his aftershave, a cool contrast to the heat from his skin. This was real, no illusion like the other night.

He circled in front of her. In his hand he held a dripping ice-cream cone, which he held out to her.

"Here, I thought you might want something after the performance."

Dia smiled and took the cone from him. "You remembered my passion for ice cream." She licked the droplets that had escaped down the sides of the sugar cone. "Mmmm, chocolate chip. One of my favorites. Thank you."

"You're welcome."

"Would you like a taste?" She faced him and held out the cone.

"No, thanks. I imagine you need to wind down. Would you like to see the zoo? I've been told the African exhibit is a stellar attraction."

"Zoos aren't my favorite things."

"Big birds. You don't like them."

"Right. Ah, well, with Mark I managed to practice on an ostrich farm. At least now the ostriches and swans and geese will be asleep, and it is a pretty evening."

Hugh seemed content to enjoy the night in silence, and as they walked side by side, Dia found herself relaxing. Her body loosened and something tight inside her unknotted.

This past week, forced to work together in such constant proximity, they'd developed a cautious relationship. They were unable to risk touching each other, but able to talk more easily each day, and even to laugh on occasion. They got to know each other in new way. Neither spoke of that night before they'd left, but it lay between them still. The bitter anger had mellowed, but the differences in their goals had not changed.

By silent accord they left the partygoers and the bands to wander into a secluded area. Wisps of fog curled around their ankles and swirled across the blacktop path. Gradually the sounds of conversation and music faded until they stopped beside a wooden fence bordering an imitation African plain. A moat surrounded it. Dia listened, but no sleepy honks disturbed the night. She was swan-free.

Hugh braced his arms against the fence top and rested one foot on a wooden rung as he gazed out over the darkened compound.

Dia leaned against the fence. "One time, you asked me what I would consider an ideal day. So what's yours?"

He didn't answer right away. "I'm not sure anymore," he said at last. "Six months ago I would have said it was to have a day where all my cases had been solved, where no one was missing, and I had hours to take my boat out for a solitary sail in summer or enjoy a good book and a fine brandy by the fire on a cold day."

To her, those sounded like plans that would entertain her for about an hour until she grew restless, or unless Hugh were sharing that boat or that fire with her. Dia refused to travel that route again. "That was six months ago? What about now?"

He cast her a brief, searing glance. "I wouldn't be alone."

Heat, sudden and demanding, coursed through her. Her lips tingled with remembered kisses, and her body softened with remembered passion. She forced herself to stay still until he looked away.

"I would also like to sit beneath the moon on a night like this and listen to a John Lee Hooker concert," he added.

"He's dead."

The look he gave her this time was mildly amused. "You said ideal, not practical. Besides, you were the one who wanted to taste every flavor of ice cream."

"True. Then John Lee Hooker it will be." Under the guise of eating the last of her ice cream, she covertly studied Hugh. He was a man of intriguing contrasts, she admitted. He excited her, just to look or smell or touch him, yet being with him like this was oddly peaceful. He seemed a solitary man, but he had fit in easily, if quietly, with her exuberant crew and he said he wanted to raise a family. She would have said he was the most honest man she'd ever met, if she hadn't seen that psychic performance.

Unless it was true.

Zeus made a sound of exasperation. Two lovers in the moonlight, in the secluded park, and the two of them stood and talked. They didn't even hold hands. By Hades, what more would it take?

He rubbed his ring and took on the form he'd used before. He bent his neck to check his reflection in the pond. A white, feathered face was reflected back to him.

Why ever had he chosen a swan to seduce Leda all those years ago? At least a bull got to stand in a field of grass. And two nights ago Dia had seemed more afraid of the bird than filled with the memory of his adoration. He rubbed his ring again, creating the image of a second swan beside him. Maybe he should try a different approach.

Suddenly the power of the temperamental ring shot out. The two images merged into a single, gigantic swan. Sleeping birds took flight from the monster. By the Oracle's laws, what was he supposed to do now? Zeus saw his massive shadow against the water, and an idea came to him.

After all, the aftermath of fear was desire.

Water lapped against his waist as he paddled with his two webbed feet. Oh, the sacrifices he made in the cause of love.

Unless Hugh truly was psychic.

Dia sucked in a breath. Here, in silence and beneath the white-gold bringer of lunacy, she could not ignore the thought that had teased her all week.

Perhaps Hugh had not lied.

Could it be true? Everything she'd known in her life—at least up to this week—said no, but everything she knew about Hugh said it was.

A psychic detective? It sounded like an oxymoron, but it had the ring of truth. With his private, reclusive nature, she could believe that he didn't talk about it much.

"Hugh." She looked up at him, and he turned, his eyes dark beneath the night.

Before he could say anything, a single crack of thunder came from the animal compound, and a flock of birds took to the air. It was followed by a honk, a honk that grew louder. Whatever was making it was getting closer—and fast.

Her heart pounding, Dia peered into the darkness. The fog had risen, obscuring her vision, and an icy tremor ran down her spine. "Do you see anything?"

"There." Hugh pointed to a shapeless gray shadow swimming toward them.

"A tree becomes a monster and a monster a mere mound," she repeated softly, moving closer to the man at her side.

"No monster," he said as the cacophony grew louder. "It's—"

"—a swan," Dia finished as the massive bird came into focus. "A bloody swan!"

And this monster was the biggest of all. Dia backed up, her heart jumping from chest to throat in the space of seconds. From its huge throat came a booming, eerie, unearthly sound. She covered her ears and closed her eyes, trying to block out the terrifying sound and sight.

Hugh wrapped his arms around her. "It's okay, Dia," he soothed, his hand smoothing down her hair. "It's a trick of the night. Moonlight and humid air and fog."

"Hugh, that is not a trick of the night!" She opened one eye. The swan was still there and closing fast. She shifted farther back, taking Hugh along with her. "Go away," she rasped.

The bird didn't listen. Dia hated the terror welling in her, but some atavistic memory kept her fear alive.

"Swans don't fly well," Hugh said. "The fence will keep it in."

"Yeah? Tell that to this one."

The bird braced one wing on the top of the fence and leaped over.

"What the hell . . . ?" Hugh started forward, preparing to meet the lunging bird.

"No, it'll peck you." Dia grabbed his arm and pulled it around her. The safety of his embrace wrapped around her. "Go away," she commanded the bird, facing it head-on.

"You tell 'im," Hugh said with a laugh as he kissed the top of her head.

The bird honked, and an eye-hurting flare of lighting struck the earth. Dia and Hugh flinched. A sharp crack sounded, like a boom of thunder.

Then silence.

And emptiness. Only the zoo, the wisps of fog, and the lunatic moon.

"It's gone," Hugh murmured, his arms still embracing her from behind. One hand trailed up and down her arm in a soothing rhythm.

For a long moment Dia couldn't move. The silence was too blessed, and for once she treasured the solitude. The feel of Hugh pressed against her was too good to push him away. She felt his lips lightly graze the top of her head and smelled his clean, fresh scent. She could feel the firm muscles beneath his soft shirt as he caressed her.

Dia gave a soft sigh of pleasure, turned, and burrowed closer. Hugh murmured something unintelligible and gathered her in.

"I didn't imagine that, did I?" she ventured at last.

"No, you didn't."

"Do you have any idea what it was I saw?"

"Simply a swan?"

"There was no 'simply' about that animal, and you are taking this awfully calmly."

"I've lived with the unusual all my life. There are some things you can't explain. You have to just accept them."

Like Zeke Jupiter? Like psychic talents? If she believed in a giant swan, why shouldn't she believe in more? "Should we tell the zookeeper one of the swans is loose?"

"Do you want to tell someone we saw a six-foot swan that disappeared into a lightning bolt?"

"Ah, no."

"Besides, that bird did me a favor."

"A favor? What?" Dia looked up at him.

"This."

Hugh's mouth came down, even as she raised herself on tiptoe to meet him.

It was a slow, thorough, claiming kiss, and Dia met it eagerly. When their lips separated, his arms tightened around her.

"I . . ." Dia stilled. "Hugh, are you vibrating?"

He gave a short curse. "My phone is ringing. I put it on vibrate mode so it wouldn't ring during your show." He made no move to answer it.

"Shouldn't you do something about it?"

"Maybe they'll leave a voice mail."

Both of them waited a moment, but the vibration continued. "You'd better answer it. It could be important."

With a sound of annoyance, Hugh let her go, then pulled the phone from his pocket and flipped it open. "Pendragon. Ronald? What . . . ? Calm down? Dia? She's right here."

He handed her the phone. Dia's insides clenched as she answered. "Ronald, is everything all right?"

"Oh, Miss Dia, I'm afraid everything is in a shambles, and I'm so sorry."

"Ronald, what happened?"

"It's Miss Claire. She's run away."

Chapter Twenty-one

"She left a note." Ronald's continuing explanation broke through the buzzing in Dia's ears. "Miss Dia, I am so sorry. I knew Miss Claire missed her mother, but I did not think she would run away."

"None of us did." Dia tried to reassure him, but she knew it wouldn't work, not if he felt as guilty as she did. She'd known there was a problem with Claire, but she'd gone on tour and hadn't given it another thought. "Read me the note." Her gut knotting and her hands shaking, she listened as he read it through.

Nothing. No clue to where she was. Claire just said that she was going to find her mother, and not to worry, that she would contact them later.

Where could she have gone? Why, why, *why* hadn't she talked?

Had Demetria made good on her threat and taken her?

"Did you talk to the other kids about where she thought she'd go?" she asked Ronald. "Or call the police?"

"I didn't know what to do. The children were asleep, and to wake them with such distressing news, I thought it best if you were here. With the police, will there be complications because their mother is gone? I simply didn't know how to handle it. So I called you. I was sure Mr. Pendragon could find her."

"Call the police, Ronald, and ask Elena and the boys what they know. We'll get there as soon as —"

"Wait, Dia." Hugh laid a hand over hers. "Ah, Ronald, just a minute."

"Do you have anything with you that belongs to Claire?"

"Um . . ." Dia shook her head, trying to think. "Her book of mythology. She left it onstage and it got packed in my things. I forgot to pull it out before we left."

"Get it for me. Give me twenty minutes. Let me see if I can find her."

"Twenty minutes? What can you—" Her voice broke off, and her chest squeezed. "Oh, no, Hugh."

"Twenty minutes." His eyes caught hers. "Ten minutes."

Trust me, he seemed to be asking. *Believe in me.*

Dia swallowed hard against the panic and the need to act. If Hugh could do what he claimed, he was their fastest, surest route to finding Claire.

If he could do what he claimed.

And she believed that he could.

She put the phone back to her ear, her eyes on Hugh. "Ronald, wait until we call you back. Okay?"

Relief flooded through Hugh that she was giving him this chance, followed quickly by fear. He didn't like at all the timing of Claire's disappearance. Was it just coincidence that it had come so close to Dia's confrontation with Demetria? He suspected Dia had the same worry.

Yet she trusted him enough to overcome her dislike of psychics and give him a chance. Could he do it? Could he find Claire? Or would she be another tragic failure? Another statistic?

The phone rang.

"Sir," Ronald said, "I forgot to tell you, Cerberus is also gone."

"You think he followed Claire?"

"It's a distinct possibility."

"Good. We'll call back within the hour."

Hugh followed Dia to the minibus with her equipment and waited while she dug out a hardback book with an elegantly embossed cover. "Ever since she studied the myths in school last year, Claire's been fascinated by the subject."

Hugh glanced at the spine. It was a copy of Edith Hamilton's book on mythology and looked well used. Inside was an inscription: *Happy twelfth. Aunt Dia.*

There would be love and pleasure associated with that volume. Hugh found a bench on the quiet edge of the zoo and held out his hand. Dia gave him the book.

He ran his hands over the smooth leather cover, the indentations of the title, the rough edges of the pages. Claire was in here somewhere, if only he could find her. If only his talents had not deserted him. Dia's presence made them stronger. Maybe it would be enough. He opened, delved deeper, and sought the soul who had held this book, who had found joy it.

Claire, where are you? His lungs clogged with smoke and he gasped in a breath. His skin burned and his throat closed as the trees and bushes faded to an indistinct mass of silver. The silver swirled, reformed into the full moon, and then the image burst upon him with sudden, vivid clarity.

His talent had come back.

The single, joyous thought sped through Hugh before it disappeared as he was immersed in the vision. Claire was on a bus, looking out the window. Through her eyes he saw the full moon and the faded stars, the same ones that loomed over his head. He felt the press of fatigue between her shoulders, and his eyelids drooped with hers. His fingers curled around Cerberus's collar.

Dumb dog, refused to go away, but she'd been kinda glad for his company. It was scary at night. The bus driver let him on when she told him Cerb was a listening-ear dog.

Claire's thoughts, not in words but in knowledge, became his.

The bus smelled of exhaust and unwashed bodies. The cloth seat was itchy and her neck hurt. Her stomach grumbled, and she reached into her backpack for a snack. A moment later Hugh tasted chocolate and marshmallow.

Where was she going? A neon sign flashed as the bus turned off into the station. Madison. She'd gone home to wait for her mother.

The bus station. Frightening at night with echoes and creepy people. Bus ticket expensive. Not enough money for a taxi.

Be strong. He touched her soul with his guidance. *Cerberus will protect you.*

He heard Cerberus's soft whine.

Could Liza be close? Close enough to come get her daughter, if she knew? He thought of the photograph, then sought the part of Liza that resided in Claire. Was that her? He followed the trace outward, seeking the missing soul, followed it to her home.

Liza. Standing on her front steps. A man beside her, but not the man from the trek. They kissed as she unlocked the door.

Lead her. The bus station. Claire. Hugh nudged gently and guided her to her daughter.

Dia stared at Hugh, who sat absolutely motionless on the bench. His eyes were open, but they neither flickered nor blinked. He'd had that gasping spasm at the beginning, then nothing. She'd even held a mirror up to his lips to make sure he was still breathing and felt for a pulse in his neck. His heart and lungs were working, but otherwise he seemed to have completely left her. She glanced at her watch. Fifteen minutes had passed.

"Hugh," she whispered softly.

No answer.

She sat beside him. He'd been like this for over fifteen minutes. Dia worried her lip with her teeth. Originally he'd asked for twenty minutes. Should she give him five more? She knew about fakery, but this was no fake. She didn't know what it was; it was completely out of her sphere of expertise. If she brought him out of the trance suddenly, would it be like one of those horror, sci-fi movies where part of him was left behind wandering the cosmos? She tested his breath and heartbeat again. Had his pulse slowed?

"Hugh," she called again, louder, and laid a hand on his shoulder.

Still no response.

She touched his cheek. He felt icy cold, as if all the heat had been sapped from him. More worried than ever, Dia gripped his strong shoulder and gave him a small shake. "Hugh, c'mon. Snap out of it," she commanded, but it wasn't she he was listening to.

She grabbed his bare wrist. That ruby-and-copper wristband, did it have some effect on the process? He wasn't wearing it. She patted his pockets until she found it, then snapped it around his wrist. Her fingers curled atop the copper, and she laid his other, unresisting hand on top of hers. "Hugh, feel this. Come back to me. You belong here. Not there. Leave. Come back." She pleaded for him to hear her.

For a moment she thought she hadn't reached him; then his fingers convulsed around the band and entwined with hers. He drew in a deep, shuddering breath, and his whole body shook and stretched, like a cat coming to wakefulness. He blinked once, very slowly, and when his lids lifted she knew he was back with her.

"What—"

He touched a finger to her lips, quieting her questions with a fleeting touch. "She's with her mother."

His voice was a low rasp, barely audible, as though it hurt to talk. "She's safe and well in Madison."

"With Liza?"

"I saw her," he said simply, and closed his eyes again.

This was no fake. Dia held his hand, convinced of that utter truth. There was nothing fake about Hugh, no illusion. He was the real thing.

Hugh was a true psychic, just as he'd claimed.

Dia's world did another one of those crazy shuffles that had become commonplace since she'd met Hugh and rearranged itself into a fresh new pattern. She felt dizzy and disoriented, unable to think or process anything beyond that fact.

"How did you find Liza? How does she look? Why did Claire leave?"

Hugh shifted away from her, so their only contact was their intertwined fingers resting atop his wristband. "Shh, Dia. Give me a moment."

She remembered now that he'd told her his senses were all heightened after one of these episodes. Seeing the pallor of his skin, she watched him carefully. He stretched his neck, the movement slow, as though his joints hurt, and he flinched when a lion roared in the background. If she ached to see him, how much worse must it be to actually experience it?

Yet he willingly went through this whenever his help was needed.

Psychics . . . love—she'd believed in neither and never expected them to touch her life. Yet here they were, all wrapped into one masculine package. She swallowed, her world reeling all over again, and when it righted she gave Hugh another careful look, glad to see that his color had returned and he was eyeing her with a steady gaze. Her heart swelled with love.

He was a good, decent, giving man. He said he loved her, but what could she offer him? A woman always on the road who was one step away from a jail cell? Some prize. Hugh deserved someone who would settle down with him and give him lots of babies. She was honest enough with herself to realize she could never be right for him.

"You're thinking again, Dia." Hugh broke the silence, his voice still low.

"Do you read minds, too?"

"Handy as that might be sometimes, alas, no." Hugh slowly disengaged their hands, and Dia stretched her stiff fingers. His grip on her had been fierce, she realized.

Hugh gathered her into his arms and let out a long, easy breath. He kissed the top of her head, then rested his cheek against her. "When you're around, I find the aftermath channels into very pleasurable possibilities," he said, his voice rueful, "but unfortunately we're not in the best of places. Call Ronald. Reassure him."

"I will; then I'm going to call Liza."

He nodded. "Confirm what I saw."

"Nope. I believe she's there, but she and I have a few little matters to discuss."

"You believe me?"

She looked straight at him. "I believe."

It was not quite dawn when Demeter slipped out of the house. This was a special time of day, as the first rays of sun rejuvenated the life-giving process of photosynthesis. She liked to wander among her plants, touching, and listening to what they had to say. Today they whispered of the full moon and the new infestation of insects—must nip that little invasion promptly—and the cars that had driven by and Hera—

Demeter stopped. She ran her hands over the tall oak that had whispered that name. She saw Hera, stealthy and sleek, rub her ring and disappear, transported to another place. She held a necklace, Demeter's necklace, a favorite of hers, and when she returned the necklace was gone.

Oh, Hera had deceived, and so well. Why? Why had she taken the necklace?

It didn't matter. The plans were set, but she would know now to watch the enemy within.

The house seemed lonely and lifeless without Dia. Hugh set down his gear and strode through the echoing halls, missing her already, though she had just dropped him off at the gate. She had gone onto Demetria's and, according to their plan, Hugh would come later as an invited guest. He knew it had to be that way, but he didn't like letting her walk into Demetria's alone.

The pieces were moving into place, and now he had one more to task to complete.

He entered the room his great-grandfather had designed. As a child he'd thought it boring. As an adult he'd recognized that it was fashioned for his talent with soft fabrics, soundproof walls, cushions, and no color, all designed to minimize the impact of the aftermath. From his pocket he retrieved the necklace that Zeke had given him. On it, irregularly shaped emeralds formed a random pattern around a twisted silver rope. It was an unsettling design, the harmony of it slightly askew, but Zeke had assured him it was Demetria's and that she enjoyed wearing it.

How Zeke had gotten it was a question the fireworks expert had avoided.

Hugh sat down in the chair he'd added to the room some years back, one contoured to fit his body. Never before had he tried to seek a soul that was not lost, and until last night he'd never tried to do more than reassure. Were his talents strong enough to accomplish their plan? For Dia's sake, he had to try—and to succeed. They had to know where Demetria kept the stolen gems.

He stroked the copper-and-ruby wristband and reminded himself how Dia had felt last night, and how he'd flown with her. How she'd told him she loved him. He wanted to believe her, wanted to believe his gifts would not fade again. He laid the necklace over his open palm, and slowly his fingers closed around the hard stones.

He felt nothing. Hugh dragged in a breath. He recalled the joy in Dia's laughter and the pleasure of dancing with her, and then tried again. His breathing slowed. He relaxed, opened, sought Demetria in the soul of the gems.

The search was unpleasant. The path he followed felt old and musty, alien almost. His skin tightened in repulsion and his mouth tasted bitter, but he forced himself to continue. Abruptly he gasped as acrid smoke choked him and his arms burned with the headlong spiral into the vision.

Demetria. He saw her; he saw through her eyes; he felt the emptiness inside her. He wanted to withdraw from that empty wasteland.

For Dia, he could not.

Demetria looked around, and Hugh felt her start. Had she detected him? He withdrew to only the barest contact and waited until she relaxed. He would have to be very careful to keep her from realizing he was watching.

He gave her the tiniest of suggestions. *Gems. Safe?*

At first he thought she wasn't going to react, for she continued talking to the caterer about the final setup for tonight. He debated giving her another nudge, uneasy that she might just get wary instead, when she completed her conversation with the caterer and left. Not reacting, not thinking, giving her nothing to notice, Hugh went with her.

His patience was rewarded. He watched as Demetria walked into a conservatory connecting her office to the outer grounds. Brick on the lower half, glass on the top, it was filled with plants of every imaginable size and shape and color. She paused a moment, then seemed to turn back.

Gems. He risked another contact.

Demetria strode over to a thick bole vine that wound through the room. The vine anchored itself in the crevices of the brick walls and spread across glass ceiling and windows. Gently she pulled one of the tendrils, tugging it from its hiding hole between the bricks.

Out with it came a jeweled box. Hugh memorized everything in sight, praying he could later pinpoint the location of the hiding place in the profusion of plants. Demetria opened the box, and in it lay what Hugh was looking for—the stolen gems and an envelope that he guessed contained the jeweler's confession, all right there in one handy packet. Except for one thing.

Her hands sifted covetously through the pile of gems, fondling and stroking. The sleeves of her dress fell back.

She was wearing his opal wristband.

Hugh sucked in a deep breath. *Damn her!*

She jerked upright, her gaze darting about the room. Hugh gripped the ruby band and withdrew to home and sanctuary. He had seen enough and didn't want to make her suspicious. He sank into the chair, exhausted, vibrating, his mouth puckering with the flavor of dust.

As Dia drove onto Demetria Cesare's property, she had to trust that the winding, smooth road led to their destination, for the thick foliage concealed everything, even the sky and sun above. The confining vegetation made her feel as if she were sinking into an emerald coffin.

The cooling greenery rendered the car's airconditioning unnecessary. Dia opened the window and drew in a breath of fresh air. The trees rustled in a whispering, soughing moan that sounded like the low hiss of voices. Her spine tightened.

Hugh's home was secluded and private and serene. This was eerie, spooky.

"Shades of *Blair Witch*, except at the center of the woods we'll find not a local legend but an elegant green bitch," she muttered.

The eeriness persisted as Dia arrived at the old house and unloaded her gear, alone except for the watchful plants. She took to whistling "Kryptonite" as an antidote, and maybe it was her imagination, but she thought the plants winced at the off-key rock tune.

She whistled a little louder.

The stage was unlike any she'd ever seen. It wandered through the room, raised enough that she could be seen, but not so far that she couldn't interact with her audience. It would be an interesting venue for her performance. She'd need a lavalier mike and a roving spot. Too bad Zeke Jupiter had other duties tonight; she could have used his expertise.

The room was immense, but made more intimate by the plants ringing it. Several had burst into bloom, adding spots of color to the endless green and a sweet scent, almost as intoxicating as incense, to the aromas of the soil and the offerings of the caterers. One of the flowers drew her attention, a plume of white so brilliant that it hurt the eyes. Dia was surprised to discover it had no scent.

"They were bred for drama, not aroma."

Dia turned at the sound of the low, cultured voice and saw Demetria, wearing a green silk outfit that reminded her of pajamas, glide in. She carried a single silver-white rose. No hybrid this, designed for show alone; the scent of the rose filled the room with a rich aroma, and the thorns on the stem seemed as if they were standing at sharp attention.

Dia had wondered when her hostess might put in an appearance. It hadn't taken long.

"All show, no action?"

"Not quite. There will be some very influential people here tonight, Dia," Demetria continued,

coming closer. "This performance will be your platform to stardom." Her voice lowered until it
matched the whisper of the trees. "Remember, too,
it can all be taken away with just a few simple
words."

"You don't have to remind me."

"Did you bring the wristband?"

"I thought it was too risky to take it while I was
staying with him. He's coming tonight. I'll make the
switch during the performance."

"And give it to me."

Dia's heart hit her ribs. That they hadn't planned
on. She was to make the switch, just in case Demetria had some way of knowing, but Dia would
keep the real band. By the end of the performance,
with Demetria exposed, Hugh could get them both
back.

"You want me to give you the band during my
performance?"

"Yes, before your finale."

"Why?"

Demetria just gave her an amused look.

Dia paced along the stage. "I've worked up a new
variation of the transmutation illusion. It's hot, I tell
you. But for a real spectacle, I'd like to use something that's valuable. Do you have something
splashy that will make a lasting impression during
the switch?"

"Something that you can switch for a fake?"

"How would I do that? I'd have to know ahead
of time what you were going to pick in order to
have a duplicate made."

"I have a jeweled dagger you can use," Demetria
said casually.

Dia's eyes narrowed. "You don't seem too interested."

"Because I'm sure you'll adjust the transmutation illusion however I need it, when I need it." She gave Dia another of those annoying amused looks. "You didn't really think I'd let such a valuable asset as you leave my employ, did you? Oh, and I do thank you for making sure Hugh Pendragon will be here tonight."

With a last pat to the white bloom, Demetria left.

Apparently Demetria's invitations were as prized as she claimed. Hugh wandered through the crowd, a drink of ice water in hand. The house was filled with the elite of Chicago and far beyond, many of whom greeted him. From some overheard conversations, they were eager to see the home of the notoriously private Demetria Cesare. Reputedly it was filled with the rare and the unusual, and the reality had lived up to the hype.

He saw Dia in the audience mingling with the crowd. She looked so beautiful tonight, dressed all in black. Glitter dusted her blond hair and shoulders, and her smile and eyes were bright with excitement.

He loved her.

She had told him she loved him.

That was all that was important, and to hell with any of Harriet Juneau's mumbo jumbo about sacrifice, and Zeke Jupiter's advice. He'd asked her once if she would choose her magic or him. Well, if he had to choose between his powers and his love, he'd choose Dia every time. If he had to give up his wristbands to keep her safe, then so be it. If life with her meant no children, then so be it.

Hugh swallowed against the aching sense of loss in his chest. Yet replacing it was a new sense of excitement and anticipation.

He watched as Dia chatted her way slowly through the crowd, surprised when she seemed to be heading his way. They had decided not to meet until it was time for the switch, yet she gradually closed the gap until she stood beside him, the musky scent of her perfume more intoxicating than any of the fragrant blooms littering the room.

"Hugh, you've got to leave," Dia whispered when she stood beside him, looking at the stage instead of at him.

"What are you talking about?"

"I think you're Demetria's target, not me. For some reason she wants you here."

"No, Dia."

"Please. I don't want anything to happen to you."

He saw a tear at the corner of her eye. "We said we'd finish this tonight. I know where the gems are, and Harry Xavier is right over there." Hugh pointed out the small, dapper man amusing the crowd with a story about the Cubs. Funny, he didn't remember Xavier as being so effusive. "We'll go on as planned."

She shook her head in denial. "I love you, and I don't want to lose you."

Hugh laid a finger on her wrist, on the warm pulse, a subtle gesture. "I love you, too. Now let's go trap a thief."

Chapter Twenty-two

Hugh slipped from the fringes of the party into the darkened conservatory. Although the upper half of the room was glass, the profusion of plants blocked the full moon. He pulled on a pair of thin leather gloves and retrieved a small flashlight from his pocket. Risking that the narrow beam wouldn't be noticed, he swept the light around. Mentally he retraced Demetria's steps, but the vines and the bricks blended until he couldn't tell which one held the three leaves with the variegated stripes and which one contained the rough dog-shaped pattern.

Action, screamed his nerves. A vine undulated in a whispering protest, and a tendril slithered across the floor to wind around his ankle. Hugh shook it off and forced himself to reenter the vision. *Think. She walked here, stood here.* Yes, there they were, the variegated leaves. *She tugged on this vine.*

"Ouch." A stinging nettle covered the vine he'd thought she'd touched, and the beastly plant had stabbed him, even through the leather gloves.

Hugh pulled off the glove and sucked at the swelling. "Damn." He shook his hand against a streak of fire spreading from the wound up his arm. Another streak shot up his leg, and he saw another nettle had reached down to entwine around his ankle. Hugh cursed. If he hadn't seen it and felt it, he wouldn't have believed it.

"I give to the Sierra Club," he muttered, but the plants didn't seem to care. They whispered and swayed and reached to hold him. The nettle slithered its way up his leg, stinging and aiming for his groin.

The plants saw him as an intruder and they were fighting back! Hugh had thought he couldn't be surprised or frightened by the strange, but his heart raced under the bizarre attack. This was the stuff of horror movies, a very primal threat. What kind of a person was Demetria Cesare that she could nurture plants like these?

He didn't have much time. Ignoring the pain, he yanked on the vine holding the gems. It resisted, but Hugh refused to be stopped by some real-life version of Audrey Two from *Little Shop of Horrors*. His body burned with a thousand stings of the nettle's poison. He wrapped the vine around his hand and gave a sharp, swift pull.

The plant came loose, ripping from the bricks. A shriek rang in his ears, although he knew no sound was audible, and the jewel box tumbled to the floor. So much for stealth.

Quickly Hugh grabbed the two items he needed from the box, then returned it to the crevice. He snapped off the light and froze.

Voices came from the hallway.

"Demetria, wait," Harriet Juneau called out.

"No! My plants are distressed!"

"The performance will be starting soon. You should be there." Harriet's voice came clear and sharp through the closed door—warning him.

"And I will." Demeter's hand hit the door, slamming it open.

Thank you, Harriet, he thought, and slipped through the doorway to the outside.

The pain raced through her gloves straight to her heart. Demeter laid her bouquet of mixed flowers on the floor and cupped the vine's damaged stem, crooning to it as she surveyed the damage Hugh Pendragon had caused. Her head throbbed with fury.

Obviously he'd gotten the confession. Well, she would find another way to bring Dia back.

Tonight it was Hugh Pendragon who would suffer, and she'd have her vengeance on the line of Hades.

She retrieved her bouquet and went over to Hera. "Your interference will not change things."

"What do you mean?"

"This." Demeter laid her hand on the vine. It whipped its tendrils out to wrap around Hera and hold her fast. Demeter saw her reach for the cloud ring, and she sent another vine to wrap her fingers.

Hera glared at her. "What are you doing?"

362

"Tonight I shall obtain the gems of Hades. His line will at last be rendered powerless, and Hugh Pendragon will live with that loss, that emptiness, just as I have lived with the emptiness of the loss of my daughter."

Hera made a disgusted noise. "Oh, get over it, Demeter. That was how many millennia ago, and you know she's perfectly happy back on d-Alphus with him."

"I shall have the power."

"Only a Soul Seeker can use it."

"With my plants, with the chemicals I am breeding in them, I think I will, in time, master that talent. Think of it, Hera, to be able to guide the thoughts and dreams of men."

"I always thought it sounded like a whole lot of work."

"I should have known you wouldn't understand." She plucked a bloom from her bouquet, a bloom so white it hurt the eyes, and gently blew out the pollen, then waited until Hera's lids drooped and her head sagged to her chest. A small amount rendered a man suggestible; a larger dose gave sleep and dreams to control.

Demeter laid a gentle hand on her hair. "Good night and pleasant dreams, for you will remember none of this in the morning." She tucked the flower back into the bouquet and went out to watch the show.

The illusions were ready.

Dia stood backstage. She was ready as well. Hair, makeup, black sequins. She patted the fake ruby in her hidden pocket, then took a deep breath. Those weren't butterflies in her stomach; those were swans.

She rubbed her hands together to warm them up, flexed and clenched, checked her costume, and then her music started. A moment later she was onstage, bathed in the familiar warmth of lights and glitter and applause. Effortlessly she fell into the routine, the magic, as always, her strength and her home.

Except she wasn't alone with her magic anymore. She had Hugh. And it was up to her to make sure he got back forever what he had lost.

When she'd done charity events or small gatherings before, she'd chosen close-up magic: walking among the guests like David Blaine did on his street-magic specials, using materials at hand, charming her viewers with her illusions, and amazing them that they could be so close and still not see how she did what she did. This stage was a perfect venue, and as Dia performed, as one illusion flowed into the next, she knew she'd never been better. If this was to be her last performance, it was going to be a stellar one.

Where was Hugh? Suddenly she found him. He had moved until the path she took would bring her right next to him. He made a casual motion that told her what she needed was in his breast pocket. Time to finish.

The music quieted to a hypnotizing drum rhythm, and the lights segued into a silvery red halo. Wisps of smoke wound through the audience. Even the room lights dimmed to match the mood.

With an easy movement, Dia donned a cloak, covering the sequins and pulling a hood up to frame her hair. In this mood, in this setting, it became a sorcerer's robe, midnight black and magic. She walked among her audience, a single spotlight highlighting her.

"Magic is among the most ancient of the arts," she said, her voice a throaty murmur that carried across the hushed audience with the aid of her microphone. "Egypt, Babylonia, Greece, all had their magicians, sometimes revered, sometimes reviled, sometimes feared. In the repression of medieval Europe, however, the conjurer entertained in the market. This was a true challenge for the magician, to provide for one man, one woman, one child, a brief flight into the amazing. Always, the keepers of magic held their secrets, and most secretive of all were the alchemists. Those who sought the transmutation. Lead into gold. Water into wine. This mystery is what I share with you tonight.

"Alchemists had their assistants, however, and I'll need some help from the audience members. You, sir, will you join me on the stage? And you, madam. You, sir." She selected a couple at random, then chose Hugh. "And I need another lady. How about our generous hostess tonight? Demetria?"

With the enthusiastic applause, Demetria joined them onstage.

"It's warm up here, isn't it gentlemen?" Dia suggested. "May I take your coats?"

Hugh and her other male volunteer shrugged out of their suit coats. Dia hung them on the coat tree center stage and deftly took what she needed from the pocket of Hugh's.

The coats disappeared in a puff of red smoke, distracting the audience from what she was really doing. Dia feigned surprise. "Oh, gentlemen, it seems your coats have disappeared. No, wait, here they are." She pulled at a bit of silk and two thin black capes appeared. She draped them over the men's shoulders. "Will this do? No? How about this?" She waved her hand and black silk turned into purple polka dots. The audience laughed. "Definitely not. Then this." Another wave and the jackets reappeared. The audience clapped in appreciation.

"Transmutation," Dia said. "Change."

She continued the act, going from one to the other of her volunteers in rapid succession, taking objects they gave her, "transmuting" them, switching them with dizzying speed that had her audience clapping. She felt, rather than saw, Hugh's small wince when she returned the fake ruby to his wrist instead of the real one. And she saw, rather than felt, Demetria's smile of triumph when she slipped the real band on.

Time for the final illusion.

"Thank you thank you, you may sit down. Demetria, will you stay here?"

Demetria glared at her, but unless she wanted to make a fuss in front of her guests, she could not refuse.

"Now, these have all been mere trinkets. Do you think our hostess will trust me with something more valuable?" Dia asked the audience. She spun around and her cloak changed from black to vibrant silver. It glittered and dazzled under the stage lights. The drumbeat picked up the pace, urging the heart to pump harder, the blood to flow faster. "Do you think I will return it, or will it stay forever transmutated into, say . . . a wand?"

One of the fiber-optic wands appeared in Dia's hands.

She looked into her audience. Hugh was waiting right next to the stage. And she saw Harry Xavier inching closer for a better look, his fingers stroking his mustache, almost as if he knew what was to happen.

She spun and twirled and brought forward a glass pedestal that had been sitting on the platform stage all night, in plain sight. A silvery cloth was draped over the lump atop it.

Dia rocked and thrust her hands in time to the driving beat. A shower of sparkles dusted the stage with brilliance. "I'm sure she's regretting her generosity right now, but before the show, Demetria let me choose something from her vast array of precious mementos."

Actually, Demetria had chosen the jeweled dagger and put it on the pedestal herself. Dia leaned forward conspiratorially to the audience. "She doesn't know I picked the most exquisite piece in her whole collection of gems." Dia flung her cape over the glass pedestal, then whipped it back.

On the pedestal sat not a jeweled dagger, but a rope of glittering diamonds—the same rope she'd stolen from Harry Xavier over nine months ago.

Very distinctive. Very obvious, even from the audience.

And Harry Xavier was sitting front and center. Shimmering. Surrounded by a shimmering, waving, golden glow. Dia blinked, looked again, and the shimmering was gone.

Xavier shot to his feet. "That's mine," he shouted. He leaped onto the stage, gesturing grandly, and snatched up the necklace. "It's mine!" he boomed. He stared at Demetria; then he pointed a dramatic, accusatory finger at her. There was a moment's pause while the audience was transfixed by the drama onstage. "Demetria Cesare, you stole my necklace."

"I never saw that before in my life," Demetria said in a snarl. "*She* must have taken it!" Her gloved hand shot toward Dia.

Hugh followed Xavier to the stage. "Then what are you doing wearing this?" He held up her hand and exposed the ruby band that he had been wearing just minutes before. "And this!" He exposed her other arm and the opal band.

Dia watched Demetria's face contort with fury.

"No! You will not take them from me!" she shouted, and ripped her arms from his grasp. She flung her hands out wide. The green gloves glowed with an eerie phosphorescent light, which shot out to all corners of the room. The white blooms shook, and their pollen exploded into the room in a yellow cloud that obliterated sight. Demeter leaped from the stage and disappeared into the chaos.

"She's getting away," Dia shouted. "She's got the bands." But the words trailed off. She could feel the pollen working on her, drawing her into the oblivion of sleep. Her mind grew fuzzy, and she wondered why she was standing here. Around her, people were dropping to the floor, snoring.

Hugh grabbed her hand and flung her cloak over her. "C'mon, Dia, get out of here. Hold your breath. Cover your face. We're higher and didn't get as much pollen."

She followed him blindly, able to see only a smudge of black and a pinpoint of jeweled blue glowing in the yellow fog.

Outside the room her mind cleared a little, enough to remember whom they were chasing. "She'll go to the conservatory."

Dia and Hugh raced, then skidded to a halt. Demetria wasn't there.

"Where could she have gone?" Dia circled, the sudden silence of the conservatory sending a frisson of fear coursing through her.

"Dia, do you still have whatever it was Demeter put on that pedestal?"

"The dagger? It's here, in my cloak." She handed it to him. "Can you find her? Even without your bands?"

A ghost of a smile crossed his lips. "With love I can."

Dia saw him grow still, knew that he sought an angry soul. A moment later he started running, and she followed.

He took them into the labyrinth of plants that surrounded Demetria's house. Deeper they went, weaving through plants that grabbed at them in a nightmare of shadows and whispers. All light was blotted out by the thick layers of leaves, and Dia was totally disoriented within minutes. Yet Hugh maintained an unerring course, following Demetria's trail.

Twice Dia thought she heard shouts and felt the vibration of pounding feet. Once her eyes stung as a plant tendril wound around a lock of hair and she had to pull free. Hugh, she saw, was scratched and bleeding, and a red welt slashed one cheek. But they plunged forward and at last they burst through to find Demetria at the side of a stream, untying a small boat, a bouquet of flowers cradled in her arms.

She spun around and her face contorted with anger. "How did you find me? You don't have your power without the bands."

Hugh smiled, cold and triumphant. "I don't need them."

Dia could sense the powerful emotions raging through him as he advanced on Demetria.

Deliberately Demetria removed the bands from her wrists and dropped them in the water.

Dia scrambled to the bank and reached into the icy water, trying to find them for Hugh.

Demetria paid her no mind. She cradled her flowers and stared at him. "No, Soul Seeker, you will not win," she whispered. "If it's visions you want, then that is all you shall have."

Dia glanced over her shoulder. As if in slow motion, she saw Hugh close in on Demetria. She saw Demetria pluck a flower from her bouquet and hold it toward Hugh's face.

A green stem covered with tiny yellow flowers.

A plant that spewed acid pollen.

"No." The denial rose from deep inside her. Dia leaped up, her hands outstretched.

Her hands. Her hands reached between Hugh and the devil plant. Her hands blocked that hellish pollen from reaching him. Her hands knocked the plant away.

Her hands.

Pain—agonizing, endless, magic-destroying pain—engulfed her hands.

370

Dia collapsed to the ground, only vaguely aware of the drama beyond the pain.

Harry Xavier burst into the clearing and hit Demetria with . . . a lightning bolt?

Armond Marceaux followed, gun drawn, a phalanx of backup men behind him.

Hugh Pendragon gathered her into his arms, with tears streaming down his face. "Dia, no. My God, your hands."

"Did she get you?" she asked weakly.

He shook his head.

"Good."

And then Hugh was carrying her, running someplace with her—Dia didn't know where. A wave of black pain passed over her, and oblivion followed.

Chapter Twenty-three

The hospital room came into focus as Dia slowly awoke. She must have been asleep for a while, she realized, because it was dusk again. For a moment she had trouble remembering what had happened; her mind seemed so fuzzy. Then as bits and pieces returned, she jolted upright.

Hugh.

Her hands.

Clumsily she lifted her arms. Her hands were encased in mittens of gauze. They hurt, but not with the agonizing pain she remembered. Did that mean all the nerve endings were burned away? Dia moaned and tried to wiggle her fingers. Was that movement? She couldn't tell through the barrier of bandages.

"The doctor says they'll be okay."

She hadn't seen Hugh come into her room until he spoke, and now she watched him walk to her bed with the lithe grace that so characterized him. Silently she held out her arms to him. He gathered her close, and Dia laid her head on his shoulder, feeling the tears come and unable to stop them.

"They'll be okay," he whispered over and over, his hand gently stroking her hair.

They'll be okay. Her hands would heal.

The flow of tears slowed, drying in the sunshine of that realization, and Dia gradually relaxed against him. He smelled so good, and his shoulder felt so good to lean on, strong and firm. She snuggled closer, content for the moment to relish the warm feel of him.

"What happened?" she asked at last, lifting her head from his shoulder and wiping at her cheeks with the gauze.

"Armond arrested Demetria. Not only did they find the gems, but some rather illegal plants and chemicals. Harry Xavier vanished after he knocked her out and gave Armond his statement, and everyone else at the party has a hard time remembering exactly what did happen, including Harriet Juneau. Most are putting it down to an excess of drink."

"So much for anyone remembering my exciting performance," she grumbled. "But what happened to my hands?"

"The river. Your hands were wet, and it diluted the pollen. I washed the rest off, so although it was painful, the damage wasn't deep. You should regain full use of them with a little time and some therapy." His hand cupped her head in a gentle embrace. "I can't believe you did that for me, Dia."

"I couldn't let her spray your face. I knew what that plant did."

His arm tightened about her. "Don't ever do something so foolish again. The world needs your talent and your magic."

She rested a hand against his cheek, feeling the roughness of the day's growth of beard. "I would do it again in a heartbeat, if it meant saving you." She kissed him. "Did you find your wristbands? Your family legacy?"

"No, we never found them."

A dark-haired man with penetrating gray eyes peered around the corner, then, seeing her awake, came in and stood at the foot of the bed.

"Go away, Armond," said Hugh, wrapping his arm around her. "She doesn't want to answer questions right now."

She laid her gauzy paw on Hugh's thigh. "It's okay. I have to answer them sometime."

Armond opened his notebook. "Demetria claims you stole the gems."

"Can it, friend," Hugh said in a growl. "You're following the wrong thread."

"I've got to ask the questions. Dia, did you—"

"She's never knowingly stolen anything in her life," Hugh answered for her.

"It's true," Dia added, "although you may find it hard to believe if you read my family history." She stretched, feeling her back stiffening, and could not stifle a yawn as fatigue overtook her again.

Armond touched her lightly on the shoulder, then nodded as though a question had been answered. "If Hugh vouches for you, we'll leave it at that for now."

She was tired of being afraid of the law, she realized. It was time she made a few changes in her life. "Those gems were taken during my performance," she blurted out.

"Dia, you don't have to say anything," warned Hugh.

"Yes, I think I do." She faced Armond. "The gems were taken at my performance, but not by me. The jeweler did it when he verified them. I didn't know about it until six months ago, and when I found out, I refused to let her use me like that."

Armond listened gravely, then shut his notebook. "That shouldn't warrant any further investigation, but we'll want to talk to you later."

"She'll be staying with me," Hugh answered.

"For how long?"

"That depends on whether you give us some privacy right now."

"I'll have to cancel the rest of my tour," Dia said, feeling the clutch of regret. "But, hands willing, I've got a date in New Orleans at the end of summer. Mark and I are doing a joint show, preparing for a European tour this fall."

Armond left, but at once Elena came bursting in. "Guess what! Mom's getting married. She and Claire and Pan came back last night and she told us she's getting married, and I get to be her attendant."

Liza followed her daughter, along with the other three children and a stocky, good-looking man with curly hair, whom Liza introduced as Julian Panadopolis. After kisses and hugs and explanations,

Hugh and Julian took the kids to the cafeteria for a drink, leaving Liza and Dia alone together.

Her sister looked tanned and fit and happier than Dia had ever seen her. "You look good," she said, voicing her thoughts.

"I feel good."

"Engaged." Dia shook her head. "Hard to believe you're taking that chance again."

"It's right this time, with Julian."

"Liza Trelawny Swensen Panadopolis. Now, that's a mouthful. But I thought you went on the trek with someone else."

"I did."

"Okay, explain. I have been hunting for you."

Liza fingered her diamond ring. "I know I should have come back, but I wanted this trip so much, I convinced myself you could handle everything. After all, you're the successful, got-it-all-together sister."

"I wish." Dia laid a hand over her sister's fidgeting fingers. "I understand; I forgive you."

"Does this mean we get free tickets to your show whenever we want?" Liza asked with a sidelong glance.

Dia laughed. "Always."

Her sister sighed. "Once we left for the jungle, there really wasn't any chance to contact you. The man I was with insisted it would spoil the wilderness experience if I left or used the emergency services, and I was trapped out there. That's one of the reasons I knew he was wrong for me; he didn't care about my family. That and the fact that all he could talk about the whole time was himself and his investments. He didn't even notice the monkeys." She

376

sighed. "But he was so rich, I thought I could be happy."

"And Julian isn't? Rich?"

She shook her head. "What's important is that I love him. I had to get away from everything—the kids, the house, the work—in order to see that."

"In that case, seems like you could have picked a spa as your getaway."

Liza laughed and scratched at a bite. "Never again will I listen to a man with too much money and time on his hands."

The words died between them, but for the sisters there was no need for words. At last Liza stood, then hugged Dia and kissed her cheek. "Julian, the kids and I will be leaving tomorrow. I appreciate your taking them in for me."

"I got to know them better. Besides, what else could I do? They're family."

"Sometimes I've wondered if you remembered that."

"I've had a few revelations myself recently."

Liza paused in the doorway. "Hugh's a nice man, and you deserve him. Don't do what I almost did and sell yourself short." She left Dia sitting alone in the bed.

Dia turned out the lights, then stood beside the window, adjusting to the blackness, enjoying the evening. Night was a friend, and tonight it whispered truths to her.

Silently Hugh rejoined her. The room was dark and enveloped them in the velvet of night. He took her hand in his. "Now's probably not the time or the place, but I don't want to lose you. I want you to be a part of my life for always."

She looked at him, at the emerald eyes and blue earring, at the masculine planes of his face. "Are you sure? I keep thinking I'm all wrong for you, Hugh."

"You're manufacturing an illusion. I have never met anyone who was so utterly right for me."

She looked at his empty wrists. "Because of the thing you were talking about? That your psychic . . . stuff comes back when I love you?"

"No. If it disappeared again, I would die inside but not because of the power being gone; because I would have lost your love. I want you for one reason only: because I love you, and because nothing is more important than having you with me. And you should stay only if you believe that and if you love me, too."

"I'll be gone a lot," she said.

"So will I. Sometimes we'll even be gone together. It can work, if we want it to."

"I'm not very domestic."

"I have Ronald. He's all the domestic anyone can handle." He took her bundle of gauze in his hand. "I know you don't want children. I don't either, if it means you're not their mother. You were willing to sacrifice your hands, your magic, for me. I won't ask you ever to give it up. We'll have a good life, the two of us."

"And Ronald."

"And Cerberus."

She closed her eyes a moment against the fire burning in his eyes. He, too, was willing to sacrifice what he wanted most for her. She imagined Hugh as the father of a little boy, dark-haired and serious, but maybe, just maybe with her blue eyes, and something inside her softened. She opened her eyes, saw him standing before her, and knew that nothing was more important.

Fears loosened their grip on her. One day she would give him that child they both wanted. Wordlessly Dia held out her hand, and she saw the shadows on his face dissipate in a moonbeam.

Hugh grinned at her. "I'm a detective. I need words and facts and evidence."

She scooted closer. "Words. I love you, Hugh. I love you so much that if you ask me to marry you and raise a passel of kids, I'll do it."

"I never said a passel," he protested. "One at most."

"Trelawnys have twins."

"Okay, two, but not if it means giving up your magic."

"I won't give it up, just adjust. What about the marrying part? Will you marry me, Hugh?"

"Yes."

She moved even closer, until her breasts brushed against his chest. She heard the quick intake of his breath and felt the familiar spiral of desire.

"Facts," she said. "I have made love to you in a car after knowing you for ten days. I have called your huge mausoleum a home and I have never thought of any place in my life as home. I offered to bear your children, when I never thought I had a mothering gene in my body. And I'm wearing gauze mittens because I tried to save your hide. If that's not love, what is?"

"What about evidence?"

She pressed against him. "This," she purred, and kissed him—long and slow and deep and more

Kathleen Nance

sensuously than she ever had, for this time there was love behind it.

"I have just one request," she said softly at the end. "That our first dance together at our wedding is the Salsa Stomp."

"Done." With a growl Hugh lifted her into his arms.

"I love it when you go primitive with me," she whispered as he lowered her to the bed and pressed his body atop hers.

"Wait until you see what I can do with ice cream," he answered, then groaned. "Dia, we can't do this. We're in a hospital."

Dia lifted her brows. "The door locks, doesn't it?"

Hugh laughed and quickly snapped the lock, then came back to her.

She wrapped her arms around his neck. "Ah, Hugh, I do love you."

"And now, my love, you can show me your magic."

At the end of August, the Cubs won their unprecedented one hundredth game, Benito Blessing broke Barry Bonds's record in home runs, and Wrigley Field set new attendance records in what everyone was calling a miracle season.

In less-remarked but still fascinating Chicago news, Demetria Cesare disappeared, forfeiting her bond and stymieing bounty hunters; reknowned but reclusive Hugh Pendragon had been spotted at the Second City venue and numerous other events around town in the company of his new and beautiful wife; Peacock Cosmetics introduced a dramatic line of cosmetics, and the CEO of the company seemed to be contemplating a merger of a more personal kind with Jupiter Fireworks.

Zeus stood in Hera's Chicago apartment watching the rising sun. It was so bright, it nearly blinded him. He missed the mountains where he'd established his current home—he was ready to go back—but this was a sight that never failed to stir him.

A fresh new day full of possibilities and potentials. Excitement, passion, danger.

He was eager for a new adventure. He patted the package waiting for special delivery. But first it was time for some unfinished business.

Hera came in, trying her robe about her, and handed him a cold cup. He took a sip. *Ah, nectar. Invigorating and refreshing.*

"We have to find her," Hera said.

Zeus took another sip of his drink. "I already have."

"What? Without telling me?" She glared at him. "You didn't go to see her. There is no telling what she will do—"

"I did the far-see only this morning," he interrupted. "While you cleansed yourself."

"Oh." Hera subsided for a moment. "What was she doing?"

"Contemplating her plants."

"Demeter? She was probably plotting something."

"Which is why we need to see her right away. Before we leave to see Dia and Mark's show in New Orleans tonight."

"Agreed. Let me get dressed."

Zeus settled in for a wait, but to his surprise Hera was back in thirty minutes. With a rub to their

Kathleen Nance

rings, they transported to Demeter's side.

She did not appear surprised to see them. Instead she waved them to a seat. "Would you like a honey cake?"

"We're not staying long," Zeus said.

Hera sat down. "I'd love a honey cake."

With a muttered grumble, Zeus seated himself. But he wouldn't eat, he decided.

"You were expecting us?" Hera asked.

"It was you who got me out of jail and urged me to flee, wasn't it?" Demeter lifted one brow in query.

Hera gaped at her.

Zeus contemplated his fingernails. "Actually, it was I."

Hera turned on him. "You impersonated me!"

"It was the only way. She'd never have agreed to anything I suggested." Maybe he would have that honey cake after all.

"But why?" sputtered Hera.

Demeter's laugh was amused and cynical. "Because we can't have one of us rotting in a prison for several hundred years, now, can we? Bound to raise a few questions."

"True," Zeus answered, "although it means you'll have to forge a new identity. Start a new life."

Demeter shrugged. "I've done it before. We all have."

Zeus looked at her then, with no vestige of humor. "A new life, Demeter. No ties, no threads to anything in this one. You lost, and I can't let you continue your mad quest for vengeance against the descendants of Hades."

382

"How are you going to stop me? Put on the Harry Xavier hologram again?"

"Like this." He reached out suddenly, took her gloved hand, and pressed his ring against the mesh. Sparks flashed from the ring and a roaring wind swooped through the room. Demeter struggled to pull her hand from his, but Zeus was stronger and he held on until the sparks and wind died. Then he let go.

The mesh glove had turned black. Demeter sat, staring, motionless. Then a single flake fell from the glove, followed by another, and another. As the three gods watched, the glove crumbled off her hand and landed at her feet as a pile of dust.

Demeter turned pale and pressed her lips together as though fighting back a swell of nausea.

"I have left you one," he said. "Continue on your vendetta and the other will be gone."

"You'd have to find me."

"I will," he said softly.

For a moment Demeter didn't move. When she raised her eyes to his, though, Zeus saw her fear and her acceptance. She nodded. "Let revenge die in peace."

Zeus rose to his feet.

"Wait," commanded Hera; then she took both of Demeter's hands in hers. "Do you need anything?"

"Just an answer to a question. Why, Hera? Why did you side with Zeus against me? I thought we were friends."

"We are, or we can be, but he is my love. Throughout all that has happened, he is my one constant."

"He's a womanizer and a jokester."

Zeus bristled at the womanizer part. And after all his efforts to remain true!

Without looking, Hera quieted him with a hand on his arm. "He says he's a changed man, and we have this little project we're working on."

Demeter shook her head. "The king of the gods has not changed that much."

"I trust that he has. Besides, with him, life is never boring."

"Passion and excitement," Zeus said.

Hera nodded. "Passion and excitement and love."

Hugh lay content and sated, holding his beloved wife in his arms. The sheen of sweat from their lovemaking slowly dried, and he pulled the sheet up to cover them. He felt her relaxing, drifting back toward sleep, and he gathered her closer, treasuring these quiet moments in their busy lives.

Her hand lay limp on the pillow. The skin was soft and pink, although a couple of puckers still marred the smoothness. He picked it up and kissed each talented finger. She'd worked tirelessly to get her hands back to performing agility, and tonight would be her reward: the kickoff to the European tour.

"You like kissing my hands, don't you?" she mumbled against the pillow.

"Yes, I do. I also like kissing your neck. And between your fingers. And your shoulder. And this little indentation at your waist." He followed each with a demonstration.

Dia moaned and squirmed.

Suddenly he stopped.

She opened one eye to glare at him. "Why'd you stop?"

"Don't you have to leave for the theater soon?"

She wriggled against him. "Not that soon."

A discreet knock on the adjoining door to their New Orleans hotel suite interrupted them. "Sir," Ronald called through the door, "a package came for you. It says 'most urgent.' And I have madam's juice."

Hugh drew on a pair of pants and answered the knock, while Dia slipped into her robe and shoved back her hair. Ronald handed Hugh a platter with a brown parcel and a large glass of orange juice. "The lad who brought it said it was important that you open it soon. I've called room service and will have a bite of supper waiting for you, sir."

"Thanks, Ronald."

"You're welcome." He closed the door and left.

Hugh brought the package over to the bed.

"Who's it from?" Dia asked.

"I don't know. There's no return address." He held it up and listened, then gave it a little shake.

"Oh, just open it," Dia said impatiently.

It took him only a few minutes to undo the sealed box and shake out the velvet box inside. With hands strangely clumsy, he opened the lid.

Inside a ruby set in copper sparkled with a scarlet passion, and an opal set in silver gleamed like moonlight.

The gems of Hades, the Treasure of the Underworld, had been returned to their rightful home.

Epilogue

Zeus reveled in the dazzling display of magic on the stage before him. Dia spun in a kaleidoscope of color and leaped up to the top of a crystal blue box. She lifted her hands as the box levitated, and fireworks of green and blue and silver shot from her fingertips. She wrapped the black cloak around her, and light and smoke exploded. An instant later the cloak lifted.

Mark Hennessy stood in her place, surrounded by a halo of red fog that dissipated with a snap of his finger.

The audience burst into applause.

The two magicians created a show of flash and romanticism in a blend of styles that flowed seamlessly from one illusion to the next. The performance of Marcus and Trelawny was a success. Next stop: Paris.

Zeus glanced over to Hugh sitting on his left. Despite the chemistry and long friendship between the two performers onstage, he saw no hint of jealousy in Hugh. The Soul Seeker clapped enthusiastically, confident of his wife's love. At his wrists the red of a ruby and the milky white of an opal reflected in the shadowed theater. Zeus knew from newspaper reports that Hugh was busier, and more successful, than ever, but he was taking some long weekends over the next months to join his wife on her European tour.

Zeus leaned over to Hera. "I'll meet you at the restaurant," he whispered.

"Don't you want to see the rest of the show?"

"I've seen enough."

Hera glanced back at the stage. "So have I."

They slipped out of their seats, then left the theater. It was several blocks' walk to Greenwood, the vegetarian restaurant where the after-show cast party was to be held.

"Shall we catch a cab?" Zeus asked.

"I think I would enjoy the walk," Hera decided.

The New Orleans night was a sultry caress. From the French Quarter to his left came the mournful wail of a lone saxophone, while on a street corner a man in a black suit held a Bible and preached the good news. He loved it here almost as much as in his mountains.

Of course, he would be happy anywhere Hera was.

"Would you like to live in the mountains?" he asked.

"My business is in Chicago."

"Are you going to be difficult about this?"

"Me, difficult? When was I ever?"

"How about that time you tricked Narcissus into thinking his reflection was an adoring maiden?"

Hera laughed. "He deserved to sit and moon for an impossible love."

"For a whole week?"

"So he lost a little weight." She pushed open the door to Greenwood. "Six months. We'll split where we live."

"Skiing and summer in the mountains."

"Spring and autumn in the city."

Inside, the spicy aroma of simmering tomato sauce and sautéing butter greeted them. Zeus glanced around.

"Joy's added a few items." Amid the decor of vegetarian posters, postcards from around the word sent by customers, and utterly tacky souvenirs, he saw a poster that read, *Vegetables. It's what's for life.*

"I think the giant cardboard moose is new."

"So is the neon 'Wisconsin Dells' light."

The restaurant was empty except for a black-haired man sitting in a corner rocking an infant and humming softly. Zeus and Hera joined him.

"Hello, Armond," greeted Zeus.

"Louis has grown so much," added Hera.

"Zeke, Harriet. Yes, he's going to be a strong one," Armond Marceaux answered proudly, his large hand gently rubbing the baby's back. "Is the show over?"

"Almost."

"Is he eating solids yet?" asked Hera.

"He gums tortillas and rice balls with the best of them."

"Is Callie anxious to get back to work at Greenwood?"

Armond shook his hand in a gesture of indecision. "She loves the restaurant, yes, but she's enjoyed being with Louis."

Armond's wife Callie owned the restaurant, but while she'd taken a year off to film a video series and have the baby, Joy, Mark's wife and also a chef, had been running Greenwood. Now Joy was going to Europe with Mark to study her culinary skills, and Callie was reclaiming the reins of the restaurant.

"I expect she'll bring him to work with her." Hera stroked one gentle finger over the baby's soft hair.

"Most likely his first words will not be *mama* or *papa*, but *peppers* and *Tabasco*."

Zeus laughed. "Is Callie here?"

"She and Joy are in the kitchen."

"Then we'll go say hello."

The scents in the kitchen were more complex, and redolent of pepper and garlic. Zeus took an appreciative sniff, then spotted the two women, red hair and brown, at the stove; chattering away.

Callie spied them first. "Zeke Jupiter, Harriet Juneau. It's been an age since I've seen you two. I hear you did exciting things with Dia's show." She gave them each a hug. "Are you going to go with them to Europe?"

"My fireworks and Harriet's cosmetics are. We're onto new projects."

"Is the show over?" Joy asked, coming over to kiss them.

"Almost."

389

"Then we'd better put the pasta on. How did it go?"

"A stunning success."

She grinned. "I knew those two would be spectacular."

No jealousy or doubts there either.

Zeus and Hera shared a conspiratorial smile while they stood to one side and watched the performers stream into Greenwood. Dia wore slinky blue and a huge smile, while Hugh rested an arm about her waist. Mark greeted Joy with an enthusiastic kiss and a "This smells wonderful, darlin', but tell me that you cooked me at least one little pork chop." Callie and Armond stood close together, their hands joined as they patted their son's back.

"Joy and Mark. Callie and Armond. Dia and Hugh," Hera said in a low voice.

Zeus clicked his tongue. "Three attempts at matchmaking, three rousing successes. By Hades, I'm good."

"*We're* good," corrected Hera.

Zeus lifted her hand to kiss her palm. "It would not have been nearly as much fun without you."

Hera cocked an eye toward Anya. "You don't suppose . . . ?" she mused.

Zeus broke into a hearty laugh. With Hera once more at his side, anything in this life was possible. "Perhaps, my love, it is time to consider another project."

KATHLEEN NANCE
THE WARRIOR

Callie Gabriel, a fiercely independent vegetarian chef, manages her own restaurant and stars in a cooking show with a devoted following. Though she knows men only lead to heartache, she can't help wanting to break through Armond Marceux's veneer of casual elegance to the primal desires that lurk beneath.

Armond returns from an undercover FBI assignment a broken man, his memories stolen by the criminal he sought to bring in. His mind can't remember Callie or their night of wild lovemaking, but his body can never forget the feel of her curves against him. And even though Callie insists she doesn't need him, Armond needs her—for she is the key to stirring not only his memories, but also his passions.

___52417-1 $5.99 US/$6.99 CAN

THE TRICKSTER

KATHLEEN NANCE

Long after she's given up on his return, Matthew Mark Hennessy strolls back into Joy Taylor's life, bolder than Hermes when he stole Apollo's cattle. But Joy is no longer the girl who had so easily trusted him with her heart. An aspiring chef, she has no intention of being distracted by the fireworks the magician sparks in her. But with a kiss silkier than her custard cream, he melts away her defenses. And she knows the master showman has performed the greatest trick of all: setting her heart afire.

Mark has traveled to Louisiana to uncover the truth, not to rekindle an old passion. But Joy sets him sizzling. It is not her cooking that has him salivating, but the sway of her hips. And though magicians never divulge their secrets, Joy tempts him to confide his innermost desires. In a flash Mark realizes their passion is no illusion, but the magic of true love.

___52382-5 $5.99 US/$6.99 CAN

Dorchester Publishing Co., Inc.
P.O. Box 6640
Wayne, PA 19087-8640

More Than Magic

Kathleen Nance

Darius is as beautiful, as mesmerizing, as dangerous as a man can be. His dark, star-kissed eyes promise exquisite joys, yet it is common knowledge he has no intention of taking a wife. Ever. Sex and sensuality will never ensnare Darius, for he is their master. But magic can. Knowledge of his true name will give a mortal woman power over the arrogant djinni, and an age-old enemy has carefully baited the trap. Alluring yet innocent, Isis Montgomery will snare his attention, and the spell she's been given will bind him to her. But who can control a force that is even more than magic?

_52299-3 $5.99 US/$6.99 CAN

KIMBERLY RAYE
A STRANGER'S KISS

Alex Daimon is the incarnation of desire, the embodiment of lust, the soul of carnality. For centuries he has existed to bring down the just and the wicked alike, to corrupt the innocent. Thus comes he to the bed of Callie Wisdom, the young heir of the witch who bound him to Darkness . . . and the girl is ripe for possession. He means to do what he's done so many times before—seduce and destroy. But looking into her crystalline eyes, Alex wishes that Callie might see some end to his curse. And introducing her to passion, Alex wonders if this time, instead of his kiss drawing his victim down into darkness, her love may not raise him up to the light.

___52462-7 $5.99 US/$6.99 CAN

Lovers and Other Lunatics
Eugenia Riley

Get Ready for . . . The Time of Your Life!

Teresa Phelps has heard of being crazy in love. But Charles Everett seems just plain mad. Her handsome kidnapper unnerves her with his charm and flabbergasts her with his accusations. He acts under the misguided belief that she holds the key to finding buried treasure. But all Tess feels she can unearth is one oddball after another.

While Charles' actions resemble those of a lunatic, his body arouses thoughts of a lover. And while Charles helps to fend off her dastardly and dangerous pursuers, Tess wonders if he has her best interests at heart—or is she just a pawn in his quest for riches? As the madcap misadventures ensue, Tess strives to dig up the truth. Who is the enigmatic Englishman? What is he after? And most important, in the hunt for hidden riches is the ultimate prize true love?

___52371-X $5.99 US/$6.99 CAN

AMANDA ASHLEY
Midnight Embrace

AVAILABLE FEBRUARY 2002!

FROM
LOVE ✦ SPELL

AMANDA ASHLEY
Midnight Embrace

ANALISA . . . He whispers her name, and it echoes back to him on the wings of the night. She is so young, so alive. She radiates warmth and goodness, chasing the coldness from his being, banishing the loneliness from his soul. In four centuries of prowling, the shadows have brought him few pleasures, but the nearness of her soft lips, her warm throat, promise sweetness beyond imagining. She has wandered unchaperoned to the moonlit tomb where he takes refuge by day, little suspecting that with his eyes alone he can mesmerize her, compel her to do his bidding. Yet he will not take her life's blood by force or trickery. He will have it as a gift, freely given, and in exchange, he will make her wildest dreams come true.

___52468-6 $5.99 US/$7.99 CAN

Sacrament

Susan Squires

Available March 2002!

From
Love Spell